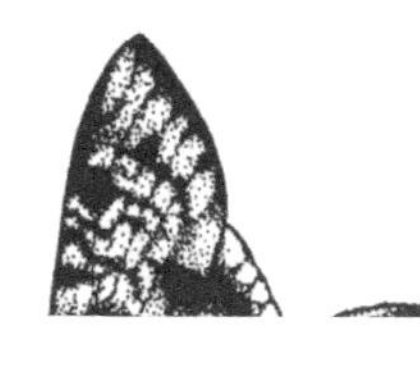

NEVER TO SUFFER

NEVER TO SUFFER

JORDYN BARNES

THE HOLLYWOODLAND SERIES
BOOK FOUR

CONTENT/TRIGGER WARNINGS

This is a polyamorous, pansexual/bisexual romance featuring a woman, a non-binary person, and two men meant for readers 18+. If you are bothered by LGBTQIA+, group scenes, or graphic sexual scenes, this book isn't for you. In fact, my books aren't for you (and no, you don't have to tell me about that). Move on.

Never To Suffer also includes dark subjects as listed in the triggers below.

Abusive relationships and cheating (not between MCs), alcohol use, drug use and discussions of use (including but not limited to marijuana and opioids), battling drug addiction, anxiety, physical assault, rape (not between MCs), blood, injury, bullying, car accident, depression, homophobia, hospitalization including rehabilitation (off page), abortion (off page), kidnapping, gaslighting, misgendering, misogyny, sex work, undiagnosed ADHD, loss of parents (off page), occult/witchcraft, physical abuse, PTSD, sexually explicit scenes.

Reader discretion is strongly advised. If you have questions regarding any of this content, feel free to reach me through my website: www.jordynbarnes.com

To those of us who wander different paths. You're not alone, and you're not lost. Don't listen to the people offering directions if they're only guiding you to conform to their level of comfort. Follow your heart and you'll find the rest of us out there waiting for you with open arms.

You are valid. You are loved.
You deserve better.

"Never to suffer would never to have been blessed."

EDGAR ALLAN POE

DICKTIONARY

Want to find (or avoid?) the open door chapters? Here is a list of chapters that get spicy!

CONTENTS

PEOPLE TO KNOW

<u>The Besties</u>:

Dani Silva: The Princess; Badass FMC of this book. She's the newest member of the friend's club, brought in after a failed date with Jamie Barton.

Chase "Cooper" Cooper: The Basketcase; Hollywood's newest mega star with a severe anxiety disorder, which has him seeing Dr. Theo Clay. This book starts about half way through Chase's own book on the timeline, meaning he's dating Dani's sister, Ren, but also actively dealing with a stalker and Ren's ex-husband. No ego to be found, Chase is just a mentally unstable golden retriever who wants to help everyone.

Steve Jensen: The Criminal; Gym owner and reformed playboy, Steve is out and proud with his husband, Ethan LaVoie. Steve is the joker of the group, but is fiercely loyal to his friends, who he knows have his back even when he screws up.

James "Jamie" Barton: The Nerd; Newly wealthy artist and dreamer with a serious brooding problem. He's survived his sister's extreme jealousy with the help of his friends and the love of his life, Alexis. He's the voice of reason for everyone in the group, except himself.

Devin "Hollywood" Cooper: The Jock; Professional goalie for the the Pasadena Fighting Parrots hockey club, he's Chase Cooper's baby brother. He's still figuring out life one hookup at a time, but doesn't feature heavily in this book.

The Others:

Alexis "Lexi" Strauss: Co-worker (read: Work Wife) of Dani and wife of James Barton. She's Dani's best friend, true crime buddy, and constant fashion project.

Ethan "Lala/Sweets" LaVoie: Steve Jensen's husband and professional hockey player for Pasadena Fighting Parrots.

Laurie Jensen: Steve Jensen's twin sister and one of Dani's closest friends/favorite person to dress. She's a lawyer who's just overthrown her father and taken over his law firm.

Renate "Ren" Silva: Dani's older sister who, through most of this book, is in hiding from her ex-husband, a violent member of a local gang.

Kennedy: Former co-worker of Dani and Alexis and former girlfriend to Steve Jensen. She's a recovering alcoholic and sex addict who works with Dr. Theo Clay as his new receptionist.

Elle Petrov: Sister of James Barton, she's currently serving time for numerous internet and identity crimes. Suspected in the murder of her father and several other crimes that weren't prosecuted due to lack of concrete evidence against her.

DANI, XANDER, THEO, & SKYLAR

HOLLYWOOD
Dani

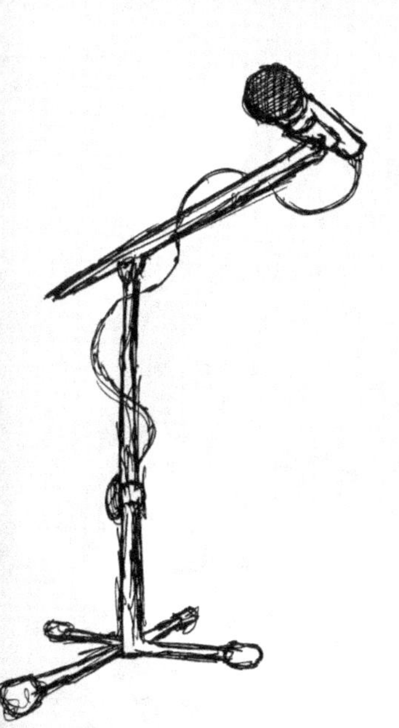

CHAPTER 1
TO ALL THE ONES THAT I LOVE

PRESS CLUB

THE OBNOXIOUS FLYER on the walls of the preppy coffee shop yells at me the minute I see it.

Is your band good enough to be the next megastar headliner?!

I read it over and over again, building my confidence each time until I'm screaming *YES!* in my mind. We're ready for fame to throw its arms open and invite us to play for the gods and goddesses of Olympus. For the world to cheer our names and wear our merch. We were born for this, for stardom, tours, and fans.

Or, that's what I'm standing here trying to convince myself to believe.

Am I sure we're ready to let that fickle bitch embrace us before turning her back on us for the next new, shiny thing? Can we handle going so big, we spend every minute on tour or sitting for interviews on global television and podcasts? Would we survive touring with each other non-stop for months at a time?

Am I ready to drop everything I know and love to make the leap into uncertainty? I have no idea, but I'd like to give it a try.

"What's got your attention? Please tell me it's not another

psychic convention or whatever they're called." My girlfriend checks the reflection of her hair in the window next to me, even though I've assured her the braids still look fine after our make-out session in the bathroom. She used to trust me, but we've been clinging to a dying relationship for weeks now. Or maybe it's me ignoring the red flags she waves in my face. Either way, one of us will break soon enough. We've got too much crackling energy between us and not the positive, fun kind. Every card I pull over the last two weeks has been a warning to let things go, but I'm stubborn.

Okay, I'm controlling. Whatever.

She smears my gloss over her pouty lips before thrusting the tube in my direction. She refuses to use my lip gloss after me if I've gone down on her.

So. Many. Red. Flags.

"It's for a contest." I nod to the flyer, refusing to break over cosmetics. I pull my phone out of my purse and snap a picture so I can upload it to the group chat. They'll laugh and tell me I'm crazy for thinking we could handle that kind of competition. But it could push us to get out of Connor's storage unit and into a real studio. Leave the small bars behind for actual venues. If we give ourselves a chance, nothing can hold us back.

Nothing but ourselves.

And maybe Rory, our bassist.

"You're not seriously thinking of entering that, are you?" Megan squints and leans close as if she doesn't have perfect eyesight. She loves drama, which makes the film industry the perfect career for her when she's on a gig. "Dani, that's a lot of money for an entry fee. We just moved into hell on earth because we're broke and you want to do *this*?"

"What are you talking about? Our awesome apartment? Right in the middle of—"

"A dump?"

"Whatever. The view—

"Of a billboard that's lit the fuck up twenty-four-seven?"

"Fine, okay, the apartment sucks. But maybe this could help? Look here, they're covering all the marketing, booking all the venues, and, if you make it to the top ten, they'll cover all travel expenses after that. That's totally worth the entry fee!"

I've read the poster at least ten times now, and each time, the adrenaline rushes through me, my toes tingle, and I bite back the grin. Our big chance right there on a flyer tacked to a wall of a coffee shop. My fingers are begging me to rip it down so no one else finds out about it, but the big, cartoonish logo of a chimp in a backward baseball hat reminds me this isn't an event you publicize on a bus stop or two. We're talking billboards on Sunset Boulevard levels of big. NotOkay Records has the pull and the money to put together something like this, something raw and untested. This isn't like those stupid auto-tuned contests on TV. Live, baby!

That terrifies me, and I swallow back the bile rising in my throat.

Odds are super in their favor that the contest will grow into a multi-billion-dollar music empire reality competition, like the singing one did years ago. Bands from everywhere competing against each other for a ticket, humiliating themselves in the process of selling out. The first year, though? That's when everything they do has one foot in reality, still about the music and the magic and not the money.

The prize payout for the top three doesn't suck though. I'm not above saying I'm in it for fame, fortune, and glory. I'm just saying I'm *also* in it for the music.

"Dani?!" I'm yanked out of my daydream so fast my vision blurs for a moment until I focus on Megan's scowl. "They've called your name like five times now. Are you going to get your coffee, or what?"

"After what I did to you in the bathroom, you could have grabbed it for me, *babe*."

Three. Orgasms.

That's how my girlfriend starts her day. I start my day getting bitched at because I won't leave my boyfriend, and I daydream too much. Ugh. She used to be fun when we first met.

"Whatever. Get your coffee. I need to go, or I'll be late for my interview." She gives me a peck on the cheek. Even that feels cold. We're still together out of spite more than anything else. "Stop it, babe. Stick to your day job." She stops and juts out a hip. "How do I look?"

"Hot," I groan. "It's only Rory. I'm not sure why you're going all out on looks, since she's basically already hired you."

"I want to look, you know, professional." I give her another look and bite back a laugh. Since when do professionals for an accounting firm wear short skirts and display mega cleavage? She crosses her arms and growls. "It's a decent job, Dani, and until I find another PA spot, or your lazy ass dickhead boyfriend gets an actual job, we need it."

My fingers flex as if I have retractable claws that are ready to come out.

"Oh, don't get all defensive. I don't mean it about Xander. I mean, I do, but I don't." She tries to play with my hair, but I pull away. "Fine. But think about what I said, okay? You don't need him in your—"

"Okay, wonderful. I'll see you at the bar after rehearsal tonight!" The fake smile hurts my face, but that's what she wants. The second she turns her back; I flip her off and stick out my tongue before I head to the counter for my coffee. My phone chirps while I'm racing to the vacant corner table before someone grabs it. Even in my chunky platform boots, I get to the table and slip into the seat seconds before another woman.

Finally, something goes right this morning.

Before I get to the messages on my phone, I set up my office for the day. I hang up my lime green and orange puffy coat on the back of my chair, position my laptop to avoid a glare, and check to see if I should add another hole to my hot pink fishnets. Once I'm finally settled and get that first sip of coffee, I start my day.

I'm not surprised the messages are all from my boyfriend, Xander.

> XANADU
>
> Hey, did you see this? You gotta do this!
> Seriously, I'll fucking rob a bank or whatever so
> you can enter!
>
> [IMAGE ATTACHED]

The flyer about the battle of the bands competition loads on my screen and this time my smile refuses to hide. The differences between my boyfriend and my girlfriend could fill a novel longer than Stephen King's IT. But Xander and I have been together since high school, and I love the little shit.

> Don't say shit like that, the g men will put you
> on a list!
>
> And yeah. I saw it this morning and sent it to
> the band.

> XANADU
>
> Oh, you think I'm not already ON a list? I'm
> probably on hundreds of lists at this point!
>
> Most of them are subscription lists for porn
> sites, but whatever! What did the band say?

> I haven't checked.

> Do you really think it's a good idea to sign up? It's so much money.

XANADU

No. No, it's a terrible idea. YES, I THINK IT'S A GOOD IDEA!

I'll pick up some side work to help you raise the money.

Tell Connor to send me the breakdown once he has it done, cause I know that math loving fucker is crunching numbers right now.

You know, Connor's kind of hot. Hotter than Megan.

> He's seeing someone. Sorry.

My phone rings and I tuck it between my ear and shoulder.

"What did I do wrong?" Xander asks before I can answer.

"What? Nothing." I check the calendar and respond to anything marked as urgent from Sam, my boss. "Why?"

"Because you didn't give me shit for saying we should bang Connor. Also, should *you enter? Where's this negative bullshit coming from? Wait, don't tell me. Megan?"*

I bite my lip and look up at the ceiling, blinking rapidly so I don't ruin my makeup, which looks fucking flawless today. I got excited when Megan invited me out to coffee this morning after we woke up. I even put my cute skirt on, the one she loves because it has this frilly edging she can play with. It's why I pulled her into the bathroom to make out, one last shot at making this work. But on that last orgasm, it wasn't my name she moaned.

Oh, Rory! Right there!

"Xander, should we be worried about this interview? About Megan and Rory?"

"Our triad isn't functional, D. So, if you need to ask—"

"I get it." I try to shake it off. "Uhm, can we talk about it later? Sam has some stuff I need to work on this morning, and I'm just getting settled in at the coffee shop."

"Hey, Beetle?" There's a brief pause filled with the sound of his sigh. It's not frustrated or annoyed like Megan's are. Instead, it's full of longing and hope for us to move on, to embrace the future. *"I don't care what she said or did, you're fucking incredible. You set your boundaries and your trust, and she's broken both more than you want to admit. Now, you're entering this competition. You deserve it. Hell, you deserve the world, Dani. I wish I could give it to you."*

"You already do, Xan."

"I wanna break up with Megan. Wanna help me dance her out of my system at a club tonight or maybe make out?" I'm sitting on my friend's kitchen counter, avoiding going home while I pretend to work. I shovel more of their leftover Chinese food into my face as I stare at the website from the flyer.

"I told you she's gotta go, and you know I'd normally be down, but I can't tonight. It's *date* night," Alexis answers as she walks behind me to see if I've left any food for her.

"Girl, you're married."

"Yeah, for two blissful years. And we still have date nights where we make out like teenagers, giggling and trying not to get caught." She grabs a bite of the half-eaten egg roll and puts the rest in the container I'm eating out of before nodding to my screen. "What's that hideousness?"

Are You Ready to ROCK?! The words scroll across the screen in a garish font and neon colors.

"Band contest. I'm thinking about entering, but it's huge and I don't know if we're exactly *ready to rock.*"

"Cheap bastards can't even hire real designers, and you're worried you're not qualified to win?" Alexis hisses as she reads over my shoulder. "Smash that god awful apply button so we can get off this website. My eyes are bleeding!"

"Hold on, I'm reading the rules!" I scan the page, looking for the keywords to tell me this is all a hoax. "The first gig kicks off a week-long music festival outside Portland. When it's over, they'll take the top twenty-five bands on a crazy-ass national tour, eliminating a band at every stop. Harsh, but epic."

"Sounds like something you and your people will crush." She hands me her credit card and grabs the container of rice. "Put it on here. I need to hop on a call with a client."

I hold up the credit card as I open the group chat, expecting them to bring me back to reality.

CONNOR

YES! I'M IN! Where? When? FUCK IT DON'T CARE!!! LET'S DOOOOO THIS!!

RORY

I'm not sure I can get that kind of time off, but I can negotiate something if I need to.

CONNOR

Fire! I'll borrow my brother's whip and we'll go in styleeeee!! We gotta do this!!!!!! Pleaaaase? Band road trip?

NOAH

His whip? You're fucking delulu. He drives a
minivan!

But yeah, I'm down. Wait, can we afford this?

CONNOR

We so can. I did the maths. We should get
some   sponsors   . Fuck, this is gonna be so

They're onboard. I can't believe what I'm reading.

> Who are you people and what have you done
> with my band?!

> I'm submitting everything now before we
> change our mind!

In two weeks, we'll find out if we really are good enough.

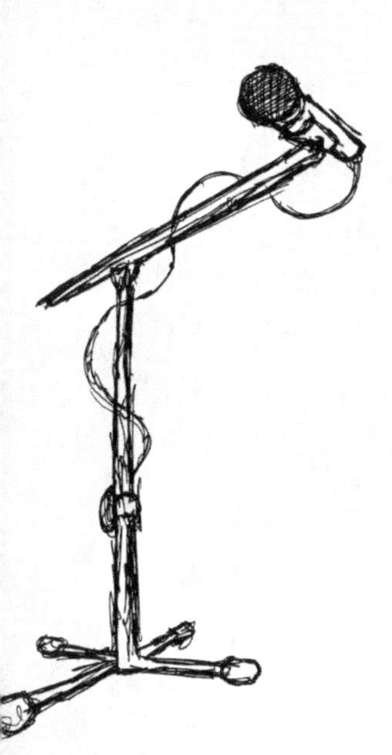

CHAPTER 2
AWAKE NOW

MR BELLA

THE FAMILIAR VIBRATION of Connor warming up his drum kit greets me and rattles the flimsy door of the studio. I'm not sure it should even be called a studio, since it's a rented storage unit full of junk from Connor's family. His mom has a hoarding problem, and instead of getting her help, his dad moves everything out here every few years so she can start her collection all over again. The stacks of newspapers provide stellar sound absorption, but the black trash bags of random crap should get tested for—well—everything.

The door screams when I push it open, and Connor swears about the light and how it burns him. Noah's in her usual spot in the corner on an old couch, notebook out and head buried. She uses this time to get the creative brain flowing, writing poems for her blog or doodling. Across the room and as far from everyone as she can get, Rory blocks out the world with her headphones and face buried in her phone. We're not a well-oiled machine; we don't even qualify as functioning co-workers. A fix for that sits at the top of the list of hurdles we need to clear now that we've gotten our welcome email for the competition.

"Sup, jerks!" I announce myself as if the loud, creaky

doorway wasn't enough. "All in favor of looking for better working conditions and winning this contest, say aye!"

"Dude, we can't afford that shit. Also, your apartment has more mice than this place does. Glass houses and throwing rocks or whatever it is," Connor teases, giving himself a rim shot before he adds, "and my unit is free!"

"Eww, don't talk about your unit!" I tease back.

"Why, cause I'm the only one in here who has one?"

"That's unconfirmed and will remain that way," Noah chimes in, tucking her notebook into her backpack and hanging it on off the giant roll-up door. "So, what's the plan, oh fearless leader of the freak show? How are we getting our asses to Portland?"

The plan doesn't exist, but I can't tell them that. I can't shoot us in the foot before we've even taken a full step toward this. In place of sleep last night, I paced and did internet searches I'm not proud of, trying to figure out how we're going to do this contest and survive. Both in terms of the stress and the cost. When Xander came home around two in the morning, he forced me to drink some tea while he gave me a foot massage and assured me we would make this work and handed me a couple hundred dollars toward Portland. He said it came from a last-minute freelance gig, which I don't bother to ask him about. Anytime I do, he shuts me out, so there's something he doesn't want to share about it. It doesn't require an office or consistent hours, so I've been envisioning him building websites for the mob.

Yo, you wanna knock some guy off? We'll knock some guy off. Check out our website, knocksomeguyoff dot com.

"I ran the numbers and did some research on the area—"

"You?" Rory scoffs. "I wasn't aware you could even add, let

alone create a budget, research costs, and—" She only stops because we're all staring at her.

"Thank you, Connor, is what she means to say, since she didn't exactly volunteer any of her free time to help." I glare at Rory, who rolls her eyes. She loves to bring all the negativity to the function. "We've already been accepted, so no need to fork out cash for demo reels or new material, so that's, you know, good? But I did send the marketing photos and some other shit."

"LA Proper takes Portland by storm! Where are we playing, anyhow?"

"Well," Connor says as he sends the group chat photos of the venue, a map, and other details. I'm pretty impressed by everything he did while I spent my time pacing myself into an early grave. "They're bringing in a ton of bands, and setting up two to three stages, and here's the location they picked. I mean, it's, you know, kinda cool. Right?"

Noah flips through the photos and snorts a laugh before staring at Connor to gauge how serious he is. "A warehouse?"

"Two warehouses! One stage and two bars each, with an outdoor stage setup for night shows. It's gonna be so fire."

"Bro, doesn't it, like, always rain in Portland or something?" Noah asks, looking between Connor and me. She's met with blank stares since neither of us have ever been to Portland to answer that. "Fuck it! I'll play in a damn tornado for a shot at this."

"When will we know the lineup or stage?" Rory asks. "Like, play one set and out or how much time are we talking?"

"They're supposed to email us a loose itinerary in the next day or two." I set up my computer and squat down to map out the motels Connor pinned, but a ding and a notification window pull my attention elsewhere. I've got a new email. It's from NotOkay Records.

"Okay, so wait, are we taking the van or—"

"Shut up!" I yell, pointing at my screen. "They've emailed us!"

"Who? Wait, NotOkay Records? Oh fuck, that was fast." Noah scrambles off her chair and runs over.

"Is that good or bad?" Marco asks as he moves closer. "Come on, open it!"

My finger hovers over the touch pad for a moment, then drops with two quick taps.

CONGRATULATIONS!

Yo, LA Proper!

Is this your lucky day, or what? You're now part of the show and the first ever Sink The Rich (subject to change) tour!

Below, you'll find a list of tour dates, venues, and information (all subject to change, so make sure you sign up for our…)

"*Sink the rich?*" Rory asks from somewhere behind me.

Connor laughs at points at the anthropomorphized punk rock orca jumping onto a yacht. "That's so fire! What does it mean?"

"How are we almost the same age and yet sometimes I feel like I don't understand anything you're saying?" I ask, and he shrugs.

"Only child?"

"Oy. Okay, remember the orcas that were sinking all those fucking yachts a while back?" Noah snickers as she explains it to him as if he were five. "And how the yacht rock bros all think they're so punk and alternative. It would have been funny like four years ago."

"My dad listens to yacht rock," Connor adds, shoulders slumping for a moment before he laughs again. "I'm gonna buy him a shirt with the logo on it. He'd get the humor."

"They'll change the name if it gets big enough. Something even more lame, like ALTour or some shit." I've been hanging around too many marketing and design firm people. I skim the rest of the email and look up at everyone hovered over me. "Guys, they want us to do three sets for the first event. Three! Are we gonna get anything played today, or should I call and tell Megan we've reconvened at the office?"

"OFFICE!" Connor and Noah shout together, while Rory groans and heads to the corner with her bass. She grabs her phone and starts rapid fire texting someone, but shoves it in her pocket when I'm a few steps away.

"See you there?" I ask and offer a smile and a wave. She only grunts back.

"Hey, I uhm, I know you're not thrilled about canceling rehearsals and all. I get that. But right now, hammering out logistics might be wiser, and you're better at that than Noah and I." If I stop and imagine what it's like talking to an active volcano, I'd picture Rory as the volcano. I'm never sure if it's going to blow up in my face or gurgle at me to remind me I'm insignificant. "Look, dumb question, but, uhm, you and Megan—"

"What about it?"

"What? Oh, I mean, I don't…How did the interview go? She worked at the bar last night, so I didn't get to see her."

"It went fine. I'll see you at the bar," she snaps, grabbing her gear and marching through the door.

"Okay. Cool. Cooooool," I mumble, following Connor and Noah out.

"What was that all about?" Noah asked, nodding toward

Rory as she closed the trunk and climbed into her fancy sports car.

"Not sure, but Megan interviewed with her the other day and didn't come home."

"Duuude," Connor's eyes go wide. "Do you think Rory murderated her? Sucked her blood out and dropped her in a dumpster?!"

Noah slaps him in the back of the head and tells him to get in the car while I keep an unreadable face. They don't need to know I imagined that scenario last night. Rory would make a terrible vampire, though. Because an accountant by day and vampire by night? Lame.

The local dive bar. Or our office, as we like to call it. The place reeks of stale beer, my shoes stick to the floor, and the pool tables haven't seen better days since at least twenty years ago. But, the bartenders know us, don't water down the drinks when we're broke, and never kick us out when we take over a table for a few hours to talk business. In fact, the second we walk in we're greeted by Bobby, a giant of a man that makes my gym bunny bestie, Steve, look like a sick puppy.

"LA PROPER!" His deep voice fills the room, drawing the letters out for emphasis and turning the few heads hiding in the dark corners. "Hey, did y'all see the competition shit going on? Some little fucker came in yesterday and wanted to put flyers up. I told him not to bother. LA Proper was gonna win the whole fuckin' thing."

"Aww, this is why we love you, Bobby!" I jump up and give him a hug.

"Drinks all around!" Connor announces as he raises his arms. Bobby gives him a look and Connor clears his throat. "Well, around the table we'll be sitting at."

"You got it. Bucket o' brews, coming your way."

"Where'd Rory go?" Connor asks an hour later when Bobby comes by, drops the third bucket of ice and bottles in front of us, and retreats to his corner of the bar to watch baseball. He's great at keeping the table stocked but not interrupting the process—or missing a pitch.

"I dunno, she dipped like ten minutes ago," Noah answers. She looks around the room and shrugs.

"Maybe she went to find Megan. Didn't you say she'd be here in like twenty minutes?" I check my phone but find no messages. "Well, whatever. We have a plan even without their help. Connor, you're on transportation and lodging."

"10-4, Captain."

"Noah, you're keeping the socials active and keeping up with updates from NotOkay Records. And I'll work on getting some new merch designs and printing. Rory can do what she always does, let us handle everything and throw money at it when we complain she's not pulling her weight." Relief washes over me, my need to over-plan and my anxiety finally taking a step back to let me breathe. I stop and look around the table at my friends, my bandmates, the people who are on this wild ride with me. "We're fucking doing this!"

Noah snaps a few photos of us around the table, even getting Bobby and the bar's logo in a few because we can't forget where we came from when we're famous. She's looking forward to documenting the whole crazy experience, and I can't blame her. This contest, this day, they'll change all our lives so much. Win or lose. Except we can't fucking lose.

After I finish my beer, I head for the bathrooms, texting

Xander with an update and asking if Megan has come home instead of heading to the bar. Before I reach out to push the door to the restroom, it flies open and I'm staring at Rory, who's tucking her shirt in as she holds the door open for none other than my fucking girlfriend, who's straightening out her skirt.

"The. Fuck?"

"Wait! I can explain!" Megan spits out as she holds her hands out.

"Oh, I fucking doubt that. Go back to the table and fucking wait, because I gotta pee before I rage. Excuse me."

I push past them both and into the room, giving them a little shoo gesture as they both stare at me, eyes wide and faces paler than normal. Once they leave, I lock the door and press my back to it, too much going through my mind all at once. I wanted to break up with her, but this isn't how I wanted to do it.

I take a few deep breaths, do my business, and think about splashing water on my face, but fuck that. I won't ruin a perfect makeup day over those two jerks. Connor and Noah keep exchanging looks as I walk up to the table. Bobby gawks at Rory and Megan as they make out. I clear my throat loud enough to break them up and slam my phone down on the table, making them both jump. I'm sure I'm supposed to be the bigger person in this situation, but I'd rather stab them both with those little toothpicks fancy bars put olives on. Who am I kidding? This bar doesn't even have toothpicks. Or olives.

"Given the circumstances that have come to light in the last few minutes—"

"Fuck, are we canceling the concert?" Connor asks.

"Nope. Rory, you're fucking fired. Connor and Noah, we'll start rehearsing bassists as soon as we can."

"Wait, what?" Rory screams as she pushes Megan off her lap.

"You can fuck Xander but you're firing me for kissing Megan? You don't own her, you know."

"Yeah, no shit. Megan, you have a week to be out of the apartment. If you had only talked to us, this could have ended much cleaner." I grab my things and glare at Rory. "And Rory, I can fuck Xander because we're in a relationship, which included Megan. Cheating is not how a polycule works. Look it the fuck up."

"This isn't fair!" Megan yells.

"You're right, Meg. I should have dropped your ass the minute you tried to pull me away from Xander. I'd never leave him for you. He eats pussy better than you do."

Megan lunges, but Connor steps between us, curling his arm around me. "We'll walk you out," Connor offers, Noah nodding beside him.

We get out to the parking lot and I'm a raging mess. Sure, I planned to break up with her anyhow, but I wanted to do it my way, not finding them fucking around in the bathroom.

"Do you think we can find a bassist in time?" Connor asks, his jovial tone extinguished.

"If we don't, we get knocked out the first week. We've already paid the entry fee. Why not go for it, right?" I struggle to keep a positive demeanor while I'm falling apart inside.

HOLLYWOOD
Xander

CHAPTER 3
OCEAN AVENUE
YELLOWCARD

"DID you speak to my assistant about the employment opportunity?"

"Yeah, I called her last week. Not gonna work out."

"What about the—"

"I've got a thing right now, mom. I picked up another app dev job and I don't have time. It's fine. And my free time is all helping Dani and the band get ready for the competition I told you about earlier." I laugh when she nods and goes back to her book. She hasn't got a clue what an app dev job is, which means it's perfect for me to hide behind. If I told her what I've been doing, she'd drop dead right here on the authentic Persian rug from the late 1800s. Who am I kidding? She'd at least have the common decency to move to the Italian marble since it's easier for someone to clean.

As someone destined for titles and abbreviations after my name, there's something refreshing when I'm given the opportunity to tell people I'm a Cam Boi for a subscription-based website making more money than they do. Or, I would make more money than they do if I posted more frequently. So far, I only bother to post when we're desperate, because I'm also working on an app that will outpace the most popular sites in under a year. I'm not lazy. In fact, I'm the opposite. But why work a 9-5 job when whipping my dick out for twenty minutes earns me more than a full week's pay at some of those places?

"Your adaptive whatever you called it isn't an honest job, Alex."

"App Dev, Mom. And yeah, it is."

For years I've wanted to go on these interviews my mom sets up for 'real jobs,' look the interviewer in the eye, and laugh when they ask why a rich kid like me didn't go to some prestigious college with polo shirts and embroidered blazers. Knowing my charming ways, I'd end the interview by giving them my link and by the end of the week, they'd book a date for some quality one-on-one time. It's an easy and effective way to show them why I opted out of college and into the adult scene. Besides, in-person hookups are always more interesting. And expensive.

I remember one of my therapists asking me why I do it when I told her about it.

*"Well, ma'am, jerking off for guys while on camera might be my calling. Far more satisfying than most jobs, especially things like law or business. And not all the guys are perverts. How **is** your son, by the way?"*

For some reason, she didn't want to see me anymore after that. Crazy. Her son still did.

I walk across my father's study to the closet, where my parents keep the few reminders that I once lived in this house. Not childhood drawings or report cards, no toys, or children's books. Clothes. More precisely, custom-tailored designer suits. A few dozen for every occasion where tight black jeans, t-shirts, and combat boots with holes in their heels won't cut it. A dozen hangers from here would easily total up to more than what Dani makes in a year at her office job, and there are at least three dozen hangers. I grab one of the black suits, a silver watch I could sell for a new car, and a purple tie before heading to the changing area.

"Alex?" My parents insist on calling me that, even though I stopped using it back when I first met Dani. "Do you remember Ronald? He's going to be at the ceremony next week. You should talk to him about your computer things."

Oh yeah, I remember Ronald. I also remember the two grand he gave me after a party a few years ago so I wouldn't say anything to anyone about what we did together. Television and movies make blackmail look so messy, unartistic, but I've got a flair for the dramatic. I keep tapes, but I don't tell them. It's far more fun to show up at big, wealthy events and watch them sweat while they introduce me to their wives and children.

Will I tell? Won't I? Could I have more on them?

"Yeah, I'll be sure to say hi to him."

"Oh, and did you hear about Amelia?" Mom calls out. "She's graduating next month and already has hospitals all over the country begging for her."

"She used to date Franky, right? How is good ole Franklin doing?" I yell back through the door while pulling up my pants, knowing it will stop the name-dropping bullshit. The cops picked Franky up in a child porn sting a few months ago and he weaseled his way out because he could afford a decent lawyer, but even the best lawyer can't wipe people's memories.

I finish looping the tie and give myself a once over. Mom will want me to wear the jacket, which works since it's where I'll stash my cigarettes and a joint—necessary evils when dealing with the likes of her people.

"Honey, don't forget that we're having that party for your

father and I next week. So please, try to behave yourself while you're here."

I bow with dramatic flair as I come out of the bathroom and present myself. "Yes, mother. Of course, mother. I shan't conduct myself in any manner thou wouldst deem unfit to thine eyes."

"Don't be like that, Alex." She doesn't look up from the book she's reading, ignoring me as I shovel handfuls of expensive chocolates and imported macadamia nuts into my mouth. "Should I send over the car to take you and Ms. Silva to the shops so you can help her find something appropriate to wear?"

Choking on Russian chocolates wasn't on my bingo card for ways I would die, but I came damn close when the image of saying that to Dani popped into my brain. She'd take my head clean off and dance over my dead body in some crazy outfit she custom made for the occasion of ending me. Even as I cough and try to catch my breath, my mother assumes it's dramatics and doesn't look up.

"No, mother," I choke out. It's more of a snarl than words. I don't like when people talk shit about Dani. Especially when those people are my parents. "Dani will wear whatever the hell she wants, and if you don't approve? It will save us all the trouble of pretending to enjoy ourselves at your big shindig when you kick us out the servants' entrance."

"Oh, you know what I mean, Alexander. Don't act like I have a problem with your...girlfriend." And yet, she always finds a problem with Dani.

I didn't plan on meeting the most perfect woman in the world in my second class of public school, but there she sat, dark purple hair fading into electric green at the ends, wild, bright makeup, and an outfit to match. I've seen men peacock for the attention of women, but that beautiful creature had me by the dick the second she flashed those big brown eyes at me. It's been thirteen years since, and she's still holding on tight. Just the way I like it.

"Yes, that will work nicely, but you should wear the blue tie. It makes your eyes brighter." She means more like hers, since we're on opposite ends of the blue-eyed spectrum. Mom thinks people will believe I'm her actual son if our eyes look enough alike. She even had me wearing blue tinted contacts when she decided mine were too gray. But most people already know I'm adopted, anyhow. "Make sure you lay out the suits you want packed for Tokyo while you're at it. Not too many. You can buy new ones while you're there, I'm sure. Those are all too old now."

"Tokyo?" I rummage around in my backpack and find an empty bag I probably used for weed at some point. Opening it confirms that suspicion from the smell alone, but it doesn't stop me from dumping the contents of the small snack bowls into it. Dani loves this kind of shit, and stopped asking me where I get it from, so she doesn't get weirded out by eating *rich people's food*.

My confusion must cut deep because when I glance up, I find my mother making eye contact. The raised eyebrow stops me mid pour, my heart thumping against my ribs. I'm not sure if it's the candy snatching or me not knowing shit about packing for Tokyo. I can take a guess, though, when she closes her book and takes her glasses off. Another conference or business meeting they're dragging me to. That's a twelve-hour flight. Twelve hours of panic, white knuckles, and sweat. Maybe I'll beat my record of hurling twice the last time we went.

"Alexander, your father notified you nearly a month ago. He gave you ample time to make yourself available and prepare for a trip to Japan. Your father wants this, and to your future, young man, depends on it. You can't—" she waves her hands around in a wild gesture that looks like she's chasing a fly. "You can't continue this unambitious and uninspired life journey. You're twenty-eight, for god's sake."

I almost correct her, since I'm almost thirty-one, but now might not be the time. I bite my lip while my brain cycles through emails and texts until the one she's talking about pops into my memory. The strategy of ignoring my father until he goes away works once in a while, but apparently this wasn't one of those times. My parents both mean well, and they tried to raise me in their footsteps. But it was more like their shadows. I don't do business like my dad. I can't speak Japanese, I hate flying. I even hate driving. I'm the worst and only person he has in mind to take over for him when he decides it's time for retirement and mimosas in Greece. As for mom's legal profession, I only want to know the laws that apply to me and how I can get around them when needed. Otherwise, I don't give a fuck or have any righteous sense of justice pulling me down that path.

That's why I didn't go to college, ditched boarding schools, and found the love of my life well outside the gold gates of Brentwood. I want to jerk off for money, and have wild sex with my girlfriend, not sit through boring people droning on about finances and the market.

"You need to start taking life seriously, Alex. You and Ms. Silva won't be able to gallivant through California like a pair of hippie nomads forever, son." She opens her books again and goes back to scanning the pages. "This nonsensical flitting about and taking contributions from the public on street corners to survive, it's indecent and idiotic—not to mention a burden on the rest of society."

"We don't take money from people on street corners, mom. Seriously?"

"You won't even tell me where the two of you reside now. I

don't think you should be living together under any circumstances, but if you must live in sin, I should know the location, at the very least." She gasps as a thought occurs to her before I can answer and looks up at me again. "Oh, Alex. Please tell me it's not in one of those tents destroying the glorious view of the downtown area?"

She'd die just to turn over in her grave if she saw where Dani and I were living, even though it's not a tent. She doesn't *hate* Dani, but she doesn't make an effort to understand us and what polyamory is, so in her mind, this is a phase, and I'll move on and find someone more suitable for the likes of our family. Mother may have lost some of her accent, but she lost little of the elitist attitude that comes from being too high up the ladder in London's upper crust of society.

"Yeah, ma, it's the orange one over in front of the courthouse. We're not in a tent, we're over in…it doesn't matter. We won't be there long. It's temporary. Only until the end of the competition that Dani's going to win. I'm working with a few new clients to save up the money she needs and extra for expenses and bills."

Of course, Dani doesn't know about the cam thing. She thinks I've been out getting odd jobs or working for my dad off and on to help support us since we got our own place a few weeks ago. I did try, I put in an honest effort. I also *do* work for my dad, but not as often as she thinks. Instead, I rigged up my old laptop, got a decent webcam, and setup an account where the depraved old fuckers can watch me for around ten dollars a month. Extra if they want to tell me what to do. It's one of the only times I've ever lied to Dani. I'm not avoiding the truth; she wouldn't leave me for telling her what I do. I lie so she won't get her own account to screw with me. She also knows when I'm going out to meet one of them. She thinks we met at work or a club. Technicalities.

"You're still ignoring my request for an address by deflecting."

"Okay, but your degrees are in law, not psychiatry. I'll message you the address later if you can get me out of this Tokyo trip so I can work. Isn't that what you wanted?"

"Not happening, kiddo." My father's voice barges into the room before he does. I assumed he took the day to go golfing since he does that almost every other day of the week. "I need you on this one. Now stop squirreling away the snacks and take the bags from the pantry. Milly can show you where they are."

"Charles, you know the doctor said those weren't good for your heart."

"That's why the candy bowls are small. Fewer to tempt me." He waggles his thick eyebrows at me and winks.

"Dad, come on. Tokyo? Can't we, like, video call or something? You know I don't understand any of the business talk bullshit."

"Watch your mouth," my mother scolds before returning to her book.

"I've got your ticket. The driver will pick you up and take you to the airport," my father says, watching me pour his snacks back out. He either doesn't smell the weed from the baggie, or he doesn't recognize it. "It will be fun, Alex. I promise! I've set up a lovely assistant for you, and sent you an itinerary of meetings, dinners, and when you'll have free time to *roam about* with your assistant." His eyebrows waggle again and my stomach clenches.

"Dad, that's...what?" My dad tries too hard to be cool, and I'm pretty sure he intended the innuendo, but I'm not one hundred percent sure. I shake my head, undo my tie, and go back into the bathroom, getting out of this stupid suit and back into real clothes. When I come out again, the conversation picks right back up where we left off.

"The driver can't taxi your son to the airport if we don't have his new address, dear. How would poor Albert know where to go?"

"His name is Alberto, Mom."

My father's mouth forms a flat line as he raises his eyebrows and shoves his hands in his pockets. "She has a point. Remedy that, would you, son?"

"I'll get to the airport on my own. Don't worry about sending Alberto." I pull on my backpack and kiss my mother on the cheek. "I'll see you guys at the party. Hopefully. I gotta get some work done so they don't shut off the power."

"You're so dramatic, Alexander. They don't turn off people's *electricity*."

Once again, I don't bother correcting her. She lives in a special world and there's no bursting that ironclad bubble.

"You're working? That's great, son!" Dad beams. If he ever figured out what I've set up, the word *disappointment* would come out and play, and I'm not fucking around with that word right now. The act with my parents requires a delicate touch, to say the least.

"Yeah, I'm still building freelance gigs, working on app development. Nothing long term, but it pays the bills, and I have a few that might, you know, take off someday."

"Well, that's a start. Bring your computer things with you on the trip; you should have ample free time to keep working your *gig* while we're there."

"Already thought of that, Dad." And all the freaky shit I can get up to in Japan. With or without my assistant. "See you later! Don't forget, Dani's coming to the party. She doesn't eat meat, mom!"

HOLLYWOOD
Dani

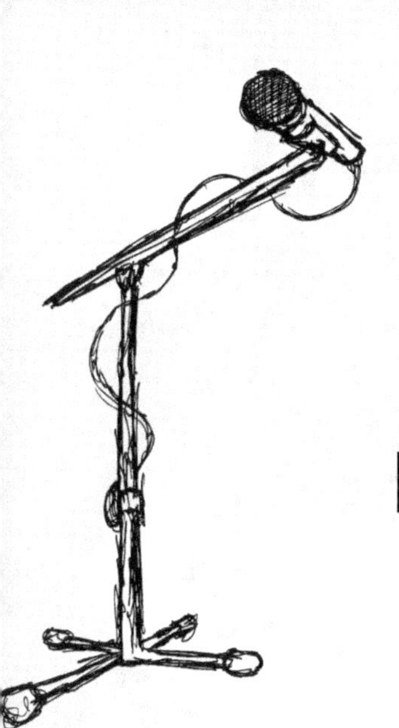

CHAPTER 4
HERE COMES YOUR MAN

PIXIES

"AHHH! THAT'S SO FUCKING GREAT!" Xander yells as he lifts me into the air, spinning us both around. It's well past midnight, and he's trying to be quiet about his excitement, but it's too much to hold in. "You're in the competition, you finally ditch Megan, AND you kick Rory out? Best day ever!"

"Okay, not exactly the response I needed, Xander. I mean, even without the whole Megan cheating issue, how are we going to do this? Find a bassist, figure out the tour, pay for this apartment? We can't do all this. We can't."

"We'll find a way. Like we always do, Beetle." He tucks a strand of hair behind my ear before his fingers trace my jaw and slide down my neck. His thumb runs over the center of my throat before he walks me backward and into a wall. His voice becomes more of a deep growl than his usual, light tone. "You know what I wanna do to celebrate this? I wanna fuck a rock star to make sure you remember me while you're gone on tour. I want you to think about what I do to you while you're tempting sexy, hedonistic fans into your bed until you come back to me."

"That's more a you thing, Xan."

"But you shouldn't miss out on the full rockstar experience. Either way, I still want you. Now."

His other hand finds my hips and slips under my skirt and into my fishnets while he still holds me against the wall. I wasn't even that horny until he lowered his voice. After that, I turned on like a fucking faucet. It doesn't help matters when his rock-hard cock pressing against me through his tight jeans. My blood becomes fire as his mouth crashes into mine, igniting my body at every point where our bodies touch. He grinds against me, whimpering when I grab his bottom lip between my teeth and bite down. It's not enough to draw blood, but enough to make him want more.

My leg wraps around him, pushing my hips up to feel him as he dry humps me against the wall. Such a strange name for something considering I'm anything but dry, soaking through my panties and his jeans, too. He squeezes my neck as he pulls away from the kiss and grins. "You taste like tequila and limes."

"I should say that's racist, but it's true."

Using his thumb, he pushes my jaw, forcing me to look away from him. Xander's a neck man, and I like to tell him he was a vampire in another life. Some days, it might let him get fake fangs and bite into my flesh to see if it releases any of the flames that have built inside me. To feel that warm trickle of blood and let him live out that fantasy. The rip and pop noise pulls me out of that fantasy as he rips my fishnets and panties.

"Xander!" I moan, low and loud, driving him on.

"I'll buy a new pair. Promise. Or better yet, stop wearing them so I can bend you over anytime I want a taste of you."

"Would you? Would you bend me over in a library and slide that dirty tongue through me?"

"Every damn day. Open your mouth." I do as he asks, and he

pulls up my t-shirt, stuffing the hem between my lips. "Good girl. Now, don't let go."

I almost do when his tongue flicks the metal bar that goes through my nipple, but I bite down, screaming in bliss into the fabric. My nails claw at his arm, but he grabs my wrists, letting go of my neck. With one hand, he pins my arms over my head, and with the other, he undoes his belt and pants. The way my hips rock forward, begging him to fuck me, makes him laugh that low, menacing chuckle that has me in a trance for him.

"Bratty little slut, making me work hard for this." He leans in, whispering next to my ear. "You'll pay for that later." He pushes into me, but not the way I expect him to. When I'm a brat, it means I want it rough, but he insists on teasing me with short, shallow thrusts. "Maybe I'll edge you tonight. Make that cunt of yours throb all night for me until you wake me up, begging for me to fuck you into the mattress. Make you cry for me while I fill your throat."

I whine through the shirt still in my mouth, screwing my eyes shut. That's when he slams into me so hard my toes lift off the ground for a moment as he pins me against the wall with his hips. Xander doesn't have a stacked body, because he's a runner. In his clothes, he looks damn near scrawny, but when the clothes come off, it's a different story.

"Dani," he moans, running his nose along mine; his heavy breath against my skin as he holds me there. "How did I ever deserve you?"

He thrusts hard and deep, still holding my arms against the wall but using his free hand to play with my clit until there's nothing in the universe but him and the way he makes me feel. I can't hold out, and he doesn't want me to, not the way he's slamming into me, full of lust and need. When he releases my arms, I fling myself around him, listening to him grunt, sucking hard on my neck as he rails me against the wall. I hold his head against me until he comes inside me with a wicked moan.

His mumbles don't always make sense after sex, like today, a handful of noises and a scattering *I love you's* as he slips back down to earth. Once he's ready, he carries me to the bedroom and cleans me up before taking care of himself.

Stepping out of the bathroom with those cute, nerdy glasses on, he flops onto the bed, quick to snuggle around me. "I love you, Dani." He leaves soft kisses along the same spots on my neck that I'm sure will have bruises tomorrow, pulling the blanket over us both. As soon as he turns on the screen of his phone, I roll over and bury my face in his chest, listening to the way it rumbles as he reads to me from the second book in the Lord of the Rings series. He does voices like he's reading to a child, but I don't stop him. It's cute. I doze off somewhere around the part with the talking trees.

Morning comes, and Xander drives us to one of our favorite breakfast spots in the valley. We leave early, so LA looks like a movie scene for an apocalypse movie, or the pandemic a few years back. No one here likes to get up before noon if they can help it. And at six in the morning on a Saturday? It's a ghost town. A few hours from now, Porto's will have a line out the door waiting to place their orders and send the worker bees into a dance down the refrigerator cases. I enjoy standing in line and watching them buzz around almost as much as I love looking in at the fruity, glaze covered cakes and tasty treats. But today, I prefer to be left alone at a table.

"You know what I wish they had? Cuban toast." Xander

laments as he places a tray of food in front of me with a breakfast burrito and torrejas. "They have everything else, but man, I could have gone for a solid Cuban toast with cheese and a cafe con leche with way too much sugar in it. Someday, I'll take you to get a non-Californian Cuban breakfast."

He sets down two overflowing bags full of delicious treats that should last us a week or more, but won't last the weekend. Cheese rolls, Croqueta de Pollo, and as many little desserts as he could get, I'm sure. This place isn't expensive if you have self-control, but he knows when I get a look at those bakery cases, all self-control goes out the window and I order one of everything. Two, if it's one of my favorites. I'm not an expensive jewelry girl, but I am a foodie with a high metabolism and a bottomless pit for pastries and sweets.

I lean over and fix a piece of Xander's hair that's sticking up. Even with day-old product in it, it's somehow still soft and inviting. The warm caramel color should be a juxtaposition to his ice gray eyes, but to me, everything about him screams cozy and tender.

"I heard it has something to do with the air in Los Angeles not being humid enough," he rambles, trying to get me to talk.

I bring the cup to my lips, feeling the burn as it slides down my throat. It needs more sugar, but it will do. "I don't know, Xan. I'm Mexican, not Cuban."

"Fair. Do you want to start with breakfast or dessert? And for once, that's not sexual. I got you that mango thing you love." He reaches into the bag and pulls out a little box and a fork, handing them to me. "Here you go."

His fingers lace between mine, and he squeezes just enough for me to look up. There's something in his face that chips away all the existential dread hounding me. Like his smile tells me this will all work out somehow so long as we have each other.

"Come on, you hot, nerdy, rich boy, let's go home and take our bed back from the mice. You can feed me sugary mango cakes all day while we watch old sci-fi movies in bed."

"Will you be naked at some point?"

"You know it, big guy."

HOLLYWOOD
Dani

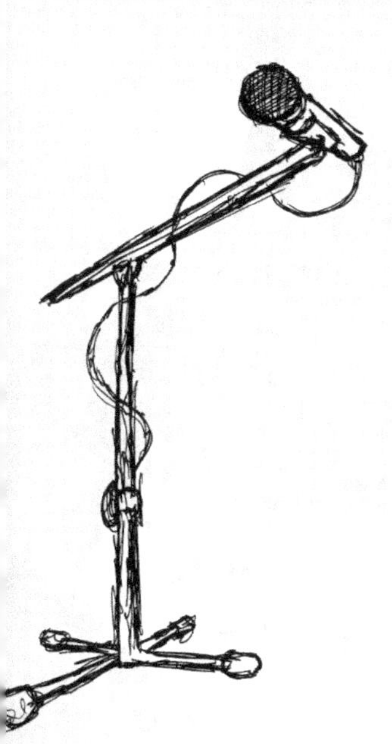

CHAPTER 5
APT

ROSÉ/ BRUNO MARS

I'M NOT sure if it's the arctic temperature in the room or Xander's hard-on poking me in the back that wakes me up after only a few hours of sleep. I shiver, and Xander's instincts have him wrapping around me, which also makes him grind against my ass. A scream comes from one of the other apartments and realize our neighbors are going at it again, and thanks to these paper-thin walls, it's like they're here in the bed with us.

A wild banshee's scream of *YES! MICHAEL! OH GOD!* has a half-awake Xander sitting upright too fast and falling out of the bed. Luckily, our bed isn't anything but a mattress on the floor, so he didn't have far to fall. The way he scrambles back up into the bed should make me laugh, but I cringe instead.

"What is it? What's the matter!?" He asks as he rubs his eyes and looks around the bed like the intruder would crawl on four legs and squeak.

Because ours *do*.

"Oh, yeah, baby. You like that? Huh? You like that?"

Instead of getting pissed off about the noise, Xander smirks and winks at me, which I can see because of the bright ass

billboard lights that flood our apartment no matter what curtains we try to hang. I used to like those neon lights and the way they formed a stain glass halo through Megan's afro while her head bobbed between my legs. Of course, now she wears her hair in braids—and she screws Rory—so I hate the dumb billboard lights.

I don't miss her, but I do feel like a failure over the entire situation. She's the fourth or fifth person we've tried to bring into our lives over the last few years for something more than a few nights of fun. Each one fails more epically than the next. Everyone since…

"We could make it a competition?" Xander's hand grips my thigh, but I only roll my eyes.

We need to move. We can't afford it—not if I'm about to go on tour.

"I'm coming!" the woman's voice screams out.

"I'm leaving," I say, shoving the covers back and climbing over Xander. He reaches for me but when I avoid him, his arms drop to the bed, defeated.

Slamming the door to the bathroom is cathartic, but the momentary joy fades fast once I turn on the shower. The hot water went out over a week ago. I wait, listening to the horror soundtrack from the pipes until it reaches a crescendo of bellows and goes silent. That's new, but I can't tell if it's a good or bad sign.

There's a creak, followed by a soft click when the door closes behind me. A heavy coat drapes over my shoulders before Xander feels his way around in the dark for an outlet to plug the small space heater into. I come here often, relaxing by the orange glow of the heater when I need to reset in a cool, dark place. Like a fucking potato.

"Want some tea?" He asks as he wraps around me again, rubbing my arms to warm me. If I wasn't so damn hardheaded, we could be in a posh hotel somewhere until they fix the water heater. Or, better yet, an apartment that wasn't an absolute shit hole. But Xander and I agreed years ago we'd do this on our own, which means no help from his disgustingly rich parents.

I came up with the idea to move out of my mama's place when we started dating Megan. Which means this, like everything else, is my fault.

"Why is it so fucking cold?"

"June gloom?" He kisses my cheek, and I respond with a groan. "Come on, D. I only wanna see you smile again. I wanna see that sparkle back in your eye and snark in your voice. This venom? This anger? It's not you, no matter how hard you try. You're pissed about Meg and Rory but fuck them." He kisses my forehead and rubs my arms. "I'm not saying you can't be upset or disappointed. I'm just saying don't let the bullshit win."

"I know. I'm trying!" I'm not trying too hard, but I've never felt depression like this. That's Xander's territory as my nerdy emo boy. Thankfully, he's picking up the slack and doing all the right things to help me through it.

I wanted this to be my year, and it's been anything but. I shouldn't have moved out of mom's house. I miss having my friends over. I'm second guessing everything I do, and Xander's right, none of this fits me and my personality.

"I'm worried about the band. The kid we found as a temporary bassist? He's…not good. Like he's okay for playing in a bar sometimes, or as emergency backup, but he's not…he's not Rory-good."

"I hate to force more facts your way, sweetheart, but Rory was okay. She wasn't impressive and she didn't fit your vibe."

His lips trace up my neck, sending the first wave of heat through my body since I walked into this bathroom.

"You're right. I should go key Rory's car. Bitch."

"That's more of a me move than a you thing. Maybe dump glitter in the passenger seat?" That gets a small laugh out of me, and he moans in my ear in response. "Damn, you smell so incredible right now. You'll figure this out, Dani. You always do. You're the best at figuring out the crazy shit and fighting back against the world. Come back to bed?"

I stick my hand under the water and pull it back quick with a hiss. Still freezing cold.

"I think I need coffee more than sex." I wait, but he doesn't argue, just keeps holding me and keeping me warm. "Xander, are we doomed to open relationships forever, bouncing between random flings and failing short-term hookups?"

I could live with that, savoring the variety life offers. I won't let anyone, or anything, tie me down to one idea or one person while I play the role of pseudo-rebel. I'm an openly queer woman in a polyam relationship, setting my own fashion trends, and I'm the lead singer in a punk band. I spend my free time attending anti-establishment protests and fighting the patriarchy.

"I don't think we are, Beetle." He gave me that nickname in high school after spotting the scarab beetle sketches on all my notebooks, and it stuck. I guess it's better than Death's Head Hawkmoth, another creature I used to draw everywhere. "There's someone out there for us. They just need to find their way home."

The longer Xander and I are together, the more I've recognized he needs stability. He doesn't come to the marches anymore, which I don't mind. He does his fighting with a computer and technology. He only did rallies and marches to show his support of me. That's something I struggle to accept from people. Support. Help.

"You mean Sky? I don't think they're coming back, babe. It's been years and they've moved on."

I grew up learning that everyone eventually leaves—especially men. I didn't get much more than six years with my father, and my brothers all left to start their own lives not long after. Xander's been the first to stick around, and, over the years, he's helped me form a second family. That isn't how he grew up, though, and even if he doesn't recognize it, I recognize how badly he's searching for stability.

"Yeah, probably." He keeps his voice soft because we're alone and he's not putting on a front for anyone to see. In this dark, cold bathroom, he's my Xander—soft and prone to cuddling for hours. He's not trying to prove anything other than how he feels about me. His hand slips down my back and when I expect him to make more of a move, he pulls a one eighty on me. "Come on, let's get out of here. We can go borrow Coop's shower, waste the day doing nothing together. Catch whatever's playing at Hollywood Forever tonight."

"Xander, you're broke, and you spent too much money last week at Portos with—"

"Or maybe I did some work around my dad's office and earned some side cash?" I stare up at him, not sure how to react. Xander has spent every day since he met me raging against the corporate machine. Declaring with pride that big paychecks and fancy cars can't lure him in. I'm one of few people who understands he's scared. He doesn't want to lose his identity to a suit and tie lifestyle because there's money in it. Other than his aunt, people with money have never done right by him. Even his parents, who still try to run his life even though he's an adult.

"I planned to take you out somewhere nice for our anniversary, but I have better ideas now. We can swing by and grab some wild new color for me to put in your hair after. Don't get me wrong, the hot pink looked sexy as fuck, but I'm not sure you're a washed-out pastel pink kinda girl." I pout, but he cups my chin, rubbing his thumb over my bottom lip. "I'll pick up more work before the band runs out of funds, I promise. I've got that computer gig I told you about, and I've been talking to the guy down on the first floor about picking up shifts with his security company if I can pass the test. I'll take care of you, Beetle. You know that."

"I don't need you to take care of me, Xan. Besides, that's dangerous shit. The dickheads in the area they patrol would take one look at your skinny white ass and, hell, I don't know. That's where my sister's ex hangs out. That's his gang's territory. I don't want you there." I lean against him, pressing my forehead against his shoulder.

"It's not patrolling, that's the best part. I stare at monitors for a few hours a night, like I do now."

"Or we can stay in, save our money. Sam won't mind if I put in some overtime while I can, and he'll let me work on the road, too. Modern technology saves the day. And the paycheck."

"You're already working too much, you're going to burn out." He lifts my head and slides his mouth over mine. "Stay here. I'll go get you some clothes."

I let out a shivering scream while Xander moves his hands as fast as he can to rinse the color out of my hair. The cold water help with the color, but sometimes, I'd rather risk the color to keep my head warm.

"Oh, I'm sure you're going to like this one, Beetle."

"We won't know until it's dry, but yeah, you're right."

He turns the water off and massages the conditioner into my hair, relaxing me almost to sleep with his fingers.

"Remember the first time I tried to do your hair?"

The snort echoes off the sides of the sink. "Yeah, the bathroom had orange splotches all over the wall and the sink, but somehow my hair didn't end up all that orange." I bite my bottom lip and lift my head. Droplets of water glide down my face, but I don't care. "Skylar had to call a friend of theirs to come fix it, so I didn't look like a Chucky doll."

"Do you think they're gone for good? Like, never coming back to Los Angeles?"

"Would you want to come back after all of that? The accident, that bitch basically getting away with it, losing Steve. I'm not sure I'd be able to handle half of what they did and stay alive, let alone return to where it all happened."

"But they have friends here. They have… they have us here. We got them through it. We were there in the hospital when they woke up. We helped them through the physical therapy." He sighs and turns the water back on, motioning for me to stick my head back under. "It wasn't the plan to fall for one another, but we did. We all did. What would be so bad about them coming back here?"

I let the thought run through my head, something I've tried to avoid in the past. It's not that I want to block the memory of them, but reliving what they went through, the sleepless nights of pain and nearly losing an arm after some bitch ran their motorcycle off the road? That's what my brain tries to remember. Xander always focused on the good and the bad, leveling out sleepless nights with stolen glances and secret touches. He'll never admit it, but my Xander is something of a hopeless romantic.

"Okay, you're all set. Let's go dry you off and see how this looks before we head out." He says, wrapping my head in a towel. "I don't wanna be late. They're playing Empire Records, and you know half these kids won't know that movie."

"We shouldn't know that movie, Xander."

"Shut your mouth, woman. It's a classic!"

HOLLYWOOD
Xander

IN THE LAST HOUR, I've had two requests to meet up, one asking for a private show, and another three telling me I need to update with more videos or they'll unsubscribe. It's typical, but it also means some people out there want to throw some extra money my way.

I check my watch and see Dani shouldn't be home for another few hours, which means I should be able to throw some numbers out and see who bites. Worst-case scenario? The private shows aren't as private as the viewers believe, with four of them in the room at once. Best case? Both in-person meetups.

I pull out the fancy box Dani got me for our weed stash out, ready to roll a joint to relax before I go on cam. Only it's empty. Not even shake.

Shit.

I'm not going to my parent's place for some uppity bullshit dinner while I'm sober, and getting drunk isn't an option. Right now, Dani and I have about twenty dollars in the bank, and we'll need that for gas. No time for the little shit. I need to go big. I crack my knuckles and open my messages to see who requested an in-person meeting. The first name isn't familiar, but the second one? Mitchell comes from money and pays well, but there's a reason he pays well.

I met Mitchell at boarding school—in fact, a surprising number of my clients came from my time at boarding school. Mitch played football for the school, and, like everyone else there, he had more money than brains. Affluent jerks learn early how to throw money at their problems rather than deal with them. Sometimes, when they're stuck in a closet or questioning which way the door swings, I get to be that problem.

The downside? I'm not rugged or athletic. I'm a fucking pretty boy with a soft voice and too much sarcasm. Eventually, they tire of hearing me run my mouth. It's taught me how to take a punch…or three. Some of these guys, like Mitchell, get off on taking things too far. I shouldn't let them, and I've used up my excuse other than some part of me likes it. It's the only reason I can imagine for going back to them so often. It's not the money, even though the rough guys always pay more. It's the contempt in their eyes when they call me the second time, or the third. Shame, disgust, anger—every bit aimed as much toward themselves as me.

Mitch's career in pro sports didn't work out, but daddy paid the right people off and now Mitch pretends to work in his cushy high-rise office in downtown LA. He found me a few years ago on the website and we've met up a time or ten.

Fuck, Alex. Your mouth feels still so damn good.

Stop crying, you little shit! This is your fault, faggot! You made me do this!

I should find out if his wife has a pre-nup agreement for if he's caught with his pants down. Maybe that would jog his memory about the time he locked me in the janitor's shed when we were eight. Three days alone, cold, and hungry at eight years old can become quite the catalyst for some nasty revenge plots.

MITCH

How Much?

$250 for ✏️💧

MITCH

Be behind the bar in 20. You know which car is
mine.

I'll bring a grand.

Blackmail gets messy. But sometimes, messy serves me well.

"A bar fight? The day you're supposed to go to your parent's house? Seriously, Xan?" Dani hisses each word under her breath, but loud enough for me to hear her. She's decorated the sink in colorful cotton balls, ranging from dark red of dried blood toward the bottom and a lighter pink toward the top when she had the bleeding under control. We've been in the bathroom for almost an hour, patching my face up and trying to cover the damage in concealer. She steps back, hip jutting out as she stares at her handiwork. "Wear your glasses. It will help hide some of the bruising that hasn't developed yet."

I nod; my lower lip tucked between my teeth like it's been since she dragged me in here. I'm fighting back the pain I don't want her to see along with all the other emotions. I'm a mirror to those assholes because I feel the same way about myself. I hate that I've become this.

I won't do it again.

The desire to scream those words—and mean them—makes my splitting headache worse. I don't need those guys. I don't need this shit. And yet, I keep going back.

"I'm sorry, Dani." Her shoulders drop at the pathetic sound. She doesn't recognize the sound of it, but I do. Childhood to me, full of fear after a nightmare. The voice begging for someone to tell him they'd protect him from the monsters.

Oh, go back to bed, Alex. I have a meeting in the morning and don't have time for your nightmares.

"You, well, you could have picked better timing, that's all," Dani sighs and kisses my head. Some days, I wonder if she realizes what I'm doing. "Let me clean all this up while you go get changed. I'll be out in a minute."

"What are you going to wear?"

"Is that you asking, or your mother?"

"Me," I answer too quickly, lowering my head again. "I… thought we could match or something."

Her scowl melts, letting the worry show in her features before she slips on her mask. "Leggings and that t-shirt dress I made from your old suit. The gray one. I love you, honeybee." She kisses my cheek and shoves me out of the bathroom.

"No, Xander, I will not sit down and pretend that your family is normal and everything is fine!" Dani barks in a harsh but hushed tone. I don't think anyone else heard her. "I wanna go home, Xander. Now."

"What? Why? It's not that bad!"

"Like your black eye wasn't that bad? Or the other bruises I had to cover up so we could even come to this thing?"

"I told you; it was a stupid bar fight!"

"Sure, Xander. And that *thing* in there is an animatronic," Dani says, rolling her eyes.

I grab her jacket from the closet before she gets to it. To judge what level of pissed off she is, I hold it high out of her reach. "Come on, this is bullshit!"

"Xander Marie Moneypenny! Give me that jacket!"

"No chance—wait, Marie Moneypenny? That's all you've got? Not your best work." I toss the jacket over my shoulder and cross my arms. She's annoyed, not pissed. To be fair, I would be, too, if I wasn't into meat and walked in on a huge ass pig staring at me with dead eyes while it slowly turned over a pit of fire. "Come on, this is seriously ridiculous. Dad asked about your band. I told him about the contest the other day, thinking maybe he could help. You're mad about that?"

"It's not! Your parents are nice, okay? They're super nice. Too nice. Like creepy aliens who want to eat all of humanity nice! Like putting out candy that's too delicious in little dishes that are too expensive to lure me into their trap nice! They're an episode of Twilight Zone, Xander!" Dani catches the sleeve of her coat and rips it off my shoulder, hugging it to her like it's the last coat on Hoth. "Their creepy routine won't work on me! Soylent green, Xander!"

"You need to cut back on the sugar and late-night horror shows, D. That wasn't Twilight Zone." I can't hold back the chuckle, even though it will only annoy her more.

"Stop laughing! There's a fucking whole ass pig outside! A PIG, Xander. On a spit! Over a fire! What the fuck kind of crazy ass cartoon world do you people live in?"

"You've been to parties like this before at Coop's house. I'm sorry about the pig; I didn't think they'd go so hard on the luau theme, but this isn't as bad as you're making it." I scratch the back of my head before dropping my arms to my side. "You've never had a pig roast before? Seriously?"

"No! Chase Cooper never once invited me to a party with a

fucking pig on fire! And he's the richest person in my life other than you!" she snaps back, crossing her arms. "We also don't eat fucking snails! Christ, I would rather eat a whole chicken nugget than anything you weird, sick people have in there. Is this a cult initiation?"

"Beetle, come on. It's not that bad, and there are some normal things, too. They ordered stuff for you, so you'd feel welcome." I nudge her jaw with my knuckle. "Or we could raid the kitchen for ice cream."

"It's probably made with something weird, like the last egg of an African Condor. What exactly on that table would you call *normal*? The lobster they boiled alive? The chicken thing I can't even pronounce? That lame ass excuse for a taco?" She wags her finger at me, becoming the spitting image of her mother when she would go off on something stupid white people did. "That thing is an insult to my people, and I should not let it stand. *Grito de Dolores!*" She throws her arms in the air, almost hitting me with her coat.

"*Grito de what*—seriously, babe?"

"Whatever, it was all I could think of." She pouts before she straightens up again. "While I appreciate the lovely spread—and I guess I do want the mac and cheese recipe—that pig could feed my entire neighborhood. Or be running free on a farm, happy. Alive! Anyway, your privilege is showing, babe. Big time!" She's pulling on her coat while continuing to yell at me in a whisper. As she fights with the sleeve, I grab her face and pull her to me into a deep, passion fueled kiss.

I've met people before that I wish had some kind of on/off switch to shut them up, but Dani has one and I've learned how to activate it. I press against her, moving her into the closet and out of sight from the hallway as our mouths come together again and again. I don't stop until she's squeezing my arm and melting into me. It's always been like this between us. We fight over stupid shit; we scream at each other; I kiss her, and it's like a reset in her head.

Sometimes. Other times, even trying it will get my head taken clean off and we break up for a week or two.

With a groan, she pulls away, smacking me in the chest. I don't let her get far though, twisting her fresh blue highlights in my fingers. She wipes my lip and shows me the electric green smudge on her thumb and smiles. If I could, I'd find the most remote castle in the world and lock us both in the dungeon, never to be seen again so I could spend the rest of my life lost in her. Even when we fight, she's the only person I give a fuck about. She'd lose her mind three minutes into our dungeon lifestyle, though. I only need the internet and some books, she needs people.

"Better?"

"No," she lies. "No, you don't get to do that, Charles Alexander Maxwell!" Real names. Now I'm in trouble. "You can't seduce your way into my head like none of this happened. You're good, but you're not mind eraser levels of good. Giant. PIG. I can't forget that. I'm going to have nightmares!"

As if summoned by Hades and our argument, my younger cousin appears in the doorway. Ginny holds a plate piled high with food and licks something with a gravy texture off her fork. She's got this innocent but angry thing going on that I can't figure out, but her grin radiates pure evil.

"Hey cuz." She draws the U out in this awkward way. "Where's the hot black chick with the cute tits you told my brother about?"

"Fuck off, Ginny."

"Oh, that's right. She wasn't enthralled with your dick the

way Dani is." She turns to face Dani with her crooked, evil grin. "You know he fucks boys with that thing, right?"

"Go…count your gold or whatever you do." I try to wave her off, but she pushes my arm like a school-yard bully, which she's always been.

"At least I have gold. You don't even have a name, loser."

"Does your father know you're drunk?" I sound like an old man asking that, but it's obvious. She's a few months shy of eighteen and has been an alcoholic for at least two years.

"Does *your* dad know you suck cock?"

A minuscule part of me wishes Megan had worked out, and I take the blame for it falling apart. She and Dani together would have ripped Ginny's head off, which would make Dani's night. Mine, too.

Megan and I never went beyond oral, but I still had her cum dripping down those thick brown thighs on plenty of occasions. And she made me come in my pants more than once while we made out backstage during Dani's shows. But I became her bisexual un-awakening—if that's even a thing. She came to terms with her sexuality and decided she only wanted Dani for herself; that's not happening. We're not asking for perfection, but we're not about to be torn apart, either.

Package deal.

"Is that seriously all you've got?" Dani frowned, rolling her eyes and sighing dramatically. "Look, when you sober up and need someone to talk about your sexuality to, come find us. Until that happens, you sound like a dumbass saying that shit."

"What the fuck? Gross." Ginny acts like I've offended her to the core, but I don't buy it and neither does Dani. She's trying to act like an adult, but the ones she has to learn from aren't impressive. "Are you some kind of groomer or something?"

"Jesus, shut the fuck up, Ginny," Dani snaps, stepping

between Ginny and I. "Open your mouth again and I'll slap the filler out of your lips even at the risk of permanently dying my hand orange from touching that fake tan. Don't cry to your daddy, just get lost. Also, that dress is fucking hideous and two seasons ago."

Ginny gawks, clutching pearls as she retreats.

"Okay, we're burning this bitch to the ground with darling cousin Ginny trapped inside. You get the gas, I'll find the lighters. Get the animals and children to safety first."

"Dani." I keep my voice soft but firm as I tuck a strand of her short hair back under her knit hat before stroking her face. She's got these brown eyes like mahogany, and I've spent hours staring into them, getting a little more lost each time. "We've been through this before. You're freaking out even though you're safe here. I'm safe. There's no reason to storm out or light the place on fire. Ginny is a—"

"Twat."

"Yeah, that."

"Xander, I—." She bites her bottom lip and bounces on the balls of her feet.

"Say it."

Her shoulders drop as she uncrosses her arms and lets them fall at her side. I pull her in and hug her tight, reassuring her because it's what she needs. It's what she always needs, even when she fights it. Dani likes people to think she's a strong, independent woman, because she is. But even the strongest women need a shoulder to cry on and someone to boost them up now and again.

"Here? A safe place for me when it never offered sanctuary to you?"

"You came here wanting a fight, I get it. The world has pushed you to your limit lately, and you're trying to reset. But,

Dani, these aren't the people you want to fight. However, if you wanna go clock Ginny, Dad would probably post your bail."

"Can we go home now?" Dani whispers. "Or maybe out to the bar? I need my people."

"Sure, Beetle. Soon. I need to stick around for a bit longer, so it's not weird. Besides, if dad has a few more drinks, I might get out of the whole Japan trip thing."

"How is it not already weird? We're these broke ass kids loitering around. We're not even worthy of being the help here."

"Not true. That one guy tried to get me to take his coat. Remember?" She gives me a sideways glare. "Dani, stop. These are your rules we're living by, remember?"

"Oh bullshit! Even before the rules, you didn't want their handouts." Her mouth drops open in anger and shock when what I said hits her before I can take the words back. "Wait! Are you saying it's my fault you're now living this life?"

Shit. I walked into this.

"Beetle, please? You're right, they're *our* rules. I didn't mean it like that. I promise, a few more minutes and you can have Steve and Ethan meet us at the bar."

"You only wanna see Ethan." She crosses her arms and pouts.

"Beetle, seriously? What the actual fuck do I have to do to make this right?"

Her face softens and her bottom lip trembles. It breaks my heart every time this happens.

"I'm doing it again, aren't I. That thing where I freak out for no reason and push you away? I'm so sorry, Xander."

"It's alright, Beetle. Come on, I'll find you something in the kitchen that's more to your taste." I give her a wink. "For the record, I'm not a fan of most of this food either. Frog legs gross me out. Who wants to eat Kermit's legs?"

She wraps around me, burying her forehead in my neck as I

kiss the top of her head. "Well, at least we didn't break up this time. Besides, what's a Maxwell family gathering without something going on that offends me?"

"Atta girl. Hey, wanna sneak off to my old room and mess around like we used to?"

"They turned your old room into your dad's office now, Xan."

"Yeah, and? Bet you'd look real pretty while I sit in that giant leather chair of his and pretend I'm some kind of big executive and you're the hot call girl on her knees." Her eyes flick up and I watch the smirk grow. There's my Beetle. "If you're a good girl, I'll bend you over that desk and have you for dinner."

"Or maybe I'm the big executive, and if you behave, I'll let you have a taste."

"Hard bargain. Why don't we try both options and compare notes?"

She bites her lip, pretending to think it over before she bolts up the set of stairs behind us. I dig into the pocket of my coat hanging in the front closet and pull out a condom. When I turn to follow her, I stop and grab one more…just in case.

HOLLYWOOD
Skylar

CHAPTER 7
VOICES

DAMIANO DAVID

THE BAR ISN'T A DIVE, or glitzy glam either, which makes it perfect for someone like me. In-between style bars like this care enough about the money to ensure patrons keep the peace and no one starts shit. I've learned that lesson the hard way, finding myself battered and bruised outside of the skeeviest of joints. And the poshest.

The hypnotic effect of watching the amber liquid swirl in my glass puts me into a state of zen. Part of that could be from the exhaustion, though. To my left sits a couple failing on a first date. To my right is a regular, here to watch the game and talk with the bartender, who's likely one of his only friends.

My phone buzzes and I glance down at the screen.

New Unread Message From: Marc

He's worried about me, but trying to give me space. I always made life more difficult for my big brother, but he always forgave me and never threw pity in my face. It will take another day before I'm at his place, and I've sent him the address of the

motel I'm staying at, like I've done every stop since Edmonton. A road trip on a motorcycle when you're in no hurry takes time.

"Okay, well," the raised voice from the man next to me piques my interest. There's a tone to it he needs to watch. "I don't understand why you think that. I'm a great guy!"

I raise my head, making eye contact with the bartender. He heard that, too, which means he's already prepared for the outcomes. None of which ends well for him.

"How's everyone doing over here?" the bartender asks while drying a spot on the bar that didn't need it.

"We're fine. In fact, we're leaving." The guy stands and drops a pair of fifties on the bar. He's an arrogant prick, but he's banking that the bartender would rather take the cash and avoid the headache. That amount of money tells me he's got more dangerous ideas planned for the night.

"Hey, let go of me," his date hisses. "You're hurting me!"

"Okay, buddy. Let her go," the bartender says, pushing the money back toward the guy. He doesn't glance around, meaning he's on his own unless he calls the cops.

Awesome. The downside of these middle-of-the-road bars rears an ugly head—no bouncers and no security. Not even the threat of a gun under the bar.

"Fuck off and mind your own business. Come on, we're leaving—" The douchebag spins around fast when I tap him on the shoulder. "The fuck is your problem?"

"They're not interested in leaving with you."

He checks me up and down, and the confusion puts a grin on my face. "Mind your own fucking business, weirdo."

Most nights I would, but I'm likely one of the very few lines of defense this woman has before he pulls her into his car. I let the dark laugh spill out of me before I drain my glass and stand to my full height, unfolding from the safety of the barstool. For extra flare, I even crunch a piece of ice between my molars and watch him try to hide his reaction.

The dickhead rocks his head all the way back to look me in the eye, but I still catch the way his neck bobs as he swallows hard. I don't like fights, I never have, but I can defend myself against one dipshit with an incel complex.

"You should leave," I rumbled, cocking my head to the side. "Alone."

"Fuck you, man." What he does next will decide both of our fates, and tonight, either option sounds like the right one to me. He scoffs and steps back. Coward. "She's not worth my time anyhow."

He rips his cheap coat from the woman's shoulders and storms toward the door. I'm happy to sit back on my stool and hunch back over my drink. No fight for me tonight, at least not yet. The night's still young, and the demons in my head are awake again, ready to dance.

"Uhm, hi." I nod to my drink instead of her, doing what I can to avoid eye contact. "Thanks for that. I didn't realize he'd turn into such a creep when I agreed to come here with him. Can I buy you a drink?"

I turn to face her, and of course, she's gorgeous. Long, curly blonde hair, big red lips, and a dress that's not leaving much to the imagination. My first thought? How much my ex-fiancé, Steve, would like her. Normally, I'd turn away, not wanting to come across as a creep, but she's not worried about the way I'm watching her. She's too busy drooling over me like I've moved to the top of her hit list.

"You have the prettiest eyes." She holds out a hand, her wrist bent in anticipation that I'm Prince Charming, ready to kiss her knuckles and take her back to my chariot. "I'm Robin."

"Skylar," I nod, but don't take her hand, hoping she gets the hint that I'm not here to make friends or get my dick wet. That pisses the demons off, which means they've noticed something I haven't picked up on yet.

"Wow, that's a cool name." She shifts the stool her date had occupied a few inches closer to me before she climbs onto it. Her hand fumbles with a straw as she sticks it between her teeth and chews. It could be nerves, until I find the deep scratches running up her arm, the bruising, and her blown out eyes.

She's high.

When she reaches for her purse, she moves like she's in a dream, knocking it over. "I'd say I'm sorry about Dave, but I'm not wasting apologies on him."

I roll my eyes as she orders herself another drink before asking what I'm having. She's too fucking high to notice the whiskey glass. Her lips pucker as she flips open a compact to reapply the bright red lipstick. That's when she notices my hand. She makes a move to touch me, but stops, hand in the small space between us.

"Wow, that's...I'm sorry, I should know better." She laughs it off, and I'm not sure if she's eyeing the tattoos or the scars. "That's solid work. Almost creepy. What is it?"

"Death's-head hawkmoth." The ink is a few years old now, but it's one I've taken more care of than anything else in my life.

"Did it hurt?" I raise an eyebrow but don't bother answering, considering I can see the ink she has peeking out from between her pushed up tits. "Why am I asking that? I have tattoos, duh."

I nod and stare forward, pretending to watch the game on TV, thankful that the person behind the camera gives the audience some fantastic shots of the batter's ass. I may not follow sports, but I love watching the boys play in those tight, unforgiving pants.

"Does it, like, have a meaning or just a cool picture you wanted to get?"

I sigh, realizing she's chipping away at my armor, and I can either walk away right now, or I'll be talking to her for the next three hours. The directions she wants to take this conversation screams danger. We could keep it cordial, and I try to convince her to get off the drugs and get help. We could fuck in the bathroom while she convinces me she shouldn't get high alone. I could fall for her pity trap and bring her back to the hotel room, where she ODs in my bed.

I turn and face her big green eyes, and she bites her bottom lip. Maybe I already feel bad for her, or maybe I want to tell someone the story I've held in for too long. Maybe I do want to get my dick sucked. Whatever the reason, I don't get up and walk away like I should.

"It's a reminder. Someone I love. Loved. Whatever it is." I nod at the bartender for another drink. I'm making mistakes, ignoring the warnings and signs I've been told about.

"Oh, did they die? I'm sorry if that brought up lousy memories. I shouldn't have asked, I guess." She giggles but catches herself.

My head shakes as the smile creeps over my face. "Nah, she's alive. She's nothing but pleasant memories."

Robin smirks and keeps asking questions. With each one, I loosen up, letting a wall come down a little more. The questions are harmless. Where do you live? What do you do? Safe questions, until she runs out of wine, and circles back to the tattoo.

"So, your girlfriend?"

"No, never got that far. She's what they call the one that got away. More like the pair that got away." I roll the hair tie from my wrist and pull my hair up while she watches. Even through the jacket, she notices my arms flexing. She licks her lips, shifting in her chair as her breathing changes. I'd bet if she stood up, there'd be a wet spot in her chair. Lucky for me, I've already decided the demons aren't winning tonight. It's her own fault. Making me talk about the tattoo puts two people in my mind that I want far more than this temptress, or the score she'd likely share with me.

"Wait, so two girls got away, or like a metaphor or something about her tits?"

"Two people." I trace my fingers over the bee on my wrist. "He...he was the reason I left my old life. The reason I couldn't pretend anymore. She's the one drawing me back, my beacon to find them again."

"Oh?" Her lip comes up on one side and she tilts her head. "Nope, gonna need more info."

"You mean you need more wine, and to call yourself a cab?"

"Aww, you can't give me a lift, big guy? All strong and tall and handsome." Her fingers slide up my arm, squeezing. "Maybe show me a few more of your tattoos." She leans over, pushing her chest out. "Or, better yet, I could show you mine."

I don't understand what people see in me, but someone once told me it had to do with the bad boy image I exude, and that I'm a soft teddy bear on the inside. I don't claim any image. I put on clothes and go through life like anyone else. Sure, I go through it with long hair, tight pants, painted nails, and a motorcycle. Apparently, I'm the rough around the edges guy everyone wants to save. Dani never wanted to save me. She said I didn't need saving; I needed to stop forcing myself to believe the lies.

My phone buzzes again. This time, it's my sponsor.

"Excuse me, Robin. I should take this." She pouts as I stand up and walk to the back of the bar and out onto the patio. I light a cigarette and lean against the wall as I answer. "Shawn."

"Hey, Skylar. How's it going?"

"I'm not dead yet, if that's what you're asking."

"I'm not. I'm worried about you. Driving from here to your brother's place in San Luis Obispo? Then to Hollywood? All on a motorcycle? You're a special kind of nuts."

"I told you; I'm making amends or whatever the fuck that step is." I tuck the phone against my shoulder and flex my hand to work out the soreness along the scar tissue and joints. I glance across the parking lot, watching the first mist from the coming rain dance around the streetlights.

"Alright, I get it. So, it's been a week since you left. How are things going?"

"I've had two…no, three whiskeys, and nothing else. I can see the hotel from where I'm standing, so I won't drive." I take a drag. "Met a girl named Robin at the bar. She's flying, but also wants to ride my dick."

"Okay, I'm pretty okay with that. Except, maybe—"

"Nah, no worries there, buddy. As soon as I go back in, I'm getting her ass in a rideshare and out of my life. I don't have time for that."

There's a silence and I don't interrupt his note taking. We planned for this when I told him I wanted to go back south, back home. I enjoyed Canada, but something about Los Angeles pulls me back no matter how far I run, or how hard I claw. I can make it work with the right people beside me.

"Skylar, are you going back to make amends with your ex, or to try to get *them* back?"

The darkness in my laugh even scares me a little. "Fuck, can't it be both? No, wait, can you accuse me of trying to get the two of them back if I've never actually *had* them?" I blow a series of smoke rings toward the giant light overhead, watching the mist turn to drizzle and growing to rain. "If you break it down to the finer points, I can't have one without the other. That goes for both the need to make things right with my ex and trying to get the people to accept me again."

"And if it doesn't work out?"

"I take my brother's offer and work for his auto body shop. I'm going there tomorrow so he can show me the place and try to tempt me away from Los Angeles."

"Good, call him, though. He's called me twice to check in on you. And think of it as a backup plan, like you said, not a lesser option."

"You know me, Shawn. Always down for a temptation or three."

"Skylar!"

"I'm kidding. G'night, Shawn."

After we hang up, I plan a way to deal with Robin while I burn through another cigarette. When I open the door, though, she's already moved on. Good for her. I pay the bartender and do the same, walking back to my motel room alone and in the rain.

I peel off the jacket and hang it in the shower to dry before I crash down onto the bouncing bed. The lights are all off, so I fish my earbuds out of my pocket, pull up my playlist, and close my eyes. The tune fills my ears seconds before her voice does, and it's not long before my fingers are moving across an invisible instrument, playing along with them.

My night-after-night routine.

Same thing every night for the last two years; since I picked up the bass again—listening and learning each new song they play. The only things that change are the rooms I'm in and the random order I play the songs. Shuffling between them makes learning the music a little harder and takes more concentration. More brain power into this means less room for another trip to the bar, a phone call, a dealer, and my life slipping away again.

The darkness of the room and the steady rain on the tin roof outside take over, pushing sleep and heavy eyes over me like a blanket. That's when my second routine begins.

"Please. Let it be her in my dreams, and not the nightmares."

I'm asking my brain more than I'm asking some god; I don't believe in higher powers. If anything, there's a handful of Loki replicas up there running this place. Nothing else makes sense, at least not to me. Why should I pray to a god that causes so much pain? Oh, and that whole bit about him only giving you what you can take? That's not a god I care to give my time to.

Too many damn Lokis.

As hard as I try, and as much as I beg, I don't dream about her.

HOLLYWOOD
Dani

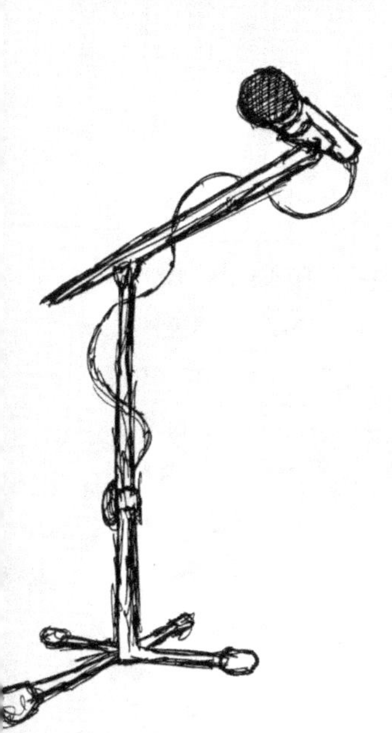

CHAPTER 8
ENOUGH IS ENOUGH
THE HIVES

"IT'S ONLY BEEN a few weeks and you're already moving back in with your mom?" the pink-haired goth girl asks me while I hold a dress up to her and scrunch my nose.

"Yep! Xander mentioned something about unsafe living environments in our notice, so maybe they won't charge us. You should have been there the other day. I woke up freezing my ass off, but by the time we tried to go to bed, I ended up sleeping in the tub surrounded by ice packs. Fucking insane." A piece of bright green fabric grabs my attention, so I grab it, presenting it with a waggle of my eyebrows to Alexis.

"No. Not green, please. It's a fantastic color for you, but I'm a pale white girl. It makes me come off as…toxic and sickly."

"Fiiiiine. I'll buy it for myself. I can work on it on the drive to Portland."

"You will not!" Our heads snap up at the familiar voice as we both smile at the gorgeous, tall blond who could be a double for Marilyn Monroe walking our way. "First off, why are you showing dresses to Lexi? You don't have the million dollars it would take to get her into one! And, also, I want it! I need something new for your show when it rolls through LA."

"Oh my god, Laurie!" I scream and throw myself around her. "I'd love it if you came to the show. If we make it that far."

"You will! Craig's bringing a bunch of guys from the gym, and I've got flyers up all over the firm." She flashes a sympathetic glance as her long, slender fingers rest on my shoulders. "I hope it's okay, but we're skipping any of the nights you aren't playing, so once we have dates, we'll buy whatever we need. We already have tickets for the finals, too, because you're making it to the fucking finale. Do you understand me?"

"Same for us, Steve, and Ethan," Lexi adds. "It depends on the Parrots' schedule, but some of the other guys on Ethan's team said they wanted to go, too."

"Oh my god, we're going to have a crowd? We need to make the finals now."

"That's what I said. So, pick out a whole new wardrobe to work on, missy," Laurie says as she types on her phone, not bothering to glance up. "Remember when we used to go watch Steve's ex?"

"Steve's ex? As in Kennedy?" Lexi questions, eyes narrowing and face turning like she bit into something sour.

"She couldn't play an instrument if her life depended on it. Except maybe the skin fl—"

"Dani! Come on, she's trying. She has a new job, and it's going well. Coop says she's almost unrecognizable now."

"As what? A porn star? Because I'm pretty sure that's her calling." My head snaps toward Lexi as she rolls her eyes and gives me *that* face. "What? That's a compliment! Porn stars are bad ass! Whatever, Laurie's talking about Skylar, who played in a band when they dated Steve. Mad skills on the bass, a phenomenal body, a functional brain, and a pretty face."

"That pretty face broke my brother's heart," Laurie adds as she eyes the clothes on a new rack. "I'd be mad about it if Steve hadn't found Ethan, but I'd also be lying if I said I didn't miss them. I hope they're doing okay. Wherever they ended up after all that shit happened. I always thought they'd end up with you."

"I heard they were backpacking through Europe. Such a fucking Skylar thing to do." I avoid the last part of what Laurie said, but the heat fills my face. I bite my lip before blurting out, "Xander wants me to text them."

"Do it!" Laurie replies.

We spend the rest of the afternoon practicing the fine art of thrifting. Or, more accurately, Laurie and I shop while Lexi plays on her phone and allows us to dress her up. Laurie has a rockin' body, but even though she's post-op, it's difficult finding clothes to fit her and complement her style. That's where I come in. Fashion school dropout, baby. Even Lexi benefits from my mad skills with a pair of scissors and some thread. She's got hips that hypnotize her husband, but standard pants off the rack fail her, and I give her more options than leggings every day.

I've even gotten her into a few dresses. And repaired them after Jamie ripped them off her.

Plus, they pay me for my time in buying me all the thrifted material I could ever want. Win fucking win. When Lexi's finally had enough of our shopping, she drags us down the street for food, but mostly to refill her coffee.

"So, what's new with the trio? I heard you've moved into the new place."

"Don't ask." I pause long enough to drop my things into the booth and drop into it. "Okay, you already did, whatever. Megan didn't work out since she's shagging Rory, our bassist. So, we kicked Megan out of our triad and fired Rory. I'm fine with that, except now we're stuck with a shitty bassist until we can find someone new who doesn't suck. But the apartment can only be described as an absolute shithole—falling apart around us and has mice. Like, so many mice."

"Daniella Silva," Laurie scolds. "Are you fucking kidding me right now?"

"About which part because that's a lot to—"

"The apartment! Is that why we haven't been over?" Laurie asks.

"Kind of?"

"You could come live with us, but I'm not sure Jamie would be okay with it," Lexi blurts out before chomping down on a fry.

"I'm sitting right here, Lexi. Did I piss Jamie off or something?"

"What? No!" She holds up her hands, a fry dangling from her fingertips. "I mean, he'd be limited to which rooms he could rip my clothes off in."

"So, we can't move in, but I'm okay with that because I don't want to see naked Jamie."

"Dude, you've seen all the boys naked at the house parties," she shrugs, holding the fry out for me.

"Fair."

As much grief as I give Xander for not having goals or a steady job, I'm a different flavor of the same problems. I've never held a job down longer than this one. At every other job, I ran away as fast as I could because it never felt like work or a commitment. Working for Sam never feels like that. I take all the time off I want; I dress and do my hair however I want, and I swear as much as I want. And now we've gone remote, so it's like a paycheck for being awesome. Sam has told me multiple times that I've got a job as long as I'm getting the work done, and I do that. It's easy. Answer phones, tell people they're fucking idiots, take notes. Done.

Laurie taps her manicured nails on the table before pointing them at me. "Ladies, we're off topic and there's a giant purple elephant in the room." We both stare at her with blank faces and she rolls her eyes. "There's a simple—and brilliant—solution to both of your problems."

"Yeah, and he's trying. It's not like he sits around all day listening to idiotic and misogynistic podcasts while playing the same game online with the same group of ten-year-olds all day. Wait—are we talking about Xander?"

Laurie's eyebrows knit together. "Strangely specific description, but no. I don't mean Xander getting an actual job. That would crush the poor boy. I'm talking about your apartment. Lexi? Isn't your latest tenant moving out soon? And weren't you telling me, like, a week ago how much you're dreading going through that process again and how you're thinking about selling the condo?"

"Oh my god, I totally forgot I even had that place."

"You forgot you own a place in the arts district? You're turning into one of them, Alexis!" I stare at her through squinted eyes and frown, laying on the dramatics for effect. "I've been fearing this day ever since you married that rich asshole!"

"Dude, James is basically your brother." Lexi giggles at my terrible southern drawl. "He didn't have a hundred dollars to his name when we met! He didn't even have enough for a motel room in Vegas when we got married! I paid for the license, Coop paid for the hotel rooms, and you paid for my kinky lingerie!"

"Yeah, but you still married him and now you're dual-income-no-kids rich, and forgetting about quaint little properties you own around Los Angeles." I grab her hand, examining her fingers. I love Jamie, and I consider him one of my brothers, just like with Steve and Coop. My boys, I call them, but I still mock them every chance I get. "Does your pinky automatically stick out when you drink tea based on the zeroes in your bank account? Or is that a conscious effort thing?"

"Oof, the pinky!" Laurie giggles. "I'll remember that question when you're a famous rock star swimming in your cash filled swimming pool."

"I kind of forgot." Lexi shrugs, sliding her tray over so I can polish off her fries, like I always do. "I don't deal with the place anymore, so I forget it exists. Besides, it's better to remember where I live now. A happy, loving, homey place my mother has only been in for a whopping five minutes."

"I get it, babes. But I love watching you get all angsty about it. Okay, back to the real shit. Laurie, what does Lexi's place have to do with me?" The kid behind the counter yells my number and I jump up to grab my food. Out of habit, I grab a handful of condiments to bring back to the apartment, so we don't have to pay for them. This shit has to stop. Dropping back into my chair, the two women stare at me like they're about to burst. "What did I miss?"

"We found you a place! I mean, my place! I mean, you should come live at my condo!" Lexi practically screams this at me, causing heads to turn. One, an older man, scowls at me from under his red hat; I flip him off and mouth the words *lesbians*. It works, and he stuffs his trash in the can and stomps out. "Isn't that an incredible idea?"

"Lexifer, I love you. Like I really, really love you and I would totally die for you so long as I go out in a dramatic and newsworthy fashion so people can say weird shit like I lit up a room. But maybe not weird enough for a whole documentary about how I was unalived by a serial psycho?" It's my worst nightmare and even told my mother to never say I lit up a room. "But like, your place? Astronomically outside of my price range.

Seriously can't afford that. Even if we still had Megan's income. But I still love you."

Laurie slides a napkin with scribbles over to me like it contains government secrets or some shit.

"Yeah, this is exactly the thing we need to get the crown jewels out of the—I don't know what this is."

"I worked out the math while you were shoving ketchup in your pockets like a foraging squirrel," Laurie answers, pointing to my pockets.

"Squirrels don't have pockets! I mean, they should. Oh, I should make little squirrel jackets with nut pockets. Not like, *nuts*, but like, you know, *nuts*. I'd probably go viral."

"Yeah, for clothing the squirrels of LA instead of the homeless people," Lexi replies, biting on the end of her straw.

"Fair. They always focus on the negative side of LA and not the cute, fun, squirrels with pockets side of life. Bastard internet trolls."

"Ladies, focus," Laurie taps her nails on the table again until we're both glaring at her in our best paying-attention faces. "Close enough. Ren, Dani. You'd pay the building fees, plus the utilities. You can absolutely afford that, can't you?"

I stare at the number for a second before shifting my glare to Lexi, scrunching my face up. "Girl, you totally paid more for this place. Please don't do some weird bullshit behind my back, like I won't notice the handout for your poor friend."

"Has anyone ever told you that you have an unhealthy relationship with the entire rich vs poor dynamic that involves a ton of projecting? Oh wait. I have." Lexi points at the number on the bottom of the napkin. "Think of it like HOA fees. I'm still the landlord or whatever, so if anything breaks, I got you. Otherwise, this isn't a handout. In fact, you'd be doing me a huge solid because if I have to deal with one more short-term rental fucker, I'm going to murder them and you'll have to help me bury the body, so you become an accessory. I didn't buy the place; I had it *gifted* to me. Remember?" She throws air quotes up around the word gifted. The courts more or less forced Lexi's mother to hand it over to her in a settlement.

"You're serious?" Nowhere in Los Angeles will come with a price tag as low as the number on the napkin. Hell, it's cheaper than anything you'd find almost anywhere without it being a total dump like we already have.

"I'll get the agreement together and email it to both of you, along with the necessary paperwork to get you out of your shitty lease." Laurie pulls out her phone and fires off a slew of emails and texts while I sit there, staring at a stupid napkin that could change everything for Xander and I. The concerts, a new apartment, a fresh start.

"I have one super important question, Lexi. Does your pastry-baking neighbor still live next door?"

"My former shrink? Dr. Clay? Yeah, I'm sure he does. I haven't seen him in a while, but you could ask Coop. He still sees him."

"Fabulous. I'm in. But, uhm, let me talk it over with Xander and I'll see what he thinks."

"If he says no, dump him again and move in. By the time the two of you kiss and makeup, you'll have all your stuff there right where you want it, and he's stuck with the leftover space." Laurie plays it off like she's joking, but I'm not so sure she is. It's a valid plan, though.

"Oh my fucking god, yes! Yes!"

"Alright, I guessed you'd be overjoyed, but I didn't think you'd go full orgasmic on me." Xander's huge smile has spread onto my face as I watch him pick up the napkin and start drawing invisible lines in the air as he does his own math. Sometimes, I hate how much I suck at math, but that's what I have Xander for. "Whatcha working on, big brain?"

"Amazing! The money you'll save on gas going to work at cafes to avoid the mice, and the reduction in rent payments, means you can afford the studio time. We can probably get the band back in there by…next month and still have enough to cover the tour."

"Or we could put it away in savings and—MOUSE!" I run across the room and jump up onto the bed. I'm not sure why I'm any safer up here since it's not even a foot off the floor and I'm pretty sure mice can jump that high. "MOUSE! Xander!"

He comes out of his math daze and runs over with his bucket, trying to trap the poor thing as it scurries around desperate for an escape. It dashes toward the bed, and I kick the blanket toward it. Direct hit! But now he's hidden under all that fabric. When he makes a break for it, Xander slams the bucket down, trapping the creature underneath.

"I'll check the traps, too. Maybe I can drive more than just him all the way out to the middle of nowhere."

I insisted on humane traps, and when Xander researched those versus the other options, he agreed. They catch the little guys with tasty peanut butter, but they can't get back out. We take them down to the public dump about five miles from here. They have diseases and shit, but I have an overactive imagination, and so I picture myself in their situation. Stuck in a trap, waiting to die of starvation or some dude to smash my head in with a hammer. Also, neither of us were smashing mouse heads. Not happening.

"Jesus, by the time we get out of here, we'll have relocated their entire mouse family to an area with much better food to mouse ratios," Xander laments as he drops onto the bucket, tapping the side and waiting for the little guy to tap back to say he's okay.

I go behind him and rub his bare shoulders and tracing his tattoos while I kiss the back of his head. "I'll call Lexi in the morning. Maybe we can move in sooner?"

HOLLYWOOD
Xander

CHAPTER 9
MASCARA

SUB URBAN

THE REFLECTION in the mirror laughs at the clown I've become. Slicked down hair, lack of piercings or eyeliner, and necktie are foreign to me. This isn't the face I see every day, the face I've grown comfortable with. The initials of the woman I love and the stars she drew on my face one drunken night that I immortalized on my flesh hide behind makeup. She taught me how to cover them so I could act the part I have in a play where I'm the only one without a script.

"Mr. Maxwell?" follows three heavy knocks on the door. "Your mother asked me to come check on you. She's waiting in the car."

"Fuck." I take one more glimpse in the mirror, reminding myself how to walk, how to talk, how to think, and how to numb myself to all of this. When I pull the door to the spare room open, I find my mother's long-time driver, Albert, standing there. He wears a ridiculous uniform. It's a costume and a farce —and pretty racist in my book. He takes a step back and holds out his hand in an 'after you' gesture. "I'm sorry she still makes you wear that."

"Oh, I don't mind. My wife loves it, and it looks damn good.

The guys in the neighborhood envy it, too, because it's fancy." The lines on his face deepen when he smiles, giving him a bit of a creepy clown appearance. It always reminds me a bit of Danny Trejo. "Besides, I don't think jeans and an LA Kings jersey will cut it when I'm driving your folks around, Mr. Maxwell—"

"Xander, man. Hell, call me Alex. Just not Mr. Maxwell. You taught me how to frame a house and grill a burger. You don't have to play the game with me anymore, man."

"Yeah, yeah, but I still need to get paid, bro. Now hurry up before your mom gets all pissy."

I'm the only person in my parent's house he'll talk to like that. He lives two doors down from where Dani and her sister lived with their mom, so he's seen the real me outside these walls. Over the years, I kind of became part of the neighborhood. They never met the polished and posh trust fund kid I saw in the mirror earlier. They only knew me as the guy Lando taught to help fix the old lady next door's plumbing when the pipes burst. The one who helped carry Mrs. Martinez's groceries three blocks when the stores locked the wheels of the buggies. The guy who'd step up and speak up when the cops came around to harass the group of teens that hung out on the street corner after school.

I glance over my shoulder, down the hall to what used to be my old bedroom. That's when the idea hits me. "Hey Berto? Do you have any clue where they put the stuff from my room?"

"Yeah, it's in a storage facility not far from here. Wait, they moved your shit and never told you? It shouldn't surprise me, kid." He claps me on the back, something he'd never do in front of my mother. "Your parents are okay people, but they're trapped in an era neither one of them lived in."

"Yeah, I keep telling them the nineteen twenties called and want their shit back."

The front door acts like a portal as we both step through. He morphs from Berto to Albert—back stiff, smile gone except for the corners of his eyes. I become Alex, the soulless meat puppet my mother and father are desperate to force me into a mold of their likeness. They're failing, but I'm not sure they realize that yet, just like they don't realize how it hurts to shove all my things into a locker the day I left. I never existed in the house as anything beyond decoration.

"Hello, Alex. Glad to see you're feeling better after the party, since I assume that's why you left early," my mother says as I climb in, though she's barely glanced at me. "Do you have to wear all that black? I'm not taking you to a funeral."

"It's the style, ma." She doesn't like when I call her that, but I don't like when she comments on my clothes. So, we're even. It's petty, but we've always traded bullshit remarks. "Hey, uhm, I forgot to tell you, but I'm picking up keys for a new place tomorrow for Dani and I. It's nice. In the arts district and I'll—"

"Oh no, baby, that's not a pleasant neighborhood."

"Okay, but we can't all live in Bel Air, can we?" I flash her a goofy grin, so she'll relax a little. "Anyhow. I'm picking the keys up tomorrow and I wanted to get some of the furniture from my old room."

My mother's brilliant, capable, legal-centric mind spends all her time doing multimillion dollar business deals and making them look easier than making a peanut butter and jelly sandwich. Not that I've ever seen her make one of those. But right now, she's staring at me as if I spoke in some broken, lost language she's never heard uttered before.

"My room. The room I had upstairs. The room I grew up in. Come on, I only want a couple of things."

"Oh, I'm sure we threw all that junk away. Why would you want your old things?"

"Because we don't have the money to get new—"

"Alexander Maxwell! Would you stop with this pauper routine, please? It's honestly driving your father and I mad. It's embarrassing, to be frank."

"Okay, but will *you* stop the millionairess act from wherever the hell people still talk like that?" Mom rolls her eyes. "Come on, Mom. It's sitting in storage somewhere; you didn't throw it out. What will it hurt if I grab the desk and a few things and put them to use?"

"Talk to your father about it. I'm not sure what he did with your things."

Her tone tells me we're done talking, and sure enough, she's silent the rest of the drive. Once we're out of the car and she's surrounded by her people, she shifts everything about herself. The way she speaks, walks, gestures, everything. She's a chameleon, going from haughty heiress in a silent film to hard as nails lawyer who will eat your soul and charge you by the hour for it. I guess we all play parts, and she's where I learned that talent.

While parading me around like a show pony, she's an expert at dodging questions like 'where did he attend school' or 'what firm does he work with' because the answer would embarrass her. These are the moments I'm the most powerful in my life. Not because of the lies, but because if I opened my mouth and told any of these people the truth, I could collapse the walls around my mother and her fantasy world. Just a few words and they'd come tumbling down on top of her, crushing her to the soul. I don't hate my parents. They're trying to what's best for me without consulting me first. They can't comprehend why I would throw away this life to 'live in a mouse infested apartment with a girl who has no future.'

They mean well, they're buried so deep in their privilege, they can't see they're wrong.

"You wanna get the hell outta here, kiddo?" The raspy voice behind me whispers as she tugs on the sleeve of my jacket. My savior. My Morpheus who freed me from the Matrix and showed me the dirt and grime of the real world: my aunt.

The doors haven't closed, and she's handing me the one-hitter and the lighter. "Aunt Melody, you're a lifesaver. Why didn't you tell me you were coming to this shitshow?"

"I wasn't, but your father told me you'd be stuck here. I can't miss an opportunity to run to the rescue of my ride or die!" She takes the pipe back and takes a hit. "God, that's so much better. So, how's the beautiful girlfriend and do we have a wedding date yet?"

I laugh a little harder than I should, but that's the weed. "No. Oh, but we're getting a new place! You have to come see it; it's fire. Arts district, too."

"Thank god! I had hoped you'd come to your senses. Mice, baby. You were re-homing mice!"

"Yeah, but it's what we could afford."

"Still holding onto that dream, huh?"

"I like making it on my own, well, with Dani." I raise a glass to a man walking across the courtyard. He swallows hard when he sees me and speeds to the doors. "Aww, shame. Mom wanted me to talk to Ronnie Boy."

"You're a mess. That's my fault."

"No, you didn't let me end up as a clone of them; it's a positive thing."

"Yeah, but are you taking care of yourself? Of Dani?" She taps the side of my head. "You've got a big brain in there, kid. It could take you far. Both of you."

"Yeah, whatever. I tried asking mom about taking some of

my old stuff from my room, and she gawked at me like I asked if I could perform brain surgery on the dog or something." I take off my jacket and toss it over the back of a chair before I dig the cigarettes out of my back pocket, offering one to my aunt. "She said Dad moved it out, but Berto said it's downtown."

"It is. I talked your dad into keeping it. When do you move in?"

"I'm going to pick up the keys today. Dani and I are camping out there tonight, so she can finally get some solid sleep before they leave in the morning. If I get the furniture, I want to move it in while she's gone so I can surprise her and so she won't have to wait till I'm back." I take a drag, the first one I've had in months, and let my head rock back. "I've been eyeing some stuff down at the discount place, too. She'd flip out. I can afford it if I get a few more subscribers, or post more."

"Tell you what, you text me the address and what you want from storage. I'll get it all delivered over there the day after tomorrow. I'm sure I can get your dad to agree to that. Hell, he's probably forgotten it's even there." Before I can counter her offer, she adds, "Don't! It's an early engagement present. Or something like that."

"I told you, Aunt Melody, Dani isn't the marrying type. It freaks her out."

"I get it, Little Bug, but an aunt can dream. And to me, you two are already married." She slaps me on the arm as she ashes her cigarette into a fake shrub. "And at least I'm not giving you shit about smoking, drugs, or asking when you're gonna give me nieces and nephews. Please, do not give me nieces and nephews. Seriously. Kids are a fucking mess."

"I won't tell your kids you said that."

"It's fine. I will once they're old enough." She laughs so loud I'm sure people inside can hear her. She doesn't care though, she never has. She's the black sheep of her family and she's passed the mantle down to me now that she's had to take up at least part of the family business. "And if your dad says no, I'll give you stuff from my place I need to get rid of."

"Any guesses why Dad wants me in Tokyo?"

"No, but he has something up his sleeve, so be prepared. My guess? He'll ask you to run the new office we're opening."

"Hard pass. A month isn't going to change that. A year wouldn't."

"Yeah, but he'll try. He wants you to have every opportunity before we pass the company off to one of my kids, since that's a good twenty years away from happening." She ruffles my hair as best as she can through the product. "That's better. Come on, lets head back inside and laugh at people."

"Do you think dad will ever just let me be me?"

She sighs, her face dropping into pity. "Make me a promise? After Tokyo, get out. Stop saying yes, stop giving them the leash. You're free, Xander. You got out, but you keep coming back out of this wild sense of duty or to spite them. I'm not sure which. But promise me you'll take that giant step away and go live your happy life with your beautiful un-wife."

"Un-wife? Dani would like that one." I purse my lips and nod, studying the dirt and cracks in the concrete pathway to avoid eye contact. "Yeah. I like that idea."

HOLLYWOOD
Theo

CHAPTER 10
MY OWN WORST ENEMY

LIT

"GOOD MORNING, DR. CLAY!" my receptionist chirps as she walks into the office, her bright red hair swaying as she sets a cup of coffee down in front of me. I glance up at her over my glasses, watching her chew her lip and avoid eye contact. "I didn't buy the coffee! So don't look at me like a disappointed dad! I got that look from my own father."

"So this just magically appeared out of the blue? Let me guess, coffee fairies?" I ask, eyebrows raised while I wait for the answer.

"Sort of? The new barista already knows your order, so he asked me to bring it up for you since you haven't been down this morning." She leans in with a smirk because she thinks she's being coy, but I'm a psychiatrist and she's not an actress. No matter how bad she wants to become one. "He's got a thing for you."

"Kennedy," I rub my temples, but she's not done yet.

"Don't tell me you didn't notice, because you noticed! Last week, when we went down for a break after Coop—I mean—*Mr. Cooper's* appointment!" She folds her arms and gives me an over

the top look of disappointment mimicking my own. "You straight up ogled him, Dr. Clay."

"First, I've told you to call me Theo and don't call Chase Mr. Cooper, he hates that. Second, I did no such—"

"And he gave you a free muffin! That's barista for let's hook up, *Theo*! Trust me, that barista used to work at the shop near the studio I worked at and he never once gave me a free muffin, and I was in there every fucking day! And I'm cute!" She stops, eyes going wide. "I mean, every gosh darn day. Sorry."

"You can say fuck, Kennedy. We're adults, and there are no patients around. It's fine."

"Right, thanks." I hired her as a favor and thought it would only last a week or two, but she's been with me for a few months now and it's been working out pretty well. She had a bit of an intervention from friends and family not too long ago, and she's cleaned up her act after dramatically driving her car through the front of her boyfriend's gym after he broke up with her. Hollywood is a wild place to be a therapist.

"But a muffin, Dr. Theo. A whole muffin!" She waves her hands as she speaks, threatening to spill her own coffee on my office floor, or me. "That's big! Like, that's almost a proposal in coffee terms! I think. Come on, you can take him to a movie, or the park, or maybe a concert! What about that concert coming up? I know you already have tickets, and I also know you and what's his name broke up months ago so get back on that horse and ride that hot barista into the vanilla latte with caramel drizzle sunset."

"I don't think that's what that saying means, and I also don't think a candlelit concert an hour away from here works for a first date." I remind myself to cancel those tickets later. "Also, Taylor and I broke up a week and a half ago. Not that I'm counting." She pouts, but she does that frequently. It's a remnant of her old self, an attempt at manipulation that does work on some men. "Kennedy, would you like the tickets?"

"No! Besides, I still have time to work on this and set you up, because I'm going to work on this. I mean, just think about it? He works right down stairs, so he could pop up for a quickie between clients after his shift. That's so fire!"

"Kennedy—"

"I overstepped, didn't I? Yeah, I'm still working on that. What? I'm twenty-six, not dead!"

"No, I think the phone is ringing, or at least my head is. Thank you for bringing me a coffee, but it's time to get to work."

She nods, bopping out of the office, and I pop open the lid on the cup and eye the bottle of whiskey in the drawer of my desk, but I add creamer instead. When I go to put the lid back on, I see a phone number scrawled across the top with a Z under it. I wonder how many times someone has called him Zorro for doing that. I sip gingerly as I stare out the window that overlooks Los Angeles, watching the people hurry to and from their offices like ants. I hate this office for its hustle and bustle, but the rent is decent, the coffee shop downstairs is convenient, and the view is brilliant.

Kennedy's right, too. The barista is attractive. Zack and I have been trading flirtatious glances for a while now. Taylor tried to use it as a reason we broke up, but he knew I'd never crossed the line with Zack. I glance down at my cup again and release a heavy, overdue sigh. It wouldn't be crossing the line if I took him out for a drink now.

I push the button on the ancient cd player and let the music fill the office. Most people would expect something light—classical or jazz. But it's been the same CD for the last few months since it came out. My fingers trace over the signature on the case as I stare at the image of the lead singer.

She's younger, probably around the same age as Kennedy, which means I'm ancient to her. I saw her at a competition last year and I bought the CD the second it came out. My fascination is borderline creepy, but it's not like I'm stalking her. Her website, yes, because I've been hoping to make another show. She has this charisma to her, this glow of confidence and strength. I'm a moth and she's the most radiant flame I've ever seen before. Maybe it's the shock-purple hair she had that night, or her wild clothes. It could be her voice and the way she commands the stage and the audience alike. She scratches an itch I haven't had in a long time and rekindled my love of music.

I meet the two clients I have on the schedule and have video appointments with two more before I get a break, which I'm grateful for. I need the distraction, busying myself helping other people solve their problems rather than dwelling on mine. Packing up a few files and sticking them under my arm, I scroll my phone as I walk toward the office door. Kennedy is already gone, she has a class this afternoon and I've been more than willing to work with her schedule to keep her on the path she's walking. She has a lot of work ahead of her, and she hasn't hit the difficult bumps in her recovery yet. My former neighbor, and patient, recommended her one day when I bumped into her at the building's trash room. The poor kid has hung onto the condo even after getting married and moving out, but every tenant she's tried has run her ragged. I'm worried she'll sell soon, and who knows what I'll be stuck with?

Downstairs, I spot an open table in the far back corner of the cafe, where I'm less likely to be bothered. I scoot into the booth and flip open a notepad, there's a list I need to put on paper before I go up and order.

Eggs. Butter. Heavy cream.

Someone clears their throat next to me. Zack.

"Dr. Clay, you do know this isn't exactly a table service kind of place, right?"

"I'm sorry, Zack. I had a thought pop into my brain and wanted to get it down before I forgot it. I promise, I was on my way up to order in a few minutes."

"Kennedy needs to teach you about voice memos. Also, don't worry, I already have your order. Should be up in a minute."

There's no sharpness to his tone, but he knows technology makes me feel like I've hit my late eighties, not my early forties. I catch him rubbing his palms on his apron and licking his lips. His dark black hair pokes out from under the knit cap and he fiddles with the lip ring. His parents own a chain of cafes in high-traffic business areas, and he's started taking night school classes to work on a business degree. The building isn't far from campus or his apartment from what little he's told me, but the pressure of running the place himself while going back to school is a heavy burden.

"I'm sorry if the phone number was too aggressive. I got a little carried away talking to Kennedy and I meant it to be a bit of a joke, right?" I'd long forgotten the phone number scrawled onto the lid of my coffee. It's somewhere in the trash under a pile of tissues from my first client's breakdown, and now I may have to go fishing it out. Shit. "I mean, I get it. I'm just a barista and you're a—you know."

It wasn't a joke, that's obvious enough a blind person could pick up on his tell tale body language. Especially when he shoves his hands in his pockets and tries not to pout. It's adorable, and I'm a sucker for his whole skater boy aesthetic. Maybe I should take Kennedy's advice?

I grab my phone off the table and unlock it before handing it over to him. "I'm less likely to lose it there."

"Wait, really?" He takes my phone with a shaky hand.

"When are you off?"

"Uhm, now? Actually, ten minutes ago, but I saw you come down so I stayed on to make sure you got a fresh pot."

"Do you have class tonight?"

"No, I decided to take it easy and not do the summer courses. I am looking into a doctorate program after this, though. Assuming I'm accepted and can come up with the money for one." His smile is shy, and I can see how tired he is from the bags under his eyes. "I hear people burn out pretty quickly, and I'm already a pile of ash and dust, but it would make my parents proud and be nice as a fall back option. And I'm talking too much."

"Nonsense. It's hard work, but it's worth it. Most of the time." I tuck my notebook into my bag and stand up. "Alright, let's get my coffee to-go and grab lunch. I may have some connections to help get you into that program. Maybe I can shed some wisdom on you while we check out the new place next door."

"Wait, now? Right now? I'm kind of, I'm not dressed for—"

"It's tacos and conversation, Zack. Neither of those require you to change your clothes. Hell, you don't even have to lose the apron."

When I get home, the sun has long set. Before I can set my bag down, the screaming begins, but she doesn't leave the bedroom. When the queen is comfortable, she stays that way.

"Sweetheart, if you keep yelling at me, I'll put you on a damn diet!" I kick my shoes off and crack my neck, watching the door. When her large orange head and accusing yellow eyes poke out from behind the door. There's no question in my mind she'd eat my face off if I died in bed. She might not even wait for me to die.

The kitchen light temporarily blinds me, so I grope around for the fridge door and pull out her food. She wastes no time hopping onto the counter when I set her bowl down, staring me right in the eyes when she knocks it to the floor. The bowl loudly strikes the tile floor, making her jump and me laugh.

"Oh, we're both having that kind of night, are we?" I reach over and scratch under her chin. "Alright, I agree."

I leave the bowl on the ground and grab what we'll need before heading to the living room and turning on the hockey game. As I listen to the commentators, I pour myself a glass of wine and gingerly place pieces of fresh salmon on a plate. I scratch behind her ears as she takes dainty bites of the salmon, fully aware that she rules this house. Unlike me, the ape-like peasant who does her bidding.

"He shoots, he scoooooores! Calgary extends their lead, up five goals to one. At this point, it will take a miracle—"

I flip the station over to the public channel just in time to watch the dead body reveal on one of those cozy British mysteries. A few years ago, I would have watched the rest of the game, but that was before I knew some of the players. Their goalie is a good kid and the brother of one of my long-time clients, but when he hits a rough patch, he skids out of control and hasn't figured out how to right the car yet.

MEOOOOOOW!

"I'm not putting the game back on. I don't care if they *are* playing a team with a cat mascot. Oh, done already? Well, I'm not giving you more." We stare each other down before I toss a few more pieces onto her plate. "So, you remember the guy I told you about? The coffee guy with the pretty eyes? Yeah, that's not gonna work out and it's all because of you."

She licks the plate clean, no response to what I've said.

"He's allergic to cats. Yeah, I probably would have had a shot tonight, but maybe you saved me from more trouble." I pour myself more wine. "So damn allergic, he had to take a pill after he sat next to me at the restaurant. So now, not only are you an ungrateful monarch, you're also a cockblocker. Cheers, Baggy."

The look she gives me as she cleans her paws reads 'you're so fucking welcome' but also 'I'll eat your face tonight with a nice Chianti.'

My phone dings, making the cat jump and brace herself to bolt again. Earthquakes she can handle, but random noises? No chance.

I'm tempted to ignore the message on my phone. After looking at the calendar on my way home, I'm expecting an earful tonight, and I'm not sure I'm in the mood. There must be a crack in the bottle I picked, because when I reach for it to refill my glass, it's half empty. Before I can decide if I should keep drinking and just finish off the bottle or go to bed, my phone has the audacity to full-on ring.

"Fuck." An entire circus goes through my mind at light speed when I see the caller ID. I knew this would happen, and still I chose to not set an alarm like she told me to do last year when I made the exact same mistake.

"*Theo!*" Her heavy French accent removes the H from my name. "*What the hell? Did you forget?*"

"No!" I did, but she doesn't need to know that. "I called earlier, but it didn't go through. I believe she's finally blocked me and moved on with her life. As she should, I don't blame her for hating me."

"*Are you serious? What kind of bullshit answer is that?! You barely had one task, ONE, and you can't even handle that? Did you set the alarm like I told you? Your phone, Theo, it could have helped you!"*

"Yeah, well, now you sound like your parents."

"Oh screw you. Call your damn daughter for fuck's sake!" The silence on the line keeps me from tipping the bottle back and saying screw the glass. She'd hear that, though, and come through the phone like a horror movie to end me. When she speaks again, there's a soothing quality to her voice and she becomes the woman I know again. *"Theo, what's going on?"*

"Marie, I've called her every year. Every. Damn. Year. And for the last six years she's refused to even give me the courtesy of answering and being a total cunt to me. I'd honestly like that more than the silence." She could never treat me that way though, I already know that well. She's a saint, like her mother, but it's easier to place blame on someone else. "Why should I call when she won't answer?"

"Because you're still her father. You're still the only parent she has left. And you know she still loves you."

I rub my chest absently, fighting to keep the flashes of memory at bay. I don't need those nightmares tonight. "Maybe it's for the best, Marie. I'm a shit parent, obviously."

"Theo, you're not a shit parent and deep down she's still the little girl who adores you. You've sacrificed for her, and she has sacrificed for you, like most families. Just call her. Please?"

"She's an adult and she's made her choice, Marie. I've left the door open and she knows—"

"If you don't call her, you're slamming the door shut. I have to go, I have an early flight. I'll be in California again in a few months, we should see each other while I'm there."

We always say that when she's in California or I take a trip to Paris, but it's rare we follow through. We're reminders to each other of what we've had and lost, of the heartache we've suffered, and of the lives we had planned before everything was ripped away from us. She lost a sister, I lost a wife.

"Yeah, we should do that. I love you, Marie." I say what she wants to hear. "I promise, I'll call Sylvie."

"Good. I love you, too, Theo. So does Sylvie."

I end the call, grab my laptop and the last of the wine, and head to my room. I need a shower, a plane ticket, and probably some porn to make up for the shitty way the day, and my date, ended.

HOLLYWOOD
Xander

THE SOUND of Dani's singing spreads out of the bathroom along with the steam from her first hot shower that didn't involve going to her mom's place. I want to join her, washing the memory of the old apartment down the drain, but she needs this, and I have work to do. Our mattress went into the trash, so I'm connecting a couple of sleeping bags, so we have some padding against the hardwood floors. Next, I should unpack a few things, not that we have much. Everything undamaged or salvageable sits in a handful of half packed boxes around the apartment, including a clothes hamper with our coffee cups and the coffeemaker.

There's a noise, and it takes a moment before I recognize the song telling me the clothes are dry. Dani hugged the washer and dryer when she walked in earlier, telling them both how much she'd missed them. She stopped when she remembered that Jamie and Alexis had made out, and more, on top of them before Lexi moved out. We've both been smiling non-stop since we stepped inside, and even without a single piece of furniture, it feels like a home.

There's a knock at the front door as the shower turns off, and

my stomach groans. Perfect timing. I tip the delivery driver the hundred dollars my mom gave me earlier today to get myself a haircut. It makes his night, and he thanks me about twenty times before I can shut the door. The smell of cheap Chinese food and MSG fills the room as I walk to the kitchen to grab a bottle of wine and two of the coffee mugs.

"Oh, bringing out the fancy glassware instead of drinking straight from the five-dollar bottle?" Dani jokes as she leans against the corner in nothing but a towel, her wet hair dripping down her face. My own private mermaid. Or well, my own until we figure out what to do next about this dating situation.

I kiss her hard, pressing my body against hers and getting the front of my shirt soaked. I would open the towel and lift her onto the counter if I had free hands. Instead, I let her push me back so we can go get some food in us. Neither of us has eaten all day, too busy with rehearsals, my mother's business event, and moving. But when Dani doesn't eat, she tries to make good on threats to gouge people's eyes out. So, I splurged on the wine and some delivery.

"So, what if we put a big, plush couch over here? Like the ones with the recliners in them and cup holders," she says, waving her chopsticks around. It's a game we play, acting out a life we can't afford and decorating on a budget we may never have.

"Okay. But make sure you angle it so we can get the projection TV over on that wall, and I can get someone to come in and run the sound system through the house. Should only be a few thousand for that, but Star Wars will sound spectacular," I reply before handing her chopsticks with a wink. "And anime."

"Love it! Oh, and a four-poster bed in the bedroom."

"Naturally," I respond before sucking down a noodle. "California King size."

"Perfect for the three of us." Dani's smile doesn't betray her. The third person she's thinking of? It's the same one in my head. "And the dogs! We'll need room for all five of them."

"Yeah, but we'll have to kick them out at night. No need for them to watch Skylar and I absolutely ruin you. And me. And them." I laugh at the images in my head, but I'm also getting hard thinking about it. "Over and over."

"I'll find something cute with lace to wear for you both. One of those old-fashioned Hollywood wraps to go over it, the kind with the big, feathery poofs at the cuff and along the bottom."

"Oh, absolutely. Anything less would be uncivilized, my dear. And besides, what else would you wear to tie us up and let them fuck me while I'm wearing that gimp suit you'd buy for my birthday?"

"Hey! Not fair! You're killing our fantasy, Xan. I'd never put you in a gimp suit!"

I lean over, shoveling some of the rice into her container of food. "Oh, but you would tie us up?"

"Absolutely. Both of you. I'll get some rope from my sister when she's back. Oh! A paddle, too." She bites her lower lip and giggles.

"Your sister? Damn. Okay, now who's killing fantasies?!" I forget about the food when she leans over, pressing a handful of kissing to my lips until they threaten to become more. She stops without warning, pulling back an inch or two.

"Do you think they'll ever come back? Sky, I mean?"

"We can hope. Something needs to put an end to this string of shit dates we keep bringing home, doesn't it?"

We go back to planning for an apartment furnished with lavish crap we'd never own, laughing and feeding each other as we go. These are the moments I wish my parents understood, when Dani and I are in sync with each other and the world of bills and responsibilities a distant memory. They understood none of my choice to live in an average apartment with a woman I would die for but would rather make love to all night in cheap sleeping bags.

I question if my parents ever felt like this for each other. Their idea of love involves a rare, robotic 'I love you' with nothing but a chill behind it. They've been together for forty years, and my aunt jokes that my conception marked the only time they had sex. My aunt taught me about snark and attitude. I don't have a drop of the ice-cold Maxwell blood running through me; she always envied that.

"Hey, daydreamer?"

"Hmm?" I hum, glancing up from the empty carton in my hand. I'm not sure when I finished it.

"Let's fall into our giant bed and surround ourselves in warm blankets. We can clean this up in the morning." She stands up and undoes her towel, letting it fall from her beautiful, tattooed body. I've traced every one of those with my tongue a million times, and it never gets old. She leans over, wiping makeup off my face using a damp part of the towel. Her smile grows as she moves to another spot, revealing a little more of the face she recognizes. "There's my pretty little nerd. That's much better."

"God, how are you so perfect?" I pull her down on top of me as I lay back, and she cackles the entire way, pretending to fight me off with weak smacks against my chest. I wrap one arm around her as the other hand gets tangled in her wild hair. I've never worried we'd turn into my parents with their cold, affection-less marriage, because in all these years, kissing Dani has never become routine. Never become just a *thing* we do out of societal norms. Each time, it's electric and sends a jolt right to my cock. I roll us to the side, protecting her head from hitting the floor before I bury my face in her neck, sucking and biting. I'm not ready to leave her behind and spend a month away from her. I never am.

"Xander? Are you already hard for me?"

"Yeah, and I'm betting you're already wet. Thinking about what Sky and I would do to you." Her hands play in my hair as one of mine slides down her body and snakes between us. Her whimpers and sighs will have my grunts and groans accompanying them soon enough.

"You should have left your tie on. Might have been fun."

"I'll bring you a closet full of ties, and you can do whatever you want with them. And me." I grip her inner thigh and open her legs for me. Two fingers slip through her, teasing her clit before sliding inside her. The slower I move, the more she begs, gripping my shirt in her fists and pulling me down to her.

"Oh fuck, Xander! You're going to make me cum too fast!"

"Oh no! I'll have to do it again, won't I?" I pull my fingers out, licking them as she giggles and reaches down to unzip my pants. My breath catches when she takes me into her hand, squeezing just enough to get that first pathetic whimper out of me. I fall forward, caging her between my arms and breathing her air while she lines me up. As I sink into her, and her legs find their spot around my hips, I can't hold back the string of obscenities followed by a litany of promises to worship her forever. Until I'm bottoming out and I'm left shuddering over her and gasping for air, the world fades away. I'm surrounded by her and only her.

I've memorized every move and every noise she'll make for me before she does, because I've done nothing but study this woman and what makes her tick since the first time we kissed. I interpret her mumbles and songs, bringing her to her highest high before I coax her down. She tightens her grip around me, and I shift my hips in response, moving in quick, deep thrusts, like she begs me to.

"When I come back, I'm never letting you wear clothes in this place. That way, I can bend you over and take this pretty pussy anytime I want." I thrust harder, both of us panting like animals.

"God, you'd be a menace. Oh, Xander...please!" Her words fail her, becoming quick, breathy squeaks as she reaches that peak.

"I love you, Beetle," I whisper against her skin. We're both close. Too close, too fast. I can't help it right now. I'm desperate for her after spending the day with those stuck-up assholes. Dani gets me; she understands who I am and loves me for it, anyway. She understands that after dealing with so many frigid people today, I need her warmth, her softness.

"I love you, too! But Xander?" Her breathy voice drives me harder. "Oh fuck! Oh shit! Can you...maybe...wear the fancy suit...more often!"

"Only for you, Beetle. But first, I want you to ruin this one. Fucking soak it for me, baby." I cry out for her as she throbs around me and my balls tighten. We collapse together in a heap on the floor, surrounded by Chinese take-away cartons, an empty wine bottle, and all our possessions. I stay inside her warmth, letting the exhaustion of the last few weeks take us both.

I can't wait for my mother to ask why I need to pick up another pair of pants from my stash at the house.

HOLLYWOOD
Dani

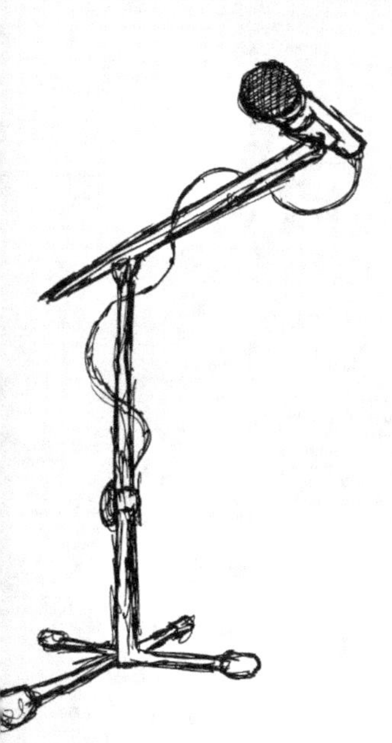

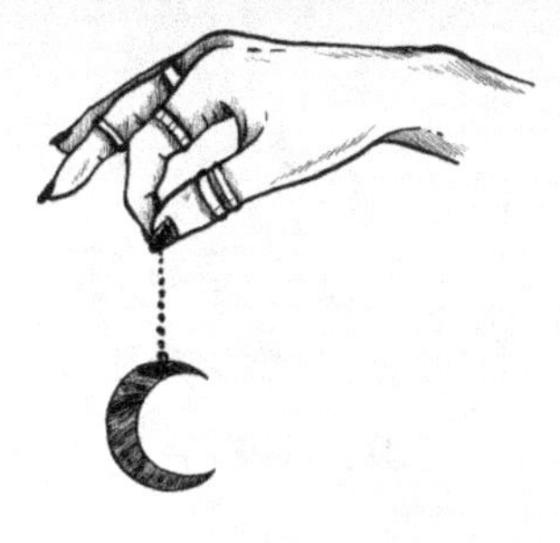

CHAPTER 12
MANEATER

GRACE MITCHELL

I HATE the expression about morning coming too early, but I understand it. Xander's arm drapes over my stomach as he snores softly next to me. I glance around and recognize the bedroom, meaning Xander carried me in here at some point last night after we dozed off. But now I need to pee, so I slip out from under him while trying not to wake him. Time to get ready for the drive up to Portland.

Or should stay here, where I'm warm and wanted. I gnaw on my bottom lip as I turn my head to face Xander's fluffy head of hair and let my mind wander back to last night, the suit, how different he acts in that world. Like he belongs there, behind a large wooden desk with some hot secretary pretending to take notes in her half unbuttoned top. We daydream about what his life would be like if he'd never met me, but he never takes it seriously. I'll talk about his big house, fancy car, and all the people taking care of anything he needs. He'll counter with the unhappy trophy wife, the kids they had out of obligation and not love, and the coldness of their conversations. No matter what illusion of richness I create, he reminds me there's a darker side behind it.

We were around seventeen when I invited him over to meet my mother for the first time. I told him to come for dinner and movies. He showed up in a suit and a giant bunch of flowers. He spent the first twenty minutes staring at us, mesmerized by the way we passed the food around, talked, laughed—not a cell phone in sight. Something as basic as sitting on the couch and talking to my mom while we watched TV was foreign to him. That's when I knew I'd never shake him; I'd shown him the world he'd struggled to find right there in my house.

I made a big show of him leaving for the night before sneaking him back into the house. Mama caught us in the kitchen, forks in hand and ready to dive into some leftovers. We were high as kites and all she yelled at us to clean up our mess together when we were done. I sometimes wonder if she meant the dishes or the consequences of our life together.

I love the warmth of those memories, and they're a core reason I'm both thrilled to have him, and terrified I'll break him. I kiss his head and grab my bag, shutting myself in the bathroom. It doesn't take long to get ready since we're all piling into Connor's van and driving the fifteen hours it will take to get to our motel in Portland. I pull on sweatpants, but don't bother with a shirt, deciding to nab one of Xander's so I can keep him close while we're apart.

When I open the door and peek out, Xander sits against the wall, messing around on my phone. I watch him for a minute before clearing my throat and announcing myself. "I don't think there are many people in this world who would sleep on the floor with me, only for me to get up and leave the next morning on a road trip."

"Would you rather stay at your mom's place, hot stuff? I thought staying here would be a bit more, I dunno, romantic?" He stares up at me, a dopey grin and his glasses both lopsided on his face. I've told him to be more careful about falling asleep with the glasses on since we can't afford new ones right now, but he still forgets. Especially when he's reading or coding. "Connor said he's running late. Come back to bed?" He holds out his hand and I take it, letting him pull me onto his lap.

"We should get this mattress replaced," I joke as he holds me. "The spring jabbed me in the back all night."

"That spring's got a mind of its own, but it wasn't your back it wanted to jab." He squeezes his eyes shut and puckers his lips, so I give him a quick, silly kiss. "But seriously, that might be a priority. I'm getting too damn old for the floor." He winces, shifting into a better position to hold me.

"You're not old." I reach up and adjust his glasses, sliding them up his face for him before I kiss the tip of his nose. "I'm worried this floor will be more comfortable than the van. Hell, probably the hotel. At least it's only Connor, Noah, and I."

"Rory wouldn't have lasted an hour in that van with you all." He pauses, his brows pulling together. "Wait, does that mean you'll miss me and our cozy little make-believe bed?"

"Duh."

"Aww. I'll miss you, too."

"Yeah, from your boujee hotel with its fancy-ass color TV."

"I'd rather have you. So, what about the new guy?"

"Todd? Ugh, I forgot about him," I groan, and he raises an eyebrow. "I don't like him, but we're making it work. At least until the first break, when we'll have more time to try people out."

He nods, turning his face away and running a hand through his hair. Xander has a specific face he makes when he's got something on his mind that he needs to let go of. He scowls and this little crease forms between his eyebrows while he stares off at something distant. Some people mistake the expression for anger, but I call it his resting dick face. He flips me off anytime I say that.

"Talk to me, Xander. Is it the trip? The new guy? Our contest? Tokyo? What has that big, nerdy brain of yours working so hard before you've had your bean water?"

"None of the above." He presses his forehead to mine and I swear this boy can see into my soul when he stares at me like this. "Well, sort of? What if this guy sucks? What if he gets you knocked out of the whole thing while I'm a million miles away? What happens then?" He shakes his head and lowers his eyes until they hide behind his long, thick lashes.

"There's always next year?" I shrug, trying to play it off like it's not weighing on my mind. I've had nightmares about it and we're all freaking out, but we can't change it. Everyone we found had schedule conflicts, wanted way more of the cut, or couldn't learn the music fast enough. It's a huge ask for little reward for the first few months. It wouldn't surprise me if we lose bands along the way because of schedules and daytime jobs, and I'm betting NotOkay Records hopes that will weed some people out well before the world tour part becomes reality.

"You guys are way too good to wait for next year."

"Yeah, well, what do you think I should do about it? Did you miraculously learn to play the bass after plugging yourself into the Matrix last night or something?"

"No. But our little game last night got me thinking, and Beetle? I think we should contact them."

I'd been thinking about that, too. But that nagging bitch of a voice in the back of my head keeps telling me I don't need that extra pain and stress right now. They left because they didn't care enough to be with us. We weren't enough to make it work. All lies I've gotten used to telling myself. "That won't work, Xan. They've got a new life now."

"Do they? They didn't go to Europe or something exotic and exciting like that. They didn't. Come on, we're single again! And we've got our own place that isn't a shithole. Enough time has passed to—"

"Has it? Where would he stay? What would he do?" I ask, worry creeping up my spine and wrapping around my brain.

"Yeah, it has. They can live with us; give this the chance it deserves. The chance we all want to take. We do, don't we?" His eyebrows jump up and down right before he tickles me, making me squirm right off his lap. He shifts on top of me, caging me in between his arms. "It's a clean slate, and we've given it years to settle out of our systems. It hasn't. Not for me, and not for you, either. They are the answer to so many of our questions, and frankly, the band's problem."

"We'd be suffocating to them. They wouldn't answer if I called," I mumble, rocking my head back. "I mean, who's saying they ever picked the bass up again? Besides, how are you so sure they're not backpacking through Europe?"

"They're not, okay. Believe me."

"Why should I believe you?" His eyes dart around because I busted him with a hand deep inside the cookie jar. "Have you talked to Skylar since they left? Am I seriously the only one who hasn't?!"

He drops his head, kissing his way up my neck, trying to keep me calm by turning me on. It's his favorite way to deal with things when I'm stressed out, and it's kind of mine, too. His hand pushes between my legs, shifting my panties to the side. He's gentler today, with soft touches and light strokes since I'm sore from last night's thorough dicking down.

"Xander, I don't have time to—"

"Connor said twenty minutes before he's here. Maybe more." He hums against my ear, shifting me so I straddle him. "As for

Sky, no. My texts have gone unanswered, but I still text them every few weeks." His eyes flutter and close while he rocks me on his lap. "Beetle, imagine it! The three of us? Fucking unstoppable."

"Yeah, we would be fucking unstoppable, in that we'd not stop screwing long enough to get anything done."

"We can make it work, Dani. The three of us." He caresses my face with one hand, his eyes begging me as his other hand makes it hard for me to concentrate. "We'd take such good care of you, Beetle. Our perfect punk princess. Worshiping you night and day, giving ourselves to you in ever way possible. Imagine waking up every morning to our mouths all over your body."

"Xander, I don't—"

"I want to take care of you, Dani. It's all I've ever wanted."

"Oh, honeybee, I get it," I reach up, taking his glasses off. They're like him, damaged enough. "Xander, I'd love that dream as much as you, but we can't get our hopes up like that. It's a dream, and we need to respect that. We can't...we can't keep waiting for them and the hope they'll decide to come back."

"Can't we?"

"And if they're playing again? What? They join the band and you're alone again." I pull his face to mine, his soft lips brushing mine as we share a breath. "I want you to be happy, Xander. I hate when you're alone, and I'll hate it more if Skylar travels with me instead of being here with you."

"I'll be okay, like now. I'll wait for you by the door like a dog, waiting for his people." He grips my hips hard, rocking me back and forth as our breathing speeds up. I listen to his soft cries that come when I run my nails over his skin and soak his cock through his boxers. "We'd find a way. We always do. We always will."

"Okay," I give in and am rewarded with a broad, toothy

smile. "I'll text them, but I won't harass them. Now, would you stop fantasizing about Skylar Beck's giant cock and use yours already? I've only got like ten minutes now!"

"Connor will wait. There's no band without you. And I haven't had my breakfast yet." He cups my face as we crash together and I glide against him, the pressure in me building like a steam train. He moves, laying me on the floor and trailing his tongue down my body. I don't fight when he pulls my sweats down and buries his face between my thighs, because there's no point. I need this.

Like he said, Connor will wait. I'm the lead singer.

HOLLYWOOD
Dani

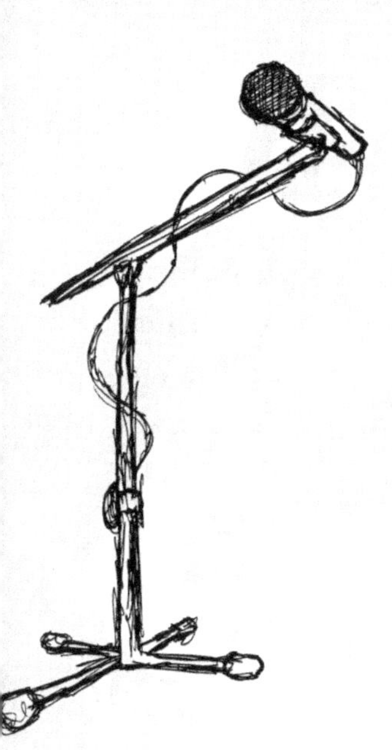

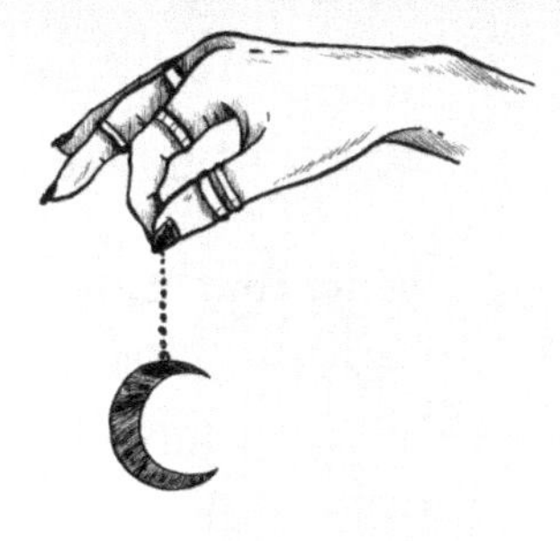

CHAPTER 13
CUNTISSIMO

MARINA

THE WORDS SIT on the screen, waiting for me to press the button and send it off to the atmosphere or wherever those things go. The words stare at me like they have for the last three hours, and that after I spent two hours trying to think of what to say, deleting messages, and retyping them.

> Skylar, we miss you. Come home?

My stomach knots, but I'm not sure if I'm more scared of them answering, or terrified that they *won't*. It's why I haven't tried to contact them before today; I'm not sure I could handle rejection from them. The simple act of not contacting them gave me permission to let my imagination run wild with possibilities. Anything I dreamed for them. But also, any nightmare. But even the nightmares weren't as hard to process as rejection.

They didn't altogether reject us; they never gave us a chance to see what would happen. For Skylar Beck, the term '*complicated relationship*' doesn't even come close to scratching the surface of their situation. But deep down, Xander and I always knew we

would come back to them, even if it took time. But do they feel the same way?

That's the deciding factor in my back-and-forth game of send or don't send. They're worth more than a shot. I press send, turn off my phone, and try to take a nap. Skylar's skills would elevate the band and bring out the best in all of us; they might do even more for Xander and I.

Every bone in my body snaps and groans as we climb out of the van and get slapped in the face with a level of humidity none of us are used to. I can feel my scalp cringing, so I grab my beanie and tug it down over my ears. I'm from Los Angeles, we don't handle rain and wet conditions well. I grab my bag and sling it over my shoulder before helping Noah get her gear out of the back. Once we have it all stacked by the side of the van, we all stand around and take in the motel.

We're going to die before this stupid contest even starts.

The ominous glow of the vacancy sign reminds me of Psycho, and the no in front of it has a persistent flash that sends either the right message or the wrong, depending on how ready you are to meet your maker. All the windows have a film to them so thick it turns my stomach. And some doors sport dents large enough to see from the parking lot.

"Shit, we're going to end up dismembered in a bathtub here tonight, gang. Good knowing you all." Connor echoes the thoughts in my head as he swallows the lump in his throat. He self-soothes by twirling his drumsticks between his fingers, and I'm jealous that he at least has a method. "Well, no point in waiting around. Shall we?"

"I go to my forefathers—" I whisper, but he only stares at me. "Lord of the—never mind. Read a book, Connor."

I dig my phone out of my pocket, turn it on, and find only two bars of reception—nothing from Sky.

"I don't think we can check into the death resort until—" Noah's cut off by tires crunching on the blacktop. We all spin around to see the shiny new Lexus pull up with its dark, tinted windows. I've seen this movie before and I'm not ready for the chase scene through the cornfield. Masked men with chainsaws are only fun on screen. The door opens and my heart races while I glance between us, trying to decide which of us has the chops to make the cut as the final girl.

The collective sigh of relief we all breathe when Todd, the new bassist, climbs out, turns to groans once we recognize him. I'm not sure which one of us will swing on him first, but it's going to happen. Connor said he's betting on me, but it might be a joint effort if he keeps this up.

"Hey, kids! We ready to rock?" He smirks, leaning against the car. "Did you guys fight a bear? And lose? Also, why the hell are you staying at the Bates Motel?"

"Oh, come on, it's not that bad! It's… charming. Quaint!" Connor tries, but can't even convince himself. "This isn't what they showed on the website, bro."

"Whatever, man, we're only sleeping here." Noah says, watching Connor jog to the office before narrowing her eyes at Todd. "Wait, what do you mean when you said why are *we* staying here? That implies you're not."

"I got a room in a less sketchy part of town. I'm not planning on dying here."

"Uhm, guys?" Connor mumbles as he walks back to the group. "Problem. Only one room left. I booked three!"

"What, and I mean this with the absolute least amount of

respect humanly possible, the hell?" Noah's arms fold as she rips Todd into a thousand pieces in her mind.

"Oh, yeah. I figured the band needed to save money and Connor can stay with me. Leaves you two ladies with a love nest to yourselves," Todd winks.

"I'll hang with you two, don't worry. Everything's gonna be fine," Connor tries to convince us with his upbeat tone, and nudges my arm. "Think of it as your old apartment; we can handle that!"

"If the serial killer comes to my room, I'm giving him directions to wherever you're sleeping tonight so I can hear you scream first, Todd." I reply, sticking my tongue out.

I am ready to redirect all my rage and aggravated energy into rocking this stage to the ground. Until Todd walked into the green room fifteen minutes before our set. No apology, no explanation, not even a boatload of bullshit excuses because, according to him, this is acceptable. Just when I don't believe it can get worse, it continues getting worse.

"Oh, cool, you're here. Where were you, man?" Connor claps the guy on the back—all smiles and happiness. I'm convinced he's high until he leans in and gives Todd a kiss that borders on pornographic, complete with Connor's soft whimper as Todd pulls away with a crooked smirk.

"Get a room—oh wait, you already have one, don't you?" I quip. "So, what do I call you on stage?"

He searches the room, only to realize I'm talking to him. "Uhm, Todd?"

"Just Todd? Like I'm going on stage in front of a crowd ready to rock, and I'm supposed to say 'and on bass, *Todd*' like it's all fine and we're cool with it?"

"I mean, it *is* my name," he scoffs, putting in a fake nose ring and eyebrow piercings before slurping down more of his iced coffee. "Rory said you guys would be dicks. I should have listened to her."

That's when I snap. Every rational, calm, fun part of me has taken shelter in the shadows, letting the other, darker emotions slither in and take control. My nails dig into the palm of my hand until I feel a warmth drip down my finger, and the heat coming off me could start a fire, I'm sure of it. I storm across the room and smack the cup out of his hand. It hits the floor, causing the top to come off and ice to fly everywhere. The cold, milky drink drips down my boots, which only adds to the raging sun burning in me.

"What the hell is your problem?" he has the audacity to ask.

"You and Rory know each other? You didn't think you should mention that!?" I don't scream it, but I add a little extra venom to her name.

"Don't do this," Connor runs over, pulling me back by the shoulders. "Come on, don't do this here, Dani. Let's get through the show, and later, we'll find a bar and talk this out."

"Talk? You want me to *talk* to this prick?" I spit out, pushing Connor off me.

"Come on, please? For me?" Connor has these big brown puppy dog eyes that he weaponizes when I least expect it. He does it because I can't say no to him, and he's laying it on extra thick right now. I hate him sometimes.

"We're all under a shit ton of stress," Noah says, maintaining her calm. "Between the move, worrying about Xander, you're under even more pressure. We can't flake out on the first night.

Take it all up there on the stage and get it out of your system the way you do, okay?"

"Fine."

"Guys, five minutes. Let's go!" the stage manager yells in the door before disappearing again.

I rip my jacket off the hook and storm out of the room, slamming the door behind me. Once I'm in the hall, I take three deep breaths to refocus all of this into the music, like Noah said. I'm not losing my shit on night one. So long as the rest of us play like our lives depend on it, we'll make it through this.

The stage manager waves us forward as the rest of the band shuffles out of the room. I wait, letting them take the lead; it's what I always do. I listen to them set up while I wait in the shadows, an eerie calm talking over as I inhale the stale beer and heavy night air. I love this shit so much. When it's my turn to walk on, the audience cheers, pumping more adrenaline through me. They're drunk, and they're ready to party. I'm pissed and ready to give them a show.

I grab the mic. "Hey fuckers! We're gonna get right into it for you since you've been waiting all day for something good. That's Connor on drums, Noah on guitar!" I turn and shake my head, motioning toward Todd. "And this is some dickwad named *Todd*. We're LA Proper. Let's do this!"

The buzz of the stage as we come off our third and final show of the week lights me up like the billboard outside my old apartment. Through the fear, anger, and uncertainty, we put on solid performances that we can be proud of. Even if we don't make the cut. I'm woman enough to admit that Todd wasn't half bad, improving with each set. He wasn't half good either, though.

After we pack up the equipment, I find three exhausted faces staring back at me, and I'm betting I'm no better. So, I offer to buy the first round while we watch the last few acts of the weekend. We navigate through the crowd to the area dedicated to the bands and nab a table in the back, ordering our first bucket of beers.

"Do you think she'll come back?" Noah tiptoes into the subject when Todd disappears from the table. "I mean, if we asked Rory and we're super nice about it. Do you think she would? 'Cause Todd was… man. He kind of sucks."

"You want her back, Noah?" I ask, taking a swig from the beer I've nursed for the last hour. "Like if she came over here right now, would you want to go up and play another set with her?"

"No," she groans. Rory and Noah never got along, but thinking back, none of us got along with Rory. "That would suck more."

"We can rework the songs, make them easier for Todd to pick up?" I try to put on a smile, but it falters. "Who am I kidding? We're headed home."

Connor puts an arm around my shoulders. "We're going home because it's between shows, not because they're dropping us. Stop being so lame. Todd will work for now, at least until we can find someone else." He tilts my head up and grins at me, half-drunk. "They've packed the house since Wednesday night. So, if you're going to think like we're going home, I'm sure NotOkay Records will host this again next year."

The pit in my stomach wants me to listen to my gut, to bow

out and come back to fight another year. Or bow out and stay out. Maybe I'm not cut out for this. Another failure in a long line of attempts to reach my dreams, only to fall. Hard.

But my heart wants to listen to Connor.

Noah flags down the guy working our area and orders another bucket before leaning in. "We need to be real, right? We're kind of broken and winging it right now. That will only get us so far before we're blown out of the water. But we still get recognition. We're still selling merch and getting the name out there."

"Do you two want to throw in the towel and let Rory win? Fine. I get it, I'll get over it, and yeah, we'll come back stronger next year," Connor replies. "But I'm all for staying in. We have a few days before the next show, and I'll work on Todd. There will be plenty of people lining up in LA. We need to get through the first couple of rounds and prove we're not losers."

"Work on Todd's skills as a bassist or work on his dick?" Noah teases, getting a laugh out of all of us. "Do you guys want the standings so far before we decide? See if they've made the decision for us?" Noah asks, staring at the bright screen in front of her.

"If we're out, are you going to tear Todd apart again?" Connor asks.

"I only spoke the truth, the whole truth, and nothing but the truth, so help me, Chase Cooper."

"Chase Cooper?" Noah cocks her head to the side. "Praying to your besties now?"

"He's played a god or something in a movie, I think."

"No, Chase played the patriotic dude's buddy or whatever," Connor corrects me before gesturing to Noah's phone. "Alright, give it to us, oh keeper of knowledge. How bad?"

We all lean in, staring at this strange tracking graphic that doesn't make much sense to me. It's hard to read the names, and I take a second to spot ours. We lock eyes for a second before checking the phone again. None of us say a word.

We're fifth. We're moving on to the next round!

HOLLYWOOD
Skylar

CHAPTER 14
OFF MY FACE

MÅNESKIN

"I'M your brother and you didn't think to pick up the dang phone and call me? Eight months and I don't hear shit from you?" He paces the hardwood floor, causing it to creak and moan in certain spots while I half-listen to his lecture. The other half of me pictures a life in this room, the room he's offering me if Los Angeles doesn't work out.

Dad bought the house a few years back as a fixer-upper project and gift to Marc. The house has plenty of room for my brother's growing family, and a studio area above the garage for Dad to live, once he retired. Dad's heart had other plans, and we lost him a month after he signed the deal. Marc took on the rebuild himself, finishing everything but this room—Dad's room.

It's a jarring time capsule clinging to the seventies with its dying breath. Either that or the room is coated in moss. That's the only thing I can think of that matches the color of this room.

"Are you listening?"

"Yeah. Yeah, I'm… Marc, what I'm supposed to say beyond I screwed up. Which I've already said." I came prepared for him to be upset, and I deserve every word. I've been a dick to everyone since the accident, and Mark didn't deserve that. Sorry doesn't even scratch the surface of healing all the wrong that sits between us. I'll take whatever he needs to dish out.

"You call me out of the blue and tell me you're in rehab in Canada? Rehab? Why don't I think it's for the arm?"

"It wasn't."

Mark glares at the bottle of beer in my hand, so I put it down on the table. "It's fine, Mark. I tell my sponsor exactly how much I'm drinking; I'm not trading drugs for becoming an alcoholic. But if it helps you feel better, I won't drink while I'm here."

"What the fuck, Skylar? Why would you do that?!"

"Well," my voice stays soft and even. I trace the hawkmoth tattoo on my hand as I talk. It's comforting when I'm stressed out. "The center in Canada had an excellent reputation, and they offered me a spot on short notice—"

"No, you asshole! I mean, why would you go through that alone and keep us in the dark?" He crouches in front of me, so we're eye to eye. "You need a support system when you leave those programs, Sky! You don't have that, do you?"

"I'm…working on it."

"Steve?" he asks, hope laced in the name. Even though Marc didn't reject my life choices, most of my family did. But they all accepted Steve. He's an idiot meathead, but he can make anyone love him with a wink and a smile.

"Not Steve. Not yet, anyhow." I stare up at the ceiling, letting my words fade away while I close my eyes. Los Angeles calls to me every day since I left. She wants me back, but my past there still has too tight a grip around my throat. I close my eyes. "Before I can stay here, you've got to tell me if *she's* here."

"Catherine?" Marc says our sister's name like it's left a rotten taste in his mouth.

Catherine dead-names me every chance she gets. She thinks I

did all this to take attention away from her, because I'm the middle child and she's the baby. She's a carbon copy of my mother, holding herself and her opinions in high esteem, thinking that social media can teach her everything about psychology, queerness, transitioning, who to pray to, and who to vote for. For years they ganged up on me, sending me pamphlets on conversion therapy, giving my phone number to random pastors, and telling anyone who would listen how hard they were praying for my soul.

"Nope. I haven't talked to Cat since Dad's funeral. She moved to Utah or some shit. I guess you haven't heard about Mom?" I shake my head, and he nods his. "She died two months ago. I found out in a letter from Cat. Can't say I miss her, but I hope she's finally at peace."

I don't believe in hell, but if it's real, I hope Mom had a first-class ticket there with no stops. Dad and Marc couldn't be any more different from my mom and sister, like two different families. They were my protectors and welcomed Steve and every other member of my found family into their lives.

"Did you get the drugs from the weird goth kid? The one dating the cute girl with the wild hair?"

"Okay, back up. You sound like one of those grumpy *stay off my lawn* guys. Or mom." I lean forward, my elbows on my knees, struggling to get comfortable on a couch that's too short for someone like me. "No, it wasn't Xander. I didn't get hooked on street drugs, okay? I went to rehab to avoid getting hooked on something worse than prescriptions."

"You were *getting* hooked?"

"It had me in a chokehold, Marc. The painkillers they gave me for my arm weren't enough, and I craved more. I had the needle in my hand, ready to jab it in my arm. But Chase and Xander found me and helped me get into rehab. I didn't plan for this to happen, or to disappear on purpose, but I didn't want to hear the disappointment in your voice."

"So, a movie star and a kid who might be a drug dealer sent you to rehab?"

"Fuck, why is this couch on the damn ground?" I stand up, ignoring his question, and stretch my back. I prepare myself for another round of lectures, but when I turn back around, he's laughing. "What?"

"Dad always said you were the dramatic one. He was right." He walks over, putting his hands on my shoulders, and stares up at me. "You see so much of the world people miss, and I don't mean because you're tall. You've always been one to find out what's inside people, and it's helped you find the right people at the right times. Including finding yourself."

"So, should I leave?"

"No," he laughs, gently slapping my face. "Skylar, I'm happy you found help. I'm happier that it worked. I'm annoyed as hell that you didn't call me sooner. I'll get over it."

"I'm sure there's a decent enough motel around."

"I'll help Marybeth pull everything out to set up the guest bed."

"Marc?" He stops before the door. "Would it be okay if I slept up here? I don't want to wake the kids up if I... uhm. I get nightmares and—"

He pulls me in for a bear hug and doesn't let go until we've both had enough time to shed a tear or three.

I can't sleep. My hands itch, my brain won't stop buzzing, and no matter how cold the room is, I'm burning up. So, I grab my cigarettes and my phone and creep out onto the back porch, glad they don't have an alarm system running to this part of the house yet. I move away from the house in case they have any of the windows open to the room the kids sleep in. I light up and pull my phone pit, expecting a message or two from my sponsor. It's been off all day, so tuck it back in my pocket while it boots up.

I'm unsettled by the silence of the backyard. People who enjoy spending time in their own minds baffle me. I don't mind being alone, but the silence becomes so much louder than any city traffic. It's also more dangerous.

My phone buzzes in my pocket.

PRINCESS BEETLE

Skylar, we miss you. Come home?

I turn the phone off again and shove it in my pocket. I doubt Xander told her about the rehab, or if she understands why I stopped all contact, but both thoughts turn my stomach. I want to answer her, to tell her I'm trying. But I'm still working up to it.

I stub out the cigarette and head back upstairs to start my nightly ritual over again.

The next morning, Marc and I are both up with the sunrise. Marybeth, my sister-in-law, told us to get out of her kitchen, so he takes me down the street to the repair garage to show me around and spend some time tuning up my bike. He's curious if I can still do this—I'm wondering if I want to.

"So, how long can we keep you here?" Marc asks after a long spell of nothing but shop noises. "I get that you've got to give LA a try before you decide if you're moving here, but I want to make sure you know we're serious. There's always a place for you, and the boys would love it. Hell, we all would."

"Thanks." I glance up and can tell by the hint of a scowl he expects more than a one-word grunt. "Marc, it's not that I don't appreciate it. I'm just not sure this place will work for me."

"Yeah, leave it to Dad to find the perfect piece of property and not notice it's full of conservative pricks. But we've found some decent people, too."

"You fit in better than I will. Either way, I'd like to head out tomorrow or the day after. A friend offered me a bartending gig while I'm getting my LA legs back."

"Where will you stay?"

"It's LA. There are plenty of places." I concentrate on the part I'm cleaning so I don't have to see him, but it doesn't do any good. "I dunno, probably a cheap motel until I can afford somewhere. Couch surf if I still have any friends left down there."

"You're not couch surfing," he sighs, tossing a rag onto the tool bench and picking up his phone. "Marybeth's sister lives nearby, and you can stay—"

"Marc, she lives an hour outside the city. I'll be okay, I promise. If I don't find somewhere, I'll call Chase or Laurie." Mark's forehead wrinkles deeper the longer he stares at me. "Chase paid for my rehab stint and checks in with me regularly. Laurie sends me dog videos on social media, and that's her way of telling me we're okay, even if it's weird."

"Promise me you'll be in touch with them and you'll tell me where you're staying."

"Sure. And I've still got Shawn on my ass, too."

"I'm not trying to ride your ass, Luca…shit… Skylar." There's an apology in the way he sighs, but he grew up calling me

Lucas. He only does that when he's annoyed or pissed off at me. It's emotions, not hurtful.

"You wouldn't ride my ass anyway, Marc. I'm a top." I wink. "Usually."

He mumbles under his breath, "Dick."

"Asshat," I return fire. He throws a shop towel at me as we both laugh and get back to work. It's nice being around him again, around people who care. It's possible I belong here. Closer to family, someone with a stable life I can look up to. But each person who walks by the shop and sneers reminds me I'd never be myself in a town like this without watching over my shoulder.

"Come on, let's get back and wash up," Marc says, putting the tools away.

I snicker at the way he adds an r to wash when his southern twang slips in. Marc was born in Georgia, and between that and years in the military, he picked up a slight drawl that got worse when he married a girl from Oklahoma. Where I ran from the military upbringing, Marc embraced it and followed in dad's footsteps. It's always been funny to me that siblings could be so different, with Marc being the macho tough guy and me being some kind of odd-ball sensitive kid.

"Worship?" I tease. "Bro, I'd catch fire in a church!"

"Shut it, California hippy." We laugh and talk as we walk the bike back to the house. He grabs a couple of hand towels out of the dryer after we wash our hands off with a hose in the yard.

"When you two finish up, breakfast is almost ready, and I've heard the whispers of the demons we keep in the attic!" shouts a tiny firecracker with long red hair pulled into a rock-a-billy fashion updo. Marybeth and Marc met in Oklahoma while stationed there, and they've been inseparable ever since.

"Sky-Sky!" Two identical gremlins with bright red hair come

bolting out of the house and head for me. I haven't seen them in at least two years, so I'm surprised they even remember me, but I guess it's hard to forget the giant who makes them fly.

"The hellions have risen! Tremble in fear!" They grab hold of my legs and shriek with laughter while I stomp around, doing my best monster impersonation.

"Okay, back inside and go set the table!" Their mom yells, clapping her hands to get their attention. I ruffle their hair before they take off for the door, still laughing. "If I could bottle up that energy, I'd get so much damn work done around the house. Oh, speaking of energy, how would you two like to go out tonight?"

"Out where?" Marc asks first, raising an eyebrow as he crosses his arms.

"Grace called earlier. Her and the boys are headed downtown tonight to check out that new bar. There's some big show going on and like five bands or something."

"I dunno—"

"Is it country music?" I ask, cringing.

"No, baby. I may be a country girl, but I'm not a country *music* girl. Come on, we'll get a sitter and show you a good time before you head off for the big city again."

"Hey, are you in a band?" a bottle blonde woman slurs as she falls against me, giggling. "Cause you're, like, in a band level hot. All brooding and mysterious…and so damn tall."

"No, just here to watch." I try to move away, but she stumbles, blocking my path.

"What do you like to watch? Because I'd let you watch me." Her blood-red lip drags through her teeth and her long, slender fingers twirl her hair. I bet she's fun, and for a second, I forget where I am and almost ask if she's got a boyfriend to join us. But she stumbles again, spilling half her beer on the floor and my boots.

"If only you weren't drunk, sweetheart. Come on, let's go find your friends. You shouldn't be left alone like this."

She pulls her arm out of my grasp and presses her tits against me. I'm not sure if she's coming on harder, or trying to stay upright. Scanning the room behind her, I try to find her crowd, but all these groups look the same. Thankfully, my sister-in-law picks that exact moment to leave the bathroom and come to my rescue.

"Monica, baby, where's Bryce? I'm sure he's looking for you, and if you keep this up, you'll start a fight." She grabs the blonde's arm and distracts her before turning to me. "Go on, find Marc and I'll catch up with y'all." She waves me off and I don't stick around.

The doors to the show swing open moments later, and a group of young girls come to sweep the drunk Monica away before they're all swallowed up by the wave of people. Either this show is bigger than I thought, or nothing else is going on in town tonight.

"Thanks for the save, Marybeth." I tap our plastic beer cups together when she catches up to us again.

"She's harmless, but her boyfriend ain't. Y'all ready to go in?" She stands on her tiptoes, watching the people still pouring into the next room.

"I'll meet you inside. I gotta hit the head."

"Be careful, baby, you don't wanna break any hearts walking around looking the way you do," she giggles and winks before she and Marc head off to brave the crowd and find their friends.

I let them get lost in the sea before I slip out the back. I've got at least half an hour before the first band goes on, and that's assuming they're on time. They won't be. Either way, it's enough time to have a cigarette and avoid the crowd. The smoking patio overflows with people in various degrees of drunk, so head out to the parking lot behind the building. I dig around in the bag on the side of my bike, searching for a small metal box, but I come up empty. Either I lost my stash, or Marc found it and threw it out, thinking he was doing me a favor. There goes the last of my low-grade weed for my panic attacks. At least until I get to LA and make some money.

"Dick," I mumble under my breath and light a cigarette instead. About halfway through, in the middle of perfecting my smoke rings, a voice cuts through the air and slices up my spine.

"That is not happening, *TODD*! You haven't learned the music we gave you!"

I blink and rub my eyes. That can't be her, can it? Maybe a ghost, or my mind projecting the face I want over that of a stranger. But that voice?

"Now *you* want to rewrite *our* shit? Why are you like every other Todd on this planet!?" she yells out. There's no mistaking that queen bitch attitude anywhere.

"Dani?"

HOLLYWOOD
Dani

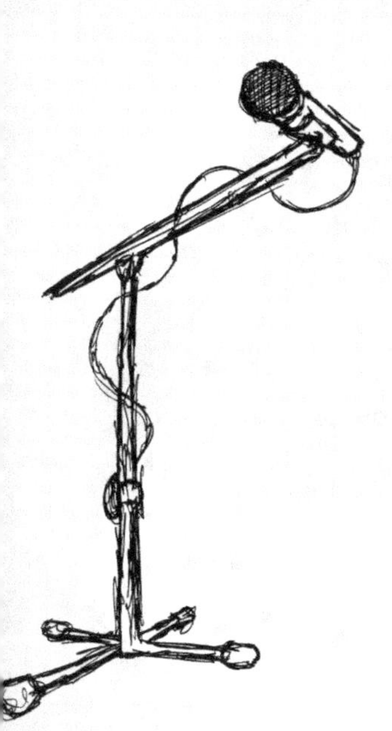

CHAPTER 15
THE ROCK SHOW
BLINK-182

"WELL, I don't care how you did it in your old band. We're paying you to play, not to write. You're temporary!" I'm so, so close to calling Xander and bawling my eyes out, because this isn't what I wanted or what we signed up for. But it's my fault we're in this spot. Last night we only avoided elimination by two votes, and if Todd screws up tonight, I may have to buy a shovel.

"Connor, can you please come here and talk to Flea's younger, far less talented idiot brother before I lose my damn mind?"

"Dani?"

I throw my head back and yell into the night, frying my vocal cords, but not caring. I can't take one more thing going wrong tonight. I cross my arms, ready for another round of verbal sparring with whoever wants to mess with me next, and turn toward the voice calling my name.

The sight knocks the breath out of my lungs. It's a trick, my mind playing games because of the stress. Interesting that it projects a sexy fallen angel with a motorcycle. Tall with long,

dark hair that spills out over broad shoulders. Pants so tight you don't need an imagination, and a jawline I need to feel between my legs. The entire package screams out to be ridden all night long and into the morning, and who am I to say no?

There's one flaw in this eye candy, and it's confirmed when they take a step a step forward, letting the glow of the streetlamp hit those rich brown eyes with their hazel centers. God, this world can get so strange sometimes.

"Skylar? Is that really you?" I scream and break into a full run. I jump into their strong, muscled arms without hesitation, and they give me that bit of an extra squeeze before they put me down and stare at me like I'm a figment of their imagination. "Look at you, baby! You look incredible!"

"No, I look like a trailer park after a tornado rips through it." They smile and it warms more than just my heart. It's been too long since I heard that voice and drowned in those eyes. "I can't believe you're here."

I've known Skylar for what feels like forever, but has only been about five years. They used to date one of my best friends, Steve—they even got engaged. They were wonderful together, always laughing and supportive. Until a truck ran Skylar's motorcycle off the road, almost killing them. When they woke up, they didn't remember the accident, the engagement, or anything else from the last two years. In the months that followed, Skylar's slow recovery took its toll on both Skylar and Steve. It only got worse when the doctors told them the fragments of memory they had recovered—about eight months before the accident—might be all they ever got back.

Xander and I tried our best to help, but it ended their relationship and a few months later, Skylar left us, too.

"What the hell are you doing here, fucker?!" I slap their arm hard enough to sting but not do any damage. "Also, where have you been? Also, also, why the shit did you ghost me, asshole?! Did you get my text?! Wait, no, backup. What are you doing here?!"

"I didn't ghost you, beautiful. I ghosted life. I needed some distance between me and everything that even reminded me of Los Angeles. I needed my life back." Their hands hold the sides of my face, and they stare at me like I'm the last cup of water in the desert. My heart flutters when soft lips press against my forehead, followed by a warm sigh of relief. "I can't believe you're here and you're real. Right when I'm trying to get my stupid head straight. Like you were sent to me."

I narrow my eyes at them. "Get your head…straight? Like, what does that mean? Were you on some kind of expedition into the depths of conversion-ville and you now go by your dead-name again or?"

They bark out a laugh, "God, no. Still Skylar, still exploring all possibilities, Beetle. You still with your honeybee, or do I finally have a shot at that guy?" They tease. I nod as they blow a cloud of smoke over their shoulder, away from me. Skylar's the only one of my friends who adopted Xander's nickname for me. At first, they did it to annoy Xander, but it stuck. "Good. Wait, are you playing tonight?"

"Yeah, it's like a tour. You should see where we've been staying the last few nights. Oh my god, it's been awful. Tonight isn't much better either. The first night we stayed outside of Portland, and Xander made me watch that Green Room movie with the Star Trek guy before I left LA, which is creepy and horrible. I freaked out for like two nights because of it, but we still ended up staying in every version of the Bates Motel that exists. Connor thinks we're gonna die in one of these dumps." I grab their arms, my eyes wide. "Please tell me the bar isn't stupid crazy with shit like chicken wire or caged dogs?"

"I missed how much you ramble. No chicken wire yet, and no signs of Captain Picard walking the halls."

"Ha. Ha. Okay, your turn!"

They pinch the end of the cigarette, letting the small chunk of burning tobacco fall to the ground and die in the puddle under their boot. "Passing through. My brother and his family live around here and wanted to take me out before I head south."

"South?"

They brush the side of my face, setting off a pyrotechnic show in my body as they stare at me for what feels like forever. I can't pry my eyes away from theirs except to stare at their lips. Skylar has these kissable, soft, pouty lips, even with the jagged scar that runs through them and the piercings. When they drag their tongue over them, I hold myself back. I kissed them on a dare once, and it solidified itself as a core memory for me. Even thinking about it now has me all warm in places I shouldn't be. If they hadn't still been with Steve when it happened, we would have done so much more than make out like teenagers in that closet. Xander would have joined in, too. He has the same tastes in men as Steve, or they go after the same men to annoy each other.

"I should have called you," they whisper. "I didn't want to get your hopes up. Either of you."

"So, are you coming back to LA? Like for real and for good?"

"I'm gonna try. I planned to give it a week or two while I worked up the nerve to call you. Guess fate had other plans."

"The nerve to call *me*?" I squeak.

"I told you how I felt and ran away. I assumed you hated me, even though no matter how far I ran, my feelings for you never changed. Even without you physically with me, you even gave me hope and restored my love of music. Your songs are the ones I play over and over, with or without the bass in my hands."

"M-My songs?" I shake the fog out of my head. "Wait, our music? Seriously?"

"It's how I kept you close. You and Xander, every single day." They wink. "I even had a gig a few weeks ago." They sigh and shake their head. "Unfortunately, the singer and drummer broke up, so it fell through. They weren't my style, anyhow."

"Too pop for your rock and roll?"

"Too hetero-normative for my rainbows, glitter, and pronouns."

"Ohhh, no bueno. Screw those guys and let that freak flag fly, baby."

"It flies so much higher with you around."

We're a breath apart, no signs of moving away from one another. The smell of their exotic tobacco, motorcycle grease, and leather mix with my whiskey and wildflowers in the sliver of space between us. The intoxicating mixture has my mind wondering if this bar has a broom closet where we can hide or if I should pull them into the van. The swarm of butterflies moves from my belly to my heart and into my throat. Now, they're threatening to jump out of my mouth and climb all over this beautiful person like I want to.

"How's everyone back…home?" Their face scrunches at the word.

"So much has changed since you left. Like Xan and I are the only things that are the same. Coop's brother moved in with him and went pro. Jamie got married, and oh my god, you'd absolutely love Alexis, she's perfect for him and they're stupidly in love. Laurie got married twice—to the same guy. Once on a cruise ship for shits and giggles and once back home for everyone else. And Steve—oh shit!"

I slam my hands over my mouth so hard it stings.

"Got married? I heard. So, he's happy?"

"He is. Ethan's the sweetest guy. Steve went on his soul-searching doom spiral and learned his soul was, in fact, not in some stranger's pants. Ethan helped him find his old spark, but we all still miss you."

"I miss you, too. But I'm glad Steve moved on. I still worry about the dumbass." Their smile reaches their eyes, which makes me smile back. So much has changed, but so much hasn't. Like me, they've earned a few more scars, added a few new lines to their face, and the look in their eye tells me things haven't been easy since they left. I'm not surprised since the last time I saw them their hand was so bad they had trouble holding the guitar let alone playing it. The depression kept them from writing music or poetry. They lost hope when giant chunks of their life were stripped away forever. Skylar has cried on my shoulders as many times as I've cried on theirs, but after the accident, the tears became sobs, gut wrenching and painful to hear. And the nightmares?

A shiver runs up my spine remembering those long nights and the way they'd scream out.

I get on my tiptoes and brush the hair out of their face, but the breeze keeps blowing it back. Before I can move my hand away, they've reached up and taken it, holding it there against the stubble and warm skin. The longer they stare at me, the closer we get to crossing a line that's ready to be run over, trampled, and lit on fire. What if the reason Xander nailed it the other night? We're searching for our third when they've been part of our lives already.

"Skylar, I—"

"Dani!" Connor's screech cuts me off from across the parking lot. It might be a blessing in disguise, but it still annoys me. "Are you coming or what?"

If you hadn't interrupted!

"Hey, break a leg up there, yeah? I'll make sure everyone in this bar has your back, Beetle."

"DANI! Come on, woman!"

"Shit, I gotta go. Stay here!" I say in a panic, making them laugh at the request. "I mean, stick around the bar, not stay in the parking lot! We can go out after and grab a stupidly early breakfast or something."

"Sure."

I narrow my eyes, but before I can say I don't believe them, they slide their jacket off and slip it over my shoulders. I pull it closed and breathe them in. We're playing with fire, making promises we shouldn't make to one another, but we're doing it, anyway. I pull them down to me and kiss their cheek before I take off running across the parking lot, holding the jacket close. I don't care that it's huge on me, I'm not taking this thing off until Skylar strips it off me.

After the show, I push my way to the back and shove open the door to the parking lot. Relief floods through me when I find them leaning against a light pole next to a familiar motorcycle.

"You stayed?" I move toward them, trying my best to come across as sexy, but I'm pretty sure I only manage stage drunk. "What did you think?"

"You've got my jacket." They wink and I hope they can't see the heat rising in my cheeks. "Same thing I've always thought.

Stunning, electrifying, transcendent, but mostly, mind numbingly gorgeous."

"Okay, enough about Connor," I joke. My entire body screams for me to jump into their arms again and beg them to never let go. Instead, I shove my hands in the pockets of the jacket, running my fingers over a set of keys I didn't realize I had. Either they still trust me and wanted to prove they wouldn't leave tonight, or they forgot their keys were in the pocket and they can't leave but don't want to make this awkward.

"Does Connor play drums or bass?" they ask, shoving their hands in their pockets.

"Drums."

"Ah, yeah, he's cute," Skylar says with a sky smile. "And he can play. I can't say as much about your bassist. Especially when his nose ring fell out." They take a step closer. "But he's got a solid band around him and a siren like you singing the sailors to their deaths in the pit."

"He's temporary. I, uhm, caught the last bassist screwing my girlfriend in the bathroom." I close the remaining gap between us, the toes of my sneakers bumping against the toes of their boots. My platforms shoes don't make a dent in the foot worth of difference in our heights. "If she'd been a better bassist, like someone I used to know, I'd have kept her in the band. Instead, I'm stuck with Todd."

"Terrible name for a bassist."

Somewhere behind me, I can hear the band packing up the van and getting ready to head out. "They're almost done packing up. I should let you get back to the band."

I take their hands in mine, my heart racing. I don't want them to leave again. "Come with us. We're grabbing dinner at one of those late-night grease traps."

They stare down at me, their face unreadable except for the tiniest twitch in the corner of their eyes. I'm sure they're about to say no, about to tell me this was fun, but we're never going to get that second chance, so why bother stringing this out?

"How about I give you a ride to the diner? We'll talk about what happens next after greasy food and shitty coffee."

"YES!" I can't hide my excitement as I jump up and scream. "I mean, mm, my favorite."

HOLLYWOOD
Dani

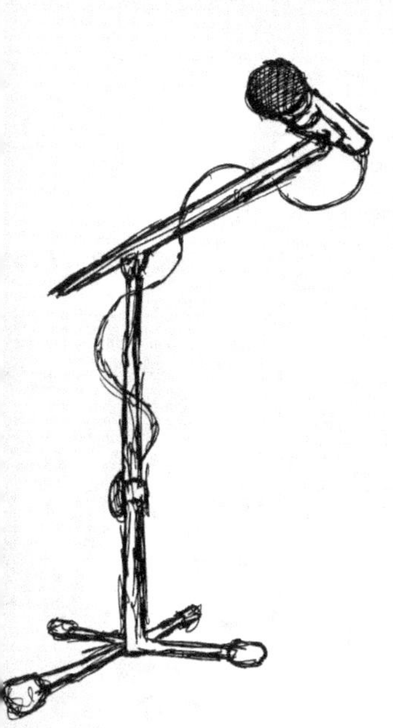

CHAPTER 16
BLISS

TYLA

HOURS PASS and it's creeping too close to sunrise by the time any of us think about leaving the diner. The muscles in my face hurt when I laugh, and there's an acrid, bitter coffee taste in the back of my mouth. Skylar's hand found its way onto my thigh and never left, and both Connor and Noah have attempted to pry into whatever this is. I shrugged, because I can't give them an answer. With a loud yawn, Connor leaves first; his arm around Todd as they stumble back to their room. Skylar and I walk out with Noah, watching her round the corner toward the hotel to make sure she gets there with no trouble.

Now, it's only Skylar, me, and the looming threat of a setting moon.

Billions of words and thoughts crash against my skull, but Sky centers my focus—their eyes, their lips, their hands.

"Dani, I need to—"

"I don't want you to go." The words run out of my mouth so fast they become one, but they aren't the words they want to hear. The heaviness of the sigh and the way they walk away tell me I've fucked up. I've imagined every hint, every touch, every glance tonight, which wouldn't be the first time. They lean

against the bike, head in their hands and shoulders slumped. I want to take it all back because I'd rather have them back as a friend than chase them out of my life again over some stupid, idiotic emotions.

Their head rocks back and their arms fold over their chest, hard biceps difficult to ignore as they hug themselves. They struggle to find words while I'm busy watching their tongue again, and how it slides over their lips. Whatever battle Skylar has going on in their head, they're losing. Now I feel like shit.

"I'm sorry, Sky," I squeak out in this pitiful, mousy voice that I've never heard come out of myself before.

"It's not you."

I don't believe them. "Did I fuck this up so bad I—"

"No! No, you didn't do anything. I…I don't know. I thought I had more time to…to figure out something I've known for a long time. Shit." They pull their hair up into a bun—icing on the cake of their entire rude body—while I'm over here struggling not to touch them. "Beetle, when you saw me in the parking lot earlier, you could have brushed me off and gone about your life. But you didn't, even though I did that to you. I walked away from everything, and you're, what, okay with that? Do you even know where I've been?"

"You had to leave. Life threw too much at you, and no one blames you for that. None of us. No matter what." I take a step closer. "Life gets messy sometimes. Look at mine. You make these plans and have these dreams about a family and making something of your life, but people do stupid shit, and your sister ends up with one of your best friends, but it's okay because… wait, where was that going?"

"Dani, you don't understand. I couldn't stay. For so many reasons, no matter how badly I wanted to. Nothing felt real anymore except—" Their mouth becomes a straight line as they take a deep breath through their nose. Their blank face can't hide the struggle behind their eyes. "I didn't want to cheat. I didn't cheat. But since I woke up in the hospital, only two people in the world have made sense to me. Neither one was Steve, and that's fucked up."

"So, you blame yourself?"

"I'm the one who kissed you."

"Steve dared you to kiss me, remember?"

"He couldn't have known how much that kiss opened my eyes and my mind." Their jaw muscle ticks as their throat bobs. If I had to guess, I'm pretty sure we're fighting the same demon right now, and I'm losing as bad as Sky is. "I lost my balance, ready to fall, ready to let go. Steve opened a door with that idiotic dare, and I still don't know if he did it on purpose. If he could see it before me. Maybe he saw it happening like the train wreck those months of recovery were, when I'd look to you and Xander instead of Steve. You two caught me when the wire finally broke."

They stare up into the starless sky and I watch them like I have a thousand times before. Struggling, trying to fight everything on their own instead of asking for help. Steve never once questioned Xander or me spending the night with Skylar in the guest bedroom, not that we did anything to question. Nightmares, pills, routines they waged wars against, and a fear I hope to never experience. The injuries and pain tried to take him from us over and over. But losing memories—the missing of chunks of their life they'd never get back—that's what ultimately broke them. Steve called us because he couldn't handle it alone and he knew Sky, Xander, and I had become close friends long before the accident. When every other memory tried to fail them, the memories of us stayed strongest in their mind.

"I left, and I fell too far to come home."

"I'll always catch you, Skylar. No matter how far you fall, we'll be there for you every single time." I sigh and drop my head, rubbing my thumb over the back of theirs and spotting a familiar image. My head snaps up, eyes locking on theirs. "Seriously?"

"I found one of your sketches a while back. You'd tucked it into my guitar case," they explain as I trace my fingers over the moth. "I wanted to make it more permanent. So, you'd both always be with me."

"I remember doing that! I wanted to give you something of mine to keep with you, just in case, but I worried you wanted to cut ties completely, so I hid it." My smile drops as their words hit my brain. "Wait, what do you mean we'd both be with you? You were always the moth and—"

They pull their sleeve back and I find the matching bumblebee on one side and the scarab on the other. I can't hold the tears back as my fingers ghost over the images. My heart lodges in my throat, because as close as I grew to Chase, Steve, and Jamie, Skylar felt like something more, something deeper.

We'd talk about nothing for hours, lay under the stars sharing our favorite music with each other, and tell each other everything. I helped Skylar and Steve pick out their rings. Skylar wanted me in the wedding party, by his side, and couldn't have been happier for them. I also couldn't have been sadder as I brushed the knots out of their hair while they were in a coma. I talked them through their past and the memories they'd lost of Steve and their relationship. I held them as they cried themselves to sleep night after night.

They helped me, too. They helped me see Xander as the best thing to ever happen to me, even when we break up. They held my hand as I testified against my sister's abusive ex-husband for the years of violence. They were the first person I trusted to read my notebook of unfinished songs and helped me finish every one of them.

I'd always known we were soulmates on some plane, but didn't know it could be this one.

"Oh, Skylar. Why did you have to leave us?" I sniffle.

"Because I needed help beyond what you could give me. Sometimes, that's how life works, Beetle." They lean forward and left the softest kiss my forehead. The feeling slid down to my toes and through my soul. "You've been calling me back since the day I left, like the siren I knew you were. Hell, I'm on my way back. I came here visiting my brother and would have left for LA in the morning."

"Why didn't you call? We've been so worried about you. Someone said you were in Europe!"

"Canada. For rehab." They run a thumb over my cheek, catching the tears. "Don't cry, Beetle. Please? I've shed enough tears for both of us these last few years. I promise, I never went a day without thinking of you two. I had to get things figured out on my own. I had to see how far I could fall without you. I had to find an end, to make sure it existed and that I couldn't fall forever."

"Will you stay? I want to wake up knowing this wasn't a dream."

"I can stay tonight."

"No." I squeeze their hand. "Not *tonight*, not sleeping next to each other after we fall asleep watching tv. Not you on a chair and me in the bed. When I say I want you to stay, Skylar, I mean more than only tonight. I mean forever."

I try to cup their face, and they take my wrists and lower my arms, but don't let go. "I left you. I never should have done that knowing what it would do to you. Knowing how many people you've loved, you've trusted, and lost. I told Xander to take care of you and never let you go. To make sure you both never forget what you meant to me."

"Stay with us now."

"We shouldn't do this, Dani. God, do I want to, but it's the last thing we should do."

"Why?" I step closer, pushing between their legs, brushing their hair back and studying a face that's been through so much. They shake their head almost imperceptibly, our mouths inches apart. They breathe me in before I lean into them, my lips pressing against theirs. A moment passes before two large hands grab my face, drawing me to them for a deeper, toe-curling kiss that will undoubtedly replace the last kiss's core memory. My arms wrap around their neck and my fingers tangle in their hair, chasing a dream that's right there, right at the literal tips of my fingers. They don't speak when their lips leave mine, and I almost lunge for more, not ready for it to stop.

I open my eyes in time to see Skylar bite their lower lip, a blush of pink spreading across their nose and cheeks. Why are they so fucking adorable? Why can't they be cruel and heartless and make all of this so much easier to deal with? Why did they have to dig their way into my heart, making themselves a home in the process if they couldn't stay?

A dozen small kisses follow. "Beetle, you've always made sense, both before I left and after. Your music healed me, but the memory of you and how you made me feel saved me. The world stopped spinning and everything stopped hurting when I kissed you. I felt like I belonged somewhere again. I found that speck of happiness in the distance and it scared the fuck out of me. But I couldn't run from it, couldn't hide. You're my north star, and I knew I needed to find you again."

"You did?"

"Yeah."

"Oh. I… Skylar, I…"

"Fuck this," they mumble before wrapping their hand around the back of my neck, pulling me into them so fiercely I don't think they'll ever let go. My eyes close as I memorize how it feels when their nose slides up my throat, their lips slide along the shell of my ear, their hand cupping my ass. I want to soak it all in. I want this to last forever, but I'm scared they'll leave again. As much as I claim to not have abandonment issues, I do. It's why I push people away before they have the chance to walk away.

Skylar walked away, and they could do it again. I'd let them so long as they give us this chance.

"Dani," they moan, digging the tips of their fingers into my hips as I hold their face, not letting go. Not letting them get away. The vibration starts between my legs and creeps up my spine, shooting bolts of electricity to the tips of my toes and the top of my head. This isn't enough. I want more of them. All of them.

"Stay," I say in a voice bordering on weak and pathetic, unrecognizable as my own. Raw.

"We shouldn't do this," they whisper, but neither of us stops our exploration. My hand slides down, savoring the groan and the way their eyes roll back as I press against the bulge in those tight jeans. "What room are you in?"

"Three ten," I barely get the numbers out and they sweep me off my feet and around the corner.

HOLLYWOOD
Theo

THE TICKET STARES at me from the counter, accusing me of being a chickenshit and hiding from my problems. The thickness of that irony could choke me. I spend my days helping other people through problems like this, through irrational fears and over-blown ideas. But when it comes to me and my own issues? I do the same things my patients do. I make excuses and bury my feelings. Therapists need therapists, too.

I glance at my watch. I could still make the flight. I can pick up my phone, get a rideshare, and be at the airport in time. By tonight, I could have a delicious meal by the finest chefs. Afterward, I'll head over to that bakery I found on my last trip to pick up those croissants Sylvie loves.

But the call never came, and I'm not in the mood for a pity trip.

I need to bake.

Baking is a meditative art form for me, putting me into a state of mental clarity and relaxation. I'm good at it, even if I'm not good at anything else in my life. In France, a lifetime ago, I had the opportunity to of becoming the next up-and-coming pastry chef, studying under one of the best in the country. It would

have been a dream come true if I'd stuck with it, but life happens. Well, more like death happens, leaving me empty and cold, with a grieving daughter and so much anger. I failed as a chef after that, and as a father.

I stride across the room and pull the fridge open. Empty. I used up the last of my groceries to keep me from coming home to a kitchen full of science experiments two weeks later. I check the cabinets to see if there's anything else I should get while I'm out, grab my reusable bags, and head for the door. As I step into the hallway, I'm met by a large couch sticking out of my neighbor's door, blocking both the stairs and the elevator. A younger guy sits on the couch, his head of shaggy dark hair in his hands and shoulders slumped.

Alexis, a former patient of mine, owns the place next door. She moved out a few years ago after getting married, and I can't blame her. She didn't have fond memories of that place. Living next to her new therapist might have been a little weird. Her sister stayed there for a few weeks before jetting off on some grand adventure; after that, Alexis tried turning it into one of those short-term vacation rental places. Last time I saw her she lamented about the stress of trying to keep up with the demands of people staying there, and the all-hours phone calls where they complained she didn't live close enough to Disney.

She had mentioned selling it, she might have rented it out to someone more long term. I glance over at the kid again, and to the stairs I can't access without climbing over the couch. My brain tells me to go back into my apartment and pretend none of this happened. Order delivery. But I'm not that kind of guy. "You, uh, need a hand?"

The kid's head snaps up, and my heart does a little tango. His eyes are a blue so light they appear gray, and full lips with their slight part—I can't help but lick my own as he stands, and I get a better view of his arms. His muscles flex under his thin t-shirt, and I swallow hard when I spot the edges of a colorful tattoo poking from under his sleeve. I'm hoping he's a kid hired to move furniture with his buddies, not my new neighbor. That could get dangerous.

"Seriously? Man, you'd be saving my ass so much humiliation and shit talking. My dickhead friends bailed on me."

The softness of his voice lures me in; maybe he's a vampire, waiting for an invitation inside. I shake that thought out of my head. Picturing him sucking on my neck will not get me groceries or get this couch out of the way. It's going to get me into a world of trouble and—

"I'm Xander." He holds his hand out. "Hell of a way to meet your new neighbor, huh? Blocking the damn walkway with furniture and shit. I'm so sorry about that."

I almost forget how humans greet one another, jerking my hand out to grab his hand and give it a squeeze. My fingers brush against the veins on the back of his hand, and his forearm tightens, giving it more definition. My mind goes blank, forgetting anyone I've shown any interest in over the last few years. This kid's puppy dog eyes, with the tattoos next to them, have my full attention. His thick brown hair and the thin line of sweat that's formed on his brow. His skinny jeans and gray henley are leaving enough to my imagination that I hope he can't read thoughts.

"Theo. Theo Clay. No worries, these hallways are a bit, uhm, tight." He smirks and I try to keep my knees from buckling, watching him size me up like a slab of meat. I'm doing the same back, so it's not like I can blame him. He's the last of a dying breed of emo kids, and he's gorgeous.

He rubs the back of his neck as he turns to nod at the couch. "I kind of planned on surprising my girlfriend. We've been living in a shit hole downtown and when I found this thing, I couldn't pass it up. I thought it would be nice for her to come home to something more than cardboard boxes and a few pillows on the ground. You know? But I'm a fucking idiot and didn't check the size."

Girlfriend? Shit.

No, that's good. He's sizing me up to know if I'm competition, not checking me out. I should know better by now. My face warms and the rush of red travel over my entire body. Reading his body language doesn't help, either. I've probably got twenty years on him, and that punches me in the gut. Time acts differently as you age, as if the world around you flexes and bends into a new reality you aren't part of. Until you catch your own reflection in a shop window and scare yourself, you don't feel the years as they pass you by. One day, you're eighteen, living life to its fullest and traveling through Europe with nothing but the clothes on your back. Blink and you're ten years older with a wife and kid. Blink again, you're listening to Hollywood's brats bitch about their lives because their parents took away their cars and made them get a job while you research retirement funds.

"So should I, uh—"

"Why don't we—"

We both go for the arm of the couch, my hand landing on top of his as we stare at each other. He's too close, or maybe I am. Either way, neither of us moves. That's when I get a flash of something familiar, something I used to see in the mirror years ago. A cockiness and bravado I long to have again. It's in his eyes and reaches his smirk.

I clear my throat—and my head—before I step away, pretending to evaluate the situation of the couch.

"Are, uh, are you sure it will fit?" I don't have time to catch my mistake as it falls out of my mouth.

"Oh, we'll make it fit." He steps up onto the couch and glares down at me, still smirking. "You just gotta push it in *real* hard. Don't worry, I can take it."

I curl my lips between my teeth and bite down to keep myself from saying something stupid. Or even worse, attempting to flirt back with the kid. *Girlfriend. He has a girlfriend. He'll live next door in Alexis's place. He has a girlfriend, and he can't be more than twenty-five, you dirty fucking pervert.*

"Relax, big guy. I'm only gonna bite if you ask." He walks down the length of the couch, hops off, grabs the other end, and winks at me. "You okay, Theo? You know I'm only teasing, right?"

"Huh, oh, yeah. I, uhm, do you have a tape measure?" *Fuck!*

"Oh, we're gonna measure it now, are we?"

"You know, to see how we'll need to angle this?"

"Buddy, I don't have any furniture, and I'm not about to measure someone else's…couch. So, why would I need a tape measure?" He leans over the arm of the couch and my heart does the tango while I fail at distracting myself by thinking of cold showers and snow. "Do you have one?"

"Never mind. I guess we're, you know, winging it."

We're reasonably certain the couch will fit with a little coaxing and brute force. He's the first to reference the sitcom from the nineties with the guys moving the couch up the stairs when ours gets stuck against the wall and a door jamb. Either he watched reruns, or he might not be as young as I thought. Still too young, though.

It takes twenty minutes before we find the sweet spot of an angle and she glides right through the door. He wasn't kidding about the furniture—or the lack thereof. I catch a glimpse of what appears to be sleeping bags on the floor in the bedroom, and the two flat pillows serve as chairs around a cardboard box table with empty Chinese food containers on top. He must notice me staring, because he hurries over and grabs the containers, tossing them in a plastic take-away bag on the floor.

"Sorry about that," he pants, a bead of sweat dripping down his forehead to his sharp jawline. This guy could be a model, but that's also true of half of Los Angeles. He reaches one hand over his head and pulls his shirt off, wipes the sweat from his face, and tosses the shirt toward the bedroom. His chest is a canvas. I've seen so many of those goofy black line art drawings that too many people regret later in life, but he's got a talented artist somewhere. Above his heart sits a scarab beetle holding a diamond. The color and detail are so intricate, I wish I had the opportunity to stare at the artwork without coming off as a bigger creep than I already am. He has others too, but beetle drawings me in the most.

"It won't hurt you." He rolls his head like he's offering me his neck, cracking it several times before he stares at me again. That cockiness back and staring at me, tempting me. "Beer?"

"I should get going. I don't want to—"

He holds his hand up. It's not threatening, it's more of a plea. "Hang on, I owe you, man. You've put up with my shit one-liners and a couch in your hallway."

Before I can stop him, he rounds the corner of the kitchen. A moment later, there's the rattle of glass and the sound of two bottles opening. As he's walking back, I can't stop my eyes as they travel down his chest and follow the tattoos and the deep V until it disappears into his low hanging black jeans. He hands me the bottle, his fingers brushing mine on purpose, or that's only my mind playing tricks on me. The bottles clink together and Xander flops down onto the couch. Winking, he pats his hand on the cushion next to him. "Come on. We worked hard getting this fucking beast in here. We might as well break it in, right?"

I don't know if he means we should sit on it, or fuck, so I keep my distance as lower myself to the edge of the cushion. It's comfortable. More comfortable than I am right now, anyhow.

"So, uh, you live next door? Or did I catch you doing a late morning walk of shame?" He wiggles his eyebrows at me. "Not that it's a bad thing, man, but I wouldn't trust whoever let you out of your bed if that's the case."

"What?!" I squeak out before I clear my throat and try again. "No. I mean yeah. Yeah, I uhm, I live next door. No walk of shame. No one…in my…bed."

"No one? That's good to know." He winks and takes a long swig from the bottle. I watch his Adam's apple bob as he drinks half the bottle before he stops. "Shit, guess I worked up a thirst. So, what do you do? Are you like a professor or something because that's the vibe you're giving off?"

"I do?" My head drops to assess my outfit. He's right.

"Oh, come on. There's gotta be some fine young student or assistant to keep you company on those lonely Los Angeles nights?"

"Only, uhh, it's only me and my cat. She's pretty much the boss." Did that sound too desperate? Why did I even bring the cat into this? It's not common for me to fumble my words like that, I haven't done it in years. Not since my first trip to Paris, the day I met *her*. Between my brain firing off warning flares and the beat my heart hammers out, I can't focus. He licks his lips, and the butterflies join the parade.

"I like cats. They're soft and warm if you treat 'em right." There's an edge to his voice, inviting but dangerous. He stares at me while finishing his beer, and doesn't stop staring as he moves closer, leaning over me with a nonchalance that's got my cock straining against my pants. "I like dogs, too, Theo. Little rougher around the edges, a little more bite to 'em."

He sets the bottle on a cardboard box while I pretend to be a marble statue.

"Am I making you uncomfortable, Theo?" The shake of my head starts slow, but the desperate need to grab his face and pull him to me speeds up the motion until I'm seeing double. "Good. Because I do intend those puns and the innuendo, if you're wondering. So, I guess what I'm asking, Theo, do you like dogs? Or are you a cats only kind of guy?"

"I—I like…what?" He's still leaning over me, and I can't hear over the blood rushing through my ears. He's so close now I can feel the heat coming off his body and the scent of his cologne massaging my brain. It has hints of something citrus—bergamot? I gasp when his hand slides over mine, taking my bottle. He licks around the mouth of the bottle and tilts his head back, pouring the amber liquid into his mouth until it's empty. I've never been so parched. I'm failing this test of my willpower.

What a fucking rollercoaster of a day. I'm not worrying about Paris anymore. I don't remember the bare cabinets and empty fridge. My brain refuses to focus on anything that isn't Xander. There could be a circus car of killer clowns piling into the apartment, honking their horns and slashing the air with their knives, and I still wouldn't be able to turn away from this guy.

His thumb grazes my chin and I'm pretty sure I get what he's about to do. The moment I decide I won't fight his advances; he swallows the beer. I swallow a mouthful of dry air and try to think of anything but his mouth, his lips, his tongue. I'm failing.

"Y-you…you said you have a girlfriend, yeah?"

"Uh huh. She left for Portland a few days ago. Guess I'm all alone, too." His hand moves to my knee before sliding up my thigh. "We've got something of an open relationship. We both like to play, and that's why I asked if you liked *dogs,* Mr. Clay."

"D-doctor. Actually."

"Oh, even fucking better. So, tell me, how'd you like me to help you out with that tent in your pants?" I nod, my chest heaving, out of my control like the rest of me. "Gimme words. Tell me you wanna play doctor, Doctor."

"Yes. Yes, I like dogs and I… I wanna…play."

"Good, because I wanna play, too."

There's no hesitation when I grab his face and bring it to mine. There's also no grace or delicate touches. It's raw. He's itching a primal need that's been begging to be scratched for too long. I pick him up and pull him onto my lap and he rides me like a bucking bull, not caring that we're both still at least partially clothed. Doubt creeps in, but he doesn't give it time to settle, pulling my face back to his and moving his hips harder and faster.

"Oh fuck! Slow…slow down."

"I got a better idea, Doctor. Take off your pants."

HOLLYWOOD
Skylar

CHAPTER 18
CLOSER
NIKI BARR BAND

WE FUMBLE with the lock on the door, and stumble inside, kicking the door shut behind us. My hands are on her face, unwilling to let go, and hers lock into fists full of my shirt. I've waited years thinking this would never happen. I'd never have another chance to make things right, make them work. I've begged every goddess and god, pleaded with the universe, and asked the devil himself for this, for her.

We break for air, but can't keep our mouths off each other, gasping in choppy breaths as I push against her and her leg wraps around mine. My fingers finally move, sliding down her body, unable to break contact until they're cupping her ass and lifting her off the ground as she lets go of the softest whimper. Which only adds fuel to the already out-of-control fire inside me.

"Tell me you want this, Dani. Tell me you want me."

"I can't!" she whines. I pull back and stare down at her, swallowing hard and waiting for the next jab of the blade to my heart. "I can't tell you I want you, because it's not that I *want* you, Skylar. That's not strong enough. I *need* you. The world isn't right when you're not in it with us."

"Beetle, I don't want to do this to you. Not again."

"Sometimes, love hurts. I love you Skylar, I have for so long now. That's why I need you, we need you. We're greedy. It's selfish of me to want this from you when I have Xander, to think I'm supposed to have both people I love most in this stupid, fucked up world. But I don't fucking care." Her eyes glisten in the streetlight that bleeds in between the curtains, and there's a familiar sting in mine. "If I can't have you, tell me now. If it's not what you feel in your heart, if it hasn't been us there with you this whole time, tell me."

"I'm broken, Dani. I'm—"

"Beautiful? Human? Trying to make it through this fucking life?" She cranes her neck and grabs my bottom lip between her teeth in a gentle nip. "Sounds like you're my type. It's like your motorcycle, Skylar. Take the wrong parts away and it won't work, but put them all together and she fucking purrs for you."

Her words have claws and hooks that sink into me, holding on in ways no one has ever held on before. Even if I walked away right now, the memory of her would never let me go, haunting me in every face, every song, every moment of my life. I've had my fair share of *what if* moments and I've blown every fucking one of them. Not this time.

Some part of my brain that's been dormant for years awakens and my hand wraps around her throat, just tight enough to make her shiver. With my thumb against her jaw, I turn her head to the side and slide my tongue over the shell of her ear. "If we do this, you're mine. My siren. My songbird. I will make you howl until your throat is raw. I'll have you on your knees crawling to me. I'll make you cry, and you'll beg for more." I move her head again and she stares at me with wide brown eyes. "And I promise you, I will hurt you, but I'll never harm you, and I will always love you."

"Those are the vows I needed. Make me purr, Skylar. Make me yours."

Teeth clash together around our tangled tongues in a hard, brutally honest kiss before I pull her away from the door. There's a shitty dresser against the wall that I clear with the swipe of my hand and push her on top of, sticking her ass in the air. Ripping her leggings down, I'm greeted by a pair of soaked lime green panties that make my mouth water. I rub her round ass before bringing my hand down hard. She jumps and gasps, trying to bury her head in her arms.

She pushes back against me, craving me inside and out. I pushed her panties to the side, running my finger through her pussy and over her tight ass as she gasped and groaned, eager for more of me. All of me.

"Let me hear you, siren." My hand comes down again, but this time she lets me hear the moan. "Can you take one more?"

She nods, "Yes! Please!"

"Good girl, using your manners already. Let's keep it that way, yeah?"

My thumb pushes against her puckered hole as my hand comes down a third time. She screams out, her arms flailing, grasping for anything she can hold on to and finding nothing but air and the edge of the dresser. "Oh fuck! Oh god, Skylar, please! Fuck, please?"

"Please what, my love?" I coo, rubbing the spot on her ass that's turning bright shades of red. "Please let you cum? Oh, that's not happening for a while. You're not ready."

"I am! I am ready!"

"You're not begging near enough yet. Not desperate and pleading to soak my cock."

She groans and I lower myself to my knees, sliding her wet panties to the side. I'm salivating for a taste of her, knowing that if I do this, there's no turning back. She'll be my new favorite drug. She'll take over every part of my life, and I'll never be able to leave her. I spread her open and shiver at the taste exploding on my tongue as I slide through her. She reaches back, grabbing my hair and holding me there, testing my need for control. I growl deep inside her and she pulls my hair in response, tightening around my tongue. When I shift my focus to her clit, she lifts onto her toes, rocking back against my face. I suck in hard pulses, my tongue lapping and swirling as she sings me a song I'll never grow tired of. Her thighs shake and her hips shift, desperate to be filled as she whines for me.

With one last flick, I release her and stand up. She glares over her shoulder, still a shuddering mess even without climaxing. She growls when I don't reach for my belt, instead licking my lips and pushing my jacket up to expose more of her back. The way my cock strains against my pants makes it hard not to impale her on it right now. I want to wait, want to make her pray for me and to me, but she's too damn inviting bent over like this in my jacket.

I lean over her, reaching into the pocket to pull out my phone when she rubs herself against my bulge with a moan and pleading eyes.

"Patience." I hold the phone up and she tenses up. "Relax, Beetle. We're gonna send this to Xander. I should have taken a before picture so he can see how badly I'm about to ruin you, but I think he'll like the handprint."

I hold her open with one hand as I take the picture. "Take a video," she suggests with a grin. "Show him how good your cock looks inside my pussy."

"You think it's that easy, do you? You just ask and I'll let you have my cock?" I grab her hair, yanking her head back. "You need to earn it."

She's shaky as she slides off the dresser and to the floor. Without direction, she moves her mouth to my jeans, kissing and groping to get her way. She doesn't know what she's asking for. She and I have done little past heavy petting and making out. Xander's at least had my cock in his mouth, but I've since made a few...modifications. She unzips me, pulling my pants down my thighs, and gasps.

"Holy fuck," she holds out the u sound and swallows hard before her eyes meet mine.

"Open your mouth and stick out your tongue. You should get used to how they feel before I make you choke on it." She does what I ask, leaning forward as I reach down, my cock in one hand, the other fisted in her hair. I hold her still as I run the tip over her tongue. She flicks against the metal balls, sliding from one to the other as my eyes roll back. Her hand replaces mine and her mouth closes around me like a lollipop, teasing and exploring the new sensations of my piercings.

"Your mouth...fuck. Dani, you're so perfect." She sucks on the head, mimicking the pulses from when I had her in my mouth and sending a series of sparks up my spine and through my brain. "You like them?"

She winks and moves her mouth down my shaft, finding the ladder and flattening her tongue against it. The speed with which she disarmed me and took control before I recognized what she had done would alarm me from anyone else. But this? I craved this since I left. I've searched for this feeling in every dream I've chased. Someone to challenge me, someone strong enough to test my limits and brave enough to allow me to find theirs.

I should have known it would be her.

"Right there, Daniella. Jesus, you're so sexy. Fuck!" I add fifty extra f's to the last word as she drags her tongue up my shaft before she impales herself, taking me down her throat. Her nails drag down my thighs, the pain an exquisite mixture to the way her throat moves with me inside her. The harder I push into her, the more she claws at me. But when her eyes flick up and meet mine, I'm done for. I can't hold out.

She gags, but I hold her there, her throat full and squeezing me. My breathing shatters as everything inside me tenses and she chokes as I spill down her throat, but she never stops. Not until I pull her off me and glance down. Her mascara runs down her face, her nose and cheeks red, and her eyes…god, those giant doe eyes. I drop to my knees and grab her face, licking the cum, spit, and tears from her chin before closing my mouth over hers and devouring her soul.

"I must look like hell," she whispers as our kisses ease back down along with our heart rates.

"You're beyond angelic. You surpass super models, nymphs, and goddesses in my eyes."

She pulls my phone out of the jacket pocket and takes a selfie with my phone. "An after picture for Xander."

I grin, "Oh, you think I'm done with you? No, love. But I wasn't prepared for how fucking well you take me, especially with the piercings. Now the real fun begins." I stand up and pull her to her feet, helping her shrug my jacket off. That won't be the last time I fuck her in my clothes.

She takes off her shirt and moves for the bra, but I stop her, taking her in. The lime green panties, the matching bra so thin I can see her dark nipples pebbled beneath the fabric. I want to taste every inch of her. I want to hold her from now until eternity.

"Skylar?"

"Yeah, my beautiful siren?"

"I'm… I want to be yours." She hesitates for a moment. "I

want to be completely and totally yours. Like, I want to let go. I've got a death grip on so much in life and I want to let go of it all. I'm so tired of holding on so tight. I want to be nothing but yours tonight."

"You could never be nothing, Dani. And I promise, you will always be *mine*." I wrap my hand around her neck, my voice low and dark. I'm trying not to let it shake, not to break, because I understand what Dani's telling me. After all these years, the pain of being apart, the unfairness of life, she still trusts me. And trust runs deeper than love.

I lift her, carrying her into the bathroom and setting her down on the counter. She makes the most beautiful noises when the fingers of one hand push deep inside her and the other hand squeezes her throat. Her wet lashes flutter and she grips me tight as I do the same to her. She comes apart for me, her cum dripping down my fingers and over the counter. She's beautiful, and even more beautiful when she lets go again, this time with my name on her lips.

There's a strange crossover with power in a sexual relationship; one a lot of people miss when they try to categorize themselves as dominants or submissive. They think being a dominant means you're in charge. What you say goes, that the submissive must always do what you say. Without mutual trust, the process falls apart and people stand a higher risk of getting hurt. A sub gives themselves over on the deepest of levels because they trust their dominant partner. They trust them to listen, to understand, to care for them, to never take it too far.

Her fingers wrap around my half-hard cock, bringing it back to life and notching the tip against her entrance.

Dani craves control over every aspect of her life, but she hides it well. She fears change, and it's rare she puts down her barriers long enough for anyone to gain admittance into her inner sanctum. She would die for her true friends, but more importantly, she would kill for them and never bat an eye. She's the beetle because of her beautiful, jeweled shell, the wild side she projects into the world. The thick armor she designed to distract from the scared little girl she never stopped being.

I push into her, watching her eyes roll back and mouth drop open. I shiver as the last piercing enters her, letting the sensation rush through us both. I stay buried in her warmth until she forces her eyes open and peers up at me.

"From now on, Beetle, I will stay." My voice shakes and my body fights the uncontrollable urge to move. "And from now on, my beautiful little beetle, with your hard shell and stubborn ways, will belong to me. Mine to love. Mine to fuck. Mine to destroy. Mine to make whole again." I won't be her jailer. Instead, I will set Dani free. We're not there yet, but this serves as my promise to her. We will be what each other needs most in life. That she can trust me, and that we'll be there for one another from now on. She'll catch me when I stumble and fall, and I'll hold her together when she's falling apart.

"You mean it, Skylar?" She pushes my head to her neck as I snap my hips and we descend into that primal chorus.

"I do, Beetle. I do."

Dani mumbles in her sleep as I slip out of bed. Grabbing my phone and pack of cigarettes, I step out onto the tiny balcony and light up. Flipping through all the pictures and videos we took has me smiling like an idiot, and, after watching them a few times, I move the files to a secure folder online. Xander taught me that trick and it's saved my ass a few times, having my important stuff kept somewhere other than my phone. It became our way of communicating without talking, using the file folders he set up for me after I'd gone. Sometimes, I'd save pictures or videos meant for him, since I knew he would get a notification for certain folders. He did the same for me. The intimacy without touching or talking had an erotic and enticing edge to it.

The first colors of the morning seep into the sky as the sun climbs over the trees to promise the world a new day and a fresh start. I don't deserve either, but I'll take it. Opening my phone again, I send a message to my sponsor.

> I found her. Well, she found me.

SHAWN

That's crazy. What happened?

I'm not surprised he's up this early since I'm convinced he sleeps less than I do.

> She wants me to come home. Her word, not mine. Home.

SHAWN

How do you feel about that?

> Like I want to try. I can feel again, Shawn. Not stressed or freaking out. Not worried about the future or what happens if I get that itch again. Just her. Just...happy.

SHAWN

I'm glad, my friend. Teach her your warning signs and call me when you can or when you need to. Give her my number, too.

I believe in you, Skylar. I always have. Hang on to this feeling.

Warning signs. I should come with a fucking label tattooed on my chest.

Danger: may become increasingly dickish with no warning, contact sponsor if patient loses interest in food, sex, or music; uncontrolled crying in the shower, chronic and sudden anxiety attacks, and long battles with self-loathing and horrific depression are common. Watch for nail biting, social withdrawal, outbursts of rage, extreme mood swings, fight or flight reactions, and fucked up drawings in my journal. Good. Fucking. Luck.

Maybe I'll do that someday. I should add the DNR order I begged for a year ago. I glance inside and see her face smashed into the pillow, makeup everywhere, and I can help but think that this time, maybe I'll be okay.

I crack my neck and put out the cigarette. Before going back into bed, I wash my hands and use some of the mouthwash Dani has by the sink. I've tried to break the nervous habit, but like I told Shawn, I can't kill all the demons at once, so I aimed for the meanest mother fucker first. I close the curtains tight so the sun won't wake us before I settle in next to Dani's warm, soft body. Nuzzling into her neck, I wonder if this sleep will end differently, if the demons will stay away, even if only for a little while.

"I love you, Daniella," I whisper as sleep pulls my eyelids down and I drift off into the darkness.

HOLLYWOOD
Xander

THIS GUY IS what would happen if the sex appeal of James Bond and the dark brooding of Batman collided and became one. Older Batman, though. When he's got those streaks of gray hair everyone knows he and Robin bang like rabbits behind closed doors. I can't tell if he knows I've been eyeing him since he found me out in the hallway, wallowing in my self-loathing for being an idiot. Okay, he's more like Superman, swooping in to save the day when all hope looked lost. Maybe I'm too much of a horny nerd.

Nerds have needs, too, though. Especially nerds terrified of flying but getting ready to board a long flight in a little more than twenty-four hours. I need something to take my mind off it, and the good doctor here will take care of that craving.

I run my hands through his short, graying hair, something I've wanted to do since he first said my name. The rolled-up sleeves do nothing to ease my raging hard on, either. Noticeable veins running through nice big, tattooed forearms as he takes hold of my hips, pushing me down and grinding against me. His hands would look fucking amazing around my neck. I bet he

fucks hard, and right now, that's what I need. I'd guess he does, too.

"Xander, you don't have to do this. I only wanted to help, not—"

"Bill me, I don't fucking care. Please, don't stop." I slide his glasses off, putting them on the arm of the couch. His eyes have swirls of greens and browns, like marble, or at least that's what I can make out from the sliver of color around his blown-out pupils. My hand slides over his thigh, brushing against the bulge and making my mouth water. The lazy, unhurried way he runs his tongue across his lips has my cock trying to rip through the seams of my pants.

"Why did you have to be so fuckin' pretty?" His deep, smooth voice has a haunting quality, but there's something more, a growl right on the edge. A beast he hasn't let out in a while that's pacing its cage.

"You've... done this before?"

His lips pull back in a sly grin and it might be the first time I'm seeing the real him. He nods, "Yeah. Yeah, I've been with dogs before. In fact, Xander, I prefer them."

Shit. I can't believe we're doing this.

I reach down between us, palming his cock as his hand slides up the back of my head, holding me to him as he kisses me deeper, harder. It's been so long since I've been with someone who isn't hiding who they are. Someone who knows what the hell they're doing with another man. I want this man to destroy me, to reduce me to whimpers and whines, to make everything else melt away.

When he throws me down on the couch, it knocks the wind out of me, but I love it. He climbs over me, unbuckling his belt and unzipping his pants before he cages me between his strong arms. I don't even try to hold back the moan as he rubs against me, or the whimper that comes out when his teeth graze against my neck.

Without warning, he freezes. His expression matches someone who's remembered they left the house with the stove on. "I shouldn't…we shouldn't do this. You're…young. Probably too young."

"I'm thirty, do you want to see my ID, or do you want to get in my fucking pants, Doctor?"

"I'll stop if you want," he whispers, but I'm not listening and he's not stopping.

"Why? Do you want to stop? Want to go about your day and get your groceries and play with your cat?"

His eyes are little disks of honey around the black, blown out pupils. He shakes his head and growls.

My nerves are pop rocks—mini explosions going off wherever our skin meets. "Take off your fucking pants and let me see what we're working with."

Our tongues wrestle for control as we grope one another, searching for ways to get rid of all the clothes between us. He wraps around me and in an almost fluid motion, he's flipped me over, grinding against my ass. His hand reached down the front of my pants and when he cups my cock, my head rocks back.

"Yes, oh god. Ah, there we go. He does like dogs!" I laugh, thrusting into his fist.

"Oh, you're gonna be a mouthy brat, are you? Well, I can fix that."

I've been told by more than one person that the best way to shut my wise mouth up is to shove something into it. Some people mean food, others, like Theo here, have something else they want me to choke on, and I'm more than willing to help him out with that. His eyes grow wide when I shove him back on his ass, and drop myself right where I need to be, between these two tree trunks he calls legs.

He swallows hard, watching me as I tease him, kissing him through his boxers and tracing my tongue along his abdomen while he helps me pull his pants down his thighs. I watch the daze take over and his head rocks back when I lick and nip at the sensitive skin of his legs.

"Ah, fuck!" he moans as I pull his cock out and give him a low whistle.

"Holy shit, Dr. Clay. You sure you were asking if the couch would fit through the doorway when you're packing this?"

"You just going to sit there and admire it, or finally put that smart mouth of yours to use?"

The deep rumble from his chest is the last sound he makes before I take him into my mouth. He stops breathing, holding the last breath he sucked into his lungs until he hits my throat. His back arches and hands shoot to my head, grabbing two fistfuls of hair and holding me down.

"Holy shit! Holy fucking shit."

My panic attacks about failing Dani are long forgotten, along with the conversation I had with my father. Maybe that's why I'm doing this, deep-seated daddy issues. What else would drive me into the arms of older men only to be shoved out of their beds before sunrise? Dani's tried to help with my near fatal attraction to older men, men who have the power that my father has. The power I could have but don't want. Now, I tell her I'm clumsy, or getting into bar fights, but it doesn't help her worry less.

Too many nights end like the one with Mitch did. Bruised, broken, and bloodied, I always end up wishing I could make better choices. I like it rough when it starts, but they take it too far. All of them do, eventually, because I make them see what they are, and they hate me for it. They pay to get off, and I pay the price for making them feel good.

Theo's hands graze my cheek, and I prepare for the worst. For the real him to beat the shit out of me after he's finished in my mouth. For the name calling and the pain, both physical and emotional.

"Fuck, you've got a hell of a mouth on you, Xander. Keep it up, baby."

Baby? They never call me that. They call me faggot, homo, queer, bitch boy. They don't call me baby.

"You're so pretty on my cock. No, that's... you're fucking breath taking, baby. That's it, beautiful. Wait, are you... crying?"

I pinch my eyes together and wait, no doubt about what's coming next while I'm trying everything to keep the tears back. The thumb wiping my face makes me flinch, but I keep going. The pain starts if I let go of his cock.

"Stop. Xander, stop!" He pulls my face from his lap, holding his hands on either side of my head as he stares at me. I can't look at him, so I brace for the impact and hope it isn't my face this time.

"Xander, I said you didn't have to do this. I meant it."

"I...want to."

"Do you? Why are you crying?"

"I'm sorry, I'll stop. I can stop. I promise."

"Oh. Fuck, I really should have seen that coming," the growl dissipates, replaced by something else. Softness and understanding. Kindness. He pulls me off the floor, but it's gentle, not painful. I still can't make eye contact with him, but damn, I want to. I'm not sure if I'm scared because it might be a trap, or scared because his concern sounds so real.

"You're safe, Xander. I won't hurt you; that's not how this is supposed to work. Those men aren't men. They're disgusting pigs and you… you deserve better."

"How did you—?" My chest tightens and I can't breathe. I can't focus. Before he can say another word, I'm on my feet and across the room, collecting our bottles and heading into the kitchen like nothing happened. The sound of the sink helps clear my mind as I rest my head against the overhead cabinet.

"Stupid fucking…" I mumble to myself, grinding my teeth together. "What were you fucking thinking? What the fucking fuck, Xander. God fucking—"

The weight of him pressing against me stops my muttering. He reaches around me, turning the water off and wrapping around me, leaving gentle kisses below my ear.

"I'm a psychiatrist, Xander. You're not the first person I've met who's suffered. Sadly, you won't be the last. But you don't have to face this alone, and you don't have to worry about that with me." I can't stop my body from melting into him. What the hell is wrong with me? Why am I like this? The hypnotic smokiness of his voice pulls me deeper into him, dragging me to a safety I don't recognize. "You're braver and stronger than you think, Xander. You're worthy of kindness and respect, and that's what you should get from these men. But you can't stop yourself, can you?"

"N-no." It's a sob filled with years of resentment and hate directed at myself. I can't hold it in anymore and I scream. "Fuck! FUCK!"

"There you go. That's good. It's a release, and that's a start." He doesn't bark at me, doesn't yell. His voice stays soft and even. "You're okay. No one will hurt you. Not while I'm here."

I'm gulping air and the tears opened a floodgate I don't have control over. The bravado has all but vanished, hiding somewhere and leaving me raw and exposed. But not scared. For once, I'm not scared. "Show me. Show me what it's supposed to be like."

"You're sure?"

"Yeah. Yes. Please?"

He turns me around and cups my face, running his thumbs across my cheeks while his nose brushes against mine. He doesn't shove his tongue down my throat, but takes his time tasting my lips, teasing my mouth open, and finally kissing me without a trace of regret or disgust. Everything slows down—my heart, my breathing, and even my mind. When I open my eyes, he presses his forehead to mine.

He stops me when I lower myself, but I shake him off and drop to my knees. Glancing up, he caresses my cheek again as I pull down his pants and boxers, but this time, when I take him into my mouth, he unleashes a moan so loud I'm sure the old lady down the hall will complain about it later.

"Oh, goddamn it." I lift my eyes, watching him grip the edges of the sink with both hands and close his eyes. I try a hum, and he moans even louder, showering me with more praise. "Atta boy, keep doing that. You're a work of art, fucking beautiful." he whispers.

I still flinch when he touches me. Each time I do, he gives me more praise and louder moans. My fingers dig into his legs as his hips rock in an unsteady rhythm. He's not tapping out, not pushing away, not angry there's a man on his knees for him. If anything, he's begging for more.

"That's it, nice and deep for me, baby. You feel so fucking good."

There's a wet pop when I release him, and he reaches down, dragging a thumb across my chin to wipe the spit away.

"Fucking. Beautiful."

"Cum in my mouth, Theo. Please?" I manage to say between gasps for air. "Let me choke on that big cock of yours."

"You say that to all your neighbors?"

"Only the incredibly hot ones who help me move couches." Even my laugh shakes. I can't remember the last time I sucked off a guy and could laugh at myself, could feel enjoyment from it. I'm not doing jumping jacks or anything, but it's…nice.

I open my mouth wide and stick out my tongue, begging for him. I crave the high his praise gives me. He takes hold of the sides of my head and slides in. When he speeds up, I gag, but I don't stop, holding his hand in my hair to signal that I'm okay while my other hand cups his balls, rolling them in my fingers.

"Oh, fuck. Oh fuck, Xander. Keep it up, baby. Don't stop."

When the telltale signs that he's about to cum start, I hum, vibrating against him. He grabs the edges of the counter and empties down my throat with a roar. When he's got nothing left, he collapses to the floor next to me with a laugh and a sigh.

"Shit, kid. I need a cigarette after that." He reaches over and ruffles my hair. I still have no clue how I'm supposed to react when he puts an arm around me. "And you, my friend, need therapy. I've got some people I could recommend."

Grabbing a box not far from us, I dig through it and pull out a joint and offer it to him along with a lighter. "Or you can take me on as a patient for a hefty Los Angeles rate and keep letting me suck your cock."

The flames dance across his face before he takes a long drag and shakes his head. "Nope." He blows out, ending the exhale in an impressive smoke ring. "I have a strict policy against taking on new patients when I'd much rather take them out for nice dinners that end in lazy morning sex and breakfast in bed. Also, it's not exactly ethical."

My heart skips and my stomach jumps. Dinners? Staying

overnight? I expected to be tossed back out into the hall when we were done, not hit on. Granted, I still ended up on the floor after, but this time, I like it.

He takes another drag and closes his eyes. Grabbing the back of my neck he pulls me in, our tongues tangling and teeth clash together through the smoke as I climb on top of him.

"Come on. We can mess around some more in the shower."

"Xander, we should—"

"Stop worrying about your groceries or my girlfriend?" I take his hand and guide it down my chest to my cock, still begging to be set free.

"Actually, I wanted to suggest we go to my place. Where I have actual furniture to defile you on."

"Oh, well, in that case, fuck me, Daddy."

"Only if you promise to never call me that again."

"Deal!"

He takes my hand before I can get up, sliding his fingers over the skin on my wrist below my thumb. It sends goosebumps up my arm. "Xander, one more thing. I need you to tell me you deserve better."

I scoff and glance away, but he doesn't let go. I listen to my heartbeat, slowing back to its steady pace while I stare at the ceiling as he continues rubbing my wrist. Everything changes, that's what Dani always told me. Nothing stays the same unless you stay the same, and man, we have changed so much over the last few months. We fight less, we stick up for each other more, we moved into a worse situation, but now we've moved onto something better instead of breaking up. Dani has her dreams right at the tips of her fingers, why can't I?

"Say it out loud."

"I deserve…better." When he tucks his finger under my chin,

my eyes drag down his arms and up his face, hesitating to meet his glare. I fight the fear and lock eyes with him.

"Say it out loud, and mean it, Xander. Believe it."

"I don't know if—Shit, Theo. How do you even know what I deserve?" I push myself up and sit against the counter again. "You've known me for a couple of hours."

"You care so much about your girlfriend, you tried to move a giant couch into the apartment for her. Alone. You slept on the floor with her in a sleeping bag the night before she left for a trip. The minute she left, you went into a tailspin."

"The hell with this. I don't need any of this."

"Whoever told you that this whole game you play of tough guy until you get your ass beat was a good idea, lied. I'm even going to guess you come from money, because this trauma screams boarding school. Also, mommy and or daddy didn't love you enough."

"They were fine, they—" I can't finish the sentence because he's hugging me to his chest.

"You deserve better than *fine*, Xander." He whispers it against my ear, rocking me back and forth on the floor of the kitchen like a child.

I don't need to be treated like a child, and if this is some weird kink he's into, I'm out. I try to twist out of his hold, but I can't, I'm stuck there.

"You deserve better," he repeats, but slower this time. "When was the last time someone held you, Xander? Told you they'd keep you safe? They'd keep you warm and protect you?" He stresses each word, ensuring I understand. Giving me no alternative but to search for the answer to his question.

Dani. The only one who ever cared about me, the only person who ever fought for me. But even she's never said it out loud. The switch he's been aiming for the whole time clicks.

The struggle stops, and my whole body goes limp. I don't have more tears to give this, not right now, so instead I shake in his arms. Rage, sadness, loneliness, all of it comes together when I can't answer him.

191

HOLLYWOOD
Skylar

CHAPTER 20
SOME NIGHTS

FUN.

THE SUN SHINES *on my face, warm and inviting. I'm coming back from checking out the last venue on our list, and I'm already planning the table layout in my head because this is the place. I've found the venue where we're getting married. Tomorrow, we're going cake tasting, which Steve hasn't shut up about since he proposed. I'm going to make him taste every fucking flavor they have until he's sick of cake.*

There's a flash. My bike drags sideways across the pavement, taking me with it. Metal screaming as it bends and twists to the breaking point. The world goes from sky to blacktop and back again. Searing pain starts in my arm and moves to my legs. Everything goes black. Someone screams; something burns. Opening my eyes, heat slices through my body and everything tastes like copper. I'm not alone. Glass crunches somewhere near my head. Why won't they stop screaming?

"Skylar? Baby, wake up. It's okay, I've got you."

I struggle to cling to the painful memories as Dani tries to wake me, but I'm losing them. I always lose them.

I don't remember Steve proposing to me, or anything else that happened in the eight months before I woke up in the hospital with pins in my arm and a tube down my throat. The doctors said my memories could come back. Spoiler alert, they didn't. Since it also meant I didn't remember how they found me, some people called it a blessing in disguise. Except I dream about it. I wake up with those last thoughts in my mind, with my heart racing and sweat soaking the sheets. Sometimes I cry, begging some non-existent sky dick to give me back what I lost. Sometimes I sit there for hours, staring at my hand and tracing the lines of the scars because I can't remember what I've lost.

Surviving has proven worse than remembering the pain of the collision, because even though I lost time and the use of my arm, I still remember the way I lost Steve and the pain I caused him, no matter how hard I tried.

I watched the video our friend Jamie shot of Steve proposing to me over and over. I watched it day after fucking day. I listened to stories of my life like a bystander, not an active participant. I hung pictures of us everywhere, so I had to see them no matter where I looked. I touched the clothes we were going to wear, visited the venue we'd picked, and struggled through months of therapy—physical and mental. No matter what, I couldn't outrun the emptiness and rage. Love and tears of joy on the screen made the hole inside me bigger, deeper, until it became impossible to fill, no matter how hard Steve tried.

He understood.

I caused his heart to break, and he never blamed me. He accepted the pain and all of my rage. He did nothing wrong—at least not that I could remember—but he took the brunt of the fallout. I gave up on myself, on us, and on him, and he accepted that fate. I couldn't find what we'd had together no matter how hard I tried, and he's the one who told me we couldn't force it or fake what wasn't there.

That's the pain I wake up to and the reason I self-medicated for so long. Today, though, I remembered something new. Someone new.

"Hey, come back to me." Her voice brings me back slowly as she wraps around me, cradling me like an infant. "Can you do that? Can you focus on me? On my voice."

It's the voice that's pulled me out of the unending nightmare before, but this time, I'm not in a hospital. This time, it's not a recording. She's real.

"Dani?" I reach out and touch her face, letting my fingers trace the edges of smudged eyeliner and feeling the corner of my mouth tick up. It's as unfamiliar as my memories, but much more welcome.

"I forgot how bad your nightmares get, Skylar. What happened?"

I bury my face in my hands, rubbing the sleep from my eyes and the thoughts from my mind. I can't burden her with this now, not after all these years. "I drank too much. Sorry I scared you, Beetle."

"Is this really how you want to start off?" I lift my head and stare up at her, and as stern as she's trying to act, the smeared makeup forces a laugh out of me. So, I sit up and cup her angelic face in my hideous hands to drink in more of her soul. She melts to my touch, and I slide between her legs, burying my head in the crook of her shoulder as I rock back and forth. I move faster when she begs me to, harder when she screams a name I never knew could sound so angelic. My name. We ascend together, a chorus of my beastly grunts and her ethereal moans reaching its crescendo before gradually returning the world. Two people, wrapped in hotel sheets the staff should burn after we leave.

After I clean us both up, tossing the towel onto the floor of the bathroom, I grab my cigarettes and head for the balcony. Before I can step outside, she's wrapping a towel around my waist while I pull her in for another kiss. And another. Until we fall together into a chair.

"Hold on," she giggles. "Wait, I gotta ask you something stupid."

"Okay, ask."

"Uhm, when did you get the, uhh, you know." She shifts and moves the towel away, staring at my cock. "Those."

"I was born with—" She smacks my arm, and I pull her back to me, deep laughter coming out of me. Gods, it feels good. "The first piercing was, I dunno, about a month after I left. Once that healed, I got the other bar done. The ladder I did right before I went into rehab. The three times I hit my lowest lows, and I wasn't sure I could still feel anything anymore. I needed to prove to myself I could feel more than numb; like I needed the pain to remind me I was alive."

"I'm sorry. I didn't mean to ruin the mood."

"You're fine. They were cathartic in ways, like that high you get from a new tattoo." She picks up my hand, tracing my death's head moth again as she listens. "They say the ladder works for self-pleasure, and the cross gives more gratification to your partners. I liked the sound of that, and the sounds you make when I'm inside you."

She kisses me, and I lift her off my lap and step out the door so I don't stink the room up. I like how it smells right now, the sweetness of her perfume mixing with the musky smell of sweat and sex. I don't notice she's staring at me because I'm lost in the landscape of puddled gravel lots and soggy trees. Not that I see them. I'm too busy remembering how everything felt last night and pushing the painful nightmare away. I want to feel like I did earlier, like a new person, re-birthed into this world to experience life and all its pain and bliss again.

She steps in front of me and undoes my towel, and it pools at our feet. "They are correct. Whoever *they* are."

"Glad you like them." She's not touching me, only studying, and that's getting me hard again. Stepping forward, her body presses against mine as her fingers trace around the metal pieces.

"We should get dressed and go get breakfast soon." She mumbles the words against my chest as I light up and suck in that first kick of nicotine. My knees buckle every time her fingertips dance along the head of my cock, exploring the piercings. "We can go back to the diner and make sure your motorcycle hasn't run off with some hot mustang or something."

"Or we can slip Connor a twenty and have him bring something back for you so we don't have to leave the room."

"Skylar, I was serious earlier."

"About what?"

"Us. About starting out this way." She steps back to stare up at me. She's not especially short, but most of the world seems short when you're 6'6". I brush her face with my knuckles and do my best to smile, the nightmare still too fresh even after our release.

"Skylar, you said you wanted to be with me, and I want to be with you too. I want this to have a chance, and it's going to be rough for a while getting used to it, getting used to each other like this. But if you're going to start off by keeping secrets, we should stop this before it gets started?"

I close my eyes and drop my head. "You're right."

"So, what did you see? You can be super vague if you're uncomfortable, but it's me."

I take another drag and watch out over the trees again. "I have nightmares about the accident. I don't remember much when I wake up, although today I held onto a little. Being with you might bring some of that back."

"Oh god, I'm so sorry. I keep putting my stupid foot in my mouth and I'm fucking this up, aren't I?"

"No! No, it's okay." I take her face again, thumb brushing over her lips. I can't get enough of her. "I can handle it. Especially when you're here, my fallen angel in your black wings."

"Are you making fun of my makeup? Because I'd like to remind you that was all your fault. I said I needed to get ready for bed and you said, and I will quote you here, 'I've waited long enough to be inside you, I won't wait any longer.' So yeah, your fault."

"I wasn't making fun of anything. I kind of dig the look, honestly. It's dirty and raw. You should keep it like this for breakfast so I can sneak off to the bathroom with you and have a little snack before pancakes."

"You officially have a higher sex drive than Xander. Insane."

"Did you call him?" I rumble into her ear.

"Is that a problem? Because you knew going into this, he was—"

"Shhh, Beetle. We're okay. I understand what it means to want you, and I meant it when I said I want every part of you. The two of you are intertwined souls. It's why every time you try to pull away from each other, you both come screaming back together from the void. When I say I want you, I'm a greedy fucking bastard. I've been too stupid to realize it until I saw you again in that parking lot. I swore I pined for LA, for what I'd lost. But I was mourning the loss of you. Dani, it's always been you. All of you. Both of you."

She starts to speak, but squeals as I lift her up and turn her around, pressing her against the sliding door. A growl from somewhere deep inside me comes out as I lean over and suck on her neck, leaving a few more marks across her brown skin.

Everything about her is a beautiful mess, from her streaked eyeliner and wild hair to the fading bite marks on the back of her legs. "He was okay with this, right?"

"If he wasn't, I wouldn't be here with you." Her sharp inhale matches the hissing sound I make as I suck in a breath and push deep into her warmth. My hand drops from her stomach, slipping between her legs to play with her clit. "Are you thinking of him while you're fucking me right now?"

"What if I am?" I'm thinking about them both and writing their names against her clit. If anyone walked through the back parking lot, they'd have a perfect view of my ass, but I wish I had a camera set up in the bedroom. Dani's tits pressed against the glass as she bounces on her toes in time with my thrusts. "What if I'm thinking about both of us inside you? He and I could have a little competition over who could make you come the most. Loser bottoms."

"Oh, shit… I … Oh fuck. Oh, Skylar!" Her moan fogs the glass seconds before her body makes the whole door rattle. I don't stop though, my fingers still strumming her as I hold her up.

"One more time, baby. But this time, you say his name while I fill you. I can't fucking wait to watch him inside you. Watch you take his fat cock like a good little girl."

Someday, we'll record the melody of her shouting his name and my moans to use as a backdrop for a song, or for me to jerk off to later. When I let her go, she walks back in the room ahead of me, a little wobble to her step, and gives me a show when she bends over to get her phone. I run a washcloth under the warm water and walk over to clean the mess I made of her, even if I don't want to. "Come here, I want to send him a picture to wake up to!"

"You should have sent him a video of what we just did."

"Pervert. But also, yeah, you're right. SMILE!" She glances down at the screen and groans. "I look like roadkill! Whatever, I'm sending it. He'll probably find that as hot as you do. Fucking boys."

"Literally."

"Shut it! Where are my pants?"

"You don't need pants." She ignores me and moves toward the bathroom, but I grab the hem of her shirt and bring her colliding back into me before I drop us both onto the bed. "I lied; I can't wait for the restaurant. I'm starving for a taste of us."

Ding.

"OH MY GOD!"

"Uh, I haven't even touched you yet."

"No, not that, this!" She holds the phone out as she giggles. Xander one upped our selfie because he's in bed with a head of salt and pepper hair against his back. I can't see the guy's face, but the way he's wrapped around him gives Xander a glow that matches my own.

XANADU

I'll tell you all about him when I'm back from Japan. Miss you, Beetle. Tell Skylar they're a cocksucker.

"Oh, come on!" I laugh. "It happened once, but to be fair, I'll totally do it again as soon as we get back to Los Angeles. Who is the silver fox?"

"I have no idea. We aren't seeing anyone right now, or, well, I mean. You, now. But that's obviously not you!" She puts the phone down and pinches her brows together. "Wait, you sucked Xander off?"

"Mhmm. Send him a picture of this as payback," I hum,

pushing her legs apart. Her stomach rumbles beneath me and I lean down and kiss it. "Alright, I hear you. Pancakes?"

"God yes!"

We weren't the only ones to have the idea of hitting the diner for breakfast, and when she sees the rest of her band at a booth, she drags me over. Her drummer either has a hangover or might still be drunk, her guitarist has a computer open and headphones on. No bassist sits with them. Dani nudges Connor further into the booth's half circle before she pats the seat next to her, but it still feels intrusive.

"Hey, come on, headphones off, out of your phone, wake up Connor."

"You can't make me!" He mumbles, folding his arms on the table and dropping his head into them.

"Where's Toddifer?" She asks, getting a blank stare from Noah.

Connor lifts his head and answers her in slurred mumbles, hungover, or still drunk. "He left last night after we…never mind. He couldn't stay on since his other band picked up a new gig."

"Jesus, we're so screwed." Noah mumbles, headphones still on. "They changed the damn tour dates again! Now, instead of a week and a half off, we're on again in three days. In Anaheim!"

"Fuuuuuuck." Connor groans, sticks a straw in his coffee, and buries his head again with the straw sticking out. Resourceful.

"That's not enough time for someone to learn our stuff," Noah scoffs. She's right, they're never going to find one in time. Even if they found one, learning an entire set overnight won't be easy, especially for a bassist. They might get the music down, but not the flow of the band or the song when it's live shit.

"What if they know them already?" I ask as the waiter sets coffees in front of Dani and I. He winks at me, flashing a coy smile. "Oh, uhm, thank you. Can *we* get a stack of pancakes and a double side of bacon? The pancakes on a different plate, though, if you don't mind?"

He rolls his eyes and walks away. Steve used to hate how often people hit on me, I've learned to ignore it. Besides, right now I'm more focused on Dani. "Beetle? Come out of that spiral for me. Please?"

"Hold on, what did you mean by that whole *what if they already know the songs* shit?" Noah asks, folding the lid of her laptop down. "Do you mean, like, begging Rory to come back or some shit?"

"No, I, uhm, I mean me. I play. In fact, I play *your* songs."

"Yeah? How many of them?" Connor slurs.

"All of them. Unless you've come out with something over the last month or so."

Dani registers what I've said, because her head moves slowly from Noah to me, eyes widening as she does. I shrug, but she grabs my face and pulls me in for a crashing kiss I didn't expect. "Oh my god, I love you!"

I smile against her lips, hoping this won't blow up in our faces.

HOLLYWOOD
Xander

CHAPTER 21

GOOD OLD FASHIONED LOVER BOY

QUEEN

WELL, that was crazy. Dani never told me the new apartment came with free therapy and a gay, big dicked, and horny as hell silver fox.

We're lying in bed, getting high while we watch the sunrise through the giant windows in his giant bed. We've slept on and off, waking up to mess around again, and falling asleep wrapped in his warmth. His arm tightens around me and I hold my breath for a moment, waiting to see if he's about to tell me I should leave, or he's ready to go again.

"We should probably talk," he whispers in my ear, sliding his nose up the shell and sending shivers up my spine.

"Unless you want to talk about what's for breakfast, or you're ready to discuss some bondage options, I can't think of anything we'd need to talk about." He groans against my ear, so I push my hips back, pressing against him. As I guessed, he's hard again. I'm not gonna walk for a week at this rate. "Oh, you mean let's talk about whether you're about to put it in my ass again or my mouth? Cause we can absolutely talk about that, big guy."

"That's so not fair," he whimpers when I don't stop rubbing against him. His boxers are already getting damp, and his hand

traces down my ribs, counting them before he follows my hips under the sheets.

He's right about talking, but I'm not great with my emotions. I'm more of a hold them all in until I explode and do something incredibly stupid kind of guy. But I've also never been in this position before. Knowing I could bump into him at any time in our hallway, and that we share a couple of walls, could make this whole thing even more awkward than it needs to be. We got our own place after the mess of trying to live with Megan, and here I am screwing the neighbor days after getting the keys.

His brawny arm wraps around my chest, holding me close as each thrust pushes new, high-pitched cry from me. Whimpers and moans follow until he shivers behind me and goes stiff. I might break this poor man.

He kisses along my shoulders and mumbles as he pulls out of me, "Xander, we—"

"You're right. I completely forgot that docking was also on the table."

"Xander," his tone has me flashing back to all the names he called me in the shower. Names I hated, but now can't hear enough. His deep, rumbling morning voice wakes my cock from its short nap. "Stop."

"Fine. Whatever, man." I twist out of his grip and try to stand, but my legs turned to putty an hour ago and the bones still aren't working right. I reach over and yank a towel off a chair, wrapping it around my waist before trying again to stand. This time, I almost make it before he grabs the back of the towel and pulls me back to him. "Fuck! Seriously?"

"Seriously." He's got that look in his eye that parents get when their kids are being assholes, until he pulls the towel open and sits me on top of his thighs. It's kind of hot.

"Let me guess." I start, my fingers playing in his chest hair.

"Oh, Xander, I had so much fun last night, but we shouldn't do this again. I like you but I'm straight, have a girlfriend—wife—whatever. Are you about to say that?"

"Not exactly what I had in mind. Tell me about your girlfriend and this open relationship situation."

"Why?"

He takes a deep breath and sits up against the headboard. "Because I also need to feel safe. Don't get me wrong, I enjoyed every minute of this, and every inch of you, but if this can't happen again, I need to know that."

"You…want this to happen again?" He rolls us over, pinning me against the mattress. I crane my neck, grabbing his bottom lip between my teeth and nibbling. He can't keep his eyes open until I finally let go.

"Depends on your situation, doesn't it?"

"You live next door, Theo. If you want this to happen again, I'm sure you can find some excuse to stop by, trip on a carpet, and fall dick first into my ass. Now, either suck it, or get off me."

"I thought we fixed that bratty mouth."

"You mean the part when you begged for this mouth last night? *Oh Xander, fuck, you feel so good!*"

"We can't use sex to avoid the subject every time I try to talk about this."

"We can. Obviously." I run my thumb over his lips until he opens his mouth and takes it in. Tease.

A familiar ring tone blasts through the apartment, but I must have left it in the other room when I went out to make coffee earlier. He leans back and I sit up on my elbows and shrug. "It's my girlfriend. Hang on and let me get that while you figure out who gets to put what in which hole."

"Vulgar."

"Admit it, it turns you on," I lean over and kiss him, and he lets me up with a deep chuckle, falling back onto the pillow while I hobble out to the kitchen counter, unlocking the screen. The band talking somewhere in the background, picking out the familiar tone of a voice I can't wait to hear in person.

"Xan! Oh my god, I have the coolest news! When do you leave for Japan?"

"Uhm in about—" I pull the phone away to check the time. "Shit, like six hours."

"Damn, I hoped you'd say tomorrow, and we could see you before you go. Did you see the pictures I sent you? Of course you did, duh, you replied. Wait, hold on!"

"Wait, what's your news?"

I don't catch her in time and the sound of fabric shifting and garbled noises that I can't make out before a voice from the past sends my mind racing.

"Morning, Xanda Panda. Guess who joined Beetle's band?" I'm instantly transported to a stairwell in my mother's office building. Skylar had come to drop something off for Dani and that's when they told me they were leaving. We went to the stairs to get high, but we never even got that far, too busy trying to rip each other's clothes off. Skylar was a unicorn, a once in a lifetime perfect match…until last night. Until Theo.

I'd wanted Skylar since I laid eyes on them, but with Steve in the picture, I wasn't about to screw with that. Steve's a damn truck and would have laid me out. I'm not that much of a dick.

"Skylar? Shit!"

"Bro, who am I kicking out of your bed when I get there?" They sound so much better than the last time I heard them. When we broke down in the stairwell after they told me they were leaving. *"Hey, coffee's here, gotta go. Oh, we made the cut, so we're on to the next round or whatever, but we'll see you soon, gorgeous!"*

"How perfect?!" Dani yells into the phone so loud I pull it away from my ear.

"Yeah, that's uhm, great?"

"That's all you've got?! What's going on? Why aren't you asking about what happened or for pictures or something?" She knows me too well, as she should. The sounds behind her become muffled and I assume she's covered the mouthpiece when she whispers. *"This isn't about Sky, right? About us hooking up?"*

"Hell, no. No, Beetle, it's not that. I'm thrilled about that and about them coming back to LA. I, uhm…nothing. I'll tell you about it another time. I'm tired, nothing more." I realize I'm missing something. "Wait, what happened to Todd?"

Her voice drops to a whisper, and I barely hear it. *"I told him to hit the bricks. Okay, he kind of quit and maybe because I bitched at him, but whatever. Are you okay? Did that guy stay overnight or something? Wait! Did he hurt you?"*

"No!" I say too fast and too loud, before I stop and take a breath. "Beetle, no, he didn't. I swear. It's…it was…

"OH MY GOD! You like him!"

"Hang on, let me… hang on a second." I cover the phone and poke my head back into the bedroom in time to watch Theo pull on his pants. There's a knife twisting in my gut at the thought of going back home, sitting there alone in the dark without him. When I notice he's looking at me in the reflection of the mirror, he winks. A rush spreads through my body like a wildfire, but instead of throwing him back on the bed, I tell him I'll be right back.

"Xander?" He calls out as I turn. When I glance back at him, he tosses me a pair of sweatpants. "Put those on if you're leaving. Otherwise, you'll kill old Mrs. What's Her Name down the hall."

"I'll be right back. I promise." When I close the door to his place, I take a deep breath. "Okay, Beetle, don't freak out on me, but I kind of, I uhm, yeah. I like him. He helped me with a thing and—uhm, we kind of—"

"You and a super hot older guy? Duh. Sky and I both agree you were glowing in that picture this morning, babes. Or, I mean, he looks older. I mean his hair does. We couldn't see much of him. Who is he? You swear to me he didn't hurt you?"

"No, he… D, it was… I've… shit, I can't even make words work right now. He's, uhm, he lives…in the building. He's… we were…"

"You were fucking all morning? That's like karmic or some shit since we were, too. They had me screaming your name, Xander. Yours. Because that doesn't scare them! It was so…"

"Freeing?"

"YES! Wait, you, too? Although, after we woke up, I needed pancakes, and that's when Skylar joined the band."

"Beetle—he, we—I cried, Dani. But like, the good cry. The get it out of my system cry. I haven't done that since—"

There's silence on the line as it hits me, but she answers before I can. *"Skylar?"*

"Yeah," I answer in a breathy whisper. "I still can't believe you found them. That you're banging them in some skeevy motel before you both come home." I laugh.

"Xan, is this…normal?"

"For anyone else, no! For the grand scheme of our lives, I hope so. God, we're the worst. I'm proud of you, Beetle. I am. About Skylar, about the competition. You're doing it, sweetheart. You're fucking killing it, and I miss you, but…we're good. Right?"

"Aw, I love you, too, Xan. And yeah, we're better than good." She reads between my words like only she can. *"And I'm proud of you,*

too. Hold on to this one. We'll figure it out when we're all back at the apartment."

There's a thud down the hall, and when I glance up, I find two giant dudes with blue jumpsuits on. They're heading toward our place, and I panic until I read their uniforms.

The movers.

Aunt Melody.

Shit!

"Dani, hey, I gotta go. I'll call you back before my flight. I love you, Beetle!"

"Xander! Fine, okay, fine. I'll talk to you later, you weirdo! I love you!"

I barely hear her last words as I end the call, shoving the phone into the pocket of Theo's sweats and walking toward the door.

"Hey, uhm, you guys are the movers, right?" They both stare at me for stating something so obvious. Any other day I'd pick a fight with them or be a raging dick, but I need these guys and I'm in too damn good of a mood to mess it up over something stupid, I said. "Right, yeah, duh. I'll get everything out of your way, not that there's much, and I'll prop the door open for you. How much did you bring, anyhow?"

One of them, the tall one with a nose that looks like it's broken looks between his partner and I. "Uh, she told us to bring everything. That's half a storage container. She said whatever you don't want, we take it back and store it again."

"Everything okay?"

I spin around to find Theo leaning against his door frame, wearing only a pair of gray sweats as he sips his coffee. I hope I'm not visibly drooling right now.

"No, I, uhm, I forgot about the furniture delivery."

"Oh, so today you have help. Good. When you get a minute,

come back and tell me what you need from the grocery store. I'm gonna go grab some stuff to make breakfast before the cat eats our eyeballs."

I don't know how long I stand there, gawking at the man, but it must be a while based on the way the mover clears his throat to regain my attention. I nod to Theo and head back into my place to move the boxes and make sure I didn't leave any obvious condom wrappers lying around the bathroom or bedroom. It doesn't take me long.

"Where do you want this?" They ask, rolling a large desk into the door, careful not to dent the desk or the wall. Based on how gingerly they're treating the stuff, I'm gonna guess Aunt Melody is paying them extra. I point to an open wall and tell them to pile everything they've got wherever there's room. That earns me an eyebrow raise as they look at the sole piece of furniture already in place.

They head back down for the next thing, and another team of two comes into the room with a chair and a small nightstand. I wanted a desk. Only the desk. Now, we're about to have a furnished apartment. Dani will either kill me, sell it all while I'm in Tokyo, or think it's brilliant—there's no way to know. After I tell them the same thing I told the first two guys, I duck out and slip back into Theo's place. He's in the kitchen, making notes on a piece of paper, and for a moment, I watch in silence. It's old school, but it's also sexy.

"Really? A shopping list on paper? How old are you, grandpa?"

"Keep that shit up and you won't get breakfast. Trust me, you'll regret that."

I lean against the wall, staring at the marks on his back. Bruising from my fingers, a few bite marks, a scratch here and there. It's a mural that tells the tale of one hell of a long night. He turns, his front equally decorated, but I don't have time to stare as his hands slide up my jawline and he pulls me in like it's our first kiss. Explorative instead of rushed, soft instead of teeth clashing against each other. My hands find his hips, squeezing enough to elicit that moan I've come to crave overnight. There's a groan from somewhere deep, like it's coming from somewhere…under the sink?

"Fuck!" He moves me out of the way and throws the cabinet doors open in time for a spray of water to coat him. It takes every part of me to not laugh, and I have to turn away and bite my finger, but he still notices my shoulders as they shake. "Yeah, laugh it up, whatever. Go get me a towel, would ya?"

"Yeah, absolutely. I'm impressed though; you took that so well Daddy. All over your face and—"

"Towel, Xander," he growls, and it's not helping make him any less hot or this any less funny.

I come back with some towels and get to work helping him. When we get the water under control, his face has turned red and the muscles in his neck look like they are about to bulge out of his skin. I slide my hand up his arm, coaxing him to relax. "Hey, take your list and get the groceries. You were supposed to do that yesterday, and I kept you from that. So go, you could use the fresh air and break from all this."

"I can't, I have to fix—"

"I've got it. I mean, I can get it fixed enough for now, and I'll come back after Japan and—" His face drops, I hadn't told him yet. "Shit, I'm sorry, Theo. Everything happened so fast and—It's a business trip, with my dad. I don't want to go. I wish I didn't have to."

"It's fine. When do you leave?"

"Uhm, in a few hours." I wince, feeling like shit.

"Do I still have time to make you breakfast?" I nod and his smile comes back. "Good."

"When I come back from Japan, I'll fix your sink for you. Like, for good, fix it."

"Do you even know what you're doing?"

"Ouch. Yeah, I know how plumbing works. That wasn't a pun or innuendo, either. Now get the heck out of here and get me some food."

HOLLYWOOD
Xander

I FLUSH the toilet and move to the sink, washing my hands before I scoop water into my mouth and over my face. They should offer me a seat in here for the rest of the flight, considering we're only halfway there and I've already emptied my guts twice. I don't even want to imagine what this would have been like if we'd taken a commercial flight instead of the company jet.

When I get back to my seat, Dad and one of his people are going through a contract while his assistant types up notes and emails as they go. Part of me thinks that's contributing to the air sickness, but that sounds too stupid to say out loud. I head toward the back, grabbing a bottle of water on the way to the couch I've been occupying since we got in the air. My phone vibrates.

BEETLE

How's the flight? You're almost there, right?

Xander: Nope. And if I hurl again, it's going to be intestines.

BEETLE

Did you take that stuff I got for you?

I swear under my breath and grab my backpack, digging through the pouch of stuff Dani makes up when I go on these trips. She used to do herbal remedies, but when I almost ended up detained for drug smuggling, she got the hint to only send commercially available stuff. About a dozen types of tea, those cheese crackers I like, candied ginger, and some over-the-counter meds. I pop open the tube and take the recommended dose before I chew on a couple pieces of ginger. If they don't help, at least it gives me something to throw up.

Forgot, but just took some.

BEETLE

The tea with the purple tags will help, too.

Okay. I miss you.

BEETLE

We miss you, too!

Is it weird I'm already saying 'we'?

Is it weird if I say no, because it kind of feels right for once?

BEETLE

It does, huh? Speaking of, how's the guy you were going to tell me all about?

I send her the screen shot from our chat after I got on the plane. A list of affirmations, a link to a new fantasy book he bought me, and he called me *baby* at least three times. Reading over it again, and knowing Dani's reading it too, has the butterflies trying to drunkenly flap around in my desolate hellscape of a stomach.

BEETLE

You know, maybe four…also feels right. I'm
glad someone else finally told you you're
fucking worth it.

I smile and open the photos from earlier, flipping back and forth between the ones of Skylar and Dani, and to the one of Theo and me. Could this work? The four of us? Should I even consider that possibility with a guy I've just met? Are we asking for too much? Asking for this to implode by adding another to the mix?

This will hurt so much if it doesn't work. Either of them.

A small part of me hoped a few hours into the flight, Theo would fade away and become another notch in my bedpost. Instead, we've been texting, exchanging pictures, and even talking about how much I hate traveling. I haven't said anything yet, but I want to ask him out, on a date. Between trips to the bathroom, I've been looking up restaurants, knowing this trip will get me a decent paycheck. Dani won't mind if I take enough out of it for a date.

Skylar. Theo. They're both too right to be wrong. But the newness of both of them could have us all so turned around they drive us over the cliff and into stupid mistakes we'll regret later, because I barely know Theo, and who knows what version of Skylar we're getting. I didn't bring Skylar up to Theo yet, either. How could I?

Hey, I think I like you and all, but there's this guy I've been craving for years, and he's railing my girlfriend so she's bringing him home. Cool, huh?

It's crazy, but so are we. It's also something I can't do much about clear across the ocean. I curl up in my hoodie Dani wears more than I do, and a shirt from Theo's closet, letting their scents come together and carry me off to sleep. Hopefully, I can stay asleep this time.

"Wake up, pal. We're about to land," My dad says as he shakes my shoulder.

I grab my things and move to one of the chairs, my head throbbing like one of those huge, deep drums. The bright light of the setting sun doesn't help my head, so I slip on my sunglasses and check the time on my phone. A new message lightens my mood.

DOC

I've heard the Kandagawa Bakery is pretty good, if you end up anywhere near it.

See you when you get back?

The flutter of butterflies is a little less drunk now, getting some solid flapping going.

I told you I need to fix that sink.

"Hey, Alex? You still look a little, uhm, pale. How are you feeling?" Dad asks, leaning over and talking in a whisper. "Did you take the stuff your mother got from her doctor?"

"Yeah. It stayed down for about an hour." I tuck my phone away so he doesn't accidentally see pictures he shouldn't. Some of those from Dani and Sky are straight up porn, and hot as shit. "Are we going straight to the hotel?"

"Dinner first, but you look like you'd rather not. Your aunt emailed me earlier, and they're switching your assistant. The other one got sick or something. I didn't get details. He should be at the airport to meet us. I've already asked him to get you a second car to take you to the hotel and check you in. We'll start fresh tomorrow morning. Sound good, Sport?"

"Sure, whatever." I don't even have the strength to respond to the outdated nickname. "I'm getting paid for this bullshit, right?"

"Uhm, yeah. Sure. Absolutely. Don't worry about it. For now, here's the company card. Don't go too wild, okay? I've got a few day's worth of meetings, so you won't need to come in right away."

"Why didn't I fly over later?"

"Because you look like shit, and I wanted to give you a few days to recover from the flight. Sleep in, go sightseeing and get a feel for things here. I'll have the assistant get you an itinerary for the first few things I will need you in the office for." He turns and goes back to talking to his people.

The plane makes a bumpy landing but gets us to a hangar. Like Dad promised, two black limos wait nearby with uniformed drivers looking ridiculous as they stand outside each one. I pull my backpack on and shove my earbuds in, so hopefully I won't have to talk to whoever this assistant is. I grab another water, my second since landing, and leave the plane. The hangar adds to my headache with its bright white lights that reflect off the even whiter walls. The tinted windows of the cars call to me, but I have to wait as Dad and his team of ass kissers go through their motions. I turn up the volume on the ambient noise meant to help my head, pull the hood over my head, and close my eyes, dozing off again as I lean against a wall.

I jump about ten feet in the air when someone's hand grabs my shoulder. "Shit, what the hell?!" I yell, pulling the ear buds out.

"I'm so sorry, Mr. Maxwell. I didn't mean to frighten you, but I did address you several times prior to breaking the boundaries of your personal space, I assure you." His posh British accent isn't what I expected from an assistant from the Tokyo office, but the company hires from all over the globe, so it shouldn't surprise me. "As your father requested, we have a car waiting for you since you'll not be attending the dinner."

"Cool. Let's get the hell out of here." I hold out my hand. "Don't call me Mr. Maxwell, I'm Xander."

"Oh, right? In that case, I'm Oliver." His crooked smile and freckles are cute, but the suit and striped tie have me weirded out. He looks like he belongs in one of my old prep schools. "I'm your new assistant, so if you need anything, please don't hesitate to—"

"Bro, what I need is a joint. I'll settle for some morphine." I rub my temples as we walk. "Can you get either of those?"

"Uhm, I should have some tablet for your head in the car. However, I'm sorry to say, I doubt we'll be able to accommodate your request for—"

"Oliver, I don't have a clue why I'm here, but I'm aware weed isn't legal, so do me a favor? Relax, would you? I'm stressed enough for both of us."

"Absolutely, Mr.... sorry...*Xander*." We shake, and he goes back into robot mode and jogs over to the car, pulling open the door for me. "We'll have your bags loaded in a moment, sir."

I turn and look at my dad, trying to figure out why I'm on this trip and why I've got an assistant, when my phone buzzes.

MELODIOUS

How was your flight?

> It landed, so I guess it was ok. Not going to dinner though, it wouldn't end well.

MELODIOUS

I figured.

If you're up to it, let Oliver show you around
town. He was very excited to meet you. He's a
good kid.

And he's single…. Wink wink.

Oh thanks, that's not…awkward!

And who types out wink wink?! Psychos!
That's who!

MELODIOUS

You're such a dick. Love you, kiddo.

Yeah, cause you have to. See you soon?

MELODIOUS

As soon as I can get free. Your idiot father has
me in about 200 meetings.

He was your idiot brother first. See you when I
see you.

I climb into the car and get comfortable as the driver loads the bags in. I didn't bring much, so they must be getting Dad's, too. While they're busy, I pull up the website and check my stats. Fifteen news subscribers, not bad since I haven't posted in a week. I need to do more, though, so we can all be covered financially while Dani and Skylar travel. Japan and a stupidly expensive hotel room should give me something to work with, a change of background scenery at least. Maybe more.

I close the app and open a browser, searching for tips on increasing my revenue and how to make money faster. The ways I've found, the legal ones anyhow, go way past my comfort level. I type out an update for a hookup or five while I'm here in Japan, but I delete it. Adding instead that I'm dropping the in person meet ups, which will piss off a few people, possibly some here in Tokyo. But after spending the night with Theo, and knowing I'm coming home to Dani and Skylar, too, that's enough for me. Solo stuff from now on.

I deserve better.

Maybe I can get Skylar to do a POV I could post to make up for it. They'll be down for some on camera fun. Maybe Theo would be up for stuff like that, too. I can blur their faces, although with all those tats, I don't think Skylar will ever be unrecognizable. The reality that I'm off the meetup market is like a boulder being lifted off of me given how they usually end. Someday, I'll be able to tell Theo I stopped because of him, but I've got to dance around a few things before I start dropping all these bombs about the guy he hooked up with.

Skylar sure as hell will, but I'm used to that. We're like an emotional see-saw. When they're up, I'm down and vice versa. I don't cry often, but I bawled like a baby around both Theo and Skylar. I hate sounding cliche, but last night opened my eyes even though it's the same shit Dani's been trying to tell me for years. Accepting I'm worthy of respect and love from men and getting to love them back? Foreign concept. Boarding schools can be like that for kids like me, messing with our heads and brainwashing us into touch-deprived perfect little Richie Rich replicas.

"Sorry for the delay, sir. We'll be headed out shortly." Oliver says as he joins me in the back, straightening his jacket and tie once he's in. I'm asleep again before the car starts rolling.

A bump in the road wakes me up to the bright lights of the city. I stare across the way and find Oliver staring at me, stiff as a board. "Oli, if we're about to spend the better part of a month together, I'm gonna need you to loosen up a bit for me. Loosen the tie…and the leash." He's got that pale complexion that lights up like a forest fire when he blushes. It's a damn good thing I'm changing my ways, or Oli would be in for a world of eye-opening experiences. Many of them are right here in this limo.

"Yes, sir—"

"See, that right there. I'm just a dude, so don't call me sir. Only my girlfriend calls me sir, and that's only when we're role playing."

He stares at his feet, shifting them awkwardly. "What, uhm, what do your, uhm, your male partners call you?"

"Male partners?" His head snaps up, and I catch that look in his eye. He thinks he's wrong, that I'm not bisexual. Maybe he heard that from my aunt, who he now thinks lied to him. I can make out the beads of sweat forming on his forehead. "Boyfriends, Oli."

"Oh, right, yes? Boyfriends."

The crooked smile that spreads over my face is genuine as the reality spreads through my body. A few nights ago, I would have scoffed and said they DO call me sir, trying to play a game with him while hiding that they call me the worst things they can think of. Now I have an answer, and it's one I want to share.

"He calls me *baby*."

HOLLYWOOD
Skylar

CHAPTER 23
WHERE IS MY MIND?
PIXIES

THE IDEA SOUNDED SO good when it popped into my head. Simple, and really a no brainer. Dani needed a bassist, and I am a bassist. I forgot to factor in that I haven't been on stage or in front of any kind of audience in years, and I don't know if my hand will make it through an entire set. I roll my neck, and lean into the mirror so I get the eye liner right. When I'm done, I lean back, and it's like looking in a time machine. One look at myself and the doubt gives way to youthful rebellion and the misguided belief that I'm invincible. I missed that feeling, and right now, it's like welcoming an old friend.

"Hey, you almost ready to go?" Connor pops his head in to check on me.

"Yeah. Oh, hey, Connor? Can I talk to you real quick?"

"Where have you two been?" Dani asks as I round the corner a few minutes later. "Oh. My. God."

"What?" I glance down at my clothes, pat my pockets. I don't see anything out of place. There's a shadow of self-consciousness creeping into my mind, telling me I'm too old for this and I look like an idiot. I shake it off. I had a plan when I picked these clothes up this afternoon, knowing how they'd look on stage.

Dani wants to kick the show up, and I'm all in. The pants are tight, with more chains and straps than a BDSM dungeon. A see-through mesh style button-up shirt shows off the new jewelry for my nipple piercings I found. One's a skeleton hanging from the post, the other is bat wings. I've wet my hair and wear it down, painted my nails electric blue, and added some bright green eyeshadow to match Dani's hair. Her eyes find and follow the leash from my neck all the way to Connor's hand as he gives her a smirk and a wink.

Compared to some of the other bands I've seen tonight, I'm overdressed, but here in the wings next to the rest of LA Proper, I blend right in. There are several men in the audience tonight that will leave here questioning their life choices after they see what Connor and I have planned. Enjoy the mind-fuck, boys.

"You're hot, and those pants are the exact tightness we're going to need for the remainder of this program." Noah explains, handing my bass out to me. Her grin grows wide, and before she walks away, she adds, "Hell, I'm not even straight and I can see...so much. Yeah, I'd absolutely smash that."

"Wait, is that bad?"

"No!" Dani screams, reaching for me, but not touching me as her fingers ghost along the leather harness. "No, not bad. None of this is bad. In fact, it's...it's..."

"At least going to earn you a set of panties thrown on stage tonight, Sky," Connor answers for her before he smacks me on the ass. "So, let's go give the people what they want. One hell of a show. Stop drooling, Dani."

"What are you freaking out over? You've seen all this. Me."

"Doesn't mean I can't appreciate you. Think we can find a closet around here for a quickie before we go on?"

I lean over and pull her in, kissing her hard until her fingers squeeze into my arm. She lets the softest whimper escape her as we pull apart. "Come on, Beetle. Let's give them the show you've always wanted. I'll let you rip the shirt off me after."

We don't run off stage. We don't even walk off. We float off, carried by the screams, whistles, and chants for more. The second I hand my bass off, I scoop Dani up and carry her over to the dingy sofa that sits just off stage. I collapse onto it, and her legs straddle as she grabs my face, refusing to let go.

Connor lets out a whoop before he and Noah crash down beside us.

Dani finally lets us breathe again, but only because we're both laughing too hard to maintain a kiss like that. "Connor!" She shouts and gives him a high five. "Bro! Oh, my god!"

"No way, couldn't have done it without Skylar!" He nods to me and grabs my knee. "You're a superhero, my friend! Also, Dani, if you three don't work out, I call dibs on this one. That kiss? Electrifying isn't strong enough of a word."

"I'm only a tiny bit jealous," Noah giggles, but Dani stands up, grabbing her face as they laugh and try to make out the way Connor and I did on stage. It's what I talked to him about beforehand; I asked his permission to try it out, and he jumped on the opportunity. Three songs in. I'm leaning over him and he looks up and nods. Neither of us missed a beat, not that you could hear us over the scream from the audience.

"I planted a seed, but your skills made it grow. Thanks for going with me on that journey, though."

"Oh, my friend, any day of the week. In fact, we'll be doing that a lot more based on the reaction it got us." he grins. "God, that whole set was insane. I need a drink. You need a drink? We need drinks!"

Dani ruffles my long, wet hair and flashes me a wink. "We owe you so many drinks, baby. Come on, the first round on me."

"Yeah, it is. It's gonna be all over you and I'm gonna put you up on the bar and lick it off, nice and slow." I pull her back to me, her nails raking down my chest through the flimsy material. "Come on, let's go before I bend you over the crate over there and add a background track to the next band's set."

"We are so recording that one day."

The crowded bar has wall to wall locals and visiting bands mixing it up and causing scenes everywhere. Every few minutes a fight breaks out over a girl, or a song, or which band will win the money. Dani and Noah have run off to the bathroom, Connor found a corner to hold court for a handful of men and women, and I'm half listening to some drunk drone on about his plans for starting his own band.

I've done a complete one eighty from the show that lit up the stage and had the audience eating out of our hands, begging for more. Almost every damn woman in the bar, and half the men, has hit on me, a few drunk enough to get handsy with me.

On stage, I've always been the epitome of cocky and brazen. I haven't found the line for too outrageous if it gets the audience on their feet and screaming for more. Taboo, illegal, sexual, none of that can stop me once the lights are on and the music flows through me. If Connor were to whip his cock out, I'll absolutely suck it to get that rush from the audience. There used to be an outlet for it when I came off the stage. Steve. We'd fuck like rabbits in closets, the car, and even a seedy motel room sometimes, to get it out of my system. Sex became an easy way to exhaust me down from the high.

That happened before the drugs. Before I understood the dangers of coming down from that high without a safety net. Because that's what performing is, a high without the dealer. Now I'm spiraling and no one here knows the warning signs because I thought I could handle this. I thought it wouldn't be so hard. I order another drink, hoping I can numb my cravings, but it's failing. Fast.

"Hey, you okay?" Dani asks, her hand dragging along my lower back. It's like ice, like one of my demons left cold burns where her fingers grazed against me. Every sensation has gone sideways so fast I can't think straight.

"I'm fine." I take another shot of whiskey, begging for a quiet darkness as I close my eyes. I should call someone, but it's late. I'm sweating and can't catch my breath. Maybe all I need is to throw Dani down on this table, rip her pants down, and bury my cock so deep inside of her, she screams and begs for more. At least the exhibitionist in me would thrive, and it could be enough of a push to get me through the night. Of course, I'd also end up in jail.

I know what I need; I know how to find it.

"Sky? Don't do this."

"Do what?" I snap. "I'm...I'm sorry."

"Then talk to me."

"I can't... You don't understand. You can't. Just... stop!"

"Understand what?"

"Anything!" I rub my temples, too aware of the migraine, too sensitive to every noise, touch, and smell. "I can't...I don't know!"

One fix. I only need it this one time. I can tell Dani after, and she'll help me. I need to get past this one time.

She reaches up and tucks my hair behind one of my ears, holding my wrist with her other hand. I'm scaring her, but I'm scaring myself more. I take a deep breath, but it's like trying to breathe in a swamp, the air too hot and thick. I squeeze my eyes shut again.

All of this can stop, all the demons can go back into hiding, safely tucked away in their bed. One fix. One night. One more time.

I need to get out of here. I need air. I need to breathe.

"Skylar, what's wrong?" Her voice sounds so far away as she tries to chase me through the crowd, but I'm on a mission, and it isn't a good one. I get outside and don't stop until I'm on my bike, turning the engine over, and kicking off the sidewalk. I doubt I'll need to go far. I can't be here and fall apart in front of her. Not again.

I rock my head back against the cold brick wall, exhaling a lungful of smoke. I called my sponsor and left a message, but didn't answer when he called back. The constant buzzing of plastic against concrete became bees in my head, never ending. Turning the phone off didn't help. Something else would buzz. Cars, voices, actual bugs. Only one thing can silence the swarm. One call, one street corner, one nod and I can be flying again, feeling that high wash through me and take away the pain and memories. It can put me back on the stage, back under the lights.

But it will push me out of her arms.

I dig the heel of my palms into my eyes, pushing harder until I feel the tears. What the hell was I thinking coming here? I can't be trusted; I can't be left alone. I'm a child no one wants in a world that makes it too easy to get what I need, even though it could kill me.

My brain hammers against my skull. I'm soaked with sweat, and I'm shivering. I'm in detox hell and I haven't taken anything.

"Fuck. Fuuuck."

Thinking about it makes my stomach knot up, twisting the booze and the beer into a monster attacking me from the inside. Brain. Stomach. Brain. Stomach. Getting jumped would feel better. I'm gonna be sick.

"Sky?"

I don't move because I don't think she's real. I've passed out behind some fucking gas station somewhere, and Marc will get a call in the morning that the cops found my body. Maybe I'm dying right now and that's why I hear her voice. I bought the drugs, took too many, and now I'm on my last big, bad trip.

"Skylar, please look at me?" She holds my face in her warm hands, but I don't look at her. I can't.

She pulls me up off the ground with Connor's help. I let them lead me across the parking lot to his van. Connor makes her promise I won't throw up, and if I do, she's cleaning it. They get me back to the hotel room and onto the bed. There's a vague sense of Dani taking off my shoes and jacket before washing my face with a cold washcloth.

"Okay, lay down. We'll get your pants off later after you sleep some of this off."

"You should go," I mumble. "It was all bullshit, everything."

"Don't say that." She walks into the bathroom, the pipes rattle when she turns the shower on, and a few minutes later, steam flowing out the doorway and into the bedroom. "Come on. If you're not going to sleep, maybe this will help."

"I should have told you."

"Told me what?"

"The drugs. Rehab. How much your voice—your music—healed me when I needed it most." I turn, taking her face in my hands and staring deep into eyes I wish I could crawl into and die. "Familiar and haunting in a perfect storm, colliding inside my soul and demanding I keep going. Every note and every word begged me not to give up, not to give in to the temptation of taking the easy way. Even tonight, the demons nipping at my heels couldn't compete with the thought of losing you. You saved me, Dani. So many times."

Her weak smile and glistening eyes tell me how messed up I am. I shouldn't have stayed.

"*You* made me fight, *you* made me hold on, and *you* made me want to feel the music again. I want to make it up to you, to repay you for breathing life into my worthless soul again. But I messed up."

"Jesus, you should be writing lyrics, but Skylar—"

"They'd only ever be about you." Every breath shakes like an earthquake, but it's my entire body, not only my breathing. "Beetle, the truth… shit, I wanted to grab you on stage tonight and bend you over an amp. I didn't care who watched or what they thought. I wanted to claim you, make you mine."

"Okay, that's hot, but what happened? Because that's not enough to make you run away."

"The show…it was too much, too fast. The power, the exhilaration, the energy. I came down too hard. I don't know if I'm ready. Ready for old, familiar streets and smells, for faces I've tried to block out, for you to…to…" I bite back the emotion, but it won't last. I can't go through losing someone else. "I wanted the high again. And I'm scared I wanted it too much."

"We'll figure it out."

"No, you don't understand. I'm scared I'll screw up again and you'll…I'll be alone again." The itch to purge the lies and hide behind them tries to take over, but I've learned how to fight that. She needs the truth. "I can't handle this. I can't do it, Dani. It's too fucking hard."

"Your sponsor said you'd probably say that. He also said I should get on your ass about not telling me what to look out for. But we're going to talk to him tomorrow morning and come up with a plan. You need a way to come down slower and smoother after the show. Drowning in shots won't work and neither will running away and scaring the ever-loving shit out of me."

"I'm so sorry," I sob, and she holds me to her. It's familiar and terrifying. "I'm scared, Dani. I'm so fucking scared to lose you, like I lost Steve. I'm scared I'll fail you and I—"

"Stop. Right now." She lifts my head, and I'm met with the stern features of her beautiful face. "This ends here and now. This marks the last time you do this shit to yourself. Now, get it into your incredible thick yet attractive head that you are not in this alone. You can't win alone. Did you listen to nothing in rehab? Where they show you that it takes a support system, not one idiot ready to make a martyr of himself. Come on, you need a shower. It will help you relax."

She pulls me up and leads me to the bathroom. When I try to handle my own clothes, she swats my hands away and cusses at me under her breath. I stand naked before her, and she takes my hands one at a time and kisses each of my knuckles before she opens the door of the shower. The water shocks my system, but only momentarily. A moment later, I'm holding out a hand and pulling her in with me. She doesn't care that her clothes are getting wet. I need to hold her, to have her against me.

"It's okay if you still love him. Steve, I mean," she says as she brushes out my hair. "You know that, right?"

"I did. Until I didn't. The accident changed my perspective. No matter how hard we tried, we couldn't ever get what we had back. The damage couldn't be fixed, and we were wallpapering over the holes left in our hearts. We drifted into a void and when I could finally see light again, I didn't have Steve anymore, only your voice to guide me."

"Seriously, I need you to start writing this shit down."

"You don't have to do this, Dani. You didn't ask for this."

"Okay, my giant emo mountain, let's get you into bed. You're cut off until you find a sponsor and some meetings when we're home." She climbs off the bed and stands in front of me. For the first time since the bar, I stare into her big eyes. "Skylar, I've watched people do stupid shit when they crave something that could kill them. You had that look in your eye at the bar, and we need to find the right plan of action. No more alcohol, though, or weed. Nothing until we have a plan. Okay?"

Her kiss takes my breath and strips me of my soul, but she replenishes what she takes with fragments of her own being, draining me and filling me at the same time. I break the kiss this time, fighting myself to pull away far enough to see her eyes again. Her fingers play in the days old beard, her touch awakening the volcano in my core, filling my veins with lava and the unquenchable thirst for her.

I understand now that she'll never let me go, never give up on me the way I give up on myself. My beautiful siren.

HOLLYWOOD
Dani

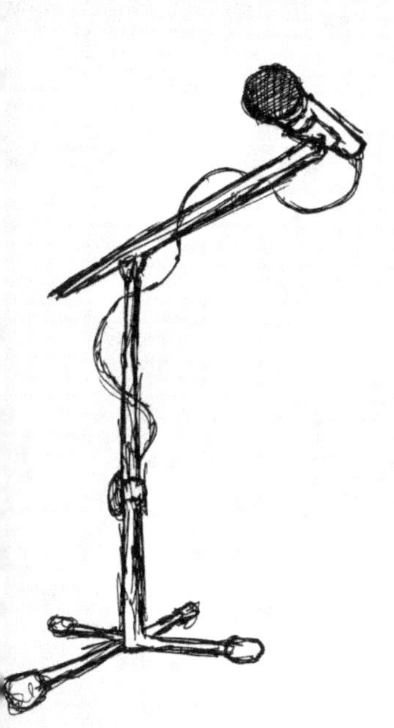

CHAPTER 24
OWN MY MIND
MÅNESKIN

"NO SHIT! You two left the bed? I thought for sure we wouldn't see either of you until the show tonight." Connor teases as he slips into the booth next to Skylar and Noah slides in next to me. "I'm gonna write a review for my noise canceling headphones. *Work like a charm when your only barrier between you and your bandmate's three in the morning mating ritual is a paper-thin wall and a shitty motel pillow some old guy probably died on. Five Stahhhs.*"

"Don't, I need coffee first!" I hold my head in my hands.

"Feeling better?" Connor asks Skylar, who might be glaring at him, but it's hard to tell with the sunglasses on. They're also wearing a hoodie under the leather jacket and have the hood pulled down low. At least they let me shave the beard down to stubble this morning, so they're not walking around intimidating everyone. They slouch lower into the seat, hands tucked deep into their pockets, but still, they give a half-hearted nod. Connor puts an arm around them before kissing their cheek. "Hang in there, my friend. We've got you and you're not alone. In fact, I'll never leave you alone after last night. And I didn't even get to sleep with you, but I listened."

It's enough to make Skylar scoff out a laugh, which I appreciate. I love my band, now that the toxic bullshit left. "So, I'm going to assume we made it to the next round after that ass kicking performance last night?"

Noah nods, flipping through her phone. "We were in second place when I fell asleep, let me check the—" There's a quick shift in her body language as I ask, and I panic. Her jaw drops open slightly, face turns paler than she already is, and her eyes slowly shift from the phone to me.

Connor noses in and his eyebrows shoot up. He might even be blushing. It's hard to tell. "That's…Holy shit! That's a video of us from last night. Skylar, you absolute specimen! Look at you! God damn!"

"What, let me see!" I come close to launching myself over the table.

"Look at the numbers, Con. It's going viral," Noah adds, tone still flat and unreadable.

Connor grabs the phone and leans in closer to Skylar. They watch a looping video compilation showing clips from last night. Skylar and Connor kissing and making out, me groping Skylar, and a nice little oral sex gesture from Noah. I remember some of it, but not all of it, and I wonder if Xander has seen this yet. If he had, he would have texted me by now.

I watch the slow pull on the corner of Skylar's mouth that becomes the precursor to the building laughter between them and Connor. They even take off the sunglasses to get a better look, of course I'm more focused on the red-rimmed eyes with their deep purple bruising underneath. It's not bad enough that the average person would notice, but I do, because I stayed up all night with them and sat up this morning trying to conceal their sleepless night with makeup. Sex took up a small portion of a night that also involved phone calls to his sponsor, too many tears, lots of holding, and a voicemail I left Chase that he's yet to respond to.

"We need more of this," Connor announces, winking at Skylar.

Noah groans, "I hate to say it but, he's right. I mean, look at our ranking last night. We came in first place."

"Don't worry, babe, you don't have to do any of it." I assure her. "You're cool as fuck looking in your own way, and that will get you plenty of attention, too. You're our token introvert; the three of us are crazy enough to do wild shit like this. It's worked for other bands." I explain, dumping more sugar in my coffee than should be legal.

"But shouldn't we be known for our music?"

"Connor and Sky making out on stage while we keep playing will get us more views faster than anything else we could do. The more views, the more coverage. The internet will build an entire world of rumors and guesses around them and people will eat that shit with a silver spoon. More views equal more listens and sales. Are they dating, who's cheating on who? Are they all sleeping together? So long as you're both okay with it. We're not forcing anyone to do anything. Understood?"

We watch the video climb over half a million views while we sit there. It's electrifying and I can't pull my eyes away, even as Skylar feeds me pancakes while they eat the bacon.

"Okay, so I'm super cool with this. How about you, Sky?" They take a moment, put their sunglasses back on, and nod. Connor flashes a lopsided grin and does a little shimmy in his seat. "Hell yeah. Best day of my life!"

My phone vibrates in my pocket and when I read the caller ID, I climb out of the booth. "Can someone send that to Xander for me? Sky, I'll be right back, okay?" He nods and gives me a sleepy smile.

"Holy shit, we're gonna hit two million!" Connor cheers from behind me.

"Hey, hold on two seconds, let me go outside!" I told Skylar I would take care of setting this up, because they need a break from everything. We all do, and you can't believe the lies that addiction goes away or can be tackled without support. That sets people up for failure. It's a lifelong struggle and unfair to handle alone. I'm glad they're finally letting me help.

"Dani? What happened?" Coop starts before I'm at the door. He's yelling, of course, and it sounds like he's on a film set somewhere. *"Everyone okay? I got part of your message, but your phone cut out. Did you say Skylar? That can't be, right? Like, our SKYLAR?!"*

"I did. Hang on!" I push open the door and wince at the blinding morning sun. Evil. Ducking around a corner, I plug one ear with my finger to hear him better over the traffic. "Hey, wait, let's start with the important stuff. Have you heard from Ren and how are you holding up?"

"No and meh," he grunts. As much as I love Steve and Jamie to death, Chase became my soul mate bestie the second we met. We tease each other relentlessly and have zero boundaries between us, and we'd both die for each other—but we've never been attracted to one another. I call it platonic soul mates. *"Still no word from your sister, but I got another sunflower token thing. Guessing nothing on your end, either?"*

"Nada. Don't worry, babe. She's a fighter and she'll mess anyone up who messes with you. Also, she loves you, bro. Like, you two are gonna make babies together and stuff! The cards told me!"

"Yeah, well, did the cards tell you I lost a movie the other day because I'm barely treading water?"

"Chase Cooper... big time movie star with the butt so cute

even my mama loves it! Get your stupid head screwed on and get those damn movies." There's noise behind me, and Skylar's familiar hand tattoos come into view as they hug me and rest their head on mine. "Look, don't you realize she's one hundred percent finding ways to watch anything and everything you put out, work on, appear in, whatever? Awards ceremonies, TV shows, magazine articles, and everything in between. She's devouring that shit since she can't have the real you! I guarantee it's keeping her going, so you can't give up on her, or yourself, now. I won't have it."

"Yeah, I guess that's a fair point. I miss her so damn much, Dani. I'm gonna marry her. Like the second I find her again, as soon as I've got her back, I'm marrying her right there. You know I will."

"I do know that, sweetie. I do. Okay, onto other shit." I take a deep breath to prepare myself. "Yes, Skylar found me, and yes, they're playing in the band now. Also, yes, we're sleeping together and stuff. Also, also, they can hear you right now, so no, I will not tell you about their dick jewelry at this moment."

"Wait, what?!"

"To which part. Seriously though, trust me, neither of us planned this. But we obviously need to talk to Stevie, and before we do that, we need your help. More accurately, Skylar needs your help. We need a place that gets them."

I love being back in my own car, with my own smells and toys that decorate it. I have a rotation of air fresheners, and the current selection of birthday cake fills the air. Skylar hasn't uttered a single word since Connor dropped us off at my car, but I don't blame them. I'd be shitting bricks right now if I had to head back to the scene of memories I couldn't access. Chase assured us Steve wouldn't be at Casa Cooper when we get there, and he's keeping tabs on him to keep it that way. We don't need him walking in before we've figured out how to handle all of this. Steve's a freak out about things and figure it out later with too many apologies' kind of guy. I don't see this as keeping secrets as much as planning out how to reveal a secret no one wants to keep.

My standard go-to option of blurting it out and dealing with the chaos won't work for Steve and Skylar.

When I turn onto the road that loops into the Hollywood Hills, Skylar finds my hand. They don't grab it, wrap around it, or squeeze it, they just find it, letting their fingers dance along my skin, waiting to see if I'll accept their silent cry for help. I do. I'll do whatever they need because they need to feel safe here in Los Angeles, and they need to be in Los Angeles if they're going to be with Xander and I. There's too much riding on one conversation we're all scared to have.

We pull up to Chase's gate and I punch in the code for access. As I park, I remind Skylar about the dogs, since Chase didn't have Pongo or Lulu before the breakup. They nod, and I squeeze their hand before I let go and climb out of the car.

"Holy shit, it's so good to see you," Chase greets Skylar with a bear hug while I distract the dogs, who are both curious about the stranger on their front steps. "I missed you, pal. You've missed so much. How are you doing? I mean, other than being back in LA and needing to find a new support group. Like, you know…whatever." He throws his arms around Skylar again, rocking them back and forth with a laugh I haven't heard from Chase in months.

"Missed you too, big brother. So damn much."

Chase takes a step back and stares, shaking his head. Skylar even does a little spin so Chase can get a good look.

"Dude, no wonder Dani's riding you into the sunset. You look great!" Chase laughs, pushing my shoulder in a teasing gesture before pointing at Sky. "Shit, Dani, I'd go play for the other team for someone who looks that damn good."

"You're pseudo-engaged, Coop! To my sister!"

"Yeah, and I'm not about to bang Sky! Wait, what's pseudo-engaged mean?"

"Ugh, when you're basically engaged, but haven't popped the question yet. And don't lie to me and say you're not. I remember what you said the other day on the phone, fucker."

"Congrats on that," Skylar's voice returns, and they even offer Chase a smile as they pull me close. It's not a possessive thing; it's a protection thing. They feel vulnerable and know I'll protect them. I'm feisty, even though I'm not worried about Chase.

"Let's get inside so no one spots us," Chase says, clapping Skylar on the back. "I made lunch, so you better be hungry."

I watch Skylar eyeing the numerous awards and trophies in the case on the living room wall as we walk by. It's odd, since the real Chase acts nothing like the persona he puts on for others. We forget he's a movie star all the time, instead seeing him as the big, goofy, squish ball who will always be there for us. Even when I watch his movies, I don't see Chase, because celebrity Chase Cooper and regular old Coop are two completely different people in my mind. I like it that way.

Sky's known him since before the fame—the same with Steve and Jamie. They all met in high school, and I came along many years later.

"Alright," Chase says once we're all too stuffed to eat any more and Skylar has started to let his guard down. I told him Chase would be fine. Why else would he have helped Skylar get into a program if he didn't still love them? "I've got a list of places that aren't too far from Dani's new place, assuming you're staying there?"

"Yeah, they'll be staying there," I answer before Skylar can question it. "We'll need a bigger bed. Okay—we'll need *any* bed —but yeah."

"Dani, you don't have to—"

"Baby! We're together. You can stay at our damn apartment with us. Where else would you stay? Huh? Here? Nope, too weird. They've got the home gym setup here, and you'd see Steve every single day. And besides, you'll be traveling with the band anyhow so—"

Chase punches me in the arm, so I'll stop talking. He's seen me go down a rabbit hole before and say things I regret, and maybe now isn't the best time for that. When is, though?

"We'll get the bed thing figured out. Crash here for a couple of nights so I can catch up with Sky."

"Gross, I had plans!" I argue. "I want to catch this local band that's in the competition with us. I haven't gotten to see them yet and they're playing the Palladium tonight. Also, I'm not living under the same roof as Devin. I'll sleep on the floor."

"Devin has a road series for the next week, and technically lived under a different roof since the pool house isn't attached, idiot. You can go to the concert; Sky and I will hang out. Okay by you, Sky?"

Skylar nods.

"And you can't move in if you don't have a bed and furniture." Chase adds. "Ethan said something about furniture for your new place the other day, maybe we can use that as a reason to meet up with Steve and E?" He flips me off before grabbing his tablet off a chair and unlocking it, showing the list to Skylar. "Take your pick. I've got the dates and times of the meetings on here, and on this calendar I made so you can keep track. I'll add you to it so you can get the info from your phone. I've also put together some clinics out here if you feel like you need to try that route again, mostly because I don't want you flying all the way back to Canada when you're already here. You can see my shrink if you want, or he can recommend someone."

"Chase, it's too much. It's all…it's…" Skylar can't finish the thought, head dropping to their chest as they bite back tears. It rips my heart open to see them like this.

"Look, punk. What happened between you and Stevie wasn't your fault, and it wasn't his fault. We know who did it and her ass is, hopefully, rotting away in prison. You're my friend, Skylar. You're a part of this family, and we want you back. Seriously. It's weird not having you around. Now, do you want to go to a meeting tonight? I can go with you. Or I can wait in the car."

Watching Chase bring Skylar back into the fold melts my heart and makes me want to throw up. Chase's natural role in life, the one he slips into so easily, is big brother. He does it with all of us, not only his real-life baby brother. Who's an idiot, but a good guy. After they pick a few meetings, I tell Chase about everything that's happened with the band, Skylar's rehab and near slip up, and the terrible plan I have for surprising Steve at work, so he won't flip the hell out on us. Instead, Chase comes up with a better plan and sets it in action before I can stop him.

Fuck. That's usually my gig.

HOLLYWOOD
Theo

CHAPTER 25
A MILLION WAYS TO MISS YOU

JAKE MILLER

IT'S NOT until I'm through the second chorus that I realize the whistling is coming from me. Whistling. Shit, when was the last time I did that? I close the file I'm working on and open my laptop to find a message from Kennedy.

KENNEDY

Details, sir! You've been back there whistling for like an hour now!

Has it been that long? I flip my phone over and find four missed messages.

BLUE EYED BABY

Good morning from the future, but also, good… afternoon?

MARIE

Call me!!!!!

BLUE EYED BABY

Which one should I wear?

[Images attached]

Ohhhh noooooo, wrong picture (wink emoji)

I almost drop the phone into my cold coffee. Bathroom selfies. Not like the idiotic ones where people take those pictures in the mirror with goofy smiles or phones blocking their faces, either. He's in the shower under a stream of water, winking at me as he holds his cock. I check the timestamp. Five minutes ago. Since he left, my morning ritual has been like this; texts, calls, video chats, and too many pictures with too much skin to be decent. Every day since he left.

> Are you trying to give me a heart attack?

BLUE EYED BABY

AYYYYY! There you are. I was worried I scared you off with that one.

> Nope……send more.

BLUE EYED BABY

Naughty. How about a video?

"Doc!" Kennedy's shrill scream pulls my head out of the clouds, but I drop my phone, covering it with my foot just in case. "Who are you talking to?"

"It's nothing! I'll… we can talk after my next client. I need to take a call."

"Uh, huh? Sure, you do." She winks, heading for the door. "Bow chicka wow wow."

I flip her off as the door closes, and hurry to pick my phone back up. We didn't have camera phones, but when I was first in Europe, we had our ways of communicating. Sexting, listening to each other over the phone, not dissimilar from now. It's been a while, though, and this isn't like riding a bike. In his ways, Xander has helped ease me into it. We've jerked off together on a video call, but we didn't show much other than our faces. I almost forgot how pretty this kid's cock is. How much it makes my mouth water. How badly I want to be inside him again.

Moan for me.

BLUE EYED BABY

You're sure I can't call you Daddy? Cause you're giving Daddy right now.

Keep that shit up and I'll have you over my knee when you get back.

BLUE EYED BABY

D.A.D.D.Y.

[Video Attached]

I watch as he fumbles with the phone a bit, trying to get a grip as I listen to the sounds of the shower. There must be a shelf or something because he backs away from the camera, waves, and steps under the water, hands roaming his chest and abs. That deep V of his hips ending in a tease where the camera cuts off. Until he takes a few more steps back and I can see where that V really ends. He's hard already, and he stares right into the camera, licking his lips as his hand wraps around his cock. I watch his hips thrusting slow and steady and eyes roll back as he teases himself, running his thumb over the tip. That brings the moan. Deep, echoing off the tiles of the shower, followed by a series of high-pitched whimpers. Those are the ones that cut right through me, the ones I could listen to for hours.

"Theo, fuck. God, you feel so good. I can't wait for you to rip me open with that cock again, to bend me over that kitchen counter and take me." Another moan dripping with sin and wicked intentions. I glance up to make sure the door remains closed, even if I do have headphones in. "Fuck me! Theo, I want you to cum on my chest. I need you to call me your perfect slut again. Please? Please tell me I can cum for you. I need you so bad."

BLUE EYED BABY

When you're done watching, call me. We can jerk off together before I have to go into the office.

[Image Attached]

A close-up of his face with his mouth open wide and tongue ready for me. "This kid will be the death of me."

There's a knock on my door and without waiting for me to tell her to, Kennedy bursts into the room. "Okay, so your new client came in, like, way too early. Do I make him wait or?"

"No, it's… fine." I close the video and pull my headphones out, scooting closer to my desk so Kennedy doesn't notice my cock straining against these pants. I type out a quick message to Xander about work, so he doesn't think I've forgotten about him. Or had a real heart attack.

"Wait! Oh my god, those are new clothes." She sniffs the air like a crime dog. "And that *is* new cologne! What's his name? Zack? Did he take allergy shots so you and him can get it on? Cause you are getting it on!"

"Get it on? Seriously?"

"I dunno, I heard it in some old movie from the nineties or whatever."

"Kennedy, you're really killing my buzz here. And no, it's not Zack."

"Ohhhh, but it is someone!"

"Yes, okay. You got me there. I'm *talking* to someone and there's interest from both parties." No amount of therapy can help someone addicted to gossip, and Kennedy could give places like TMZ a run for their money. I'm surprised she doesn't go work for them. "But it's nothing you need to concern yourself with."

"Both parties? Interest? Lame! But okay, fiiiine. Your three o'clock just walked in. Late, as usual. Oh, and Chase called. I booked him for four fifteen, your next opening. Video call since he's on set, but he called it kind of an emergency."

"Fine, that will be fine. Kennedy?" I'm about to go back to my files, but stop. "Did I whistle for an hour?"

"At least. Like, you saw Mrs. Klein out and as soon as she was gone, you started. Pretty much been going strong ever since. You're good at it though, so I'm not complaining, but I don't know the songs, so I can't sing along."

LA Proper. I've been listening to their music again since I found out they were in that ridiculous, exploitative competition. Leave it to me to be the one shrink in LA whistling punk rock songs as a sign I'm falling for someone.

Am I? Falling?

I hope the band has a decent lawyer to get them out of whatever contract they had to sign to do this shit. The video of them from the show last night has hit record views because of their new bass player. The guy's got skills, but he's also got this stellar stage presence that pulls you in, which fits them better than the last guy. Doesn't hurt that he and the drummer make out. I missed the Orange County show; it sold out in minutes. But I've already purchased a pair of tickets for their next closest show and finals party they're doing here in Los Angeles months from now. Maybe I can bring Xander along.

"Oh, speaking of music, here!" She pulls out a handful of tickets. "This guy I met gave them to me, but it's not my scene. He only wants in my pants. But you go to a ton of live shows, so maybe you want them or someone you know can use them?"

She thrusts them out toward me. "I don't know the bands. Take your new boo!"

I take the tickets with a smile. No point in arguing with her when she doesn't care if I go. She needs the temptation taken out of her own hands. I wish I could tell her how proud I am of her for this step, but she's the type who doesn't do well with that kind of praise. I give them a quick glance and see they're for tonight.

"So?"

"Hmm?"

"The lucky person! I want deets!"

I tuck the tickets into my desk drawer and turn back to my computer. "It's…seriously nothing to dwell on. We haven't known each other long, and I don't know where this will end up. There's a few, uhm, complications? Things we'd need to iron out before he and I could move to the next step."

"Oh. My. God. He's married?"

"No, not exactly."

She sits in a chair, scooting it closer before propping her elbows on my desk and batting her eyes at me in anticipation. A big bag of popcorn would complete her look as she sits there, expecting me to spill everything out to her. I would love to wax poetically about Xander to someone, but not to Kennedy.

"I'm a little…busy." My phone buzzes, my fingers itching to pick it up. "Very busy, in fact."

Her jaw drops. Shit. "Dr. Clay you cad!"

"Cad?"

"Yeah, I've been reading my mom's romance novels and they're, well, regency."

"Interesting. Now, if you don't mind?"

She rolls her eyes and finally leaves, saying something about going downstairs to get a coffee and some food. I flip over my phone and there are two new videos and a message from Xander.

BLUE EYED BABY

Was that too much?

No, baby. I'm just…work is making it hard.

But don't stop. I look forward to watching all of these later tonight.

BLUE EYED BABY

It's not your work making it hard, it's me

Dinner when I come back? Like, out, not you cooking again.

You don't have to answer me right away.

I rub my temples as my brain plays a game of Pong with the answer. If I say no, will he stop talking to me? If I say yes, am I crossing more lines I can't come back from? What am I afraid of? Other people are going to think whatever they think, and it's not like it's something they can take my license away for. Xander is an adult, thirty, if he told me the truth. Eleven years isn't even something to make people look twice here in Los Angeles. And I deserve to have a chance at happiness again. Don't I?

I type out and answer and hit send before I can second guess myself any further.

Yes. I'd love to.

Let me know when you're back. I'll pick you up at the airport.

BLUE EYED BABY

Call me later? I don't care how late it is. I'll be up.

In more ways than one

I uhm, I miss you. I hope that's not too much.

Not at all, Baby. I miss you, too.

Maybe he said that too quickly. Maybe I answered it too quickly.

I groan, leaning back in my chair and releasing a slow exhale. What am I doing? I'm forty-one! That's far too late in life to dip toes back into those polyamorous waters. But how much different could it be from what I had before. I loved the woman who became my wife, but she knew I had other needs. Hell, she's the one who invited Gio, a friend of hers from school, over to the apartment. He moved in with us a few weeks later, each of us having a sexual relationship with the other. I thought it would end when Élodie and I were married, but Gio stood there, by our side through the wedding and the birth of Sylvie. We were in Paris, the city of love, and I thought it would always be like that. The three of us were raising Sylvie, getting a house together, filling it with affection, openness, and happy memories.

The only thing that kept me clinging to that last thread of sanity after the accident? Knowing they'd been together when they died. Knowing they hadn't been alone, and they'd been with someone who loved them in their final moments. It didn't take me long to realize losing them like that meant I was utterly alone in ways I couldn't have imagined. Poor Sylvie spent more time with her grandparents than me because I couldn't hold it together long enough. I saw too much of Élodie in her curious eyes, too much of Gio in her laughter, even if her genetics don't match his. She will always be ours.

If I can stop screwing it all up. Xander might be the answer to that. The one who can steer me back toward true affection again.

I open the chat again and scroll up, not to the naked pictures of him, but to the one he took before he left the two of us in the car. The serious lines of my face are replaced by a genuine smile, my walls down, and a sparkle in my eyes. Then there's him. Crooked grin and nerdy black glasses, nothing but hope in his face. He said that's what I gave him; hope. Well, that and a damn good night.

I have my answer and it's yes. I'm falling for those pretty blue eyes, the snarky attitude, the desperate need to be understood. Even now, sitting in my office, I long to be back in bed with him, holding him to my chest and whispering against his soft, fluffy brown hair.

A notification interrupts my daydream, reminding me I'd gotten a text from Marie, too. Groaning, I slide to the phone app and call my sister-in-law back.

"Theo! Oh, thank God you called. I was worried something had happened to you!"

"No. Well, yeah, something has happened. All good. What's up Fifi?"

There's a long pause and I'm not sure if it's the connection or her until her voice comes back. *"Theo, are you baking?"*

"Not yet? Why? Need me to whip something up for you? Ship it to Boston, New York, wherever you are this week?"

"Oh no, no, no. What I called you about, it can wait. You called me Fifi." I stop, realizing I call her a childhood pet. Fifi Marie. I don't even remember how we came up with it, but it's what Élodie, Gio, and I called her. With a French accent, it's cute. Fee Fee Mah Ree. *"Tell me what has you so happy and yet not in the kitchen?"*

I laugh, but it's not a surface laugh. It goes through to my ribs, it comes from my center, from a frozen piece of my heart that's finally getting the chance to feel some warmth again.

"I, uhm, I met someone. He reminds me so damn much of Gio. Hell, his eyes are that same steel blue." Maybe that's why

I'm opening up to him, the idea of him combined with how much he looks like the love I'd lost. I hope I'm not projecting. Gio sure as hell didn't fuck like Xander, though. God, that mouth is made for—

"Tell me everything, Theo!" She pulls me out of my daydream again. I've got to stop doing that. *"I'm so damn happy for you! It's about time."*

"Marie, I've dated since them."

"No, you've had a series of terrible, awful, boring affairs. You would call me and still sound sad. Hell, you called me from their beds and sounded sad. This has a different feel to it. Maybe à l'amour! Does he have a name?"

I sit back and look out the window, watching the traffic. "Xander." The name slides off my tongue as smooth as butter, and I can't stop smiling whenever I say it. "His name is Xander."

HOLLYWOOD
Xander

CHAPTER 26

PANIC ATTACK

THE GLORIOUS SONS

I WAKE up to the alarm I miraculously remembered to set, still exhausted from a late-night phone call with my new personal psychiatrist. My shower takes longer than it should, daydreaming and jerking off to the thought of him and how he looks at me with those hazel eyes. I hurry to get dressed, and take out the foundation and concealer Dani taught me how to use, getting to work covering the tattoos on my face and neck.

Once I put in the contacts and slick my hair back, I complete the transformation. I grab the rings out of my bag and slide them on. They're not special, they're not even expensive, but they give me just that bit of assurance that I'm still me under all this bullshit. I snap a picture and shoot it off to Theo with the caption: What do you think of your corporate boy toy?

Stepping out into the hallway, I find Oliver there with his arm raised, ready to knock. With a wink, I walk past him and to the bank of elevators, pulling my jacket on as I go.

"You coming, Oli?"

His hurried footsteps run past me, and he jabs the down button. "Sorry, Mr. ...err... Xander. I hadn't anticipated you being as...punctual. Especially after how late you were out last night."

"Bro, just because I hate being professional doesn't mean I'm bad at it. I've been doing this shit since I was five. Relax." I rub my temples, still unable to shake the headache I've had since landing here days ago. Listening for the doors, Oliver taps me on the shoulders. I open my eyes again and I'm greeted with a bottle of pills I can't read, but the graphics I recognize from back home. Finally, the good stuff. So far, I've only had the generic shit Oli's been giving me from a first aid kit he found in the office. "Oh shit, I love you! I got like two hours of sleep. I can't adjust to the time difference and trying to find the right time to FaceTime my new man? Impossible, bro."

"Most people have trouble adjusting to the time difference when they contact friends and family back home," he assures me with a smile. "These are the strongest tablets they had in the shops."

"You're a lifesaver." I open the bottle and pop three into my mouth, swallowing them dry and regretting that a moment later. I should have checked to make sure they were the coated ones—they're not.

Oliver escorts me through the building and across a pedestrian bridge, avoiding the morning rush of pedestrian traffic. It reminds me of an ant farm, everyone moving with purpose toward their individual goals in life. I hate everything about it. When we get to the offices, my father already sits behind a giant oak desk that makes him look both older and smaller than he is. Enormous windows look out over the city and modern furniture that clashes with his desk fills the room.

"Ah, Alex! Glad to get you into the office. Sorry it took an extra day; contract negotiations are a bear."

I replay a conversation with Theo about boundaries in my head and take a deep breath. "Dad, these trips gotta stop. I'll let you and mom parade me around LA, but no more travel, and only on my terms."

"Right. We can discuss that later."

"I don't want to *discuss* it, Dad. They're done."

"Fine. Let's get through today before you throw any more demands on me, though. I have an announcement to make, and I need to focus on that. So will you." He picks up a stack of files and looks at Oliver for the first time. "Oliver, please take five minutes to acquaint my son with the new computer system and get him signed up."

"Signed in, sir, and yes, right away." Oliver nods and moves across the room to a large cabinet, pulling out a drawer that has at least five new tablets still in their pristine white boxes. He turns and nods toward a door in the back of the room. "Follow me, I'll get you set up in your temporary office while IT runs their updates."

Not once in all the years I've been playing business with my father has he ever given me an assistant, an office, or a single piece of technology. When Oliver walks me into a space adjacent to my father's, more than one warning bell goes off in my mind. I try to shake off the feeling, flopping down on the couch across from the desk. My hands cover my face, and contemplate passing out, but Oliver announces he's done, and when I check my watch, I've spent fifteen minutes lost in my mind.

"Just in time, sir, here's your tablet. You should be capable of completing the registration and setting your password since you're more computer savvy than your father. But if you run into any hiccups, let me know. I'll be sitting behind you through the meeting."

"Behind me?"

"Ah, executives and special guests only at the table. The

assistants will all be in the back to not cause any distractions or disturbances."

The immense size of the room takes my breath away, and Oliver makes it a point to introduce me to at least a dozen people. I promptly forget all their names before I even take a seat, and by the time my father comes in to start the meeting, my leg bounces so fast I could use it to power a small city. Nothing feels right about this. I should have kept my passport with me and had a backup plan for a flight home.

"My friends, shall we begin?" My father says to the mostly male table. I take a deep breath, assuring myself that I'm over-reacting and jumping to conclusions. "There's no need for me to bury the lead on this. Most of you know why we're here today. As of last night, Maxwell Corp became the new home of Tanaki Industries. Even with the ink barely dry, we've begun to implement procedures and transition staff to new positions where needed to ensure this goes smoothly."

There's clapping around the table when my father pauses to take a drink of water. My tablet vibrates and I glance down.

MELODY MAXWELL

Stay calm and remember where you are.
Trust me.

When I try to look down the table at her, she has her head down, typing furiously on her own tablet.

"Now, for the best part of that news, at least for me. Our new branch here in Tokyo will need leadership, and while our company isn't hurting for options, this one will need a unique appointment. Because of the reputation Tanaki Industries holds, I wanted to make this a fresh, bold pick. I want someone with fearless ideas who understands the new age we're entering and can tackle the evolving opportunities this venture will bring. The choice didn't come easy, and I spent many hours mulling it over and discussing it with my closest partners in this business, but in the end, only one choice made sense. May I introduce the new C.E.O. Of Maxwell Industries, Tokyo branch, my son, Charles Alexander Maxwell!"

My face drops and I choke on my own saliva as I stare up at his big smile. People around the table are clapping, and I can't hear a damn thing over the high-pitched screaming in my ears. My father motions for me to stand up, but if I do that, I'll bolt for the emergency exit the second my ass leaves this chair. I stare at him from my seat, stunned into silence.

"Ah, I caught him by surprise, folks. Now the cat's got his tongue. I'm sure Alex is eager to meet all of you as he settles into his new role." He flashes me a look I've seen more than once from my parents. Disappointment. "Alright, with that out of the way, let's get onto the strategies for—"

He drones on, but I'm distracted by the messages popping up on the tablet Oliver gave me what feels like hours ago.

Congratulations, Alex!

Welcome aboard!

Can't wait to meet you, Charles!

Where are all these coming from!?

I glance around the room and notice the camera coming down from the ceiling. My father didn't announce that to the room of executive ass kissers, but to the whole damn company.

When my aunt finally looks up, she mouths, "I didn't know," before tapping on the edge of her tablet.

MELODY MAXWELL

The gift. Hurry! Before he cuts us off.

My brain cycles through the thousand things she could mean. My office? An assistant? No, it's something else. Something bigger. Why would I need a gift if my father—SHIT. I pull out my phone and type frantically, hoping the message will send.

> I'm not leaving you! Don't believe anything they tell you! The furniture was a payoff!

I hit send and watch the bar slide across the screen. I'm not even sure if she's been home yet, so she may not have a clue what I'm talking about, but at least there's some warning. The bar stalls halfway through sending and stops. This isn't good. Since when has my father had enough tech know-how to lock me out like this? He couldn't even come up with this idea, he can barely send an email without crashing the security system.

> Unable to send messages. Please try again.

I smash the button again, but I get the same results. I check the agenda and, sure enough, there's a fifteen-minute break after this. *Fifteen minutes.* He ruins my life and thinks it will only take fifteen minutes to smooth this over and make it right. When the meeting ends, I don't even wait for him, bee lining to his office and already pacing when he walks in, my aunt and Oliver close behind him.

"What the fuck?!" I scream. It feels good, especially since the door hasn't closed yet.

"Alex, I can explain."

"Yeah, I don't think you can. Tricking me to coming here, thinking you can buy Dani off with some furniture, broadcasting it to the whole damn company, and blocking my damn phone?"

"Alex, you're thirty years old! You have no job, no future. We've put up with your games, we've played along in some cases, but not anymore. I will not allow you to single-handedly ruin the Maxwell name and reputation."

"I refuse the position. You can shove it right up your pompous asses, every damn one of you pricks." I storm for the door.

"You can't leave Japan, Alex. I've frozen the credit card and told the plane it doesn't leave under any authorization but my own." His voice doesn't tremble, it doesn't even raise. The calm is unsettling.

"First off, fuck you. Second off, I will find a way home. You can't keep me here!"

"You are home, Alex." My father spreads his arms wide like he's Jesus at the last supper or some shit.

"*LA* is my home. *Dani* is my home!" I scream back. "And while we're at it, my fucking name is *Xander*."

"I'll give you two weeks to finish your freelance jobs, settle up, and close out your dealings with your clients. After that, you'll be here in the office full time with Oliver and Melody, helping you get accustomed to your new role." It's like he hasn't heard a word I've said, like my opinion and my life means nothing to him other than to move it around like a chess piece. He plays at shuffling papers around on his desk, his way of ending the conversation and dismissing me. "Son, if you continue to act defiant, we'll cut you off completely and you'll hear from our lawyer about arrangements for back payments."

"Back what?"

"We took you into our home, clothed you, raised you, gave you every opportunity to succeed, and you've done nothing but squander everything we've done for you. If nothing else, we'll be seeking repayment for every cent we've given you, in whatever format, since you turned eighteen. The legal team has the paperwork drafted."

I pull my wallet out of my back pocket and slip two hundred-dollar bills out, slapping them down on his desk. "Here, keep the change."

"Alexander—"

"No! You want to talk about back payments? How about the therapy sessions, trauma, and humiliation? The years of being raised in a cold, heartless home and the abuse I lived through at those damn schools you sent me to. You knew what would happen to me. You always knew. And when I tried to tell you, you told me to stop being so dramatic." I can't control my voice or keep the tears back. "You want dramatic, *Dad*? Fine, you have no son. You don't deserve one. Get another dog."

I don't wait for a response, walking out the door and slamming it shut behind me. I expect him to yell after me, chase me down and threaten me more, but if he does, I don't hear him. Before I can press the button for the elevator, a familiar hand reaches out and presses it for me.

"Uhm, you probably don't want to see me right now, but Melody had a feeling it would come to this and asked me to, well, look out for you."

"Look out for me? You mean convince me I'm wrong?"

"No, not at all. I am only here to help you with navigating the city, translations, and procurement of necessities. When your aunt realized what your father planned, she asked me to keep you safe. Nothing more."

"Alright, let's get the hell out of here. I never want to see this place again."

"Anywhere in particular you'd care to go?"

"Yeah, actually. There is. I need some pain therapy."

HOLLYWOOD
Dani

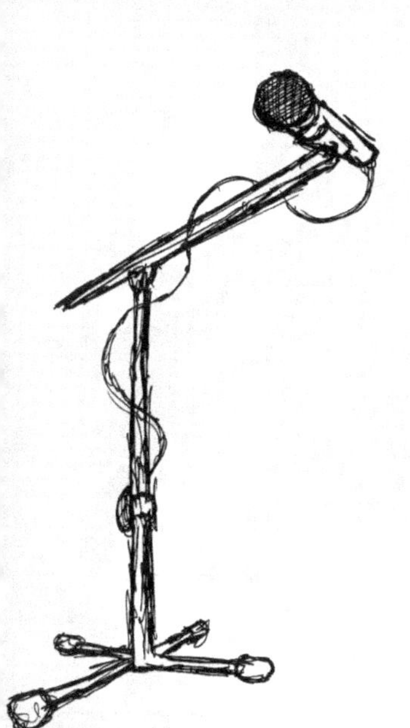

CHAPTER 27
YOUNG & DUMB
AVRIL LAVIGNE, SIMPLE PLAN

I AM A CUCUMBER. No, I hate those fucking things. What else is calm and cool? Cactus? No, but maybe the cactus fits a little better. I'm not cool and I'm sure as hell not calm sitting here in the mall food court. I'm prickly and scared and I will stab someone if they try me today. Yeah, I'm all cactus, baby.

This would be easier if Xander wasn't ghosting me. He does that when he goes on these stupid business trips, but I haven't heard from him in like two days. It's annoying, but it might be my fault since my phone got jacked up. Just like this mall. How did people ever find these places cool?

I'm a sucker for vintage things, and even more so when I'm a nervous wreck. Sadly, mall food courts are now considered vintage, and so are the restaurants in them. I've overpaid for a slice of pizza, a soda, and a side of garlic knots because it comes with memories of my mother, sister, and I all going to the mall together as kids. Mom would give all her quarters to Ren and let her watch me in the arcade. I look back at those times now and wonder how the two of us never got abducted.

Coop suggested somewhere public for me to meet up with Steve and Ethan, hoping it would prevent a Steve level global

meltdown. My leg bounces so hard it's difficult to take a drink, so I do a few breathing exercises like I watch Coop do all the time. Manifesting the outcome where all of us are happy and refocusing my energy into what I'm going to say to Steve when he finally gets here. If he shows. He better fucking show.

"Okay," I whisper, pulling up a picture of Steve and Ethan on my phone and leaning it against my drink so I can pretend I'm talking to him. "I can do this. Here we go. Steve, I love you and I'm so glad you have Ethan, a man who fits you so perfectly and makes you happy. I'm sleeping with your ex-fiancé."

Ugh. My shoulders slump and I cover my face with my hands and groan.

"Steve, you and I are besties, and we share a lot of…no, that's not… shit."

"Hey, punk bitch. Who're you talking to?"

I grab for my phone, knocking my drink over and spilling the syrupy goodness all over the table. Thankfully, it didn't land on anyone, and Ethan runs to get us a few napkins while Steve helps me collect the ice.

"Why did you have to sneak up on me!?" I shriek.

"I'm sorry, I didn't know you'd jump like that!" Steve defends himself.

"Of course I'd jump, you asshole! I'm in a shopping mall, on my fourth soda, plus I had two coffees and a cookie from the pastry place already, and you snuck up on me!"

"Here, I've got it." Ethan puts the napkins down, soaking up as much as he can. A janitor noticed us and comes to the rescue with a wet rag and a mop. By the time we're done, and I've got another soda—which Steve said was a terrible idea, but I didn't listen—I'm ready to give up, go home, and hide in the hope that Steve never finds out what's going on. Fat chance.

Instead, he slides into the booth next to me and pulls me in for a big brother hug. "Okay, jump scare. Why am I here at a mall like it's the nineties again? Wait, does this place have a music store?"

"A what?" Ethan asks, his face scrunched up and glaring at Steve like he grew an extra head. "Pumpkin, nobody has music stores anymore. Are you gonna ask me to go to Blockbuster on the way home, too? Pick up some video tapes?"

"Don't start with me, child! Wait, did you ever even go to a Blockbuster Video?" Steve asks.

"Yes, fuckface!" Ethan shoots back.

"Only yours, baby." Steve leans on his elbows and stares into Ethan's eyes. I'm not sure if he's about to kiss him or trying to read his mind. "Did you ever rent something that wasn't animated?"

"Fuck. Off." Ethan emphasizes each word by pointing his finger at Steve.

"That's a no. I'm such a perv and a cradle robber. How does your mom even like me, Sweets?" Ethan rolls his eyes as Steve leans back with a sigh and takes a drink of my soda. "So, spill it, other kid. No, wait, you already did. Tell me why I'm here."

"Uhm," I cringe, wrapping the paper from a straw around my fingers, unwrapping it, and doing it all over again. "So, you know how, like, the world is super weird and when you think someone is cool, the world takes them away? And you're all like, bro, that sucked, but maybe I'll see them again someday, and you find a rock that reminds you of your friend and you keep it and—"

Ethan reaches across the table and slides the drink away from me, eyes wide and blinking rapidly. "Enough caffeine. You're worse than me on a three-day sugar binge."

"Hold on, I'm still stuck on why you have a rock," Steve says, scratching his head.

"I don't.. It's not a…it's a metaphorical rock!" I fold my arms on the table and let gravity take my head. "I can't do this!"

"Alright, we'll be serious. What do you need to tell me, D?"

"I can't tell you! You're gonna hate me!"

"Because your band went viral?"

I can't move. My head won't lift off my arms, my lungs refuse to take a breath, even my leg has stopped bouncing as what he said hits me right in the gut.

"Laurie sent me a text the other day about it, said you and your band did something and it blew up. Cool, right? I mean, Laurie told me not to look it up and that I should talk to you about it first. Didn't make much sense, but I'm not going to screw with my sister." He tries to look under my arms to find me, so I turn my head enough to make a sliver of eye contact.

"I'm sorry, Stevie," I mumble into my arms. "I mean, I am, but I'm also not. I don't know how that works. How I can be sorry, but also unapologetically happy for this. I've been rehearsing what I need to say, how to tell you, but I can't get it right. I can't find the—"

"Spit it out. Rip the bandage off."

I close my eyes, covering them with my hands. "Skylar came back. They're in my band now, and we're sleeping together."

I have no idea what Steve does next because not only are my eyes closed, but the blood rushing through my ears mixes with the echo chamber of the food court, and I go temporarily deaf. I've stressed myself out so hard, I can't make out words anymore and I swear I can feel the room buzzing in my teeth. Time means nothing because I can't even concentrate enough to count the seconds as they tick by. I usually only have time distortion like this when I'm high, not from stress.

"Come on, open," Steve coaxes, prying my hands away from my face. The anger, disappointment, and hatred I expected never come. His words are soft and a little choked as he pulls my hands away from my face and I crack open one eye enough to see Ethan holding Steve's hand across the table. His squeeze forces me to realize his other hand has a hold of mine.

"There you go. Look at me, Dani. I heard you, I did, but I want to hear you say it again. Slower. One thing at a time."

"Uhm, Skylar joined the band and—"

"Stop. Back up."

"Right. I fired Rory from the band and the guy we found sucked bad, and we were at the gig. I flipped out at the new kid and when I turned around, I found Skylar standing there in the parking lot." I take a big swig of my drink, a failing attempt to quench the desert in my mouth. "They were visiting their brother. I didn't even know their brother lived there! We, uhm, we slept together that night. And the next day, they joined our band because Todd quit."

"Todd? Terrible name for a bassist. How do you even introduce that?" Steve grumbles before he shifts to that big, cocky grin. "They still play, though? Skylar? That's great. That's amazing."

His hand releases mine, rubbing my back in slow circles. The knuckles on his other hand are white from how hard he's squeezing Ethan's fingers. Ethan can take it; he's a pro hockey player who gets in fights and stuff. I don't understand the game, but they try to teach me whenever I'm around and the Parrots are playing. I enjoy going to the games, though, especially now that Sam and Chase have a suite with free beer and food.

I risk it and let my eyes wander up to meet Steve's.

"Seriously, it's... okay. We're good, Dani."

"I never did anything with them before. Like when they were with you. Okay, I mean, I kissed them, but you were there for that and you were the one that dared us, anyhow. I thought they went to Greece! How could I have known? Wait, they said you sent them music?"

I can't help myself, letting all my thoughts spill out of my mouth as they form in my brain. They're not rational or fully developed, and I keep hoping I can stop before I say something that will cost me one of my best friends. I give him grief all the time, more than Jamie or Coop, but that's because Steve means the world to me. He's my safety net. Jamie plays my dad figure; I disappoint him regularly, and he tries to keep me in line. Coop became my twin brother even though he's like a billion years older than me, we're constantly picking at each other, but no one should ever come between us for their own safety. Steve's the favorite brother, the one I go to with my problems, the one I complain about Xander to, the one who understands me on the deepest and most real level. I can't lose him. I can't lose any of them.

"I did. Do. They never respond, but I get notifications when they open the emails. It's communication in our own way. Same with Xander and Coop."

The look on his face shifts, and that's what makes things a little clearer for me. "You…you still send my songs?"

"Every time a new one comes out." He pats my back. "I get your music first, because you always send it to me first, and I send it immediately to Skylar in the hopes it will push them back to playing, to recovering. What happened between Sky and I…"

"It wasn't your fault, Stevie," I whisper, trying to maintain eye contact even when he looks away again.

"Yeah, I get it. I mean, I get it now, but back then I convinced myself I imploded our relationship. Now, well, because of you and your weird voodoo shit, I kind of believe the accident, the breakup, all of it served a purpose." He glances across the table and smiles as Ethan's face turns red and he looks away. "It brought me Ethan. It forced me to learn who I am and accept myself, flaws and all. When I reminisce about Skylar and me, I can't guarantee we'd still be together now."

He reaches over and smacks the brim of Ethan's hat, and when he looks back at Steve with those wet, emerald eyes before the tear falls, I almost join him in crying. "I fight for you every day, Ethan, and I always will. That's the difference, because I never fought for Sky, not like I could have. I let him walk away because, deep down, I knew after the accident, our relationship had an expiration date. A day where we'd have nothing left to give each other. With you, I'll never run out of steam, or love, and I'll sure as fuck never let you go."

"Gross," I tease, pushing Steve's shoulder before he leans across the table, cups Ethan's face, and plants a big old pornographically hot kiss on him, knocking his hat to the floor. It's cute to watch, especially since Ethan still hasn't adjusted to life out of the closet yet. He's getting there, but he still looks around to see who's watching when they separate.

"Love you too, Stevie," Ethan smirks, picking his hat up off the ground.

"And what do you mean, gross? You admitted to sleeping with my ex. Dirty whore!" Steve pushes me back with a laugh and no real force behind it. Steve owns a gym and has arms bigger than the trunks of the dying palm trees in Mama's front yard. Massive. "So, if you're telling me this because you're worried how I'll react if I had found out on my own, which I appreciate not doing, what else? Don't hold back."

"They're here, in Los Angeles. We crashed at Coop's house last night since I don't have furniture, and Sky needed a meeting."

"Okay, that's hilarious. Your triad piece used to be my piece. A meeting?"

"N.A. They're…struggling with coming back. Seeing you." Steve's face drops into serious mode as he goes quiet and listens. "Also, Xander found someone while we were playing in Portland. Maybe Megan ended up opening our eyes to see what we wanted in the world, or the universe finally felt awful for how shitty it treated us. New apartment, new people, newfound fame. So much has changed in what comes down to a few days."

I'm not afraid of the speed of the world, I'm used to that. My father died unexpectedly when I was young, and within six months, my sister got married to her douchebag abusive boyfriend, my mother's apartment got condemned by the city, and I got my first bedroom when we moved in with my sister. Life enjoys throwing things at me to see how I react, and I like to believe I've got mad reflexive skills to move with it. Maybe that's why I couldn't hold down a job before I dropped out of art school and fashion school. Maybe I pretend I don't like change, but secretly I thrive on it, on the chaos and the uncertainty. I guess Xander and I constantly breaking up with each other could also circle back to the way I handle life.

"Speaking of your apartment, we have some stuff in the SUV," Ethan disrupts my train of thought, sending it down a ravine in a fiery ball of doom, the ideas onboard never to surface again. "Nothing crazy, some furniture we, uhm, need to clear out."

"You're clearing out furniture? Sick! I love your—why are you clearing out furniture?" I glare at Ethan, knowing he'll break first. "Out with it. Or I'll start making assumptions. They'll be wild, too. Things like you're pregnant and that's not even possi —OH MY GOD! HOW DID YOU GET ETHAN PREGNANT?! Or Steve? Who's the daddy? Mommy? Fuck, I don't even know what I'm saying anymore!"

Ethan's deer in the headlights look as Steve doubles over and almost falls to the floor.

"Don't, uh, don't tell Coop yet," Ethan mumbles. "We've still got too much to figure out before we're really doing this, and we want things to settle down in his world, and your sister's, before we go for this. But yeah, we're...well, we're thinking of adopting."

I throw my arms around Steve and squish him as hard as my scrawny arms can. "Oh my god, this day keeps getting crazier! Furniture, babies, exes, sex, and rock-n-roll!" I squeal and slam a hand over my mouth. "I really need to cut down on the caffeine today."

"Yeah, come on. Let's go spruce up our place so my ex can rail my other ex while my husband and I go pick out babies from a book. What the hell world do I live in now?" Steve teases before he brings me in for a tight hug. "Don't worry, kiddo. We're good. But you three are going to need a bigger bed."

"Especially if it's us four. Life is so wild right now."

HOLLYWOOD
Xander

CHAPTER 28
FIGURE IT OUT

ROYAL BLOOD

THERE'S a cathartic serenity that comes from the repetition and the sound of the needle as the artist goes to work. It's a small piece, probably my smallest one aside from the stars Dani drew, but it's as important as those doodles.

You. Deserve. Better.

When I go to pay, I'm surprised my card works and that my father didn't find a way to freeze my personal accounts. Although, he doesn't know about this one since I use it for my money from the sex work. I tip the artist and grab his card; there's a solid chance I'll be back for more therapy if I'm stuck in Japan much longer.

"So, uhm, does it mean something?" Oliver asks, finally loosening his tie when we climb into the limo. The tattoo artist got a few shots of sake into him, giving him a red nose and a slight slur to his speech. He shuffles around in his seat, reaching into the console next to him and pressing a button. There's a whirring, and a door pops open to reveal a mini bar. Oliver

grabs a small bottle before looking at me and gesturing to the bar.

"Whiskey. Neat." I lean forward and take the glass after he pours what looks to be about six shots into it. Either Oliver wants me drunk, or he doesn't drink and has no idea how any of this works. My headache has come back, so I rub my temples. Maybe I should have ordered my drink on the rocks.

"Oh my, you have them on your face as well?" He asks, gesturing toward my face with the bottle of pills for my headache.

"Hmm?" I check the glass and realize I've rubbed off the makeup covering my face tattoos. I shrug and take the pills, popping three of them. "Yeah. My girl drew them one night, and I went out and made them permanent. I need to tell her what happened. She's gonna lose it."

I dig my phone out and there's still no service, so I shut it off to save the battery. I haven't been back to the hotel yet; sure my father has a team waiting on me. Oliver said my aunt hasn't been in contact either. For now, my father's threat stands, I can't leave Japan. I yawn, realizing the late hour and how much time has passed since we left for the office this morning. Everything hits me at once and the adrenaline has run out. I'm exhausted.

"Maybe we should head back to the hotel and face whatever awaits?"

Oliver's mouth curls into a devious grin that reminds me of the Grinch, and he leans forward, his elbow almost missing his knee all together. He opens his mouth to speak, stops, and I'm worried he's about to lose it all over the back seat. I don't expect it when he gets up and moves across to sit next to me. I also don't expect his arm to drape over me like we're long-lost frat brothers.

"If I might be so bold, Xander. This poses a fantastic

opportunity. Money, power, fame. But there's one tiny problem." He leans in too close, gripping my knee and squeezing until I wince. "I wanted that job. I've earned that job."

"What? What job?"

"The one you turned down like a spoiled brat. Your idiotic self would run the company into the ground in days, if not hours. Ten fucking years I've worked for your family, learning everything I could about the company, them, you."

"Take it! I don't even want it."

"That won't work, my sweet, but far from innocent, boy. You see, your father hopes it straightens you out. Your whole life, a clean slate." He smacks my leg and laughs. "He thinks while you're in Japan, you'll find a docile wife, and stop puttering around with, well, everything else. I should know better, though. That's why a convenient illness took your original assistant, the one he'd hoped to find in your bed. I, of course, volunteered in her place, and they had no other choice."

"Straighten—what?" My words are oddly thick in my mouth, sounding odd and slurred. "Are you kidding me? He wouldn't do that."

"Ah, yes, that part might be my fault. I've been slipping him hints about your sex scandals and elite families being dismantled by them. Dismantled by you and your busy little cock. Well, not little, I suppose. I've seen the website." He slides his hand up my leg and I struggle to push it away. "Your father bought into the propaganda of the rise of homosexuality and how it ties into pedophilia. Your parents might have the riches, but my god do they live in a bygone era. Clueless about the world."

I lunge, trying to get away from him, but he pushes me back into the seat and looms over me. It makes no sense. I'm bigger than he is, but I can't fight him off. "I may have recently let it slip about your girlfriend's trip to the clinic and how close they came to shelling out millions to keep the bastard child out of the headlines."

"You son of a… why?"

He holds his fingers up to shush me, but misses his mouth by a good four inches. I'm gonna throw up, I can feel it building. I stumble across the seat, somehow getting to the window and pushing the button. The cool night air on my face keeps what little I have in my stomach right where it is.

"I kept one last secret from him, though. Well, at least one. The one where you go around waving your cock at the camera for money. How the men you meet pay you for sex and leave you a battered mess in the gutter. My god, when I tell him about that! Show him his son in your true form, a pathetic whore and a punching bag?"

The air isn't cool anymore. It's ice cold, like the blood in my veins. He holds his sides as he laughs, and I'm questioning if he's drunk at all. How long has he played me? Did his accent just slip? He's next to me again, his hand on my chest. "Don't worry, love. Dear old dad doesn't need to know. We can keep it our little secret if you play nice. I wasn't very happy when you canceled all your dates here in the city. I had several brilliant ones lined up for you to give myself some cover. But you threw that option away. Or did you?"

He gets on his knees in front of me, running his hand up my thigh.

"Get the hell off of me! What—what do you want from me?"

SMACK!

My cheek burns, and he grabs me by the jaw, squeezing tight. "You will shut your whore mouth, listen to me, and play the good little son. I take care of the business and clean up the mess you're about to be in. We show your father you've become a team player, thanks to me taking you under my wing. You pretend you're now interested in the company and give me half your salary. Oh, and you'll be my own personal whore, keeping me satisfied every night. Your father won't need to know that part, and your aunt has already tried to push me in your direction."

"No—"

"Yes, Xander. And you'll agree to my terms, so I don't release the rest of the videos." His hot breath on my face makes me gag. "Maybe I'll keep your girl and that gorgeous looking doctor out of it, too. If you perform well enough on your knees for me, *Baby*."

My ability to form sentences stops working, and I can't do much more than stare at him and his dumb, freckled face I want to punch. "I'm not... I won't do... Fuck you!" I'm not even sure if the words make sense or if they're slurred noises.

"Oh, no. Not tonight. In fact, you wouldn't be awake for it if I did. You've only got a few—"

His voice drifts further away, which doesn't make sense since there are three of him now.

The world goes black.

I wake up to living nightmares, or to a vague idea of what's happening to me when I'm not awake. Flashing lights, voices, Oliver, others. I can't remember what's happening most of the time, nor do I want to. I've yet to wake up anywhere familiar, but every time I do wake up, I'm in hell. Too many people. Too many hands.

I shouldn't have come to Tokyo. I shouldn't have left Dani. I should have stayed with Theo. Do they even know I'm missing? Does anyone?

"Oh, good morning, sunshine. How are you feeling? I hope Mr. Sato wasn't too rough on you." Oliver's voice drips with sarcasm the way the syringe in his hand drips with whatever he's been using to knock me out. I try to shake my head, to pull my arm away, but he's stronger and not made of jelly. "Now, come on, beautiful. Don't fight. Do I need to remind you what happens when you fight me? Who am I kidding? You shouldn't remember a thing I've done to you since the limo."

The garbled moan that comes out of me when the needle pricks my skin doesn't even resemble the words I'm trying to say. But I'm sure he gets the idea. He laughs.

"It's a shame you don't remember. We've had some excellent times together. Well, I have, anyhow. And some of your clients, too." His laugh sounds strange, face distorted like I'm looking at a clown in a funhouse mirror. "This isn't going to knock you out, but don't get any ideas because you're not going anywhere. Not yet. Not until we come to an agreement."

"Let go of me." It comes out something like legfmah, and I can't lift my head.

"Hmm, I may have used too much sedative earlier. Let's stick to *yes* and *no* from you." He smiles, slapping the side of my face lightly. "It's my first go at kidnapping, you know. No, I don't suppose you do know that. Oh, and good news, they've realized you're missing! Only took them three days."

He drops something next to my head. It smells like a newspaper, but I can't tell. The world spins, and dips sideways when he picks my head up again, pulling open my eyelids like they do in the movies. He pulls a ski mask down over his face and takes out his phone.

"Eyes open, love. They need to see you're alive if I'm sending proof of life. How about we start with ten million? Are you worth ten million? No, I don't think you are after that outburst at the office. Let's play it safe and say three."

"Money?" I barely understand the word I spit out.

"Yeah, money. Isn't it always money? Oh, money and spite. My parents worked for your father for years, were laid off, I couldn't afford to stay at the boarding school, so I came up with this crazy plan to work here blah blah villain origin story type stuff. The problem was, I can't blackmail your father on his deeds alone. He's too…boring. Your family are white bread, mundane people, Alex—err, *Xander*. You, on the other hand, are a wildcard. A warped vigilante collecting pieces for your game until you have enough to take down the strongest of castles, aren't you?"

I shake my head, a mistake because it starts the world spinning.

"Why are you going after all the small chickens? You already have access to the big, fat, golden egg-laying hen! Your father holds the power and the money. Everything would have been handed over to you if you'd kept your head down instead of sucking on every rich prick you could find." He takes a few photos before releasing my head to check them. "You're doing everything the hard way, because you're an idiot."

"You should have kidnapped my aunt."

"She has security, or I would have." He pulls my computer out and sets it on the bed next to me. "Open your files and I'll give you—"

There's a sharp pain across my face and I try to keep my eyes open, but I can't. He swears at me as I pass out again.

My eyes don't respond when I try to open them. My arms weigh too much to lift them. My mind dips in and out of consciousness at intervals I can't discern, giving me limited function. The only constant is his voice, and that offers no comfort, only the promise of pain or darkness.

Or both.

Something flashes when I convince a sliver of my eye to open. It reminds me of the apartment and even the vague memory of mice offers comfort. I'd welcome one of those little bastards crawling over my foot right now, telling me this has all been a nightmare and I'm still back in Los Angeles. I force my eye to open more, and those hopes fly out the window. It's a flashing sign outside, but the writing isn't English. I haven't been this conscious since the limo.

A door opens quickly and slams shut, but I'm not sure if it's in the next room or ten floors away. I'm screaming at my body, begging it to move, but where the hell would I even go? My head falls to the side, and I find my backpack with all my things dumped out a few feet from me. The phone sits close enough to reach if I could just move my damn arms.

Footsteps grow louder and I slam my eyes shut, pretending to still be asleep when he stomps into the room, muttering to himself.

"You really screwed everything up, you prick." He comes closer, his hot breath on my back as he looms over me. "Why are you this big of a fuckup?! Why won't your father PAY ME?!"

Holding still when he yells unexpectedly isn't easy, but trying to fool him into thinking I'm passed out when his heavy boot connects with my ribs should earn me an Oscar. The second kick almost blows my cover when it forces the air from my lungs in a violent cough.

He's still, but the sound of his breathing tells me he's watching me, seeing if that woke me.

"Whiney little twat. You had everything, and you threw it away for what?" Oliver has gone back to rambling and starts pacing the room. "Maybe I should kill you? Dump your body in a river somewhere or drive you out to that forest and hang you from a tree. Who would question it? Who would care about you?"

He'd do it, and right now, I couldn't stop him. He's wrong, though, because people would care. Dani. Theo. Skylar. Melody. The names I keep repeating to myself whenever I can. The people I want to see again. They're what keeps me hanging on when there were a few times the darkness became a little too comfortable, a little too easy to slip deeper into.

"Oh, now there's an idea!" He rummages around in my things, but I don't dare open my eyes. He steps close again, gripping my hair and pulling my head up so violently, hot pain runs along my scalp and down my shoulders. He lets go and my head drops to the floor with a painful thump. "Well, look at that. Facial recognition still works, even with all those bruises. Guess it's used to you looking like this, isn't it?"

His footsteps head away from me, and I chance a look. He's on my phone. My heart races, hoping there's any kind of connection wherever we are. One phone call, one internet search, one read message. It won't take much for my aunt to find me, and he's said they know I'm missing, so she's looking.

"Useless," he whispers, dropping the phone on the floor and grabbing my laptop out of the backpack. He opens the lid and smirks, turning to face me again. I shut my eyes again, hoping he didn't notice. He slides over to me, climbing onto my back. That's when I realize I'm naked. His laughter turns my stomach and triggers fear to rush through my entire body.

"I'll miss having you around, but I've decided exactly what I'm going to do with you. Don't worry, you're going to love it. Well, you probably won't love not getting paid, but you'll be used, beaten, and thrown out with the trash when they're done with you. Just the way you like it."

He squeezes my neck and bites down on my ear until a trickle of warmth slips down my neck. I hear a zipper and feel tears I can't control anymore. "What do you say, Xander? Should we have one more tryst before I hand you over to the traffickers? Your videos should be enough to entice them, even though you're older than they usually like. Someone out there will want you." His body stiffens against me, then shudders.

"What the hell?"

He climbs off me and I risk opening my eyes. The strangest sensation of relief floods through me when I notice the screen on my phone light up with an incoming message before he grabs it, shoving it into the backpack with my computer.

"Stay here, not that you have much of a choice." He leaves, pulling the backpack on as he walks away.

HOLLYWOOD
Theo

CHAPTER 29

NOTHING BREAKS LIKE A HEART

DAMIANO DAVID

I SHOULD HAVE KNOWN BETTER than to get involved with Xander. But sometimes, the heart convinces you to take a shot you're guaranteed to miss reminding yourself life sucks and there's no escaping it.

I've left a few voicemails since he stopped answering my texts. I'm sure he's moved on, either finding someone better, or maybe his relationship with the girlfriend isn't as open as he led me to believe. I pick up my phone, stare at it for a few seconds, and set it back down again before I make a move for the kitchen. A few minutes later, and I have everything I need for an emergency baking session, now for the question I should ask myself. Is this for before or after the call? Or both?

Baggy purrs, wrapping herself between my legs like she senses my stress, which I'm sure she does. Although, she probably hopes I start stress baking now so she can get whatever falls on the floor. Sometimes, she thinks she's a dog.

Shit, even thinking about cats and dogs reminds me of Xander. I grab my phone again.

> Look, as a concerned neighbor, can you at
> least tell me you're okay?

My finger hovers over the send button, and finally, when I accept that the words aren't going to send themselves, I mash it and flip to the phone app. Sliding down through my contacts to the S names, remembering too late that I don't have her listed under Sylvie. She's listed under P for Pixie. It rings until her voicemail picks up, which I expected, and yet, I still don't have a message prepared, so I stumble through one.

"Salut, Pixie. Ça va? Look, I'm supposed to say I'm sorry. Marie already yelled at me, but you're an adult. I don't want to lie to you. I knew it was your birthday, and I didn't call. I made that choice. I, uhm, I figured you didn't want me to, and I wanted to respect your decisions. The problem is, now I feel like shit.

Sylvie, I miss you. I'm going to put this out there. I'm booking a flight, and this time I'm getting on the damn plane. I'll leave a week from tomorrow, which gives you time to think it over. If you want to see me, I'll be at the cafe at eight."

Je t'aime, Pixie. Even if you don't show. Always."

I toss the phone on the counter and lean against the sink in time to watch Baggy jump up next to me and beg for love. Or food.

"Yeah, it's stupid. I'm stupid. I'm screwing this up with both of them, aren't I?" I rub her ears, and she rumbles, pushing against my hand. "I mean, I'm doing the best I can, aren't I? No, you're right, I should have called her, and I should have left him alone. But...shit. Everything has blown up in my face." My phone buzzes and I'm too quick to snatch it up, only to see it's neither of the people I'm hoping for.

KENNEDY

Coffee this morning?

No, I'm taking my morning calls from home. Be there in a few hours.

Glancing over at the cooking supplies, I wave them off and go back to the couch to answer emails and check my schedule for the week. Before I get to that, though, I close the window with the flight information from Paris to Tokyo, and book my ticket to Paris for a week from today. I send a message to Kennedy to revise all my appointments that week from in person to online or reschedule them. Next, I shoot off an email to Marie to tell her I'll be in France and give her the dates in case our paths happen to cross.

There's a buzz from the kitchen, and when I glance over, I can make out the light of my cell phone. I'm sure it's Kennedy again. Just as I'm about to go back to my emails, it buzzes again, so I walk over to see if it's anything important.

Political ad junk. As I swipe to delete the message, my phone lights up with an unknown number, and I end up answering it accidentally.

"Uh, hello? Dr. Clay here."

"THEO! It's Xander," he slurs into the phone.

"Xander? What the hell, are you okay?" I thought I'd be upset with him, tell him he could have called or texted, maybe yell a little. But there's something off about the entire situation. As quickly as my emotions rocketed up to a high from hearing his voice again, they're now taking my stomach and plummeting down.

"I… I fucked up. I'm uhm, I'm sorry about not calling. I don't… I don't know where I am. A hotel I think? Fuck. I'm so sorry, I just, I searched for you online and found your office. I tried to call, but it was

the weekend, and then I had to beg the shit out of the girl who finally answered. Oh, weird story, I know her—anyhow, I just, uhm—"

"Xander, take a breath." The word baby desperately tries to fall out of my mouth, but I don't want to rock the boat. "Have you been drinking?"

"I'm sorry," the words crack, followed by a sniffle and sobs. *"I'm, uh, shit! Everything's gone wrong and...and I don't know what to do. I just—I needed to hear a voice and Beetle didn't pick up. I don't know where I am or when he's coming back. I can't think straight. I need someone to tell me it's going to be okay. She hates me. She's gonna leave me for this."*

"Xander, what happened? What's—" my voice drops, and without thinking, I go into therapy mode. "Xander, did someone hurt you? Did you meet up with someone while you were there?"

I've dealt with awful cases of abuse in my career, but I've always found a way to keep my personal opinions out of it, to take a step back and not get pulled down into that darkness. But asking Xander if he slept with someone else and let them use him again becomes a ten-inch serrated dagger I've plunged into my own gut and started twisting to see how it would feel.

The silence on the line knocks the wind out of me, and I slide down the cabinets and onto the kitchen floor. I need to keep my head, pull myself out of this and compartmentalize it. I prepared for this, didn't I?

"Theo, I...I don't think I...I'm scared," his words quaver until they break apart into a wail and I listen to him breakdown over the phone. *"I'm scared. I don't know where I am, and he drugged me. Shit! I hear him. He's back. I need to go! Don't call this number!"*

"Xander? Xander!" I shout into the phone, heart stuck firmly in my throat. "Xander? Hello?"

The call ends and I'm left with silence and questions.

"Good morning, Doctor Theo!" Kennedy's chipper voice reminds me of nails on a chalkboard this morning, I shouldn't have come in. "The weirdest thing happened this morning, like right after I texted you about coffee. I answered—"

"Kennedy, push my clients back. I'm busy and I'm not to be disturbed." I head for my office, stopping to turn back and add, "If anyone from Japan calls, you interrupt me, understand? Anyone! Otherwise—"

"You mean, anyone like Xander Maxwell?"

Weird story. I know her.

"Yes!" Wonderful, more questions to race through my mind. Kennedy and Xander are closer in age, but out of the millions of people in Los Angeles, I never thought the two of them would have a history. Before I can ask, the door opens, and my first client comes in.

"Oh, hey Doc. Am I early?"

"Yes, Parker, you're always early. Excuse me, I need a few minutes to get things in order," I tell him, and turn back to Kennedy with a whisper. "We need to talk after Parker. Try to reschedule what you can. Interrupt me if Xander calls, or anyone calls about him, understood?"

"Yes, sir." She gives me a salute.

She's never seen me like this, a hectic mess losing control. I've been on the phone with a police department in Tokyo who think I'm crazy. I've tried to call Alexis to see who she rented the apartment to and if she has any other contact information. Every time I try to call Xander's number, which has been about every two minutes, it goes straight to voicemail.

Don't call this number back!

In my office, I toss my bag next to my desk and head straight for the bathroom, splashing cold water on my face and taking deep breaths. Clients can't see me like this. I'm supposed to remain calm, steady. I cover my face with a towel and take one more deep breath in, holding it for an eight count, and slowly release it. When I open my eyes, I at least look less frazzled than I'm feeling. Now to get through the day without telling half of my patients to buck up and stop their bitching so I can go find my boyfriend.

Jesus, he's not even my boyfriend. Good luck, me. Today has gone straight to hell.

I place a quick call to a friend of mine to see if they can help, but I doubt I'll get far sending an American investigator a case based in Japan when I don't know a damn thing about Xander that's any help. An hour goes by, one client down and no interruptions. Kennedy messaged me a few minutes ago saying my next client agreed to reschedule. I settle in behind my desk, entering the name Xander Maxwell into the computer. Nothing helpful. I try the long form of his name, Alexander and—bingo! The screen fills with articles, pictures, videos, and blog links.

Also, holy shit.

Charles Alexander Maxwell. The son of billionaires Charles and Victoria Maxwell. Those names I've heard before, hell, anyone not living under a rock has heard of them. Xander shouldn't be sleeping on the floor of a cheap ass condo in the arts district. He should own the building while he lives in a damn castle. What the hell is going on?

There's a knock on the door and Kennedy pops in. "I'm going downstairs to grab lunch. Want anything?"

"How do you know him?"

"Dude, you need to switch to decaf if you're going to come at me like that. Who?"

"Xander. Alexander Maxwell. How the hell do you know him?"

"I used to chill with him, and I knew his girlfriend. She's tight with Steve, so I haven't seen either of them since that whole break up mess where I drove the car through the front window of Steve's gym. He dated Steve for a bit. Maybe they only fucked. I dunno."

"Steve?"

"My ex? Steve Jensen. Owns that big ass gym in the valley." My brain isn't making connections like it should right now, giving her nothing but a blank stare. "For shit's sake, doc. Go home. Steve and Chase Cooper are besties. Steve married the hockey player, bro, the cute one. Well, they're kind of all cute. I prefer the goalie. I should have banged him at that Halloween party instead of—"

"Kennedy!"

"Sorry! I've had way too much caffeine."

"Fine. Just focus for two minutes. Xander might be in trouble. Do you know how I can get a hold of anyone close to him? Are he and Chase close?"

"Nah, I don't think so. He spends most of his time with Dani. How do you know him?"

"Danny?"

"Yeah, Dani Silva," she says, like I should know who the hell she's talking about.

"Can you get me *Danny's* number, please?"

"Sure, hang on."

Some days I'm trapped in an old Abbott and Costello sketch comedy about baseball when I talk to Kennedy. She's a bright kid when she wants to be, but that's her biggest problem. She doesn't want to be.

While I wait, I call the US Consulate again and the police.

Neither of them knows anything about Alexander Maxwell, but they gave me the number to the Maxwell Corporation's Tokyo office, which I have, and called three times now. They keep blowing me off.

"Here you go. Dani and Xander are, like, always together." She pops her gum as I continue to stare at her. "Can I go get lunch now?"

"Yeah. In fact, you're free for the day. I'll pay you for the whole day, but you can cut out now. Leave the front door unlocked in case a patient comes by."

"Sweet, sure. Good luck finding Xander, he's a tricky bitch to pin down." She heads out the door, adding, "Call me if you can't reach Dani. I'll check with my ex, the dickhead."

She calls all her ex's dickheads, so that narrows nothing down. I need to figure out who this Danny guy is. I should have asked him more about his girlfriend, because just *Beetle* won't help me at all.

I continue to read about Xander, or Alex, as he's called in most articles. As I'm digging around, the front door opens, and the familiar sound of a vacuum cleaner fills the hallway. The cleaners mean it's well after six and I've fallen deep down the internet rabbit hole. I hurry to pack up my things, nod to the crew who smile and wave, and head home where I can continue this expedition. The entire ride home, I'm replaying everything that happened between us in my head. The furniture delivery, flight to Japan, business trip —all that makes more sense now than it did before, even though I didn't question it. The sleeping bag, cardboard boxes, and the thrift store couch? None of that makes any sense at all. I nailed the detail about the boarding school, though.

Who the hell is Danny?

When I get home, the counters still have stacks of cooking

supplies on them from this morning. I never got around to cooking a damn thing, getting lost in my head. I leave it for now and set up my laptop after I feed Baguette and grab a bottle of wine. And a second, just in case.

My phone rings when I'm almost on the couch, so I dump both bottles on the cushions and pray they don't slam together and break. Running across the room, I grab my satchel, digging my phone out in such a hurry that I don't look at the caller ID before I answer.

"Xander?" I yell, panting and hopeful. There's no response, and when I pull the phone away, I notice it's a text.

Maurice: Your daughter is in a cult. Call Marie.

I stare at the message on my phone, not quite sure how to react to news like that. Maurice is my father-in-law. He took in Sylvie when she decided to stay behind in France while I moved on and began a new life here in Los Angeles. Like Sylvie, I don't talk to Maurice much. He blames me for the death of his daughter and claims I took her down a road of debauchery, ruining her. He's a bitter old man, but he's been there for Sylvie when I wasn't.

Your daughter is in a cult. What the hell does he mean by a cult? Why did this have to happen now?!

As a therapist, I've coached people through escaping cults or dealing with their children or close family joining cults, but I never imagined I'd have to walk that path myself. I pull up my sister-in-law's number, pop in my earbuds, and press the call button as I head back to my computer.

"Hey Theo! How's your new man?"

"Hi Marie. Uhm, later?" My voice cracks, but I'm hoping she didn't notice. "Have you talked with your father lately? Or Sylvie?"

"No, not in a few days. I had business in Chicago and only got back to New York this morning, though, so what have I missed?"

I open a new tab on the browser and type my own daughter's name this time. "Maurice sent me a message. It said, and I quote, 'Your daughter is in a cult. Call Marie.' Nothing more."

"Shit. She's not in a cult. Papa doesn't like her new boyfriend, Luca. He's sweet! Young, attractive Italian boy, always talking about yoga, meditation, and those new age religious beliefs. But it's France, and he's Italian." She tells me what little she knows about him, more than I knew before. He's a musician, like Sylvie. She met Luca at university and they hit it off. Apparently, they've been dating for two years.

"Okay, well, if you happen to hear from her, can you let me know?"

"I will. Papa probably told her she can't see Luca anymore and when she fought back, he decided to take a leap off the deep end. You know how he can get. Are you still coming next week?"

"Maybe? Things here are—complicated. I don't want to bring my drama into her life when she already has enough of her own, by the sounds of it." I struggle to not add *again* to the end of that statement.

"Theo!" Marie catches me before I hang up. *"She's a good kid. Try to be here, okay? Let me know."*

"If she wants me there, I'll drop everything. I promise."

I end the call and stare at the phone, the computer, and the supplies in the kitchen. I don't want to bake; I want a drink and to get the hell out of the house. Everything in here reminds me of my dead partners, my daughter, or the man I'm falling for who might be in trouble a world away. No one will tell me anything, no one will even admit he's in Tokyo, missing, or even exists.

I grab my keys and go somewhere to clear my mind.

HOLLYWOOD
Dani

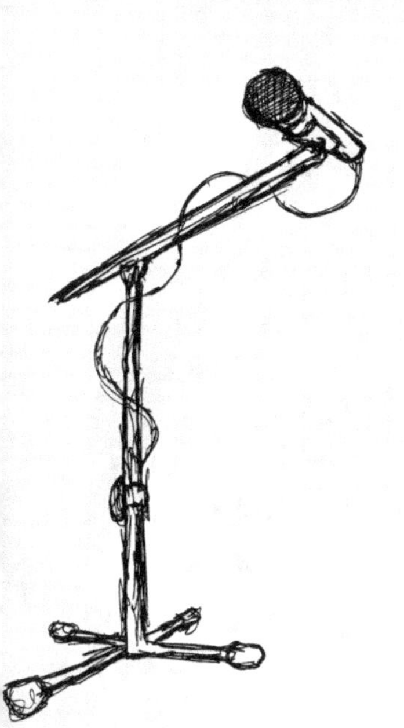

CHAPTER 30
CATCH THESE FISTS
WET LEG

I HAVEN'T BEEN 'HOME' yet, so I'm not sure what state Xander left the place. I'm not too concerned about it since he's not a slob, but that doesn't mean he didn't leave out a giant dildo, edible nighty, or a new pair of handcuffs for us to try out when he gets home. Not that the men I'm bringing over would even bat an eye at any of that, but I would. Sometimes Steve can forget about who I am, and I enjoy bursting the innocence bubble he puts around me when that happens.

"Okay, so, uhm, shield your eyes!" Neither one of them does. They only continue to stare at me as they hold the table I'm hoping to use for sewing. "FINE! I have no responsibility for the state of this apartment since I haven't seen it in like two weeks!"

I push the door open, and my jaw drops to the floor.

"Guess you might not need all this stuff after all?"

"I don't understand. Lexi said there wasn't any furniture, and there wasn't the other night. Just sleeping bags and boxes." I stare at the couch, and while it's not fresh from a showroom floor, it's still big and he shouldn't have spent that kind of money without me unless—I close the door and double check

the number. I lock and unlock the door. "Shit, this *is* my apartment!"

"Okay, open her back up. There's still some room and we can help you get things organized at least," Steve says as he directs Ethan and the desk inside. "We need to move some things around and make this place livable. Because right now, you've got a lovely warehouse chic going. Bravo."

"Whatever! I can't believe he did this! He knows we need the money for bills. We can't afford this!"

"Hey, maybe it's not as bad as you think!" Ethan tries to cheer me up as I drop onto the couch. At least it's comfortable. "I mean, look. This stuff isn't new, so maybe he got it at a good price? Like an estate sale or something?"

Estate sale. For whatever reason, those words slam into my brain and jar something loose. I hop up and open a few drawers before I run my fingers over the tops of a few items. When I spot the desk in the bedroom, I scream out. "I know this furniture!"

Steve and Ethan exchange a look before they glare at me. "Like, in an animated way? Do they come to life and sing about your dinner, or?"

"It's Xander's. Like from his old room."

"EW!" Steve pulls away from the dresser he's leaning against. "You've done dirty things on these!"

"Shut up, loser!"

Ethan's low whistle reminds me how short of a time he's known us. He takes the room in again and shakes his head before he punches Steve in the arm. "Maybe I went for the wrong jackass that night. This is expensive stuff. Since when is Xander loaded?"

"Oh, shut up!" Steve chides. "You're a multi-million-dollar hockey star and Dani's made him take some kind of weird vow of celibacy or some shit."

"Poverty," Ethan corrects, and Steve rolls his eyes.

"Not really," I correct the tall, blonde himbo and he shrugs it off. "I mean, I make us work for what we want, which he's cool with. Like, he doesn't take things from his parents and not pay for them. And yet, I guarantee he didn't pay for this shit."

Steve's goofy grin fades away as he takes my shoulder and looks me in the eye. "Dani, he's paid for every piece of this shit. It wasn't with money. Trust me. If anything, they owe him this ten times over for everything that happened in those schools they sent him to."

"I never thought of it like that."

Ethan hops on top of a table and makes a few suggestions about where the furniture should go. He's talking about maximizing the space and creating a natural flow while I'm having a mental breakdown over Xander, what Steve said about paying for it in other ways, and how I'm going to explain all of this to Sky when they get here. Steve knows me too well, though, and the next thing I know, I'm wrapped in his arms and swaying back and forth like a little kid dancing with their older brother or father. They're still talking and laying out my apartment, but at least I'm calming down.

"Look, sweetheart," Steve croons a few minutes later as he dries my eyes. "Sometimes, you gotta let the poor kid do his best. He did this to surprise you, to make sure you were coming home to more than empty spaces and that sleeping bag in the corner. It's from his old room, right? So how is that any different from us giving you our old stuff? Knowing his folks, they had it stuck in a storage unit somewhere collecting dust. It's recycling. If you're smart with it, give it some paint and upgrades, it's upcycling. And maybe you two can sell some of it."

"I'm just, I dunno. I'm losing it, Stevie," I sniffle loudly. "Skylar's hurting, and I can't fix them. Xander's doing shit that's going to get him into trouble, and this whole apartment thing. My sister still hasn't come home. The tour is so insane. I'm just—"

"Tired?" I nod. "Of course you are. You're putting everyone but you first. Empty pitchers can't fill other people's cups."

"What?" Ethan scoffs. "Jesus, Stevie. *You can't pour from an empty cup.*"

"Yeah, that's what I said! Now, help us get this shit organized. When we're done, we're going out to the bar, getting drunk, and the three of us will make out on the dance floor to whatever live band they booked until they kick us out." Steve whispers.

"We're not getting kicked out of another bar, Pumpkin," Ethan yells from somewhere in the bedroom.

"Watch me, asshat!" He smirks until something comes flying out towards him. He ducks out of the way and yells again, "I love you!"

My heart beats with the baseline of this song as another band rips the doors off the place and gives the crowd one hell of an intro. I've always been a fan of kicking the show off in the most epic way possible, and this has me wanting to move my body with the rest of the people who've come to the show early. By the time the set ends, I'm a dehydrated mess and I've lost Steve and Ethan. They're probably in the bathroom doing incredibly hot stuff to each other. Which makes me wish Xander was here.

Maybe it's time to make some bad decisions that I will possibly regret when I wake up in the morning. There's no better place to start than the bar. A few people in the audience recognize me from the viral video, and I'm stopped for pictures and autographs on the way to quench my thirst—that shit will never get old, no matter what Coop says. I love being recognized, sharing the love of music, and feeling the excitement radiating off our fans. It fuels my creativity, satiates the extrovert in me, and gives me the energy I need when I hit the stage. I haven't been giving myself any love lately and I needed this.

"Hey, Racket!" I yell as I run to the bar and jump up to give the bartender a hug. It's not the easiest maneuver, but I'm not letting a bar get between us. Racket has saved my ass from creepers, played the wingman for both Xander and me, and of course, always given me a strong pour. "I didn't know you'd be here tonight!"

"Of course I'm here! The money doesn't suck and, eventually, the music will be okay, too."

"Eventually? Those guys were pretty good!"

"Nah, they ain't got shit on you guys." He doesn't ask what I want, putting down a bottle and filling a shot glass next to it as we talk. "Where's the boy toy? I hardly ever see you without him, unless you're on a split again. In which case, should I be looking out for numbers?"

"He's… on a trip. And for once, I don't think I should get numbers tonight. Stevie and Ethan are here. They'll give me shit for it. Plus, Conner messed up my phone."

"Your ancient phone? Get a new one. You replace bassists more than you do phones." He slides my drinks over. "Tell Sky I said Hey, I caught that video of them at the show."

"They're gonna be playing with us, and I don't only mean the band." I give him the best wink I've got, which sucks.

"Girl, you got a wild life, you know that? Never change."

I make a show of glancing down the bar, surprised when I land on someone. He looks familiar, and he's brooding, which means he's my type. Broad shoulders, powerful hands, and there's something about that salt and pepper hair giving me all the right vibes. "Uh, hold that thought on the numbers."

He follows my stare and laughs, slipping into a terrible Australian accent. "Cricky, even when not on the hunt, the mantis has spotted her prey. This member of a particularly rare and elusive Silver Haired Brooder species appears lost, drawn away from his herd of elder millennials that would protect him from her punk rock princess style. The huntress can't ignore the instinctual pull to mate with the creature in the darkest corners of her inner sanctum. Will he be capable of evading her attempts and cry it out at home, alone? Or will the power of the mantis prove too strong, as she rips his head clean off after mating, leaving me a mess in the back room?"

"Dude, you have got to lay off the nature channel. Seriously. And I have NEVER left you a mess. Prick." I lick my bottom lip before pulling it through my teeth. It helps me think. I'm a little out of my element. Older guys are more Xander's thing. If he were here, he'd stalk this prey with me, and it would be all over for this poor guy, like Racket said. It's not like I'm going to bang the guy, just some making out and dancing. "Send him a drink."

"Yes, ma'am!"

I push my boobs up as I watch Racket pour a Jack and Ginger and head over to the guy who hasn't even raised his head to look around. How does anyone do that? Sit in a bar full of raucous bands and fans without being swept up in the commotion and camaraderie? My brain cannot wrap around that idea, which is part of why I'm drawn to him. He's a mystery, a puzzle box, a thing I need to take apart while he takes me apart.

Confusion lines his face when the drink slides in front of him, and he looks down the bar at me. There's interest. I'd be lying if I said I didn't squeeze my legs together as he stood up from his barstool. He's taller than Xander, shorter than Skylar, and he might beat Skylar in an arm-wrestling competition. Which I'd pay to watch.

"I'm told I have you to thank for trying to get me drunk?" His velvet laced voice has me hooked already. He reaches out and puts the drink on the bar, and I get a look at his tattooed forearms. The ink goes further up, but he's wearing long sleeves, and they're only rolled up so far. That's when I notice he's wearing a dress shirt. And a vest.

A dad? At a rock show? "You look familiar, but—"

He shakes his head with a deep, dark laugh. It's sexy as hell. "We met once, last year. I'm surprised you remember at all"

"Last year?" I squint harder and lean in. The smell of cinnamon and a freshly opened barrel of expensive whiskey surround me. "Did we fu—Wait! I do remember you! You were a judge at that St. Patrick's battle!"

"A last-minute addition when the original judge called out sick." He smiles, but it's forced. "I, uhm, had hoped your band would win. Sorry it didn't work out. You were good."

"*Were*? Baby, we *are* good! Besides, that got us a gig that paid pretty well." I laugh and touch his arm, feeling his muscles tense and quickly relax. "Here to judge more bands?"

"Drowning the sorrows of the day." He takes a drink, licking his lips with a deliberate slowness. "It's fortuitous to meet you here, though. You made a lifelong fan of me that night." I get the sense he's hiding something. Maybe he's a serial killer and I'm his next victim, but I'm not getting the murder-y vibes from him. Famous last words.

"Fortuitous, eh?" I cock my head to the side. "Then why do you look so bored?"

I have this sudden urge to know more, to get inside his head, to find his broken bits and put him back together. My curse in life. I can spot broken men with deadly accuracy, but I can't keep myself away from them once I find them. It's why I never became a therapist.

"Troubled mind. The atmosphere helped improve my mood over the last few minutes."

"It's the drink, isn't it?"

"It's the company, too. You're easy to talk to."

"Yeah, I have that effect on people. Bringing out the party in everyone and everything. The Midas touch of fun." I reach out and run a hand down the buttons of his vest. "I like your look. Not a lot of guys show up to these straight from their day jobs, and those that do, don't have the hot professor look going for them. In fact, if you added glasses, I don't think I'd be able to resist you."

Without a word, he reaches into an inner pocket of his vest and slips on a pair of black-framed glasses, completing the nerdy professor illusion. I can't stop myself from imagining being sandwiched between him and Xander. "You're the second person in the last few weeks to tell me I look like a professor. Although, I'm not convinced it's a compliment."

He tips back his drink before sliding the empty glass across the bar, nodding to Racket for another. He turns to face me, dark hazel eyes staring into my soul. Fuck. Me. I may have been wrong about the *not having sex at the club tonight* thing.

"Do you believe in fate?" He asks.

"Is this about to be a bad pickup line?"

"Not intentionally. I hope I don't come off as a creep, but it's possible I was meant to come here tonight. To see you." He chuckles and shakes his head. "Yeah, that sounded better in my head. I meant talking to you, nothing more. It's helping my mood."

I'm trying to tamp down the warning bells going off,

reminding me of all the true crime I listen to that say he could be a stalker or worse. Can someone be too hot to be a murderer? No, people thought Ted Bundy was hot. "Wait, how many names do you have?"

"Names?"

"Like, do you have a serial killer middle name? John Wayne Gayce? Mark David Chapman? Teddy Bobby Bundy?"

He laughs, a deep, real laugh this time. "You know way too much about serial killers. I've also never heard him called *Teddy Bobby* before. But no, I don't have a middle name. I'm Theo."

"Nice to meet you, Theo." I take the hand he offers and go to shake it, but he turns my hand over and kisses my knuckles instead. He's good, and he's gonna murder me one way or another if I sneak him backstage. "So, what's with the brooding?"

"Ah, you don't want to hear all that shit."

"Hey, maybe it will inspire a song. Who knows!"

He nods, flashing me a beautiful, but sad, smile. "Well, I met someone and thought we hit it off. Today he called me. He sounded drunk, and he didn't make any sense. Sent me into a tailspin, but now I can't reach him. I also forgot my daughter's birthday. More like avoided since she doesn't talk to me anymore. We've fallen too far apart." He swirls his drink. "Sorry to trauma dump on you. Guess I needed to get it out."

"Yikes, that's rough." I take another drink, deciding how to unpack that. "I hate the drunk calls; it puts too many doubts in your head! Like, should you trust what they're saying? Are they playing a cruel joke? Does it make them an asshole?"

"Or, the worst possibility of all, they didn't even like you to begin with."

"Ugh! Seriously." I shake my head and get an idea. "You know how you get past drunken gaslighting? Dancing."

"I'm not really—"

"It wasn't a request."

He gulps down his drink and I wink at Racket before leading the mysterious man out into the buzzing hornets' nest. This is punk music. Most people thrash and jump around, starting a mosh pit that borders on a mindless mob. Those people enjoy the music, but they don't live the music. They don't welcome it into their body and soul, willing it to take over.

I close my eyes as the singer's dark, raspy voice fills the room, letting myself go. Vaguely curious if Theo stands there like a confused weirdo or if he—the large hands on my hips answer that question, as he presses his fingers into my skin and follows my lead.

HOLLYWOOD
Xander

"XANDER?" The voice breaks through the storm in my mind, but not enough to wake me. "Come on, Bug, wake up for me. Please? Xander!" My body shifts and I force my eyes open, but they're struggling to stay that way. Like quicksand, the harder I struggle to wake up, the deeper into the nightmare I fall.

"Oh bug, what have they done to you?" It's my aunt's voice. A moment later, she kisses my head and whispers, "Sorry about this, you can pay me back for it later."

The sensation of drowning in a frozen pond does the trick, and I sit straight up, gasping for air as icy water drips from my forehead. I wipe the water from my eyes and glance around the room. I'm on the floor with a corded phone in my hand.

"What…how did I get here?"

"Come on, we'll figure that out later. I need to get you out of here. Now." She rummages around, throwing clothes that aren't mine in my direction. I glance around, hoping for some sense of familiarity, but my brain only sends signals to run. Get out.

"Where am I?"

"We've been looking for you for a week. A week, Xander. Your father has losing his mind. What happened?"

"I don't... I don't remember..." I'm still not fully awake, still trapped with one foot in the world of darkness that likes me a little too much to let go. But I remember there's something important about my backpack.

"Later, clothes, baby, now!"

I glance down. *Why am I naked?* If panic didn't have control of my brain right now, embarrassment would, but I don't even care at this point. I'm a tapestry of bruises, dried blood, and cuts, but I don't remember how I got them. Every time I move, pain shoots through my entire body. Melody helps me off the ground and pulls a pair of jeans on me as I wince and whine.

"How did you get here? Did you see who did this?" She's asked questions since I woke up, and I don't have an answer for any of them.

I flail around, pulling the comforter from the bed, searching everywhere and finding nothing. I drunkenly stumble around the room, checking the closet, drawers, and bathroom. No backpack.

"Xander! We need to go!"

"What the hell is going on, Melody? Where am I?"

"You're in a shitty hotel in an area of town that didn't even exist to me yesterday, Xander. Your father wasn't sure if it was a kidnapping or a sick joke you played as payback. You turned on your phone, that's how we found you."

"My...phone?" A spike goes through my head, and I grab my face, dropping to my knees.

"I've got you, bug." Melody holds me until the screaming stops. My screaming. "Oliver said you were having headaches, what are you on? What did you take, Xander?"

"Oliver?" There's something wrong with her face, like she wants to smack me but hug me at the same time.

"Yes, he saw you last, so security questioned him. He said

you had him drop you off at a bar and he hasn't seen you since." She bites her lip, and I shake my head as she whispers, "He said you were going there to...to meet a man. To...Xander, why do you let them do that to you?"

I search around the room again, slower this time. Condom wrappers. Empty bottles of wine and alcohol. I can stop shaking when my eyes land on the empty bed frame and the mattress ripped off of it and left on the floor. I don't want to remember, but I have to.

"Oliver. I remember. It was him, he... he..." I grab my head, pressing the sides with the heels of my hands as hard as I can to squeeze the memories out of my brain.

"That's not possible, Xander. Oliver said—"

"I can't remember—No, it was him. He did things..." I don't recognize my own voice. Even as a child, I never had this much fear, this much pain laced into it. I've never begged like I'm begging her now. "Please, don't make me remember."

"What did you take, Xander? I need to call a doctor. You're covered in bruises and—"

I turn and grab her shoulders, begging her to listen to me. "I didn't take anything! I swear! I left dad's office and I...I..."

I try to remember, too much static in my brain makes it difficult and my mind wants to protect me from whatever happened over the last week. When I go to scratch the itch on my hand, I find Theo's words.

You. Deserve. Better.

You have them on your face, too?

"Tattoos. I got a tattoo. Oliver found me a tattoo place. We were there for like an hour, tops! The guy kept feeding sake to Oliver until he couldn't walk straight. When we got in the limo. He asked me about... my tattoos. The job."

I grind my teeth together, struggling to bring more memories back.

"He…He knew about Dani and…Theo…but it goes blank. I can't remember. He showed me a mini bar. He gave me whiskey and pills for my head. I remember the floor, watching him take my backpack. He took my computer."

I can't find anger in her face about what Oliver did, only pity. She doesn't believe me, and that's a punch right to the gut. Like Dani, I don't lie to Melody. I may not tell her everything, but I don't lie to her. Whatever Oliver's done or said has made her question me.

"Sweetheart, Oliver claims you seduced him, got him drunk, and…took video of him as blackmail. You forced him to take you to meet some man."

"No. No, that didn't happen. I'm not lying, Melody. He handed me a drink and the next thing I remember, you're tossing a bucket of ice water at me! He gave me pills for my headache."

"Grab whatever you need. I'm taking you to the airport."

"Airport? No, someone needs to go after Oliver!"

"I need to get you home, Xander. Safely." She strokes my face and her eyes well with tears. "We saw what you were letting those men do to you, what you were doing to yourself, what you did with Oliver. Your father broke down and went into a rage. I didn't see it had gotten this bad, Bug. If you can't tell me the name of the client you met, I understand. But we need to get you home."

"He…saw?" I stumble into a chair. The possibility of my parents finding out always existed, but they weren't supposed to. Knowing they've seen it, seen how depraved I get, that's not something parents should see. Even if they are shitty parents.

"I'll get the jet cleared to take off and—"

"I can't. The backpack has my computer, my ID, and my passport. I don't have anything."

"How did you get so careless?" She pulls her phone out and taps rapidly before handing it to me. It's this room. Oliver. Me. Quick, jerky cuts and…

"No. No, this didn't happen. He…" Flashes come back, hitting me like a truck. "Hands. Men. They tied me up. They—" I sprint for the bathroom. When I'm done retching, I close my eyes and focus.

Dani. Theo. Skylar. Dani. Theo. Skylar.

I need to get back home.

I repeat the mantra that kept me alive. When I open my eyes again, I get up and stumble to the other room, pulling on a t-shirt and keeping my head down I don't want to think about what did, didn't, or might have happened. I can't stop shaking. I can't catch my breath. They'll believe me, even if no one here does.

"Oh, Bug. What did they do to you?" She marches across the room, digging her phone out of her purse and unlocking it before holding it to her ear.

"Alec, I want you to keep Oliver in the building. Search his room for a backpack with my nephew's things in it or anything else that he shouldn't have. Search his car, his house, everything, understand?" There's a pause while she glances around the room and lowers her voice. "Check for used condoms, wrappers, anything of the sort while you're at it. Anything with DNA. Pictures of everything and bag it up. Do the same in this room. Do not involve the local police in this until I say."

When she hangs up, she stands in front of me and holds her arms out. I fall into them, letting her perfume take over my senses. "I'm sorry, Xander. I'm so sorry. I just, the videos, they broke me and I… I'm sorry. Come on, I'll get you somewhere safe until we can figure this out."

I've gone over what I can remember as many times as I've traced the tattoo on my hand. Bits and pieces coming back, but nothing I can grab and hold, nothing I can make stick. I want to scream. I've worked myself into at least three panic attacks since I've been stuck here in this hospital room, and I'm not even sure how long I've been in here. Ten minutes? An hour? Most of the day? I'm fighting my own mind, trying to remember and not sure I want to remember.

The handle on the door jiggles, and I watch my aunt and one of her buff as hell security dudes walk into the room, locking the door behind them. Melody drops a plastic bag on the table before walking around the bed and cupping my face to stare into my eyes.

"How are you, Bug?" She wipes the tear streaks from my cheek. "I'm working on getting a hold of Dani, but I also want you to get checked out by a doctor I trust, okay? Oh, and I brought some food. Nothing too crazy, some rice and steamed vegetables until you're sure you can stomach more."

I nod and glance over at the guy still guarding the door. It takes me a minute to register that he's holding a bag. My bag.

"You found it!" I take a closer look. "What the hell happened to it?"

"We found it about a block from the hotel where you were. At the edge of a pond. Your phone and a few other things were inside, they're getting cleaned up now, but I've brought a temporary phone in case we can't get yours working again. No laptop, though, and no passport." She takes the bag from the guard and walks it over to me. She pulls out my glasses and slides them on me. The world coming back into focus makes me a little nauseous for a minute since it's been out of focus for too long.

"I need to call Dani."

"You do. I spoke to her earlier while you were resting, and I've told her what happened. Well, some of it. I offered to fly her out here—"

"No! No, she… she can't. I don't want her to see me. Not like this. She needs to stay there, she's on tour."

She nods, holding my hand. "Do you remember anything else? Has anyone threatened you recently?"

"Seriously? Damn, Melody, I'm a gay sex worker. I get threats almost daily. Someone has threatened me my whole stupid life, and take a guess who most of the threats come from? Your people! They tell me I better keep my mouth shut about what they did to me. A week later, they're telling me when and where to meet them next so they can do it again." I grab the bag and fling it across the room, watching it slosh against a wall and fall with a sick, wet sound.

It started in high school out of something I could loosely call necessity. I needed to get the hell out of that private school, away from their cult. The fastest way for that to happen involved getting caught with my mouth around a star athlete's cock. I'd already done that plenty of times. Of course, I wanted the guarantee that I'd have some leverage after getting caught, so I made sure the coach joined us, too. Nothing like the school's biggest donors walking in and catching my cute self getting spit roasted in the locker room. Funny how they walked in right when I needed them to.

When the kids' family, the school, and the coach paid my family off to keep everything covered up, I learned I could use sex as both a weapon and a suit of armor. I learned secrets are both dangerous and expensive when they involve the right people. I should have also seen that my parents allowed that cover up to happen rather than believing me, finding me help, or standing up for me. Theo had it right, and I chose not to see it until now.

"You need to tell me everything, Xander. It's been difficult for you since you were young—"

"Difficult? I've been stripped naked and shoved in lockers, beaten, spat on, and forced to do shit to stay alive because of rich assholes! And this time? They drugged me and Oliver let them… he let them ra—" I stop, unable to say the word. "Melody, I'm not one of them, and they can tell. They smell it on me. I'm not one of their cult members, so I'm expendable. I'm trash." My fists ball up. I want to find Oliver and end him with my bare hands.

"I'm so sorry, Xander. I should have noticed."

The laughter takes a moment to build, but then I can't stop it. "Someone knew. But that doesn't matter because I embraced it. I have so much dirt on every one of those bastards. I hope everything on that laptop gets out. Every shred of it. Every video of some multi-billion-dollar CEO with their cock in *my* mouth." Tears stream down my face and my voice wavers, but I can't stop. I need to get this out. "Every picture of them on top of *me* instead of their wives. Every single god damn image of what they did to me when they were done. Every bruise and busted lip Dani cleaned for me. I didn't give two shits about the money. That's why I never told Dani. Revenge, Aunt Melody. Revenge against every pompous prick hiding behind their stacks of cash and lawyers. That's why I did it, and I'd do it all again."

My nostrils flair as I stare down at her, showing her the dark side of me I've never let her see before. The side Theo uncovered after one night, hell, after less than five damn minutes. No one in my family understands. How could they? They don't see me. They're just like the boys at school, I'm nothing to them. Disposable. Replaceable.

A man comes into the room and whispers something to Melody, handing her a tablet. She turns it around so I can see a still frame of the video she showed me earlier. "What is this?" She asks, pointing to something in the upper corner.

"I don't know." I cross my arms dismissively, done with this shit.

"Xander, stop being like that. This isn't the hotel room."

I grab the tablet and stare at the screen. When I zoom out to see the full frame, my head cocks to the side. "What the shit?" I switch over to a browser, and Melody watches as I open the subscription site I'm part of. I flip through thumbnail after thumbnail of videos in search of a specific one.

"Did any of them ever threaten you?"

"Melody," my voice barely whispers now as I concentrate. "I'm thirty years old, and I've been doing this shit since I was sixteen. Twice in fourteen years I've been with a man who didn't attack me—physically, verbally, or legally—after we were done. *Twice*. If you don't believe me, ask Dani. She's covered and uncovered enough of the injuries to help me hide them from my parents. They all threaten me eventually."

"She didn't stop you?"

I stop scrolling, glancing down at my hand. Theo's words. "I thought I deserved it. That's all I knew, Melody," I explain as my eyes and fingers get to work again. "You saw how cold my entire childhood was. You tried to warm it up, but that wasn't enough. My screwing around and getting smacked around caused about ninety percent of the breakups between Dani and I and— FOUND IT!" I play the video, scrubbing through it until I find what I'm looking for. It's the exact background from the still Melody showed me. "He edited it. He found the videos that would work and edited his own sick shit into it. That's part of why he needed my computer, to get to the unedited video."

"But—"

"He doesn't care who else I have evidence of, Melody, he wants Dad. It's some revenge plot of his own, he called him the goose that lays golden eggs or whatever. He kept telling me I'd gone after the wrong people."

There's a knock at the door and the security detail escorts a middle-aged man with a bag into the room.

"Dr. Hayashi, thank you for coming," my aunt greets him before pulling him to the other side of the room to talk in whispers. While they talk, the security guy comes over next to me and hands me a phone. It's not my phone, so I don't take it right away, but he pushes it into my hand.

"It's a burner. Untraceable. Your aunt arranged for it until we can get your phone back up and checked out. She didn't share the number with anyone."

I grab it, turning it on and punching in Dani's number. Voicemail. "Beetle, uhm, it's me. I just… I miss you and I love you. I'm okay. Maybe. I'll call you back later. Don't trust anyone, especially my parents or any fuckwad named Oliver."

I hang up, not caring how cryptic that would sound.

"Xander, Dr. Hayashi wants to check you out and test your blood, make sure whatever he used has cleared your system." I'm still stunned that she believes me, my parents wouldn't have listened to any of this. "Xander, do you want him to run a—"

"Don't." I drop my head, shaking it and turning away.

"You're sure?"

I don't answer. If they do a kit, it makes it real. I can't go through that, not without Dani. I also don't want them telling me how many there were. Melody hugs me again, tears in both our eyes now.

"He'll take good care of you, Bug. I'm going to make some calls and get that video analyzed and figure it out. If you need anything, I'll be right outside with security. No one will hurt you now. Not again."

HOLLYWOOD
Skylar

CHAPTER 32
BONNIE AND CLYDE
RED LEATHER

I SNEAK INTO THE BEDROOM, making sure the door doesn't make a sound when I shut it. I even tuck the phone under my shirt to dull the light of the screen while I find my way to the bed, where Dani snores loudly. It's cute, and she only does that when she's drunk. Pulling the covers back only enough to slip in next to her, I kiss the side of her head and lay down to stare at the ceiling in the hopes that I'll sleep.

Dani rolls over, throwing her arm over my chest and nuzzling into my arm.

"Did you two have fun?" She mumbles.

"Yeah."

"What'd you do?"

"Uhm, don't worry about it, go back to sleep."

Her head pops up like a prairie dog, it's too dark to see anything but the silhouette of wild messy hair sticking out everywhere but my imagination fills in the gaps. I bet her makeup is still on but smeared to give her that cute raccoon appearance. I'm also guessing she's squinting at me, trying to make out my expression in the dark. I can't hold back the laughter over the mental image.

"Okay, see, I wanted to go back to sleep until you told me to not worry about it and decided to laugh at me. What am I not to worry about? Why are you laughing?"

I crane my neck, nudging her nose with mine before tenderly kissing her. She's been at the bar, I can taste the whiskey behind the mouthwash. "How did it go today with Stevie?"

"You're changing the subject."

"Mmhmm." I reach over, letting my hand find her skin under the blanket and following it up her body. Some people won't mess around unless it's dark in the room because they're ashamed of their bodies. After the accident, I insisted on it, not wanting to see the disgust in Steve's eyes when he got to my scars. It didn't take long for me to understand how stupid that was. In the dark, people notice things they wouldn't with the lights on. Like how I'm focusing on my rough skin and scarred body, worried she's disgusted every time she touches me. I should focus on her body, smooth and warm against me.

"Why are you changing the subject?" She asks, her hand sliding up my chest. "Why are you shaking?"

"What are you worried about, Beetle?"

"Oh, I dunno. My incredibly hot and sexually fluid bedmate telling me not to worry when he's gone off and spent hours with my incredibly hot idiot of a bestie and didn't even invite me to watch?"

"Bedmate?" I pull back, wishing I could see her better. "Is that all—"

"No! I didn't want you freak out. And we hadn't talked about what to call each other."

"Do we need titles?" I kiss her again, slower and deeper. She lets out an adorable groan when I pull away again. "Can't we just *be*? Exist in each other's orbits without worrying about what people think we are or aren't? We're two people, exploring the universes in each other's eyes as our souls fuse together."

"That's a lot to say. Especially when I just call Xander my boyfriend. How about calling you my partner? Too old west or a nineties buddy cop movie? Yeah, it makes you sound like you need a cowboy hat or a slobbery dog or something."

"Yeehaw," I laugh, holding her hand as it stops over my heart. "Daniella, I don't care, really, as long as you call me yours. And you're welcome to come and watch Chase and I tomorrow," I reply, pulling her on top of me. She giggles, but it's cut short when I shift and groan in pain.

"Skylar? What's wrong?"

"It's…nothing. I'm a little sore. Been a while since I went that hard. Does a number on my back."

"Stop! Did you—"

"Spend a few hours in the gym trying to one up each other while going over the plan to keep me from slipping? Cause if that's what you were going to ask, yes. If you were going to ask if I bent his cute ass over the bench and took that man's innocence. No. Not that I could anyhow."

"You were working out this whole time? Wait, what did you mean? The last bit? About Coop's ass?"

"Daniella, you're so crass sometimes—it makes me hard," I giggle, tickling her ribs.

"Stop! Wait, did Steve? Come on! Who was it?"

"You wanna know?"

"Yes! I wanna know who took that straight as an arrow man's booty v-card!" She wiggles her ass and leans in close. We're not going to sleep anytime soon.

"Well, how do I put this?" I waffle between shock or tact. Shock will get me smacked, and maybe I want that right now. "Okay, your sister tied him up and pegged him in a hotel."

She sits straight up, hands on my chest to balance herself. Instead of waiting for her questions, I roll us both over, spreading her legs wide before I push her panties to the side. She sleeps in a big t-shirt and panties, I find that a million times sexier than naked. My fingertip dips inside, sliding through her until she shivers. Dani isn't patient when it comes to sex, moving her hips to try to push me deeper. But I don't let her have what she wants. I prefer to tease her until she's a mumbling mess.

"Careful, Beetle. I don't want you coming apart until I tell you it's time."

"You're a tease. Who told you they did that?"

"Chase told me. He told me all about her little bag of toys and how they went to some hotel in the middle of nowhere." I tease her clit with the pad of my thumb, slipping two fingers into her while I talk. "He talked about her strap-on and how she made him suck it, how she much he begged her to fuck his throat and called him a good boy. How much he liked it."

"Keep talking!" She moans, nails dragging down my back. "Details."

"Details?"

"Whatever, make them up, I don't care. Don't stop talking about it!" She demands.

"Are…you fantasizing about Coop while I've got my fingers inside you?"

"Oh, because you won't when I get a dildo and shove it in your ass?"

"Fair. Do you promise?" I curl my fingers, stroking them against her g-spot.

"Yes! God, yes! More!"

"I've got a better idea, how about a different fantasy? One that could happen. One with you, on your back, and my head between your thighs." I kiss her bare stomach where her shirt has pulled up. "Xander behind me with his thick cock in his hand."

Her head rocks back as I work my tongue up her torso, nudging my way under her shirt to those perky little tits of hers. I swirl my tongue over her nipple, and it hardens to my touch. I pump into her harder and faster, listening to her moan and the beautiful sounds her wet cunt makes for me. I've put the picture of Xander in her head and she's running wild with it.

My fingers slip out of her, but before she can bitch about it, I flip her over, pressing against her ass. "I'm imagining us on stage as an entire arena of people watch me strip you naked and take you from behind while Xander devours your sweet pussy." I swirl my wet fingers over her clit, pinching her nipples with the other hand.

"Oh GOD! I need you! Please, Skylar? Pleaaase?"

I run my fingers through her wetness again, bringing my fingers to her lips and pushing them into her mouth. She sucks them clean, sliding her tongue over them while I rut against her ass. I'm desperate to be inside her, let her warmth surround me. I hold her still, letting my shaft slide through her slickness as I bite along her neck and back.

"Spread your legs and keep your ass up for me." Once she's in position, I lean over and spit on her tight hole, sliding my tongue over the puckered skin while I strum her clit. "Remember to breathe, Daniella."

"Skylar, I've… I…" I press a finger into her, and she screams out, back bowing and nails dragging down the bed.

"Good girl. It won't be tonight, but someday soon, you're going to beg me to bury myself in this perfect ass. Xander and I will fill you up until you're drunk on our cocks and praying to us." I push deeper into her, letting her stretch around me.

"You're too big for that. Oh god. Oh my god! Please!"

"See? Already begging for it. But I need your mouth tonight, Beetle. I want you to play with yourself until you can't take it anymore while you choke on my cock. I want your tongue sliding over these piercings, while you're on your knees, praying for me to let you cum. I want your cunt soaking wet before I spread your legs wide and listen to you beg to your god."

"S-Sklyar? You are my god!"

"You say that now, but when I'm done with you, you'll believe it in your soul." I tease her entrance with the tip of my cock, desperate to be inside her no matter how much pain I'm in. She's my drug, she'll help me forget. "Say my name, Dani."

"Sky!"

I pull out and she reaches for me, clawing at my arms. "Say my name, Dani."

"Skylar!"

My hand wraps around her neck as I tease her with only the tip, watching it drive her to the brink. I squeeze herder, and she screams for me. "OH GOD! SKYLAR! MY GOD, MY DARK DEITY, MY SAVIOR! PLEASE!"

"Please what?"

"Ruin me. Claim me. Please, use me."

I thrust into her and the oxygen leaves the room for a moment of painful bliss. She sucks in a shattered breath and arches her back. Nails rake down my arms as she gasps and begs for me. My tongue laps at the sweet sweat beading on the skin of her neck. I lean back and my hand comes down in a crack, timed to my next thrust. Now it's my voice singing her praise in the dark.

I don't have long before my back will give out, but when she cries out, I can't say no. I bite back the pain, keeping it out of my voice as I thrust into her.

"Come for me, Beetle. Come all over my cock, soak the bed

for me, love." I'm holding back. I'm coming apart at the seams, listening to my name on her lips while she squeezes me in her vise. I smack her round ass again, leaving an angry red print I wish I could see, and it sends her rocketing into space, her whole body shaking as she drips down my thighs.

"Good girl." I whisper to her as she comes back to the real world. I climb off the bed, hiding the pain in every movement until I stand upright, and the pressure fades. "Now get on your knees and open your mouth. Your blasphemy has only just begun."

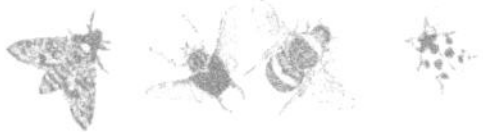

"If Skylar wanted something to sink his teeth into, I could have made some dinner before they went to bed last night," Coop says when Dani walks into the kitchen, lifting the steaming cup to his lips as he reads his tablet.

"Huh?" Dani asks, eyes bouncing between the two of us. I pour my coffee and keep my head down, joining Coop at the table. Dani spins around, finding her reflection in the door of the fridge and gasps. The perfect, clear bite marks on her neck are a beautiful combination of horrifying and incredibly hot.

"You *marked* me!"

"Yeah, I'm not gonna pretend I'm not a little jealous." Coop answers before I can. "Your sister has left a few—"

"COOPER! I already heard about what she did to your ass, I don't need to hear about the rest of you."

Coop spits his coffee across the table, choking on it as he laughs, and wipes up the mess. "Jesus, really? Now I gotta change. Maybe I should take back that new phone I got you after that bullshit? Don't let Connor drop it in any more beer tubs, okay?"

"Aww, you're the best." She flips him off, then blows him a kiss.

"When are you two asshats leaving? Not that I don't love having you here and all."

"In a few hours. Now that we have furniture, I figured we'd get some groceries and lock ourselves in the apartment until we leave again," Dani explains, getting her own cup of coffee and a replacement for Coop's. She hands me a bottle of pills. "I already called a nursing hotline; you can take these. They'll help your back so you can stop pretending you're okay."

"Thanks, Beetle," I kiss her cheek as she leans over.

"Good, some peace and quiet tonight. Although, damn, you two were putting on a show last night."

"I thought you soundproofed your room!?"

"It is," he smirks, but doesn't hold it, sighing. "But I sleep in the loft now. The bedroom is too empty without your sister." He looks out at the pool to hide the glisten in his blue eyes. "Do you want to leave your bike here, Sky? Probably safer than street parking."

I nod, but they're too busy flipping each other off. I swear they both become eight-year-olds when they're together. I duck out long enough to get Dani's new phone and start setting it up for her. Once it's ready, the missed messages hit. Ten missed calls from an unknown caller, a few from Steve, and one from Connor.

"Something wrong?" I ask when her face scrunches up.

"Yeah, I'm pretty sure I didn't give my number to the guy I made out with last night. But I have like a million missed calls."

"Sounds clingy," I reply, scrolling through the social media feed on my phone. With a laugh, I turn the phone around and show Dani a picture of herself hanging all over some guy at a bar. Even without seeing his face, he looks familiar. "This guy?"

"Yeah, him. Dark and broody with this whole professor thing going on. Made me wish I had a skirt and a yardstick." She winks at me when I adjust my position after picturing her bent over and waiting for a spanking.

"Bring him home next time. He's hot. Also, I wanna watch that happen."

"Skylar! But yeah, that's fair. Alright, he also left three messages. Let's see how weird it gets!"

"Dani?" Our eyes lock at the sound of Xander's voice and the fear it's laced with. *"I, uhm, tried to call you. Look, shit… shit got weird and I'm in, I think I'm in trouble."*

"Skylar, oh my god!" She holds her phone up and shows me the timestamp on the message. It's from yesterday morning. Almost twenty-four hours ago. All the missed calls show as yesterday.

"I'm not sure where I am," his voice continues, growing shaky the more he says. *"I uhm, I love you. I think it was Oliver. I think he did something. I don't know… I don't—"*

The call cuts off. Followed by three minutes of near silence that we all listen to more than once. Chase gets on his phone texting someone to see if they can figure out how to get the number. Dani presses the last voicemail and holds her breath. I hold mine, too.

"Dani, I hope this is your number, because it's the only one I can find." It's a woman's voice. *"We found Xander, and he's going to be okay. He said he tried to call you, so I'm sure you're frantic right now if he managed to reach you. Here's my number. Call me back as soon as you get this."*

She holds the phone to her chest, waving both Coop and I off as she takes off down the hall.

"I wonder what she means when she says they *found* Xander. I don't think that can be good." Coop's dog, a big white and brown pit, joins us, nudging Coop's leg and going into a sit position. "Crap, thanks, Buddy. Almost forgot."

"Huh?"

"Oh, not you. The dog. You should bring Pongo up to Dr. Clay next week. Maybe a psychiatric service dog could help you out. Like, he just told my dumb ass to go take my meds. Chase gives the dog a couple of scratches before he gets up and goes back into the kitchen.

He's doing his best to distract me, which I appreciate, but my eyes haven't left the doorway. It's ten minutes before Dani comes back, tear streaks running down her face. She comes straight to me, climbs into my lap, and hugs me close. "I've got you, Beetle. Take your time."

"I called his aunt. Some guy drugged him and tried to blackmail his dad. Stole his computer, phone, passport, everything."

"Holy shit!" Chase shouts.

"They checked him out of the hospital a few hours ago, she's going to have him call when he wakes up again."

"Alright, love," I rub her back for a minute before standing up, taking her with me. "Let's get you fed and get to the apartment so we can get everything ready for you to go. I'll come with you, if you want." She nods into my shoulder, and I hold her tight until she stops shaking.

HOLLYWOOD
Xander

THE HEAVY RAIN falling when I land fits the mood as I grab the few things have and leave the plane. I'm numb, to the point that I don't remember any of the flight, but I didn't sleep. I didn't get sick, either. Melody agreed to handle everything, but it took her a week to convince the police I should go home. I've done nothing but wallow in the toxic pool of loathing ever since she found me, and the only bright spots have been the texts from Dani, Theo, and Skylar as they tried to keep me from drowning.

Headlights flick on across the private parking lot, telling me where to go. Someone gets out of the car with an umbrella, but I don't bother to wait, putting my head down and leaving the shelter of the hangar to walk through the rain. I tried to think of it as a baptism, a cleansing of all my filth by the LA sky as it greeted me. As we get closer and I recognize him, my heart perks up, drumming a little harder until it's lodged in my throat. Will he yell at me, be disappointed, and tell me how stupid I was? I guess if he planned to do that, he wouldn't have bothered to come here in the first place.

"Hey, baby." He wraps his free arm around my shoulders, hugging me to his warm, dry body. I've dreamed of this, of the

comfort of his thick arms and the safety he's promised me over and over.

Just get home, Baby. We'll take care of you from there.

I've walked through the last few weeks in a trance I can't escape. Even now, I'm not sure if I'm here with Theo, or in a dream my mind created to protect me. "Come on, let's get you out of the rain. Are you hungry?"

I shake my head. I should eat since it's been over twelve hours since I had anything, and that wasn't much more than rice. Dani begged to come get me, but I wouldn't let her cancel her shows. I'm not even sure why I asked Theo to pick me up when I had so many other options, but they would have judged me. But I deserve that.

You. Deserve. Better.

His hand slips down my arm and finds mine, threading our fingers together and pulling my eyes from the ground where my shoes have adhered to the asphalt. He's staring at me, but I can't read his expression—I don't trust myself to read it. The rain beats down around us as we stand there, neither of us making the move toward the car.

The umbrella clatters to the ground, and, in an instant, he's cupping my face in his large hands. "You didn't deserve anything that happened to you, Xander. Do you understand me?" He reads my mind. "None of that was your fault."

I squint against the rain and nod, but it's obvious I don't believe him. He doesn't argue with me, not with his voice, anyhow. Instead, he lowers his head to mine, pressing our lips together. I don't fight him, but I don't move to embrace him or even drop my bag as the rain falls harder. When he finally releases me, he kisses my forehead with more tenderness than I've felt since I left his arms the last time.

"I'm here when you're ready, but only when you're ready."

He picks up the useless umbrella and we head for the car, where he holds the door open for me.

I don't speak the entire drive, staring out the window and watching the lights of Los Angeles reflect off the wet surfaces. A few minutes into the drive, I reach over and find Theo's hand, holding it tight because it's all I can do right now. He doesn't let go until we pull into the brightly lit parking garage under the building. I hide from the overhead lights, hoping the darkness will swallow me up so he doesn't see me.

"Come on, Xander. Let's get you upstairs."

"My girlfriend is upstairs. I'm not sure I'm ready for—"

"That's fine. Like I said, your pace, when you're ready. But I'm not letting you sleep out here in the car when you're soaked to the bone. Let her back in, Xander. Let one of us back in. Please?"

I finally turn and let our eyes meet. He reaches up, brushing his thumb across my bottom lip, avoiding the large cut in the middle. "This from the fight you picked?"

A few days after the hospital, I snuck away from security and walked. I wasn't going anywhere specific, and I ended up finding the darker side of Tokyo. Maybe that's what I wanted to find, the dark, dingy bars where the tourists don't dare go. I drank myself stupid, and the fight came to me. I never even swung on the guy. I let him hit me over and over again. That's what made the cops agree to send me home.

"I don't want to talk about it," I mumble, lip quivering against his touch. "Call me by the other name, Theo. The one only you call me."

The corner of his mouth lifts in a crooked grin. "Baby?" I nod and he leans in. The kiss barely grazes my lips before he whispers into me. "You're *my* baby. No matter what."

I hit the button on the seatbelt and throw my arms around

him, climbing over the center console, desperate to be in his arms. I'm scared, I'm cold, and I'm wet, but for the first time since I left LA weeks ago, I don't feel alone. It's not enough, though.

"Take me home, Theo. Take me to bed. Make it all stop." I beg him each time our lips pull apart. I grab for his shirt, desperate to get it off him, but he catches my wrists and holds me until I melt into him, giving up the fight and sobbing into his chest.

"It doesn't work that way, kid. Experience should tell you that much." He dries my face with the gentlest touch I've ever felt. "Let's get you home, okay?"

He walks me upstairs, holding my hand the entire way to my door. There's one last kiss before he walks further down the hall, standing in his own doorway. I watch him unlock his door and push it open as I hold my hand up and knock on my own door.

"I'm right here if you need me, baby. No matter what time it is."

I nod and he disappears inside as the door to my apartment flies open and Dani stares at me. I'm shutting down again, the fear taking over because I'm not sure what to expect or how she'll react to all of this. She lunges at me, her arms around my neck and in my hair as she holds me to her, doing her best to crush me.

It reminds me so much of when Theo held me, but so different, too.

"It's you! It's really you. Oh my god, Xan, you had me so worried! We finished the show and came right home so you wouldn't come back to an empty apartment." She pulls back, taking in my stray dog aesthetic. "You're soaked! And your eye, Jesus. Get in here. We'll get you a shower and something to eat. Do you want some tea? I can order pizza, whatever you want."

"Can I just go to bed?" I mumble with my head down as she tries to take my backpack. I grip it tight. There's nothing in there worth hiding anymore, but it's all I have left from the worst weeks of my life.

"Okay. I'll, uhm, I—" She walks toward the kitchen, holding her stomach and trying to hide the fear. Melody told Dani everything. That's the only reason she's acting like this, not blowing up at me for being an idiot.

"Beetle? I—I'm sorry?"

Slowly, she turns to face me again, but this time, I drop my bag and shuffle to her, burying my head in her neck and letting her hold me. I need to do that more, to not push her away when things get hard and when I'm the one who needs someone to lean on. It's not only her, either, and I reach a hand behind me. They haven't said a word since I walked in, but I can sense them standing there, waiting to be told it's okay. They're going to be part of this, too. I need them. All of them. Just like Theo said I would. He just doesn't know how many of us there are yet.

Fingers brush mine and I grab their hand as they press against my back, holding us both in their strong arms.

"Whatever you need, love," Skylar's deep whisper fills my head. "We're here for you."

I wake up to a throbbing headache, the arm that's been across my chest all night still there, heavy and holding me to reality. I've never had nightmares, not even as a kid. But after Oliver drugged me, they're all I have. I hate that Skylar has so much experience with them, but they've been helping me through each one. Never getting angry or telling me to get over it, only reassuring me I'm safe and loved. They've refused to leave my side, no matter how loud I yell or how hard I fight back. It's been like this for three nights now.

I turn, laying on my back to stare at the ceiling, but the arm moves, and the hand caresses my face. Deep brown and gold eyes sparkle out of focus until I nod and close my eyes. Their parted lips meet mine, and they're softer than I remember.

They stop and pull back, nudging my nose with theirs, brushing my cheek with their thumb. "Good morning, love."

I offer the slightest smile and a pathetic grunt, but I still haven't found my words unless I'm fighting the nightmares or screaming to be left alone. I don't want words, not mine anyhow.

"Dani's getting ready for work. She needs to get out of the house, and I told her I'd take care of you, that okay?" they whisper, their mouth moving down my jaw as a hand dances through the patch of hair under my navel. I nod, closing my eyes as their hand slides under the band of my sweats and knuckles brush against my hard cock. Only I could scream at terrors all night and wake up with morning wood. "Do you want me to—"

I nod, shutting my eyes. They're careful, moving slowly and checking in often. They kiss down my chest, following the same path their hand already traveled but now with their tongue, my breath catching every time their teeth drag over my flesh. They push my sweats down and take me into their mouth, and I move the blanket back so I can watch them suck the tip of my cock, licking the beads of pre-cum already forming.

It's the farthest we've managed to get without me breaking down and wanting to throw up. They reach up and hold my hand, and I grip it tight.

I can do this. I want this. I deserve—love.

I forgot how good they felt, every part of them. Being near Skylar makes my skin hot and my brain fizzle. Their head disappears further and mine falls back onto the pillow as they flatten their tongue and lick me from balls to tip. They nip and tease anywhere that pulls a reaction from me, leaving nothing out. I want them to consume every part of me.

"Is this okay, love?" They ask, their eyes meeting mine as I lick my lips and nod again. They take all of me into their mouth, bobbing up and down until they slip a finger into me at the same time, and I swear I'm about to black out. They check on me again, stroking their saliva up and down my cock, squeezing and twisting their fingers before they slide a thumb over the tip. My mind becomes one of those sparklers they give kids on the Fourth of July, sizzling and shooting off sparks without a coherent thought.

"Skylar," I add a hundred extra syllables to their name and my back comes off the bed. Before I register the sweet smell of vanilla, a soft, familiar mouth closes over mine and Dani's fingers play in my hair.

"You two are as pretty as I expected you to be," Dani says.

Why did I ever leave? Why do I still give the wrong people control, even after all these years?

"I need you," I whine to her, and she answers with a soft smile and a softer kiss.

"I can't wait to see how my little bee begs for Skylar's surprise later," she says with a wicked grin, letting her robe drop to the floor so I can see that smooth, soft brown canvas of tattoos.

I trace my fingers over her hips. "Show me now. Make me forget everything but the two of you."

There's a wet popping sound and Skylar lifts their head, motioning for Dani to climb on top of me. They help her straddle me, squeezing my cock as she lowers herself onto me. "Good girl." They whisper against her skin before they look down at me. "We're gonna make Xander feel so damn good. Show him how eager you are to please us. Aren't we, my pet?"

"Yes, master," she moans, biting her lower lip as her hungry eyes land on mine.

"Tell him. Tell him who you belong to."

"You. Both of you. I serve you both." She means it, too. She shifts, bending over and offering Skylar her ass. "I'm your plaything. Please? Please, sir?"

"Not yet. Xander gets it first. Take care of him," they say, turning Dani to face me again.

"Wait, the surprise is Dani's ass?" I ask, still groggy but cupping Dani's perfect small tits and pinching her nipples hard, the way she likes it. She repays me by dragging her nails down my chest. Skylar controls her speed, moving her hips and holding her throat. God, they look so hot together. "Please tell me we're going to do her together?"

Dani giggles as she rides my cock and holds my hands to her chest. A moment later, Skylar's fingers push into me, spreading me. I grab Dani's hips, rocking her harder, my hips hammering into her. They're both watching, waiting to see if I need to stop or if this breaks me. I won't let it. I close my eyes until the world becomes a hornet's nest. They pull their fingers out and Dani stops moving.

There's the unmistakable click of a cap opening. "Don't forget to relax, okay, lover? I'll stop anytime you need me to." I can only see the edge of their face as they watch me over Dani's shoulder. My eyes shoot open, and I gasp for air when they push against me. My back arches so high Dani almost falls off, but Skylar helps her stay balanced.

"What is that?!" I whimper.

"I'm barely in, my love. Do you want me to stop?" Skylar

chuckles, still pushing something inside me. If that's his cock, he's added accessories.

"Fuck! No, don't stop. Please don't stop!" He pushes further and I stop breathing before I yell again. "JESUS CHRIST WHAT IS THAT?!"

"Shh, relax, love. It's only me…after a few modifications."

"Xander," Dani hums, leaning down until her tits brush against my chest. "Trust me, you're gonna like it even more once you relax."

"Is it too much? We don't have to do this if—"

"Shut up and keep going! Holy shit. HOLY SHIT!" I cup Dani's ass hard, bouncing her on me, desperate as every nerve prepares to explode. I yell out anything and everything as they slowly push deeper into me, allowing each metal piece they're shoving inside me to quiet another part of my mind. The deeper they go, the more of me I'm getting back. I don't understand it, but I can let them stop. I can't let that sick fuck Oliver take this from me, take them from me. If I give myself to Dani and Skylar, maybe it will all go away, and I can be myself again.

Dani's hips rock again, making my head swim. "You're so pretty like this, Xander. I missed you so much."

I'm a pinball machine, and Skylar's cock wants the bonus round, hitting all the bonus bumper spots. Long asleep nerve endings come to life, flashing and sparking as Dani pushes my legs down, riding in steady waves. We moan together as Skylar fully seats themself inside of me and I'm hanging onto my girl for dear life right up until our mouths crash together again. Skylar's watching us, reciting poetry, cooing in Dani's ear when she sits up again, and I can only scream the one word left in my brain.

"MORE!"

I lose all control of my body when the thrusting starts, long and slow. My mouth drops open, my hands hold Dani with a mixture of desperation and passion while she bounces, and Skylar plays with her clit. My eyes roll to the back of my head like a shark. When I open them again, Dani's screaming her way into an orgasm while Skylar bites her shoulder and finds the pace they want to set. I'm lost in a den of sinful pleasure. I'm a mumbling mess of obscenities and prayer as they both tear me apart.

"Your greedy ass is swallowing me up, love. I take it you approve of the piercings?"

"Stop talking, but don't stop!" I yell, grabbing hold of Skylar's arm because it's the only part of them I can reach. My other hand finds Dani's, locking our fingers together as push me to the brink of oblivion, riding and thrusting me deeper into the mattress. "Oh, shit! Oh, Skylar! Oh, fuck I'm gonna cum, Dani!"

"Show him how you pray to me, Beetle," Skylar coos, and I watch as they dip their hands between Dani's legs again, strumming her like a bass guitar. Her head rocks back onto their shoulder as she unleashes the most beautiful series of moans I've ever heard.

"Xander, please! Please, I need you so bad."

"Tell him, love," Skylar's other hand wraps around her throat, squeezing. They're talking to her, but their swirling, brown, blown out eyes are staring through me as the thrusts become deeper, and they nip at her neck. "Tell him what you are. What you want."

"I-I need to be a good girl for you. I need to p-please you," she sputters, clenching my cock inside her. "Please? Fill me with your cum! I want to be your... your whore!"

If my brain were a computer, it would be flashing a 404 error. Dani and I never had roles in sex, always letting the power belong to whoever wanted it. But watching how she's giving so much of herself to us—*ALL* of herself to us? I don't have words for how magnificent she looks. She yells out, nails scratching me as her body convulses again. It's heaven or a dream, I can't decide which.

Skylar releases her and she drops to my chest. Arms wrap around my neck as she shakes and mumbles. I watch Skylar's muscles flex and twist as they speed up, destroying every memory I have of the last two weeks and replacing it with nothing but them and what they're doing to me right now, in this very minute. I can't hold it anymore, grabbing Dani and cling to her as I pump everything I've got into her, and she whispers her thanks. I'm not sure if she's had a gap between the last two orgasms, or if she's slipped from one to the next. I also don't care. My body is a volcano, and the whimpers in my ear telling me we've destroyed her ignite my core.

"I missed you so much, my lovers. No one felt right after the two of you. No one felt this incredible." There's a rare quality to Skylar's voice, putting it somewhere between a demon and an angel. I'm also convinced their words alone could have me seeing stars. But their cock? It's sending me to new dimensions. "Now I have you both and I never want to let go."

"I love you, Skylar. I love you!" I squeak out between pants for air as he tears me in two. "I'm sorry, I'm so sorry. I shouldn't… I shouldn't want… oh god! Oh, fuck! Yes!"

There's only one thing missing, one touch, one person. "Theo…shit. I need… I want… Oh god!"

Skylar's head falls back, and I could swear the most beautiful black wings spring out as they pump deep into me. They yell my name, yell that they love me so much as Dani whispers it drunkenly into my ear. Then the darkness takes over.

HOLLYWOOD
Dani

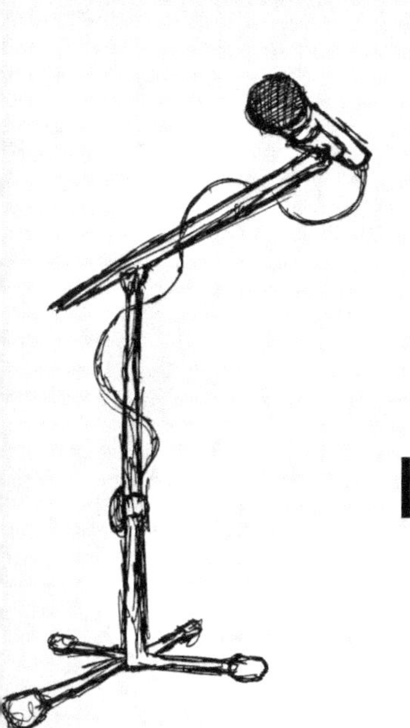

CHAPTER 34
I CAN'T ESCAPE MYSELF

THE DARE

I WATCH XANDER'S BEAUTIFUL, long eyelashes flutter open while I'm dabbing his face with a cool, wet cloth. The smell of cinnamon, sugar, and coffee heavy in the air. "Oh, there you are, my sweet boy."

"Hey," the hoarse word falls out like he's drunk. "Guess who went and got their dick pierced? Skylar!" I giggle and kiss his forehead before leaning back to hand a steaming mug to Skylar, who's sitting against the headboard. Xander watches me, trying to make sense of movement again and realizing he's lying in Skylar's lap. He stares up at them with a dopey grin. "Oh, hi! You got your dick pierced!"

"I noticed," Skylar teases, then brushes the hair out of his face.

"Okay, black for my dark moth. And extra sweet for my honeybee." I wink as Xander sits up to take his mug in shaky hands. That's why I didn't fill it. "Okay, before we talk about Sky's dick railing so hard you blacked out...how do you feel?"

He opens his mouth to answer, but a knock at the front door cuts him off. I groan and growl as I hop off the bed, complaining the whole way to the door. "Ugh, I'll get it. They've got to fix

that stupid gate before I throw one of these survey people down the damn stairs. It's like, what, ten in the morning in Los-friggin-Angeles and they—Oh!"

"You?"

"What are you doing here? And how did you find me?" I ask, ready to pounce.

Skylar and Xander stumble out of bed and rush into the room. Clothes be damned, apparently. Xander skids to a stop behind me on his shaky Bambi legs.

"Theo! Shit! This is—" Xander looks around the room. "It's exactly what it looks like."

"Dr. Clay?"

Skylar and I both look at one another and ask the same question. "You know him?"

"Oh, boy," Theo sighs, his eyes bouncing between the three of us like a beach ball in the stands of a baseball stadium.

"Wait, you're not here for me?" I ask, my brain trying to make sense of his appearance at my door. The unexpected scent of melted butter hits me and I forget everything else. I can sense the fresh baked goodness within my reach! "Okay, well, I'm still taking your peace offering, because it smells... delicious and flaky."

"Do things smell flaky?" Xander asks, missing the point entirely. I don't care though, it's good to hear his voice breaking through the shadow that's covered him since he got home.

Moving the towel out of the way to behold a steaming pile of croissants triggers a memory. "Holy fuckballs, you're the baking neighbor therapy guy!"

"I am the baking neighbor, yes. And uhm, I... came to see him." Theo smiles softly, nodding to Xander. "But the pastries are for, uhm, everyone. I guess. Glad I made extra."

"I…am so confused," Skylar says, grabbing a pillow and covering himself.

Xander leans over me, pulling Theo to him for a deep, hot as hell kiss. "Maybe you should come in before things get any weirder." Xander offers.

"AHH, YOU'RE HIM, TOO! You're salt and pepper bedroom hottie and baker neighbor?!" I yell, unable to stop myself.

"Again, yes. Dr. Theo Clay, to be more exact on who I am."

"Okay, come in now. Please?" Xander asks him.

"Yeah, come in because I have soooo many questions. Why are you here with pastries? How does everyone here know you? What bizarro world do I live in now? Can I expect pastries on the daily?" I bombard him in rapid fire interrogation, but don't move to give him room to come inside. Xander may be ready to welcome him into our home, but I'm not so sure I am. Even with my mouth full of sugary, flaky goodness. "Ah! They're chocolate filled! My weakness!"

Xander grabs my hips and spins me around, so I face the couch. I cradle the food like a baby, protecting it like a hobbit protects their pantry. Skylar sits beside me, and I come close to snarling about them being my precious snacks when he moves to take one. I've got to stop watching Xander's fantasy movies.

"I couldn't sleep last night, worried about you. So, I baked. I thought about leaving them here at the door for you, but I didn't want anyone taking them." Theo explains to Xander before glancing over at Skylar and me. "I didn't realize you were the girlfriend, Dani. He only ever called you Beetle. When Kennedy said your name, it didn't click that she meant D-A-N-I instead of D-A-N-N-Y. I also didn't expect you'd have company."

"Yeah, guess I need a referral for a different therapist," Skylar smirks.

Lightbulbs are going off above all our heads like some kind

of cartoon, as we all connect the dots and realize everything has been an intricate web of coincidence from the start.

"Maybe I should go."

"No!" Xander yells and grabs his arm. "No, please. I…please don't go. I can explain! Well, some of it."

"You're sure?"

"Yeah, please? They need an explanation, too. It's—everything went sideways."

Theo looks down at their hands, his fingers tracing over the words below Xander's thumb. I hadn't noticed the new ink yet with everything else going on, but the entire scene gives me butterflies and giddy feelings. Until Theo's shoulders slump and I panic. He might leave after this.

"GET IN HERE!" I scream. "Sorry, I mean, you shouldn't… can you come in here before Xander cries or whatever? We just got him back!"

Theo nods, brushing his knuckles over Xander's cheek. "I told you I'd wait until you were ready and ended up barging in like this. I'm sorry, Xander."

"It's okay. I promise, it is. You can make breakfast to go with whatever you baked if it would help. You know, being in the kitchen and cooking or whatever?" Xander offers before leaning in and kissing him chastely on the cheek. I'm melting into the couch faster than this butter melting in my mouth.

"Sure, baby."

"Excellent!" I yell.

Xander blushes and kisses Theo again before whispering, "Good, I'm starving, and Dani can't cook eggs without the shells getting into the pan. She also burns the bacon."

"LIES! I can cook bacon and eggs!"

"No, you can't," Skylar agrees with a laugh. They grab a

pastry and run off to the bedroom, pillow still covering their front, before I can smack them.

"Baby?" Theo smiles at Xander and I want to kick my feet so badly. It's a miscommunication rom com happening in my own living room. "Put on some pants. It's…distracting."

I've kept my mouth shut for over an hour now as Xander fills us in on Theo and some of what happened in Tokyo. Okay, that's not true, I've been shoveling these croissants into my face like its popcorn and I'm watching the movie's big reveal scene. That's when I notice they're all looking at me. They've gone around the room, but I haven't told them my part of the story yet.

"We met a few years ago at one of her shows," Theo offers as he picks up the coffee mugs and plates from the coffee table. "I judged her band, and I've kind of been obsessed with her voice ever since."

"So that's not creepy at all. Are you a stalker?" Skylar asks from their perch in the window across the room as they blow smoke out of the apartment. They've only said a few words here and there, since they've had the least amount of contact with Theo. I'm hoping they're okay.

"What kind of terrible stalker misses all of her inner circle when they're a part of it already? I'm sure we're even in pictures together if you go through enough of Chase's parties, since I've made an appearance or two over the years."

"Coop's parties?! No way!" I scream, jumping up in my seat and almost knocking over the few remaining goodies. "When, which ones!?"

"Uhm, let's see. They were both Halloween. I went as Negan from the walking dead one year and—"

"HOLY SHIT! I REMEMBER YOU!" I slap my hand over my mouth as they all stare at me, bursting into laughter. Even I laugh at that, and it's good to see Xander smiling again, even if he keeps grabbing his ribs when he does. "Bro, Xander got so wasted that night, he kept begging me to go hit on you. There were so many baseball bat innuendos!"

"Shit, I remember that!" Xander says, leaning back on the couch and running his hands through his hair. "So, when I was, uhm, gone, did you two...you know? Did you hook up?"

"No. We came close. At a bar a few weeks ago. He definitely rubbed his dick against me a few times, but you were all he wanted. Thousands of miles away and still a cockblock, Xander!"

"I didn't know?!" Xander yells back, hitting me with a pillow.

Theo shakes his head and disappears around the corner and into the kitchen. I wait a few minutes before following him out there and I find him drying the dishes and stacking them up. "You didn't need to do all this, you know. But I do need to thank you. For taking care of Xander when he needed someone he could trust."

"Don't thank me, Dani. Things are...complicated."

"We're...not okay, are we?" Xander asks as he joins us, his sad puppy face back. Theo's heavy sigh speaks volumes, and I listen to Xander's heart shatter into a million pieces as his bottom lip quivers.

"Baby," Theo starts, but stops himself.

"I understand," Xander says, shoving his hands into the pockets of his hoodie and backing up against Skylar. "Thanks, Theo. For, well, for everything. I'm sorry I couldn't—"

My heart breaks and I remember that saying, how some people are only meant to be in your life for a short time and those people make the biggest impacts. Or however it goes. I used to think that would be Skylar for us, a flash in the pan we couldn't replicate no matter how hard we tried.

"No! You two can't break up!" I yell, looking between the pair.

Theo steps forward and puts a hand on Xander's shoulder. "You have a long road in front of you, Xander. Even without me there with you, you won't walk it alone. Look around the room. You've got your support system. You're the Tin Man, on his way to Oz so someone can fix your broken heart. Dorothy and the brave Lion by your side every step of the way. You'll make it, baby. I know you will."

"Isn't that a little too on the nose?" Skylar asks. Theo looks up at them, and Skylar's arms wrap around Xander protectively. "Because if that's the narrative you're going for, it sure as hell explains things. Like why you'd leave him."

Xander starts to argue, but it's too late because I'm jumping on this bandwagon. "You're right, Skylar. By the Doc's own logic, that makes him the Scarecrow, dancing around like a moron with no brain and running away from the three people sent here to help. Three people who live right next door."

"I'm not the one who—"

"Oh, if Doctor Dark-and-Broody wants to tell me he doesn't need help, I'm gonna lose my shit laughing." I walk over, stepping into the space between Xander and Theo, glaring up at him while I poke my finger into his chest. "You cried for him, Theo. You said it yourself at the bar after we danced. You told me you wanted me that night, but you weren't ready to give up on the guy you'd only just met. Xander, right? It had to be."

"Yes, but—"

"Why are you running?" I question him in a harsh tone.

"I'm not the scarecrow and I'm not running! I'm—" he sputters.

"Oh, you're the man behind the curtain. The architect of the house of lies? Maybe your daughter had it right when she bailed on you so you could have your little pity party and wear your emerald glasses to see the LA skyline?"

"What?" Xander's voice comes out as barely a whisper, and I bite my lip. He didn't know about Theo's daughter.

Sky lets go of Xander with one hand, holding it out to Theo. "I'm Skylar, and I'm idiotically in love with these two people. I'm the only one you haven't made out with, so I'm a bit of the odd one out. Maybe that's your problem right now. Me." They wink at him and kiss Xander on the head before pulling on their jacket. "But I'm also out of cigarettes. So, I'm going to take a walk and give you an opportunity to un-fuck this a bit. I'd appreciate it if you'd stay here and help our Beetle take care of our Bee. Figure things out if you can, because something tells me your analogy isn't far off. If that's the case, we've all got a long, winding road ahead of us, and we're going to need all four of us to get through."

"Are we getting a dog?" I ask nibbling on another croissant to keep me from any more outbursts.

"He has a cat," Xander mumbles.

Theo chuckles, shaking Skylar's hand. "I'll do my best to be here when you get back."

Theo and I both reach out and take one of Xander's hands, leading him back to the couch. His face paler than usual, and he's spiraling. I've seen it before. It reminds me of Coop, and how he taught me what to do when Xander goes so deep into his own mind it's like he's not even here in the room with me. But before I can start the routine, Theo beats me to it.

"Xander, I need you to listen to my voice," he says, squatting in front of Xander and putting his hands on his knees. "Focus on that for right now, nothing else, alright? We're going to work through this together. Okay?"

Xander nods absently and I squeeze his hand before I brush his hair out of his eyes. "I'm sorry I didn't—"

"Stop, you're not the one to blame. Let's start with the basics. Can you tell me five things you can see right now?"

His eyes stay down, unmoving for the longest time, and the seed of panic growing in me. He's gotten like this before a few times, after his 'dates' come close to putting him in the hospital. He's gone days where he refuses to leave the bed and stares at the wall until I force him to eat something and drink water. I watch the slightest movement in his eyes.

"That's it, honeybee. Take your time."

His lip trembles again as he fights a pout, but manages to croak out, "Skylar's bass guitar. Dani's records. Dani's pink bunny slippers. The stupid stuffed monkey. Your watch."

He insists he doesn't need to go through the rest, but Theo makes him anyhow, telling him it's best if he breaks out of the cycle completely instead of shortcuts. He squeezes my hand to let me know he's okay when they're done, and I brace myself for the tears. Breakups never get easier, and Xander has a bad case of falling for people harder than he cares to admit. I wish I could give him everything he needs, and I hope that maybe with Skylar it will be a step easier to heal. The problem is, I suspect Theo plays a part in Xander's healing, too.

"Okay," I break through the brief silence. "So, like, why can't you and Xander stay together?"

"Dani, that's… you know that won't work. We're a package deal. We always have been."

"Yeah, and he likes me, too. Like, seriously, he wanted to bend me over a bathroom sink and have a—"

"Hey! Come on. Can we not?" Theo holds his arms out, but Xander and I stare at him. "Wait, this is…normal?"

"Duh. We tell each other pretty much everything. Hell, he's got videos and picture of Sky and I together."

"Well," Xander flinches. "Sort of. I've, uhm, I've not been totally honest with either of you about…something. I've, uhm, I'm a… I kind of…shit," he groans, putting his head in his hands and mumbling. "I'm basically a sex worker. No, I AM a sex worker. At first, I only did on that one subscription website, and a guy offered me extra for a meetup. I'm not meeting dates through work or clubs, Dani. They're… I'm… I sell my body."

I raise an eyebrow and give him an incredulous smirk. I expect the same from Theo, but when I find the glint of tears as his lips fall open. His eyes drop to the floor, and he shakes his head. Because today, we're all learning things we might not want to know about. So much for waking up to amazing sex, but this isn't as bad as Xander's continuous, fitful nightmares.

"Xander, are they the men who hurt you?" Theo asks.

Xander nods, and Theo responds by reaching out and pulling him into a hug.

"I did it for a while before I met Dani. A few guys I knew. I got on a website, no meeting. We needed money to fix Dani's car, and I convinced myself it would only happen once. We'd meet up, have sex, and nothing else. He offered me five hundred dollars. But I didn't stop there. The money came too easy, and we had bills to pay. I stopped in Tokyo. I stopped seeing them for you, Theo. I thought I could do this," Xander cries into his shoulder while I wrap around them both. "You said you'd be there for me. You said no one would hurt me again. I'm sorry. I'm sorry, Theo."

"And I will, Baby. I promise I will. You're okay."

"No, I'm not! Normal people don't do this!" Xander yells, but when he tries to pull away, Theo holds him tighter.

"Xander, that's not true," Theo presses his lips against Xander's head, and my heart breaks and melts at once while they rock together. "You're not the problem. Society is. I'm so sorry the world did this to you. I'm the one who's sorry, baby."

"So," I cut into their moment because I can't hold back. "That means you're going to give this a shot, right? See if we can all hack it together?"

They both look up and stare at each other, but eventually, Theo nods, and I kiss each one of them on the cheek.

"Good, cause you two are cute as hell together. I don't know if I want to throw up or let my heart explode over all this mushy shit."

HOLLYWOOD
Theo

CHAPTER 35

HOT STUFF

BLUE OCTOBER

XANDER'S BEEN under my kitchen sink for the better part of an hour now, swearing and banging on things. He promised he'd done this before, so I'm staying out of the way and working on some client files in the living room while Baggy goes between the two of us, begging for food. The plan we made involved a lazy Sunday morning and not much getting out of bed, but when the sink broke again as Xander tried to make coffee, he made it his mission to get it fixed.

The kid can't function without his coffee.

"Be right back," he calls out as he speeds through the room and out the front door. In some places, the adjustment happened in smooth, graceful steps as if we'd always been a cohesive unit. In others, bumpy might undersell the issues. Through all of it, though, everyone agrees Xander has never been happier or tried harder than he has over the last month.

I've changed in many of the same ways, too.

The front door opens, and he runs back in with something in his hand and goes back to work. He's so focused, he doesn't notice he's left the door wide open. I'm wondering how long this will go on before we knock down part of the wall and join our

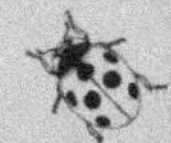

places. I wouldn't be against it, given the number of times I've had to remind him that he should put pants on before going into the hall.

I hit send on the last form I care to fill out this morning and shut the front door before Baguette gets any wild ideas about the glorious outside world full of new smells and possible food sources. When I get to the kitchen, Xander's standing at the sink and looking down the drain. His damp hair sticks out of his backwards baseball cap. He decided to let it grow, even if it drives him nuts—hence, the baseball caps. He calls it his first true act of full-blown rebellion against his parents in years. Face tattoos he jumps at, but missing a haircut? He's got an interesting rebellious streak, to say the least.

He's also put some of his weight back on since the post-Tokyo depression era. Although it's more muscle than before since he goes to the gym with Skylar and Chase a few times a week. I'm sure as hell not complaining about it, but I am wondering if I should join them, or maybe their friend's gym, so I don't spend the entire time ogling Xander.

Or Skylar.

Xander drops to his knees, climbing halfway under my sink. His hips move to the music, and so do the muscles in his back, making the ink along his ribcage do their own little dance. His shoulders flex and he swears loud enough for me to hear it. When he pops out of the cabinet and stands over the sink again, I can't take my eyes off him. He hasn't noticed I'm standing there as he sings along to the music. I don't even care that he's off key because I'm too busy staring at his shoulders and how defined they are now.

I watch his body flex as he leans in, shining a flashlight into the abyss while sticking his ass out like an invitation. He's going to need to finish this later.

Without warning, I walk up behind him and pull his sweats down below his cheeks, grinding against his ass as I attack his neck with my mouth.

"JESUS! Bro, you scared the shit out of me!" He says after he jumps, knocking his head against the cabinet. He takes off the hat and rubs the top of his head, his shaggy hair falling around his face. "Now? I'm almost done, Theo!"

"Yeah, and I'm just getting started. Also, it's Sunday, baby." I roll my hips against him as I suck on his neck, holding him tight.

We now call Sunday's fair game days. Neither of us were getting a damn thing done except each other, which included skipping out on work or getting groceries. So, we decided that one day every week, we couldn't say no to each other. It helps make saying no ordinary life things easier, so long as we don't keep those things until Sunday.

I blindly dig through the random stuff drawer and find the bottle of lube we keep in there. There's a few stashed in different spots throughout my place, and his. The snap of the cap turns Xander into Pavlov's dog as he leans forward, offering me his ass.

"That's better. Look at you, Baby. So ready for me to be inside you." I push a slick finger into him, and he reaches out, grabbing the counter with a groan. Xander makes the most beautiful noises when we're together. High-pitched whimpers. Groans that break down into needy pants. Whiny little pleas begging me to fill his tight ass. I understand why he makes such good money on that website, and I'm proud of him for not giving up on something he enjoys. If my baby wants men to throw money at him for jerking off on camera, I'm fine with it. So long as he sticks with his rules about nothing in person, which he has.

"Yes, sir. I'm always ready for you, for your big cock to stretch me wide open for you."

"You keep talking and it's going in that pretty mouth of yours." His body jumps like I've sent a shockwave through him when I curl my finger and massage that spot.

"Theo?" he whines. "Can you do something for me?"

"What do you need, baby?"

"I want it to be hard today. I want you to let go again and fuck me like you want to. Like you've been afraid to do since I got back." He looks at me over his shoulder, those beautiful blue eyes hypnotizing me. "I'm ready. I promise."

I run my nose up his neck and wrap my fingers around his throat, not squeezing, only resting there, testing him. "You're sure?"

"Yes," he nods. "I'll tell you if it's too much. I promise. I just need it. I need to remember the good pain again. To show myself I'm not made of glass, and I won't break."

I pull him back and slam him against the refrigerator, hearing the glass bottles on the door clang together from the force. My hands are in his hair as he fights me for dominance, only to give in a moment later, letting me shove his sweatpants down his thighs and kick his legs wider. I line my cock against his slick hole. He grunts, pushing his hips back.

"Shit, do you treat all the plumbers—Ah!" It's not the right sound to make me stop and think I'm hurting him as I push the tip in. "More!" He begs, so I give him all of it in one thrust. There's pain in his cry, but only on the edges. Only for a moment. I grab his hips, thrusting into him so hard, the refrigerator lurches with every thrust. He can't speak, and when he tries, it's gibberish sprinkled between whimpers and moans.

"This what you need, Xander? Your teasing ass fucked so hard you can't even scream for me?"

"YES!" His panting breaths and whimpers match my thrusts, melodic as they drive me harder. "Harder, Theo. Make it hurt!"

My hand comes down on his bare ass and the noise he lets loose ignites something dormant in me. I wrap around him, rutting into him as I squeeze his throat tighter, cutting off his airway. I've never been this wild and mindless, never allowed myself this freedom before Xander. I'm reduced to my most primal needs and the thrill of being with him. It's this craving in the back of my mind, the drive to take him as hard as he'll let me and claim him as mine. "You wanna fucking tease me like that? Huh? You wanna flaunt yourself like a slut? Leaving the door open so anyone can walk in here and have your tight ass?"

"I'm sorry, sir! You should punish me for being bad."

I grab a fistful of his hair and yank back hard as the growl works its way through my chest. "You're mine, you understand that? Your mouth. Your ass. Your whole fucking body. All of it. Mine."

"Yes, sir!" he whines, face smashed against the cool metal and twisting with pleasure. Fear has no place here, not with me, which means he can explore the things that get him off more freely. And I can wake the beast inside me.

Even my grunts are animalistic, like someone—something else has taken over. I drop my head to his shoulder, biting down on his smooth pale skin, having enough presence of mind to avoid his tattoos. I squeeze his throat and leave behind fingerprints where I've held him tight.

"Oh god!" His shaky voice whines. He's crying, but he hasn't said stop, hasn't shut down.

"Is this what you want? Your tight ass punished so hard you can't sit down after? Tell me. TELL ME!"

"Yes! Shit! I need you to... oh god... please!" He chokes on his words until one comes out as clear as a bell. "More."

I spank him so hard even my hand stings before I reach around and grab his cock, pumping it hard. His warm, sticky pre-cum drips down my fingers and his head rocks back. "You like being my fuck toy, don't you? Like me deep inside of you, making you beg for me."

"Yes!"

"Open your mouth, Xander." He does, more weak grunts and moans spilling out of him until I slip my fingers into his mouth. "Clean your cum off my fingers, you dirty slut. Atta boy. So damn needy."

I wrap an arm around him, the other pulling his head to the side by the hair. I bite the base of his neck as I speed up. His body tenses against mine and his hips try to buck. He begs and cries out each time I pull out, only to sing my praise when I hammer back into him. My hand comes down for a third time on his hot, red ass, leaving a handprint as his guttural moans turn once more to gibberish.

"Cum for me, Xander. Cum on the damn counter so I can make you lick it up."

His hips jerk against nothing, thrusting into the air. My eyes drop in time to see ropes of white decorating the cabinet doors as his body goes limp and his legs shake. The knot inside me lets go and I fill him like the animal I've become, still sucking on his neck and holding him up. Still rutting against him like I'm trying to breed him—taking him like an animal until I've had my fill.

"Oh! Oh shit!" Another wave of cum spills down his legs and onto the floor. He lets out a strangled whimper when I pull out, like defeated prey giving one last yell before he collapses into my arms. As I shift his limp body, he struggles to wrap his arm around my neck. I lift him off the floor and he nuzzles against my neck.

"Sorry about the mess," he pants. "I'll clean it up later."

I admire the destruction of my kitchen, watching his cum dripping and smeared over the door of the fridge and the lower cabinets. We've turned the room into a passionate Jackson Pollock art installation, and I don't regret a damn thing.

"I'll take care of it, baby. And you." I carry him back to the bedroom and lay him down on the bed. He reaches for me with shaking arms when I leave to run him a bath.

"Wait, where are you—?"

"Don't worry, baby. I'm not going anywhere." I leave soft kisses on his bruised lips. I fill the bathtub, and he winces when I lower him into the warm, soapy water. I use a soft cloth and wipe his chest and face, and make sure he can reach the cold bottle of water I've set on the edge of the tub.

"You alright?" I ask, brushing the hair out of his eyes as he lays his head against the side of the tub, his nod almost imperceptible. I lean over the edge, using a washcloth to clean his body before I have him sit up to wash his hair. When I'm done, and he looks as though he's about to fall asleep, I kiss his head and stand. "I'll be back in a few minutes. Yell if you need anything, okay?"

In the kitchen, I get out everything I need while listening for any noise coming from the bedroom. I have four things cooking at once: eggs, toast, bacon, and waffles. A few minutes later, I push the door of the bathroom open and set the tray down across the tub. He's asleep. Peaceful and angelic, I could sit here and count the freckles across his shoulders for the rest of the day if I didn't need him to eat something.

"Hey," my gravelly voice echoes off the walls even in a whisper. "Come on, you gotta eat, Xander."

His eyelids flutter open but can't pull themselves all the way open. "Nooo. Just…sleep."

His blank, vacant stare concerns me, and I question if I went too far. But he manages a sleepy, crooked smile and I breathe again. I dip a hand into the water and grumble at the cold.

"I don't think I can stand." His wink gives me small comfort in knowing we're okay, or at least hoping we are. I pull off my shirt and lift him out of the tub like a child, wrapping a robe around him and carrying him to bed before I bring the tray in for him. I brush his hair with my fingers as I feed him, and when he's done, I clear the food away. He falls asleep in my arms, and I never want to let go.

It's only the second time in my life I've ever felt this way about someone else, a connection, a pull stronger than lust or magnetism. It tells me to hold on to this person and never let them go, all I've ever wanted. The last time I felt this, I was eighteen and in my second year in France. Even when they lowered her into the ground five years later, I tried like hell to join her, to hold her one more time and make it last forever.

Feeling it again scares the absolute hell out of me. Knowing that I could lose him—lose all of them—in a heartbeat only amplifies the fear. My phone rings in the other room, and I slide out of the bed, careful not to disturb Xander. He needed sleep after that. Padding to the charger in the living room, Baggy tries to trip me as I get to the phone. Maybe she tried to warn me, because I'm not prepared for the name that comes up on my screen.

Incoming Call From: Pixie

"Hello, err, Bonjour? Sylvie?" I spit it all out like it's one word, in case she hangs up on me.

"Allo, Papa. I got your message about my birthday."

"Pixie, that was…that was months ago."

"I needed to take my time and think about what you said. I've been fighting with Pépé, and it's made life troublesome. Do you think we could still meet sometime soon? At the cafe again?"

"Yes! Yeah. I need to book a flight and a room." My mind races like a locomotive with no breaks. "I'll call you back as soon as I book the flight. Next week? I'm sure I can find something."

"Okay. I will see you soon."

"Pixie?" I wait, listening to see if she's hung up. "I uhm. You can bring him, if you'd like. Luca. Marie told me about him and, I uhm, I'd love to meet him."

"I would like that. Shit, my taxi has arrived. We'll talk later. Goodnight, Papa."

When the phone clicks, my legs give out and I miss the couch by inches, bouncing off the cushion and to the floor. Xander stumbles out of the room like Bambi and finds me on the ground, phone still in hand. His mouth moves, but it sounds like the aftermath of a bomb exploding, noises muffled and far away, that loud ringing the only constant.

"I need to go to Paris."

HOLLYWOOD
Dani

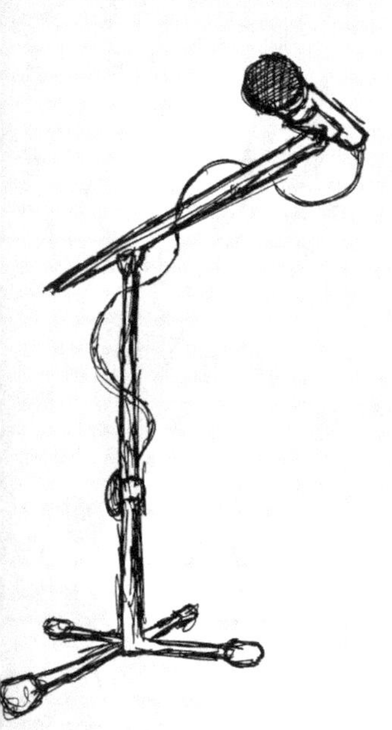

CHAPTER 36
PARTY 4 U
CHARLI XCX

STEPPING INTO THE GYM, I'm greeted with a wave from the receptionist and the offensive smell of CrossFit. Normally, I don't mind hanging out here, but those people go all out, and watching them makes me need a nap and a bag of candy. And to decorate the room in those little tree air fresheners like that one horror movie.

"Hey, Dani!" Yells Kylie, a bubbly blonde who works for Steve's gym. She runs around the desk to hug me. "How's Ren doing?"

My sister came out of hiding a week ago in true Silva fashion. A blaze of glory, blood, and gunfire. She's been in and out of surgeries ever since. None of them major once they got the knife wound under control. Coop's been with her, partially because of his own injuries, but mostly because he can't stand to be away from her. It's disgusting, I adore it.

"Recovering and blissfully in love. She and Coop have a trip to Europe planned once the doctor clears them both to travel again. Which means even through a psycho stalker and a gang banger ex, my matchmaking skills are ah-maze-ing. So, you need to get hooked up?"

"Nah, I've got a girlfriend," she giggles and nods across the room to this absolutely gorgeous older red head that could bench press me and throw me through a brick wall any day. "Anyhow, Steve's between clients, so he's probably in the break room. If he's not, he's in the office. Be careful if you check in there, though. Ethan has a key to the back so he can sneak in unseen."

"There's a joke in there."

"Yeah, there is. Craig comes up with a new one every few days. The rest of us don't bother going back there and page Steve over the intercom to avoid the accidental walking in. Seriously, he needs to get that lock fixed."

"Thanks for the heads up." I head for the back area and down a long hall. I still poke my head into the open office door to make sure he's not in there and find it empty. Someone starts rummaging around in the break room, so I follow the sounds. At the back counter, facing away from me, I find a mountain of muscles with tufts of blonde hair. The logo of a parrot stares at me menacingly from his green hat. "Stevie!"

"D! Hey stranger." He leans back and gives me a fist bump before I pull out a chair and sit on the back of it with my feet in the seat. "How's everything going with the new living situation?"

I bite my thumbnail as I consider how to answer, since it's a loaded question. "It's…weird?"

"Weird as in the stripper pole and sex swing are getting installed next week? Or weird, like you're sleeping on the couch?"

"What? Why are those my only two options?! I dunno, it's just weird. I'm used to always having Xander. But now? Sometimes I have Xander there, sometimes I don't. Sometimes I wake up to Skylar, sometimes they're hiding out on the fire escape."

"What about you and the Doc?"

"Epic make-out sessions when we're alone, but I don't wake up with him. So, like, even that's weird! He wants to take it slow with Sky and I, even after he basically jumped into bed with Xander."

"It's only weird because you're trying to make it fit into a social structure it's never going to fit into. You, them, hell, even Ethan and I, we don't fit neatly into categories, and it pisses people off. Screw those people. Don't worry about what makes them happy! They're boring in bed. We need to satisfy ourselves before we give two shits about the people who vote against our rights and chant out derogatory shit."

"Yeah, I guess." He pulses the blender a few more times before popping the top off to taste the green sludge. I study his face, watching the different muscles in his neck shift as he evaluates the taste. He turns to offer me a blender full of something green and toxic looking. My lip curls up when I take a sniff and push his hand back. With a shrug, he turns back around and pours the liquid into a cup decorated with donuts and sprinkles and pops a lid on it. "Dude, how do you drink that stuff?"

"This isn't even for me, but it's not as bad as it looks." He takes a long look at me before crossing his arms. "You're living with three hotties who love to screw, and you're worried about who sleeps where? Get a bigger bed! But that's not why you're here. Out with it, why are you all bummed out? Did the tour go to shit or something?"

"More like bleeding us all dry. Skylar's even working two jobs right now, but neither one can be done remotely. There are so many things I didn't factor into it all. Laundry on the road, buying new clothes to replace the stuff that got ruined doing laundry on the road." I hop off the counter and mindlessly follow him through the gym and into his office, still talking. "…maintenance on the van. Connor getting high and raiding the mini bar. Helping to pay for Sky's therapy sessions. Xander's back to doing what he does, but less of it."

"Trying to do all that shit on your talent and good looks isn't going to work, sweetheart. Not yet anyhow. Going viral helped for a short burst, I'm sure, but did you monetize it?" He raises an eyebrow, and I shrug in response. When Steve goes into business mode, he transforms into a different person, and he knows what he's talking about.

Before he can explain, Kylie's voice on the intercom cuts through the screaming metal music to tell Steve to come up for his next client. He nods to the door and walks me to the back of the gym. Before he opens the door to the parking lot where he knows my car is, he stops by a large bulletin board.

"Here, take this. It's for an influencer I work with. They're an enormous help with the social media and marketing of the gym been." He unpins the flyer and hands it to me. "I've been meaning to pull it off for you next time you came around."

"Bro, phrasing. I don't ever want to hear about you pulling anything off."

"Yeah, you don't want to hear about it because you'd rather watch." He grabs imaginary hips and thrusts against them. "Oh, baby, just like that, yeah, baby! Take that cock, Ethan, yeah!"

I roll my eyes and give the most dramatic sigh I can manage, channeling my inner valley princess. "How are you even married?!"

"I've got a big dick and I beat your boyfriend to him?" With a shrug, he pulls the flyer from the board and hands it to me. "As for the money situation for the band, the gym can totally sponsor you guys."

"I'll get right on that, Stevie." It's tempting, but the offer tastes like a handout, and I'd rather drink the green death stuff than take a handout from my friends. I hate being the only broke one in the group, and I miss the days when Coop was the only one of us with money.

"Don't be like that, jerk. You know damn well we don't think of you as a charity case. You're our family. Annoying, bratty, stubborn family." He pulls me in and hugs me to his sweaty, smelly t-shirt. "In this family, family helps family out."

"Inspiring."

"Shut up, you sound like Ethan. Besides, you'll pay me back when you're some famous rockstar by getting me backstage passes so I can post it all over socials and annoy people! Slap some of our stickers on your equipment boxes and the van, get Connor or someone to wear our shirt a few times. Or getting Connor and Skylar to come pose for some pics to promote the gym?"

"You're married, perv!" I pull away. "Ah, you're messing up my face with your man sweat!"

"Your face has always been messed up! And I'm married, but I can still look! Besides, I'll tell Sweets about it, and he'll teach me a lesson that involves me in his jersey and a belt—" There's another page for Steve, this time louder to ensure he hears it. They probably think he's in his office with Ethan doing the dirty. "Shit, I gotta go. Say hey to Sky for me, oh, and say *hello* to Xander, too."

"I thought you were over your playboy ways?!"

"Tigers and stripes, baby. Go take care of Skylar and the boys. I'll take care of your money issues."

"Woooow!" I spin around in the hotel lobby. It's not the Ritz, but it's better than anything we've had in months. "Uhm, can we afford this shit?"

"We can, but not at every stop," Connor explains. "I figured we could use a little pick me after making it to the top fifteen. Oh, and the sponsorship checks are all cleared, which means spending money while we're here in Boston."

When Steve offered to sponsor the band, I didn't realize the gym could crank out that kind of cash. Or that he'd get our friends Coop and Jamie to add to the total. Even Coop's little brother, Devin, got a collection going in the Pasadena Parrots' locker room that earned us a few grand, a bunch of merch sales, and a roll of hockey tape that Skylar and Connor fought over.

"We also got a load of cash dropped off at the bar for us the other day. They didn't leave a name, but bartender Bobby said she was smoking hot."

"Bobby refers to anything with boobs as smoking hot, Connor."

"Whatever. BAR!" Connor takes off for the hotel's lounge.

"He's going to get us thrown out before I even get you naked and tie you to the bed, isn't he?" Skylar asks, their hand holding mine.

"Duh," Noah replies as she pulls her suitcase behind her. "But it's cool. There's a motel down the street that's probably more used to the noise complaints the two of you cause."

"Touché?" Skylar replies.

Noah follows after Connor, but Skylar catches my hesitation as I mumble to myself, chewing on my thumbnail. It's a lot to take in right now, and I don't only mean the nicer hotel. As ready for all this as I thought I was, I'm questioning everything that's happened in the last few months. Questioning if I'm the one who isn't ready to take this big step. What if I'm the one who's been holding us back because of my own pride? I could have asked the guys for money a month ago, before any of this shit happened. I could have let Xander get help from his parents instead of living in a shitty apartment. I could have been less of a stuck-up bitch about things that never mattered. I should have admitted I'm scared, and yet, I still haven't.

"Hey," Skylar's deep, gravelly voice does two things for me at that moment—pulls me out of my own head and makes my knees weak. They tap the side of my head. "What's going on up there, Beetle?"

"I dunno, worried about Xander, I guess. My sister, too."

"Mmm," they squeeze my hand, and I turn to face them, running my fingers through the stubble they didn't shave off this morning. "Your sister has Chase. Xander has Theo. I have you. At home, we all have each other. Well, without your sister and Chase. That's why this will work, Dani. It's what you said you couldn't find. You didn't expect it to come in two different packages."

"Yeah, I guess."

"What's really bothering you?"

"I don't know."

"You remember that conversation we had in the first hotel room we shared? The night the world finally made sense to me again? You said we shouldn't keep secrets if we want this to work."

I close my eyes, pressing my forehead into their chest and fighting back tears when their arms fold over me. My protector, my shield, my shadowy moth, hiding me from my demons and drawing their attention away with flashy wings. I should have seen it in them years ago. Like Xander became my fighter, my guardian, my honeybee. I wonder what Theo will be if he accepts his new place in our lives. Would he act like an ant? Strong and determined? Or the mantis, patient and mindful?

"I'm scared. I'm not ready for this."

"For the show?"

I shake my head and glance over my shoulder to the bar where Noah joins Connor, who's already got three people lured in by his stories and vivacious energy. We've grown closer during this competition—we've had to. At least three bands have dropped out over the last few weeks, and that's when the true nature of this contest finally stepped into the light. It's not only about the music and being able to play for the crowd, but also about making it through the rough patches without losing the glue holding each band together. Changed dates, canceled venues, flat tires, blown amps, and everything else that's happened during this tour can chip away at a band if they're not strong enough.

"Skylar, if we don't win, what happens to us? If I miss a lyric or mess up a note, I could ruin all of this. What if I say the wrong thing in the post interview or we can't get the tire changed so we're stuck on the side of the road and the hoard of zombies overwhelms us while we're trapped there, and I never get back to see—"

"Woah, woah," they cut me off and crouch down to look me in the eye. Their hands cool my face as they hold on and wait for me to focus on them. "Daniella Silva, you are my black winged angel, my siren on the jagged rocks, my scarab beetle meant to guide me through this journey and onto the next. This tour could end for us tomorrow, but it isn't the end of us. You're too focused on this one path while ignoring the thousands of other options.

Kick down the doors that stand in your way until you find the one that leads us where you want to go."

"Why do you always sound like a fortune cookie?"

"Too many self-help books that didn't help." They kiss my forehead, holding their lips there until my hands wrap around their wrists. "Are we good, Beetle?" he asks into my hair.

"Yeah," I breathe out with a nod. "Yeah, we're good. Come on, I need a drink before we call and check in back home."

"When you get back, it might be time to talk to Theo. We've both seen the way he calms Xander, even on his worst days. I'm not saying he'd be your therapist, but a wise ear for you to whisper whatever's eating you up inside?"

I sigh, rocking my head back until it clicks. "This from the one who tries to avoid Theo by hiding on your perch outside?" I regret it the moment I say it. I'm not trying to be mean, just stating the obvious.

"I don't want to be the wave maker, Dani. Of all the fragile pieces on the board, I'm the steadiest right now, the most supported. You and Xander are the two with wobbling bases. Theo and I will figure each other out in time, and neither of us has to rush."

"I'm not wobbly! I'm fine! I'm better than fine." I hope he doesn't hear the shake in my declaration. "Come on, let's go get a drink."

HOLLYWOOD
Skylar

CHAPTER 37
DANCIN' AROUND

MEG DONNELLY

I'M in the middle of one of Xander's epic fantasy novels he left out on the table, enjoying the rare quiet of the apartment, when the door handle turns, and Theo walks in with a tin of something he made from scratch last night. His being here reinforces my idea of the pattern of life he lives. If Xander spends the night at Theo's, they're together most of the day and we don't see much of them. If Xander spends the night here, I can almost set my watch to Theo's appearance the next day with something delicious and fresh baked in his hands. He's not intrusive. I don't even find it that weird, just something I noticed from my view in the background. If Theo's noticed any patterns like that in me, he hasn't mentioned it, although since he's not my shrink, he doesn't need to notice me at all.

"Hey, Doc," I don't bother looking up from the book or climbing inside. "If you're looking for the kids, they were gone before I got back, so I'm not sure when they plan to be home. Date night."

"Yeah, I got the calendar reminder earlier. I wasn't planning to cook anything because of that, but, well, I didn't want to disappoint you by not coming over."

"So, you noticed your own habit?" That gets my attention. I put the book down and lean in, curiosity getting the better of me. Theo doesn't come over for me, I'm an afterthought. That title doesn't bother me since we're all still adjusting to this whole situation. In all fairness, I haven't extended an olive branch of any kind either.

"I, uhm, thought you were headed out to France?"

"I am," he answers with a slow nod. "Not for a few days, though. Baggy must know, too, because she's been MIA since I got home and finished cooking these. She does that as soon as I get the luggage out and pack."

"She'll be in good hands, Doc. She and Dani both have the same care instructions: feed them and pet them until they're happy." I run my hand through my hair, trying to figure out what we do next in this awkward dance, but he takes the lead, walking over and holding a box out to me. Reflexes say I should take it, thank him, and leave it on the counter for Xander, but my gut says there's something else going on here.

"I noticed the other day that you were a fan of the pistachio macarons. So, knowing they wouldn't be here to eat them before you get a chance, I made you some. Call it an ice breaker, of sorts."

"You made them...for me?" I take the box and read the handwritten note he's left on top. "*Skylar's, do not eat these if your name isn't Skylar*. Pretty sure you could put these under lock and key and Dani would still find a way in. Uhm, thank you."

It's awkward. Neither of us is sure where to go from here. Do we shake, hug, or keep staring at each other for all eternity? Guess it's my turn to take the initiative. I slide over and pat the pillow next to me. "Care to join me? Xander rolled this for me before he left. I haven't gotten around to it yet."

I hold up a joint and he takes it and nods before climbing

through the large window and onto the fire escape. I love old buildings. They've all got built in patios perfect for some fresh air if you're not a dick about it. I grab the bottle of wine I brought out with me early and set it between us.

"It's not French, or even that good, but—"

"Doesn't matter. Wine and coffee share a lot in common, Skylar. The company you're with can make a fifty-cent cup taste like it costs a million dollars. You'll keep the memories long after you've forgotten the brand."

"And here Dani thinks I'm the wordsmith. I might make use of that saying." I pour some wine into a coffee cup and hand it over to him. "Don't worry, I'll keep it out of the lyrics. For now."

"Do you write any of her songs?" He asks, sniffing wine and taking a drink. "The lyrics, I mean."

"No, I leave that all up to her. Well, more like she refuses to relinquish that responsibility."

He nods, and the silence falls over us for a while. Adjusting to each other's company will take time. I light my smoke and hand him the lighter. It's a rare, nice day in Los Angeles, if you stick to the shadows of the buildings. The triple digital temperatures of summer are gone, but we're not into the cooler months yet. We might get lucky and get a cool November next month.

"How are you doing with Anna? Are you two getting along?" He asks, lighting the joint and taking a deep pull.

"She's been wonderful. I had to call her from the road a few times with the way the tour has been, and she's handled the odd hours of my…breakdowns with grace and kindness." He holds the joint out to me and I stare at it for too long before taking it.

The thick, smooth taste of the weed comforts me more than my cigarettes. Nothing like the skunky shit we used to buy from dealers when I was a teenager. The months-long break means it hits harder than I'm prepared for, bringing me down to a mellow I've been trying to replicate for a while now. I pass it back, blowing out smoke rings. Theo does the same.

"You should know," Theo says as I offer him a macaron. "I had ulterior motives coming over here today. I almost chickened out. Twice." I grab the bottle of wine and top us both off before he says anything else. This might be an intervention or him gearing up to give me a speech about the quad not working and how I'm the problem. I'm gonna need a drink. "I'm trying to figure out the other sides of this box, and how we connect."

"You'd rather it be a triangle, I assume?"

His head tilts to the side before he reaches over and takes one of the macarons, staring at it. "You know, I have a strange ability to relate to people through food easier than I do emotions sometimes, which, for a psychiatrist, can be problematic. I also don't waste my time, talent, and ingredients on someone if they're not worth it. If they're not someone I want to connect with in some way. My issue isn't that I want a different shape or number, it's that I'm too stuck in my own angle to see everyone's place in the shape we're making."

"I...don't think I understand."

Theo picks up the box and pulls out the tray of cookies, setting them aside and pointing to an edge of the box. "This represents you, and I'm on the edge opposite you. We both see Xander and Dani, but our edges can't see one another. Unless we do this."

He folds the box, collapsing it into itself, flattening it. I take it when he hands it to me, turning it over in both my mind and my hands as what he's saying makes more sense. He's not leaving or asking me to leave. But I'm not sure what he's talking about yet.

"You should stick to food metaphors. But how do we get here? To a place where we can all see each other's edges?"

"Well, that's the reason for my trepidation. I couldn't figure it out, and that bothered me, which led me to baking, which had me grabbing pistachios, something I rarely use. I didn't question it; my heart told me I needed to bake for you. The skipped beats, the sweaty palms, the way my mind buzzes around you. You're not Xander, or Dani, you're a high school crush I don't know how to talk to."

"I'm confused again," I set the box aside. "Usually, it's me who confuses people."

"You shouldn't." He holds out a hand, palm up, and gestures toward mine. When he takes my hand, he draws in my palm, like he's reading it or something. "Skylar, I'm using too many colorful descriptions and bullshit to say something simple. You are someone I don't know well enough, but I like you enough to cook for you, and I trust you. So, I'd like to ask you out on a date."

My eyebrows shoot up and for once in my life, I'm at an utter loss for words.

"Romantic chaos offers so much when people open their minds to it. This also wouldn't be my first polyamorous relationship, although we stopped at three people before. I assumed more people would be too much, but that's wrong. I'm amazed every day at how much more stable and capable we are together." He brings my hand to his lips and my heart flutters. It could be the weed, but I doubt it. "Skylar, I've watched you and Dani hold Xander up when he's ready to fall, and a moment later, he's by your side when you need that tender touch that Dani isn't comfortable with. You all have a role in this family, and it's beautiful. I want to be a part of that, a part of all three of your lives, not only Dani and Xander's."

"You...do? I'm sorry, I prepared to hear you recite a list of reasons why I am the problem, that my past would eventually bring negative influences on Xander, that my feelings toward them were jaded by trauma to my mind."

"Those are your inner demons; they're wearing a mask to fool you into thinking it comes from me. From a professional standpoint, I believe your accident did bring you three together, but not because of mental trauma. You had a massive shift in priorities, and it hit you fast. You're not the first, although you were lucky enough to know where to go from there. You were afraid to commit to it at the time, also a normal reaction."

"Would you mind if I show you something?" He follows me inside and I push a shelf to the side, revealing markings on the wall.

"Mural?" He asks, stepping closer.

I trace along the wall with my finger. "Door. It represents the hope that we can all pull together and become one. I also thought Baguette would appreciate having access to two kitchens."

"So would Dani. I've been thinking of doing this. Have you checked the wall?"

"Yep, we should be clear. I did a bit of framing and carpentry work growing up. Dad worked in contracting."

He steps back, taking it all in. The door would end up just off both kitchens, connecting the dining rooms. "Perfect. Let's do it."

"What? Now?"

He checks the time and nods. "How long does it take? Five or six hours?"

"You, uh, don't do much building, huh?" I shake my head with a laugh. "If I run to the store, we can probably have it done in a couple of hours. Assuming we don't hit any weird. Electrical wires, plumbing, dead bodies."

"Okay, let's hope there's no dead bodies, but uh, here." He unlocks his phone and hands it to me, a level of trust clearly established between us. "I'll work on clearing out anything in the way on my side. Order whatever we need. Get it delivered and put it on my card."

"You're serious?"

"I am. About the door, about us, about becoming one. Yeah."

An hour later, I wrap up the first stages of the new door frame, which isn't anything more than a big ass, door-shaped hole in the wall. While we wait for the wood and other supplies to be delivered, I peek through to watch Theo working in his kitchen, measuring out ingredients with precision. He's a machine in there, and I have to admit it's sexy as hell watching the muscles in his forearms flex while he works. Brains and skills.

"That's how you handle the stoner snacks? I expected a pizza and a bag of popcorn or something." His head snaps around, almost knocking over the bowl he's stirring. "Sorry, didn't mean to spook you. What are you making?"

"Strawberry jam for a Fraisier cake." His tongue swipes across his lips as he stares at me, reminding me I took off my shirt a while ago. I duck my head down, trying hard not to blush. "Do you want to try it?"

He beams with pride and pulls a spoon out when I nod. He holds a scoop up for me, his other hand under it to catch anything that drips. The intense flavor that explodes the second it hits my tongue has me moaning before I can stop myself. "Doc! I could eat this all day. This can't be only jam, it tastes too good."

"Well, for one, we're high. But also, those are fresh

strawberries, so that always helps." He grins up at me, and I catch the faintest dusting of pink on his cheeks before he turns away. "The, uh, door looks nice."

"Thanks." Now it's my turn to look away, my ears burning.

He reaches up and my heart slams into my ribcage as he swipes his thumb across my bottom lip, pulling back a bit of the jam. He goes to grab the towel, but I catch his wrist, staring him right in the eye as I close my mouth over his thumb, sucking it clean.

"Wouldn't want to waste a single drop from you, Doc." I say after popping his thumb out of my mouth.

There's a split second when we both stare at each other, waiting for the other to make the first move. I'm not sure which one of us pounces first as we both bust forward, our mouths slamming together as our bodies fight for dominance and fewer clothes. It's a fight I'm too close to losing as he pins me against the counter and undoes my belt. I'm kissing him again, ready to give up the struggle and let him take the lead, until a knock at the door freezes us both.

"Should we ignore it?"

"Could be important," he counters

"More important than this?" I reach down, cupping his bulge as I nip at his lip.

Before he can answer, there's another knock, this time more urgent. "I'll be right back. In the meantime? Why don't you take your pants off and put your hands on the counter for me?"

Well, fuck me.

Xander didn't tell me he found himself a *daddy*. I wait till he's across the room before I give him a whistle. He can see me when he turns, but the counter blocks the important part as I let my jeans fall to the ground with a quiet thud.

"Don't make me wait too long, Chef."

"A quick learner. I like that."

"Excuse me, sorry to bother you. Are you Mr. Lucas Fitzpatrick?" The young kid at the door asks.

"Shit," I swear under my breath and head toward the door. Theo watches my hands as I walk toward him, re-button my pants and grab my shirt. I could swear he groans when I pull it back over my head.

"Don't worry. Just means we start all over again." I wink and turn to the kid. "That's not my name anymore."

"Shit, I'm so sorry! You're right, I read the wrong line!" The kid jerks the envelope out, eyes darting between us as he tries to work it out in his head. "I'm supposed to deliver this."

I take the envelope and, sure enough, it says my name and my dead name. I hate how archaic our government enjoys being. I glance up at the kid and his eyes still dart between us, trying to figure us out.

"We're roommates," Theo enlightens him, rolling his eyes as he tucks his hand into the back pocket of my jeans and giving my ass a squeeze.

"Right."

Under normal circumstances, I would play along and make a fun show of it, but I'm too distracted by the name on the envelope. It's a law firm, but not any law firm. It's the one that represented me when we tried to go after the woman who caused my accident. I can't focus. A dark curtain comes down over my vision. The air in the room turns thick with smoke and everything smells like gasoline. I can hear the sizzle of flesh, and I know it's mine.

Theo catches me before I hit the ground, and I don't register when he helps me to the couch until he comes back with a glass of water and a look in his eye I've seen too many times before. Pity.

I open the letter, scanning it as much as I can with my hands shaking the way they are.

"Do you need to talk about it, or?"

"There's new evidence in my accident. The lawyers want to talk to me."

HOLLYWOOD
Dani

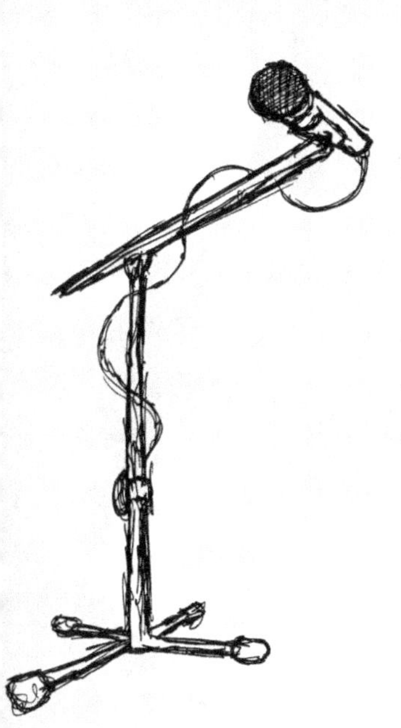

CHAPTER 38
THEREFORE I AM

BILLIE EILISH

WHY CAN'T I get this right? I rip out another piece of paper from my notebook and chuck it behind me somewhere to start over again on the next page. Our songs are boring, so I need to write some new ones and get everyone in the studio as soon as possible. If I don't, we run the risk of losing people's interest the longer we're in this competition.

"Ugh!" I groan loud enough to feel like a release, tearing that sheet out to start a fresh one. Maybe that's my problem. I need to start on a sheet I've already used. I glance over my shoulder and shake my head. That's idiotic. The stack of papers on the shelf has four new songs, a few chorus options to add more lyrics to, and a sketch for the album cover. But I have more to do. I've also made three new outfits. Well, half-made, those need finishing, too. Since my sister came back, I've been splitting the time between my family here and my family in the hospital. It's cost me too much time, and while I've appreciated the breaks and my sister being back, it's been chaotic. Ren's going to be fine. Do I need to be at her bedside every friggin' day?

Where the hell did that thought come from? It's my sister and Coop! Of course, I have to be there every day. What's wrong with me?

"Come on, Dani," I cheer myself on. "Only five more songs and you can take a break. For editing!"

There's a soft tap on the door before it creaks open. I don't bother to look up, too busy with my chicken scratch writing. A low whistle starts behind me before the un-crinkling of paper.

"Dani, how long have you been at this?" Skylar asks.

"Uhm, I dunno. Since I came in here to work and not be disturbed a few hours ago."

"A few hours ago? Love, have you looked out the window?"

I pry my eyes from the paper long enough to see there's no light coming in the room, but dive back into the writing. "Okay, so open the curtains."

"They are open. Come on, you can't be creative like this. Besides," they say, unfolding another piece of paper from the floor. "You're throwing away good stuff here. And murdering trees."

"They're in the notebook. They're already dead. And that stuff sucks."

"Is this one about Xander?"

"What?" I spin around in the chair and they're standing there with their arms crossed. At their feet, wads of paper resemble a snowball fight in our room. At least a hundred sheets lay all over the room. "Shit."

"Yeah, now put the pen down."

"Skylar I just—"

"Daniella, if you don't put that pen down right now, I'm going to tie you to the bed so you can't even touch your notebook. I'll leave you like that to make you take a break and torture you at the same time."

"You...wouldn't?"

They raise an eyebrow, daring me to try them. Instead, I put the pen down with a heavy sigh. "Fine. Five minutes."

"You've been in here for twelve hours, Beetle. You're done for the night." They sit on the bed, patting the spot next to them, so I trudge through the room, somehow avoiding any paper cuts on my bare feet. I flop down, letting my back bounce off the mattress.

"Need to talk?"

"No."

"To anyone?"

"NO!"

They lay back, nuzzling the side of my head. "Not even Noah?"

I turn and look at them, my face scrunched up. Why would I need to talk to Noah? She's handling all the postings on social media, which I've been sending her images for twice a week since Lexi taught me how to use a few programs.

"She has a notebook overflowing with songs. They're solid. Some could use a bit of finesse from you, but they absolutely fit our style.

"Great. You already know *our* style, so why don't you help her clean them up?" I snap.

"If you want. I could." They don't take the bait, remaining calm and even. "If it helps you breathe."

They're doing that on purpose, ignoring my snarky responses and attitude. I turn my head and look at the desk, the pile of papers, the invisible clock ticking away as I lay here getting no work done.

I gasp at the cold metal of their rings when they take my face and turn it back toward them. They let go of my chin, letting their finger trail down my throat to my shirt, which they slowly unbutton down to my bra.

"Take it off," they growl. I protest, but they give me that look. "Now. Or I rip it off, and you won't like the consequences."

I groan and sit up, reaching behind me and unhooking my bra and pulling off my shirt. Before I can ask what they want next, their warm breath kisses my spine seconds before they do. From my tailbone to between my shoulder blades, they move at their own pace. It's how they force me to slow down, but I'm too far into this manic state for that to work.

"Take off your shorts, leave the panties. Get on the bed on your hands and knees."

"Sky, I really—" my words are cut short by their hand around my throat, squeezing. That shouldn't make me as wet as it does.

"Open your bratty mouth now." I do, and they spit onto my tongue, pushing my mouth closed with one finger. "Swallow."

Another thing that shouldn't turn me on the way it does. Nothing they've done crosses a line. I've never even use the word to make them stop, only begging them for more, to take it farther.

"Now don't say another word—don't even open your damn mouth—until you're told. Shorts. Off."

I stand, letting my shorts slip down my legs before I crawl into the bed as they demanded. My panties on full display should anyone walk in the door.

And that's when Xander gets home, as if Skylar could hear him coming. The door to the bedroom opens and Sky calls out, knowing Xander came in Theo's door. The scuff of his shoes gets closer and there's muffled talking. I'm tempted to run over, shut the door, lock it, and go back to work, but I'm more interested in seeing what Skylar has planned for me now, since Xander's home.

The bedroom door opens wide, and I peek over my shoulder, finding all three of them standing in the doorway, ogling my ass. I didn't even realize Theo had come home from work, but he's in his lounge pants, which means he's been home for hours. Like Skylar said, I need a break.

I give them a little shake and a wink. Xander looks ready to pounce. So does Theo. But Skylar? They have something up their sleeve, even if they're not wearing a shirt. "Don't move, pet. Understood?"

I nod, and to my surprise, they go for Xander, pushing him against the wall in a breathless kiss full of passion and silent praise. Theo and Skylar both race to cup his cock as they bite, lick, and kiss one another. Skylar and Theo grunt while Xander lets out a series of high pitched swears. They grope each other and dry hump right there, across the room and out of my reach. I need to touch them. When they break apart, Skylar holds Xander's wrists against the wall with one hand, the other wandering all over his body. Theo drops to his knees, unzipping Xander's pants and tugging them down, doing the same with Skylar before standing again. Next, it's Xander's turn to get on his knees as Skylar pushes him down.

"Open wide, pretty boy. Eyes on our bratty little girl over there. If she moves, we're going to tie her up and fuck right on top of her." They give me a sideways glance and a wink, reminding me they'll do what they're threatening without a second thought.

Xander releases Theo's cock from his pants first, and my jaw drops. He's not as long as Skylar, but he's thick, like a damn horse. I'm not sure how Xander walks after that thing's been shoved inside him. Next, he turns and pulls Skylar out of their boxers, teasing the piercings with his thumb as he looks up at them both, waiting for direction.

"I've changed my mind," Skylar announces, their fingers dancing over Xander's puppy dog face. "Stand up, beautiful."

He does, standing beside Theo as they exchange a look laced

in confusion until Skylar faces me, dropping to his knees with their eyes locked on mine. They take Xander's cock out, licking a thick stripe up the underside of his shaft all the way to the head. It pulls breathy moans and whimpers from Xander until Theo's mouth muffles the sounds with long, slow kisses.

I'm stuck in place, my heart racing while I watch Skylar's tongue flick the tip of Theo's cock next, and I'm even more helpless when Xander grabs Skyler's hair, pushing them down onto Theo. "Suck it, don't stare at it," Xander quips, earning him a solid smack on the ass from Skylar.

Even from their knees, Skylar's control shines the brightest. The puppet master, stroking and sucking until the two men are his to control, begging for release as Sky switches from one to the other, before taking both together. I'm stuck watching while the wet spot on my panties grows every time they look at me.

"Just like that, Xander. Let her see how good I make you feel." Skylar hums between them. I strain to see more, but they've shifted and all I can see are the backs of Theo and Xander.

"God, Skylar. That's it," Theo praises. Before putting an arm over Xander's shoulder and pulling him closer. "That's it. Look how well the two of us fit. Like you were always meant to be ours."

"You want this, don't you, Beetle? Want to watch us cum all over Skylar's face while you soak your panties?" Xander asks, his eyes rolling back along with his head. He struggles to bring his eyes back to me. "You're so wet, Dani. Don't stop, Skylar. I bet we can make her cum without touching her perfect little cunt."

Skylar sucks in a deep breath as he lets Xander go with a pop, their hands jerking up and down as they watch me from between the pair of men. "Another time, handsome." They stand up, kissing Xander again before directing him over to me. He climbs up behind me, spreading me open, and shoving my panties to the side before he slides his tongue through me. Meanwhile, Skylar climbs in front of me, kneeling and taking hold of my head to direct it towards their dripping cock.

"Your turn, pretty girl. Since you won't listen to reason, we'll teach you to stop being so hard on yourself. You're going to be cock-drunk for days." They push down on my chin with their thumb, pressing their piercings to my lips and sucking in a deep breath when I lick the pre-cum from their head. They rock their hips in a lazy, uncoordinated circle, and when I see their eyes, they aren't watching me.

Xander's nips and teases don't last long, and soon he's buried his face inside me. It's heaven, but when he grunts and moans hard into me, I almost cum on his face right there. His fingers dig into me as he rocks back and forth, his breath shaky as he struggles to maintain his focus, and so do I. I want to turn around, to see what's happening. I want to see what Skylar sees.

"Oh! I can't! Holy shit."

Theo growls from somewhere behind me, "You can take it, Baby. You always take me so well in that perfect little ass."

"If you can't," Skylar adds. "I'm going to handcuff you both to the headboard and make you watch while Theo and I play, and you won't be allowed to come. Now get your face back into that cunt."

Xander feasts on me like a man on a mission, which when I figure out why he's rocking the way he is. The sound of slapping skin grows the more Xander moans, and I squirm. Xander's tongue writes poems inside me, lapping and sucking on my clit while I gag on Skylar as he holds my head down, humping my face.

"God, you're so tight, Baby. Do you like my cock spreading

you wide like the whore you are?" Theo groans, his voice getting tighter with each word. "And Dani, Skylar looks so damn good down your throat." A hand comes down on my ass and I let out a squeak.

"Ahh," Skylar breaths out. "Theo, harder. Spank our little nymph's ass harder. She liked that."

There's a loud smack and Xander groans deep, and a moment later, the stinging heat of Theo's hand comes down on me again. Xander's fingers pump into me and his mouth pulses on my clit harder with every spank we're given. It's all too much. I grab Skylar's thigh, digging my nails in as I try to balance on one hand.

They pull out of me, a line of saliva the only thing left connecting us. "Theo, Xander," they bark, and without another word, I'm left untouched, my head pivoting. They can't leave me like this, so close to the end. "Get in the bed."

Climbing in next to Skylar, Xander kneels in front of me, pulling me up so I'm kneeling, too. My eyes lock with his as Theo positions himself behind Xander, impaling him on that impressive, thick cock. Lava bubbles deep inside me as I watch Xander's mouth dropping open for a fury of beautiful noises.

"You good, Theo?" Skylar asks as Xander's head rocks back to Theo's shoulder and his hands latch onto my hips, pulling me closer.

"I'll be better when Xander starts fucking her instead of just sitting on my dick."

"Oh, shut it, old man." Xander yells—his words and breath shuttering. Skylar reaches between us, wrapping his hand around Xander's shaft, and lifting my leg with his other hand, sliding Xander into me like I'm a rag doll. "Dani," squeaks out of his mouth in the softest, most angelic noise I've ever heard from Xander. It's part praise and part plea, all in one word.

Skylar laughs, and the deep vibration of it does nothing to stop my swimming head. He moves behind me, his soothing voice wrapping around me, but I'm so far gone I can't make out the words. I gasp at the cold, wet sensation and release a groan the likes of which I've never heard come out of me before as they push inside of me.

"Breath, lover," Skylar whispers. "You're going to take a lot more than my finger."

"W-what?" Before he can answer, Theo bucks and Xander's hips move in response as he squeezes my hips, sending a wave of pain and pleasure through me. The movement between the three of us starts off sloppy and awkward, but we fall into a rhythm that matches Xander's moans and pleas. I cup his face and our eyes meet. Without a word, we share a moment of bliss before he lurches forward and covers my mouth with his.

"Are you ready? Both of you?" Xander breaks our kiss and nods with half-opened eyes, his hands reaching behind me and cupping my cheeks to spread them apart. "You know the word, Beetle. I'll take it slow."

The instant their head pushes into me; my back bends and my head slams back. The pain isn't what I'd expected; curling my toes as I scream out their name. My legs shake, threatening to give out, but Xander helps to keep me upright.

"I told you this ass belonged to me, and I meant it. Now, sing for us."

"I… can't. Too full! Oh, hell!" A few minutes ago, I couldn't find words for my lyrics. Now I can't even remember how words work as we become a writhing mass of grunts and groans with my screams mixed between them.

Xander grabs my face, and when I open my eyes, I can't believe I've never seen him look this beautiful before. His blissed-out eyes and their slivers of blue, his pretty mouth gasping and whimpering. The way he stares at me melts the icy wall I'd built around my heart these last few months, and I hope my face matches his and shows him how beautiful this is. I throw my arms around him, both of us shaking.

"You're doing great, Xander. Taking me so well, like a good boy should. Making our girl moan like the slut she is," Theo praises, leaving soft kisses up Xander's neck while reaching out for Skylar and wrapping his hand in their hair.

Xander and I never stood a chance, reduced to putty between these two powerful bodies as the pair watch each other. I watch it in Theo's eyes and hear it in Skylar's breathing, telling me how close they've become when I wasn't looking. What else have I missed while trapped inside my mind, refusing to let anyone in?

"God, Dani, you're so amazing. You both feel incredible!"

"Do you want to cum for her, Xander? Fill your queen bee?"

"Yes, please!" Theo smacks Xander's ass and his body goes tense, his cock pulsing inside me as I squeeze him tight. Skylar and Theo both thrust harder, and I find myself in a galaxy of far away stars as I come undone around Xander, collapsing in his arms. Skylar lets out a primal yell first as he reaches his climax next.

"That's it, baby. Take it all. Take every drop of me. I'll make sure Theo fucks my cum back into you."

There's another loud groan and Xander shudders, his grip on me tightening. But the world disappeared already, and everything melts together. I can't tell one orgasm from the next as they coax them out of my limp body. Different arms wrap around me, and I'm lowered to the bed, legs spread wide. Skylar's hair tickles as it drapes over me, his mouth closing around my breast. Xander's long, slender fingers tease my overstimulated clit while he whispers to me. I let out a pathetic gasp when the bearded face buries itself between my legs. Every movement is soft and caring, sending me deeper and deeper into the serene dark. My eyes close and I'm covered in a warm blanket of sleep.

I wake up in a fresh shirt and panties, with Xander wrapped around my front, and Skylar my back, and Theo's hand on my stomach. They're all softly snoring. I wish I could stick this moment into a time capsule and open it whenever I needed the lift. I should go back to work. I should, but I'm far too tired now to think. There's always tomorrow.

HOLLYWOOD
Theo

CHAPTER 39
FRENCH GIRLS

DOVE CAMERON

WE BUILT A DOOR, and it opened a world to us all. The four of us slipping into something of a routine lifestyle together. It's a beautiful dynamic, and, outside of the bedroom, none of us fight for dominance or attention.

Xander started talking about what he remembers in Tokyo, but only to me. He still refuses to see another professional about it. The nightmares persist, but the intensity has dialed down a few notches. He's still on the website, but in his free time, he's working on his own program and site. He works hard, especially when the trail of his attacker, Oliver, goes cold. But he's trying not to let it take over his mind.

Skylar's progress has been slow, but when the needle moves, it jumps several degrees. Xander or I take them to meetings regularly, and they've done excellent work with the therapist I recommended. They're even down to three cigarettes a day—when they're not stressed. The lawyer's visits put them on edge, and they can't help but look over their shoulder every time we go out, cringing away from certain sounds and making themselves as small as they can so no one will take notice of

them. I've made sure they get a little extra praise when I'm with them; they deserve it.

They're both giving me the strength I needed to buy the ticket to France and book the hotel for two weeks. Xander almost choked on the words when he told me to go for it, but we made a promise to talk every day while I'm gone. I've even opened up about my wife, our lover, and a little bit about Sylvie, too. It hasn't felt like letting go of them, like I had imagined it would. Instead, it's as though I've invited them back into my life, sharing stories about them and keeping them alive within me. Skylar said I should tell some of these stories to Sylvie, and they're right. Maybe that's where our disconnect lies.

Then there's Dani. Our little lost queen beetle, as Skylar calls her. She's wandering around in the dark, scurrying under the furniture when we open the door and try to shed light on anything she's going through. A silent fighter who teeters on the edge of a breakdown but doesn't see the cliff, doesn't know about the jagged rocks below her. She blames everyone else, but the real problem lies under her hard carapace. She's run out of room to store the pent-up feelings, and now, even the little things have nowhere else to go. I've warned both Xander and Skylar that she's in for a rough ride when the shell cracks and she's left vulnerable and exposed. The problem is, she takes it out on Xander because she thinks he can handle it. That may have worked before Tokyo, but since his return, he's not stable enough for that. Not yet.

We'll be there for her when she needs us most, keeping her protected as she licks her wounds and rebuilds her armor. Some people only know how to handle stress one way, bury it deep inside. Until she breaks, we're doing what we can to hold the house together for and around her.

"Skylar! Theo! Where are you, dickheads?" Xander comes

bolting into their place, before running through mine like he's on fire.

"What? What is it?" We both hurry out of the bedroom, pulling clothes back on and finding him waving his phone around, the biggest grin I've seen on him in months.

"Oh, sure, you couldn't even wait for me? Don't care, this is too incredible!" He runs over, shoving his phone in our faces. Skylar grabs his hand to steady it as we both try to read, but neither of us understands what the hell we're reading. "It's the investor I told you about! The one who wants to see the site I built! He wants to meet with me next week and go over logistics and—Holy shit, I sound like my dad."

"Happier. You sound way happier than your dad," Skylar points out, even though neither of us has met Mr. Maxwell.

"God, this is gonna be epic. I need to prepare. I need to practice the pitch, go over the deck again, and check the coding." His face drops as he looks between the two of us. He's gone from happy to looking like he's going to lose his lunch in point three seconds. "Oh, shit."

"Woah, deep breaths, love," Skylar coaches, putting a hand on his shoulder and making a breathing motion over their own chest with the other hand. "In and out. That's all you need to do right now."

"No! I need a suit. I can't borrow yours, either of you. Mine are all with my parents. Well, all but that one, but I threw out the pants. Shit, Dani ripped the jacket up and turned it into a dress for one of the shows. The vest, too."

"Okay, let's go get you a new one." I offer. "My treat. We'll call it my way of investing in your sales pitch. But that means I also get first dibs on ripping it off you."

"Smooth." Skylar laughs. "Also, the thought of bending him

over a desk with a tie shoved in his mouth to keep him subdued? Perfection."

Xander shakes his head. "You two are worse than me, I swear. Also, no office. Please, do not let me get an office."

The conversation about offices, suits, and business in general continues as we pile into my car and head down to the fashion district. I've had a few clients that work in the area and they love to tell me I should come by sometime and see what they do, so I'm going to take them up on it for once. We head to see Sage first at her shop in Santee Alley. It's early enough in the day the crowds haven't hit their peak yet, but it's still bustling as the shops open. This place resembles a carnival of colors and fashion, everything from high end, custom pieces to knock off sports jerseys and bags all next to each other in cramped stalls down an open-air corridor.

It takes us a while to find her stall, losing Xander to a cologne stall once, Skylar by a candy vendor, and both in a stall packed with replica vintage t-shirts. When we do find her, Skylar's eyes light up and he dives right in, flipping through fabrics and colors across the spectrum. When Xander freezes, I take his hand and introduce him to Sage. She takes a few measurements and disappears somewhere in the racks of clothes.

"I don't know if any of these work for me," he laments, cringing at the three-piece suit hanging on the wall. "I don't want this. I don't want suits and offices."

"Oh, you'll want an office," I promise him, cupping his face and kissing him a dozen times. "An office with little surprises everywhere. A place for Skylar to tie you up and remind you who's in charge. A place for me to hold you down while you tremble below me, begging for me to fill that pretty ass of yours harder."

"Oh, I like the sound of that office," Skylar says, appearing from nowhere with a handful of ties. "A nice couch where Dani can ride you, and some added soundproofing to keep your assistants from hearing too much."

"I'm gonna need a lock on the door. Wait, I said no office!" His eyes light up as the flick between us and he reconsiders his stance. "Okay, but Dani gets the desk first. My desk. Not my dad's, not someone else's, mine. I'm gonna eat her for lunch one day, papers everywhere, phones ringing, and her, spread wide and dripping for me."

"Seems fair," Skylar replies, picking up a tie and holding to Xander's eyes before taking his hands and wrapping the tie loosely around them. "Get this one."

"He hasn't even picked out a suit yet!" I laugh, nudging Sky's arm with my elbow.

"Who said anything about wearing it with a suit?" They wink at me before they go back to the labyrinth in time for Sage to reappear with four suit bags.

"Okay, so you're like a perfect size for these, which is amazeballs, since I haven't been able to show these off since fashion school. By the way, I used to go to school with your girlfriend. We had a class together. Don't let her fool you into thinking she can't do menswear, because she's fucking boss at it. Seriously. Absolute fire."

Xander's crooked smile and soft pink cheeks make my heart flutter. We need to help Dani and him work through whatever they're going through, because those two are something beyond the normal constraints of love and affection. For now, we focus on the bags, though. Or, more importantly, what we're about to find in them.

His jaw drops when she pulls out a beautiful black jacket with studs decorating the pockets, a handwritten message filling one side of the chest, and beautiful matching details making sparse appearances on the other side. He blinks rapidly, gawking at me before looking back at the jacket.

"Try it on, bro!" Sage offers, holding it up for him. It's damn near made for him. "I need to adjust a couple of things to make this work for you, babe. But seriously, look at how boss you look? I'd work for you!"

He looks in the mirror and, for a while, he can't speak.

"I've never seen *myself* in a suit. It's always been someone else, someone I pretended to be to fit in. Someone I didn't recognize and didn't want to be. I don't feel that right now."

"Yeah, your grandpa ain't wearing my suits. I mean, unless he's like super rad or whatever." She stands on her tiptoes and glances around the shop before looking at me again. "Doc, please, oh please tell me I'm gonna dress that tall, broody, and beautiful creature that came in with you, too. I mean, seriously, you let me dress these two. I'll throw in a free suit for you."

"I'm down. I need some new stuff for the road. Sexy me up, baby!" Skylar answers before I can, holding up a vest covered in chains, buckles, and studs. "This place is a punk's wet dream and a corporate dickhead's nightmare. You're a saint, Sage."

"I aim to create chaos and confusion!" She yells, throwing her hands in the air. "Let's get to work!"

"I guess we're in business," I finally answer. Xander and Skylar each kissing my cheeks as Sage hugs me.

The plane touches down with a jerk, jarring sleeping passengers awake, which included the two children sitting right behind first class. I don't normally fly first class, but I had enough points and figured what the hell. The food blew my mind, but the privacy sent my imagination on an adventure. Xander would love this, and I could keep him busy enough to not think about it. At the least, I'd be able to hold him through it, snuggled into the small bed together.

I text him when I land, and he sends me a picture of Baggy eating salmon out of his hand. I should tell them not to eat in the bed, but the sweet face he makes in the next picture melts my heart. I don't know what brought us together other than a couch in the hallway, or if we'd have found each other eventually without the couch, but I can't imagine my future without him now. All of them.

Climbing into the cab, I get a text, but this one isn't from Xander.

PIXIE

Papa, we're running late. Maybe twenty minutes. Please wait for us!

I'd wait all night for you.

I almost add in that I have waited all night for her. Two nights, in fact. Taking shifts with Gio sleeping on the old, uncomfortable chairs in the hospital while her mother was in labor. Sylvie hadn't been interested in joining the world, too comfy. She took her time, and Élodie handled it like I never could. When the time finally came, and the nurse tried to tell Gio he had to leave, Élodie threw a fit and I locked arms with both Gio and I. He was as much Sylvie's father as I was in our eyes and hearts.

These are memories Sylvie's grandparents can't share with her. Even my sister-in-law, Marie, can only share so much. I've deprived her of knowing not only me, but Gio and Élodie, too. I reach for the photo album in my backpack for the hundredth time, ensuring myself I remembered it. Xander found the book on top of my suitcase and brought it to me in the bed with a bottle of wine. Flipping through the book offers a magical, tactile connection to the memories. Especially with Xander curled in my arms as I went through my entire history in France. In some ways, those days happened in a different universe long ago. But I've found connections to this life, to these new people I've opened my heart for.

I reach further down in the bag and find the empty box I brought with me. I don't know if it will be empty on the way home, but I wanted to try since Sylvie has Élodie's wedding ring, and the rings Gio and I wore to symbolize the three of us belonged together. I don't expect to get her mother's, but Gio's? I want to put that on Xander's finger so fiercely I can't breathe when I imagine it. The entire situation has moved so fast—faster than Élodie or Gio. But I can see them in his eyes, like they're a part of him.

After I drop my things at the hotel, I grab my coat and head down the busy streets of Paris. Again, I find myself picturing Xander here with me, the weight of his hand in mine as we walk the historic sites, taking him to all the museums and restaurants before hopping a train out to the countryside for a week or two between the grapevines. I never sold the land we owned out there, but I have no idea what shape it's in now. I hope the flowers from Élodie's garden have taken the land back, making it beautiful but mysterious. Land, like the love that blossomed there, lost to time.

I laugh at the poetry of the thought. I've been spending too much time with Skylar. They'd love it here, too. So would Dani. I should stop by the old house and see how much of it still stands.

At the cafe, I order a coffee and a box of pastries. At home, I give most of what I bake away, but here? Oh, these babies are all mine here. I'll buy more for Sylvie and Luca if they want anything. I find a seat at a corner table where I can look out over the street, watching the sunset and the glow of the streetlights filling the night. My phone buzzes, so I check it in case it's Sylvie again.

BLUE EYED BABY

You're going to do great tonight, and someday, I'm going to meet her.

Tell her all those stories you told me about them.

What if she cries? Like you did?

BLUE EYED BABY

Hold her like you did me, big guy. Only, you know, not the making out and sex part, obviously.

I miss you. And your smart mouth.

BLUE EYED BABY

I miss you, too.

How's Dani doing?

BLUE EYED BABY

I retreated to your place. She's on a tirade right now about Skylar's smoking and how the band would fall apart without her.

Hang in there. She's got to break soon. make sure she's not alone when she does.

BLUE EYED BABY

We'll take care of her. You get your daughter back and enjoy yourself. Call me later if you want.

I'll call you tonight when I get back in.

I type out the words I haven't said to him yet, and delete them. They'll come out in time.

"Papa?"

I glance up from my phone and I'm staring into the eyes of my Élodie. The phone clatters to the floor as I stand, hugging Sylvie as tight as she'll let me. She even hugs me back. I can't stop the flood of words and affection. "I'm sorry, Pixie. God, I'm so sorry. I'm going to try harder. I promise you, I will."

When we finally pull away from one another, she takes the hand of the young man standing next to her. A lopsided grin forms on my face as I stare at him, knowing exactly why Sylvie's grandfather claimed she'd joined a cult. This kid's entire aura screams Italian. The clothes, the hair, his entire look. It reminds me of that lead singer of the Italian band that won Eurovision a few years ago. I laugh, because Skylar has the same Italian swagger, and looks like he could be that singer's much taller brother. Luca holds out my phone with a smirk.

"You dropped this."

"Luca, I assume?" He nods as I take the phone and tuck it away. I won't be looking at that for a while, I can tell. "Nice to meet you, I'm Theo. If you've met my father-in-law, I offer you my heartfelt apologies. He and I disagree over too much, and always have, so I feel your pain." My eyes bounce between them, pride bubbling through my chest. "Sit, please. We have so much to catch up on."

HOLLYWOOD
Xander

CHAPTER 40
HAND THAT FEEDS

HALSEY, AMY LEE

DANI HAS ABOUT ten more laps in her pacing before she'll wear through the floorboards, and we'll give our downstairs neighbor's a free skylight. She won't tell me what's bothering her. Every time I try to talk to her, she snaps and goes back to pacing. We're supposed to go out today, a date with only the two of us, but she's canceled for the fourth time in two weeks.

The tickets to the zoo I can exchange for another day, again, but the play she wanted to see closes tonight. I'd spent the last of my money from Tokyo on those tickets. I couldn't look at that money in my bank and not see Oliver's face or hear my father's screaming. I should have turned the money down when my aunt sent me the check. If it had come from my father, I would have.

Storm Dani changes trajectory and veers for the kitchen, slamming the door to the fridge a few moments later and stalking back to the living room empty-handed. We had hoped she found a way out of her funk, but the more we try to help or be there for her, the deeper into herself she crawls. This morning, she lost her shit on Skylar, and they left. They texted me from Chase's house to let me know they're okay, but giving her space.

"Why are you just sitting there?" She yells, so I slowly glance

up from my book, half expecting her to be yelling at a plant or a bird on the windowsill. But it's me.

"Uhm, I'm reading?" I hold the book up and shake it.

"Is that what you do all day when I'm at work? Sit around getting high, play video games, read your stupid fantasy books?" She snarls, waving her hands around to emphasize whatever point she's trying to make. "Maybe, if you put the smallest effort into—"

"Dani, I was up till three in the morning working. What do you want from me?"

"Some fucking support! Do I have to do everything myself?"

"You don't do everything yourself. What are you freaking out over?"

She storms over to a stack of papers, straightening them before shoving them in a box. Next, she takes a vase of week-old flowers, throwing them in the trash—they could have lasted a few more days. She continues storming around the house, picking off every little thing that offends her, mumbling about a mess that never existed. Theo suggested she get tested for ADHD, saying she displays several signs, but she laughed him off because there's no possible way she has ADHD in her mind. The closet full of half started, never finished projects might like to argue with her about that, but I sure as hell am not.

"I don't have time for this!" she looks like she's about to cry. Like she wants to scream into the void for an hour or so. I wish she would. Instead, she slams drawers, mumbling under an audible level, and occasionally lets out a guttural yell, storming out of the kitchen. "Why is this shit still here?"

"What shit?"

She waves her hands around the apartment, exasperated that I'd have the gall to ask such a question. I glance around, not sure what she's getting at.

"The blood furniture! My reverse dowry! The shit your parents thought would buy my silence when they tried to take you back to their castle of lies!"

"That's accurate yet dramatic. Uh, mostly because it's all we have. I told you, when I'm making some more money working, I'll replace it. For now, I mean, we could sell it, I guess. But that's just—"

"Working or *working*?" She throws air quotes up around the last word, crossing her arms and staring at me. I'm not sure how to react to that since she already knows I was up coding and building websites all night. She also knows I'm trying to stay away from the subscription site for now, maybe forever. Or until get funding and launch the competitor site.

"Okay, I'm gonna give you some space and—"

"Blow fifteen other guys behind my back? I'm sure Theo's real proud of that, dating a guy like you."

Theo's proud of me for it. He tells me that every night, and how much he appreciates me and how hard I'm working on myself. Dani hasn't said a word about the site, or me sleeping with men, both things she knew about. She didn't know about the money for sex, but she knew I already jerked off for subscribers. The boyfriend we had never stuck around after they found out.

"What are you saying?" My voice stays even, but she can tell she's hit the nerve she's aimed for all morning.

"You know what I'm saying! Do you wait for us to go to work and suck some stranger's cock in an alley, begging him to punch you in the face for it? Did you do that so you could blow the money on those fucking tickets? That's appropriate, isn't it? Calling them *fucking* tickets since that's how you got them?"

"What the hell, Dani?" I shift so I'm sitting in the chair instead of across it, leaning on my elbows. I don't like raising my voice to her. But Dani's a yeller when we fight. She goes for the lowest hanging fruit, the hits she knows will hurt the fastest. We haven't fought like this in months, though. "Is this because of the suit? Because I didn't come to you first?"

"No! But maybe it is. Who the hell cares about what I have to say, anyhow?"

"I do! I always have!" My mind races. This can't be about the stupid suit. "Theo took us out there to get clothes because you're busy, Dani. I didn't want to put one more thing on your plate. Hell, I want to take things off it! I'm trying!"

"You couldn't even ask, Xander? You went behind my back! You went to my former classmate; do you know how embarrassing that is?"

"I got one suit, Dani. One. Because she told me how amazing you are at making menswear. You know how many times you've made anything for me in the last fourteen years?"

"Oh, screw you, I've… I made you… It doesn't matter!"

"It does matter! Jesus Christ, Dani, I've got nothing left to give you, nothing."

"What's that supposed to mean?"

You. Deserve. Better.

Theo's words play in my head, but I never expected I'd use them against Dani. This isn't who she is. This is—I stop my excuses before they can form. She holds everything in until she explodes, and when that happens, I become her verbal punching bag. She spits her venom, and I've built an immunity, but she's found the weak spot in my armor. I'll always fight for her, always. But I'm tired of fighting against her. Against who she's always been.

"Dani, this isn't about the kitchen, the furniture, or some fabric you didn't sew together with your own hands. You're scared about Skylar, and probably still pissed off that he left when he got addicted, that we weren't there for him. You think we failed him? I'm struggling with that, too. But that's the past. Are you upset about Theo, or stressed about your sister? If that's the case, we should talk, not scream." I shake my head, hoping this isn't falling on deaf ears, but I'm already seeing that it is. "Don't take it out on me! Don't hide your fake rage behind the money I earned in—"

"You expect me to believe that you went to Japan, told your dad where to shove his promotion, and they still paid you? That's bullshit, Xander. How stupid do you think I am? You don't have a job, so you must have gotten the money somewhere. You're screwing them again, aren't you?"

I close my eyes and take a slow breath, repeating the mantra I've said for years in my mind. *She's not mad at you. She's taking it out on you because you can take it. I can't take it today, though. I should never, again.*

"You don't mean any of this."

"Maybe I do! If you hadn't—"

"Please, I'm begging you, Beetle. Please don't do this."

She lets out something between a growl and a scream before she storms into the bedroom, slamming the door shut. I pull out my phone and send a text to her.

"Fine! I'll go stay at Theo's!"

"What good does that do? There's a giant hole in our wall!" She yells through the door. "Besides, he's in PARIS! With his DAUGHTER!"

"You know what? The hell with this, I'll go to Paris." I mumble, as I stand up and start grabbing my things. "Get as far away from you as I can, since that's what you want!" I shove my laptop and my book into my backpack and yell back to the door, "I'm not doing this anymore, Dani, I'm not. I'm done. Figure your shit out and let me know if you want me to bother coming back, or if we're done. Because I can't keep doing this. I can't keep giving you this."

"Giving me what?" She snaps, whipping the door open so she can stare at me.

"That safety net that says I'll come back, because this time, I won't. You'll be adding me to that list I've tried so hard not to be part of. The long list of people who've walked out of your life because you pushed them out."

I don't wait for her to respond; I don't want her to. I storm for the door, rip it open, and let it slam shut behind me. I stand there in the cold, dim hallway. This part never gets easier for me, and I don't think it does for her either. She understands each time it happens, I'm pushed closer to the edge, closer to letting go of us. She tries to beat the system by pushing people out before they can walk out. Forcing them out of her life so she doesn't need to face her own demons. But I'm always there, always willing to take one for the team, to let her work it out of her system knowing I'm a yo-yo and I'll only go so far before I come spinning on back to her.

But I've brought scissors to this fight, and I'm cutting the string. It's the worst possible time for this to happen, which makes it the best time for it, too. I wait in the stairwell for her to leave for a Skylar-less rehearsal before I head over to Theo's empty apartment and pack up everything Baggy needs. She hates the carrier, but I coax her in there with salmon.

I hate doing this. The whole idea of not coming back to Dani rips my heart out, but a night alone may remind her that what she's asking for might not be what she wants.

I sit in the bedroom under the window, stroking Baggy's soft fur to help her relax in the carrier. The tears won't stop as I force myself to picture life without Dani, trying to convince myself I could make it on my own. "I guess I wouldn't be on my own, would I Baggy?" I say, wiping my face with my free hand. I glare at the wall. Knowing she's right there on the other side isn't helping matters. "But I couldn't stay here. You think your dad would move?"

MEOW!

"Yeah, I don't think so, either."

Usually, when she throws me out, I set up a long-term hookup. Someone who will let me share their bed for a week or two. My friend's list isn't long, but friends who would willingly put me up for a few nights? I have even fewer options there. I have one I trust enough to know he won't expect special favors or beat my ass when I try to leave. Small victories, I guess.

Baggy lets out a low mewling noise as I climb down the stairs with her and load her into Theo's car, screaming her displeasure that I'm taking her. Or she's pissed she's out of salmon. I strap her carrier into the back seat, making sure she's secure before I climb in and pull out of the garage. I'll be back, but I'm unsure what or who I'll be coming back to.

HOLLYWOOD
Theo

SYLVIE, Luca, and I closed the coffee shop that first night, and again the second night. On the third, I watched them both play in a production at their college, and I cried like a damn baby when Sylvie performed her solo. Marie sat next to me, holding my hand and crying with me. We went for dinner and drinks after, laughing and talking about music and art. It was the first time I broached the subject of her mother since I'd gotten there, not knowing how it would go over.

"Your mother, if you don't mind me talking about her, would have been so proud to hear you tonight, Pixie. Absolutely beautiful and haunting, you're a natural in that chair, becoming one with the cello and moving the audience the way you did. And you, Luca, Christ, man. How long have you been playing?"

"I started playing violin at five. My mother insisted I play something, anything. She thought piano, maybe. But I liked Sherlock Holmes, and when he played. I loved the sound of the music, haunting yet peaceful. It made my heart leap with joy one moment, and weep the next."

I watched the pair squeeze each other's hands, taking the compliments in stride with only a little blushing. Sylvie circled

back to what I'd said earlier, "Do you really think Mama would have been proud? Of me, of all of this?"

"More than proud, sweetheart. I can see the three of you now, playing together at the house with—"

"Mama played? What did she play?"

My heart gets lodged in my throat as the smile slides off my face. I glare at Marie, but she avoids looking back, playing with her napkin and avoiding the question I'm about to ask her. The hell with that, someone will have to answer. If I have to find Sylvie's grandfather and force it out of him.

"Sylvie, your mother played both the violin and the cello. She was practically a savant. She reached first chair violin before she left university, and her cello skills had invitations coming from orchestras all over Europe." I let out a long, slow breath from my nose, closing my eyes and shaking my head. The heat rising from my collar must show on my face because Marie squeezes my leg under the table. "I'm sorry, Pixie. I don't want to cause a rift, but...fuck. Maurice should have given you those instruments. I kept them, cleaned them, made sure they would be in perfect shape for you if you ever wanted to play. He promised me he'd give them to you. I thought—I thought you were playing her cello tonight. I truly did."

She's silent for a while, a single tear falling that Luca quickly swipes away with his thumb. He whispers something to her, and she nods, lowering her head.

"Dr. Clay—"

"Theo."

"Yes. Theo. Sylvie's grandfather tried to stop her from playing. Said it would be a disgrace, among other terrible things. He's kept everything from her, things she knew her mother or you had left for her. She has only a single picture of the three of you and a man she doesn't know."

My heart screams as it shatters. I want to march to the village outside town, pitchforks and torches style, and drag Maurice out of his home and into the street. I trusted him. I turn to Marie again. This time, she has the courage to look at me and purse her lips, looking for pity.

"I tried, but you know how my father can be since losing Élodie."

I'm about to lose control when a soft hand settles on mine, giving a gentle tap the way her mother used to. Looking at my daughter again gives me an idea that might go over better than murdering an old man in his own home, but I make myself a promise. Tomorrow, I get everything we left for Sylvie, no matter what.

"Sylvie, I don't have much. In fact, all I have left of that time is the memories and the pictures in the book I brought with me. If you'd like, if it's okay, I'd like to grab a couple bottles of wine, head out somewhere quiet with the three of you, and tell you about your mother. And about the man in the picture? He's Giovanni."

"Wait," Marie holds up a hand and I nearly growl at her for it. "I want you to do this, to tell them everything. I'm not trying to stop that. But it's late, and those memories will take us through sunrise. Come to my house in the morning. I'll make us all breakfast; we'll have all day to talk. After the memories, we'll start planning on how to get your things from my Papa. Okay?"

We're all reluctant, but we nod. We say our goodbyes and Luca says he and Sylvie will pick me up in the morning. In the hotel, I can't sleep. I'm an ocean of emotions, one wave of joy and pride, followed by another of rage and guilt. At two in the morning, I try to call Xander, but there's no answer, so I leave a message. I toss and turn until sunrise, get ready, and I'm downstairs a full twenty minutes before Luca and Sylvie are supposed to be here. I try Xander again, leaving another voicemail, but this time I'm less surprised. It's close to one in the morning there, which means he's probably in bed with Sky and Dani, or playing video games. So I grab a coffee and partake in the French tradition of people watching while I wait.

"…and that probably means Maurice hates you as much as me." I explain to Luca as we all crowd around the coffee table with the picture book spread out. It's open to a photo of Gio holding Sylvie after she was born. He's nothing but smiles and joy. Looking at the picture, I'm reminded of the pride that welled inside both of us when we first saw *our* daughter. "Sylvie, have you told him your middle name?"

"I…have a middle name?" She stares at me, stunned. "I only know my first."

"Marie, by the end of this trip, I think I'm going to murder your father. Sylvie, your full name at birth was Sylvie Fiorella Duponte-Clay. It drove your grandfather insane because he's a close-minded prick." Marie puts a hand on my arm and I wave her off. "Look, what I'm trying to tell you, what I've been trying to tell you, our lives were so much more intertwined than you know. We loved him."

"Like, what, an uncle or close friend?"

"No, sweetie. Like a husband. We, the three of us, shared our home, our lives, our love, and, well, everything else. You were *our* daughter, equally so in our eyes." The gears turn in her head and she grabs the book, flipping back a few pages and pointing at the rings Gio and I wear. "Yeah, we couldn't get married, but we didn't need a piece of paper to share our love. They matched your mother's ring, all three of our names on the inside. Here." I pull my ring out of my bag, dangling the chain out for her to catch it.

"You still have it?"

"I still wear it. Well, I did. I will again, but that's another story."

She swallows hard, pulling out the chain that's around her own neck revealing a ring that looks similar to her mothers. Luca pulls the picture of baby Sylvie, her mother, Gio, and me out, and points to the ring. "It took a lot to figure out, but with Marie's help, I tried to recreate the ring your wife had when I… well," he lowers his head, hiding his smile.

"What?!" I shout and Sylvie jumps, eyes wide as she stares at me. For a second, she's not sure if I'm livid or elated. I'm a little of both. "You don't have the ring? You made a replica? Shit, you proposed to her, didn't you?"

I'm grinning from ear to ear when I stand up, kissing them both. Words are lost on me, and I wish Skylar were here to say something profound and poetic. After the tears start to fall, I kiss Sylvie's forehead and whisper, "I'm so happy for you both. You have no idea how happy I am. No idea. And I'll get you that ring back, I will."

My phone buzzes and I reach for it on instinct. Sylvie must catch something in my face or my body language, because she asks if I'm okay. I'm not. I'm worried about Xander and every time my phone goes off, I'm grabbing it in the hopes it's him.

"Sylvie, I have a favor to ask. I'm going to Maurice's tonight, and we'll get everything back. You can keep as much of it as you want. All of it except one thing. I have no right to ask since you lost him, too. Maurice scrubbed so much from your memory, even though Gio loved you as deeply as your mother and I did. I want Gio's ring back. I want to give it to… to the man I've… I've…"

She doesn't let me finish, standing so fast she nearly knocks her chair over. Her arms come around me, followed by a soft giggle. "On one condition," she says, holding my face and giving me the same serious look that her mother used to when she wanted me to know she wasn't kidding. "I want to meet him."

"We can arrange that, but there's more than just one."

"Papa!" She snickers.

"Xander, Skylar, and Dani."

"All boys you love?"

"Xander is, yeah. Skylar is non-binary, so we call them the person we love. Dani is a woman." I pull my phone out again, showing her pictures where they at least have enough clothes on to be decent. It's tricky sometimes. I find one of Xander and I, from the night he got on the plane for Tokyo. We'd barely known each other a day and already I knew he changed me. Changing my whole life. "That's him."

"So, you love him more than the others?"

"Not more, no. It's not a competition. I love them all in their own ways, but he found me first. He's the reason I let myself fall in love again."

"Your father called me," Marie interrupts. "I couldn't believe how happy he was. Like being young again and hearing him call me about Gio or Élodie. So much love in his voice, just like now. Just like you two." She looks down at Luca, and back to Sylvie and I. "We should go. Papa will be home by now and it's time he puts this foolishness aside. His daughter loved an American as much as she loved an Italian."

"Why does he dislike Italians so much?" Luca asks.

"Ah, because he is a stubborn old man. His father left his

mother for an Italian actress. Then Papa fell in love with his own Italian woman, who left him at the altar. He's held a grudge against your country ever since. Absolutely stupid. He only found more hatred after Gio moved in with Élodie and Theo. He couldn't understand and thought it made Élodie look...dirty. He's a Catholic, and they can be so strange sometimes, I swear." She picks up the dishes from lunch, turning before she gets to the kitchen. "Theo, after we deal with Papa, I have something to show you."

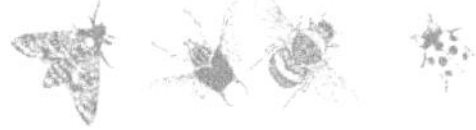

Maurice yells at me in French. I yell back in broken French and English. He yells some more. When Marie steps in between us saying the neighbors are about to call the police on us, Maurice finally backs down and lets us into the house. It's another hour of heated arguments, but less yelling, before Marie and Sylvie have Luca and I leave. When we're allowed back in, Maurice is gone, but he's told us to take whatever we want. Or, at least, that's how Marie puts it. So we do. Marie leads us to the attic, where we find the instruments and boxes of gifts I'd sent for Sylvie after I'd left. We find toys she never got, packages and presents they hid from her, and a lifetime of memories I promise to explain for the rest of my life if I have to. It's no wonder she didn't want to talk to me. She thought I'd abandoned her, and her grandparents helped fuel that belief.

We pile everything we can into Luca's car, and even fill Marie's. The last few boxes come with me in a cab. The neighbors watch the whole thing, probably happy Maurice is moving. They're less happy when they realize he's not. After we unpack the boxes into Sylvie and Luca's apartment for them to go through, we're all exhausted and ready to call it an early night.

"One more stop. I promise, it will be worth it. We'll grab some wine and snacks on the way and we can eat there."

"Where?"

"Somewhere Sylvie needs to see. You, too."

It doesn't take me long to recognize the path she's taking, pointing out different places along the way that Sylvie has seen her whole life but never knew she had ties to. The first restaurant I worked at. The place her mother and I met. The first apartment we shared with Gio. As we leave the city behind for more rural roads, I stare at a landscape that's hardly changed in the years I've been gone. Sylvie falls asleep leaning against Luca, and he nods off shortly after that. I check my phone again, but still nothing from Xander. The calendar says Dani and Skylar have a show tonight, so I don't want to bother them. I'm only here for another two days before I head back home. Hopefully I hear from him before that.

The crunch of gravel as Marie pulls off the main road pulls me out of a dream with a start. I glance around, my brain still a little foggy about where I am and why I'm in a car.

"Have a nice nap?"

"Yeah, sorry about that. I didn't mean to—" My thoughts screech to a halt when she turns a corner, and the house comes into view. I had pictured it with weeds and flowers overtaking it through the years, but it looks the same as it did in my rearview mirror when I finally decided I couldn't take anymore and went back to the states.

"Where are we?" Sylvie asks as Marie puts the car in park. She gasps and sits upright, pointing out the window to a wooden swing hanging from a branch. "LUCA! Oh, my god! I know this house. I know that swing!"

"Gio hung that up for you. Took him three weeks to convince Élodie that you wouldn't kill yourself on it. You were so scared the first time; he held you while I pushed you both."

"I—I remember that. I believed it all a strange dream I had, not reality." She pushes the door open and runs across the backyard past the swing and to the tree where our initials are all carved. "You built me a house! My own little house, and I loved it so. It sat there. Oh, and over there we had a table where we painted together, all of us. I used to paint the sun, always the sun. Mama painted flowers. Gigi. I called him Gigi!"

I hold Marie's hand as I watch Sylvie's childhood come back to her. Marie hands her a key, and she runs inside and up the stairs, Luca right on her heels.

"I've been paying a local boy to keep the place up. He and his father live on the farm down the road. Now you can stop staying in hotels."

"Or I could give it to Sylvie."

"No, Theo. This place is yours. Besides, what would she do way the hell out here in the middle of nowhere? This place doesn't even get the internet!"

"Yeah, well, that wasn't really a thing we cared about back then."

"No. You should bring your new family here. Let them meet your ghosts, because Élodie and Gio would be so damn happy for you."

"Thank you, Marie. For telling me to call her. For helping with Maurice. For this."

"You took care of my sister. You loved her. At least I can do this for you."

The next few days are a blur of sorting through boxes, finding the rings, and trying to remember all the little details and stories for each new thing we uncovered. There's still more. So much more. I wish I could stay a few more weeks, but Xander's silence has my mind racing, and I don't want to risk it knowing how on edge Dani has been. My family here is safe and happy. My family back home is cracking under the pressure, and it's time for me to go home and get to work. I'm more determined now than before to make this work between us, to have the family we need and deserve.

As the plane takes off and I leave Paris behind once again, my phone buzzes. I normally don't pay for the Wi-Fi on a flight, but I wanted to be available if anyone called. I turn the phone over.

LOVE

I know you're headed home, and I'm not sure you'll get this. Xander took off a few days ago and won't return our calls. He took Baggy, so I'm sure he's okay. He wouldn't do anything that put her in harm's way.

Dani's a mess. We only made it through to the next round because the other band all got sick and had to drop out. It was bad.

Sorry to dump all this on you. I just didn't want you walking in blind.

I'm sorry, Skylar. That's a lot to deal with on your own. Call me if you can or if you need to. I'll let you know as soon as I land, and we'll sort this all out.

We'll get through this. It's just a bump in the road to test our suspension.

LOVE

Good thing I know how to fix those.

Be safe, we miss you. And your cooking.

HOLLYWOOD
Skylar

CHAPTER 42
UNSHATTER
LINKIN PARK

"DANIELLA, OPEN THE DOOR."

"No!"

"I'll take it off the hinges if you don't open the door." We've been communicating through the bathroom door for twenty minutes and I'm tired of it. *Communicating.* I guess that's what I'll call it since it's more or less been me checking on her, and her telling me to go away. Words have been spoken, but to say it's conversational is overstepping. "Dani, come on. You don't need to do this alone."

"I do!"

I rock my head forward and it thumps against the door. This is the part of relationships no one likes, and sometimes, it's the part that ends them before they can begin. This is the kind of shit I'll bring up when people want to talk about all the sex I must have in a poly relationship. Yeah, there's sex, but there are also four distinct personalities going on a journey of emotions with each other. Sometimes—most of the time—they're not in sync with each other. There's no way to plan when one, or all of us, is sad, depressed, and unwilling to budge.

"Beetle, I want to help you. If you open the door, I'll go away, or I'll hold your hand. I'll stop talking and listen, or I'll tell you stories till you fall asleep. I'll do whatever you need, but love, I need this door open before I can. Please?"

There's a shuffle of movement, the lock clicks, and the door whips open so fast her loose hair flies around her head in the breeze. Her red eyes and nose scrunch up into a scowl and she pushes past me with a grunt.

"Dani?"

"WHAT?!" she spins, teeth bared. "I opened the fucking door. Now, what the hell do you want?"

I don't move, I don't even speak, I just look at her. Her mask of anger melts away and her eyes fight to find more tears to cry, but she has none left. I hold my arms out and, with more hesitation than I'd like to admit, she comes back to me, slamming into my chest so I can wrap around her. Theo's due home soon from his family. He doesn't know volatile things are right now. More explosions are imminent, along with more tears once her body has time to replenish them.

"I only want you to know you're safe. You're going to get through this, and when you're ready, we're here for you. But I won't let you lock yourself away like that. I can't. The worst things happen behind locked doors."

She sniffles, reluctantly moving her arms around me. It's more holding on than hugging, but I'll take it.

"Do you want to get out of here for a bit?" She nods against my chest. "I need to go meet up with everyone. We're going to the Irish bar near Steve's gym. Why don't you come with me?" She nods again as I rub her back in slow circles. "Do you want me to help you get dressed?"

Her head pulls back, and she looks up at me, resting her chin on my chest. "Can we go find Xander after that?"

"Yeah, love. We'll come back and get Theo, and we'll find our little lost boy. I promise."

There's a thunk from somewhere outside the bedroom before Theo calls out. I lean over and kiss Dani's forehead, giving her one more squeeze before I let go over her. I always hate letting go of her. It never seems fair.

"I'm gonna go shower." She nuzzles her face against me, wiping her dried tears on my shirt. "I'll leave the door open."

She grabs her things and turns on the water while I go out to find Theo leaning against the frame of the passageway we built. His face looks a little softer, but he also looks like he needs about a week's worth of sleep. "Permission to enter the fight circle?"

"Permission granted." We embrace, but it's more than a hug. It's *welcome home. I'm sorry, things are crazy. I missed you.* I read between the lines of the open book that is Skylar as we hold each other up. "You picked a hell of a time to come home. I'm sorry, it's not a warmer welcoming committee."

"You're more than enough, Skylar." His gentle words set my heart pounding. There's so many ways to say *'I Love You'* without using those exact words, and usually, they're deeper and more meaningful. He kisses my cheek and we finally part as he looks around the apartment. "How bad?"

"Well, I finally got her to open the bathroom door. She's showering now, and I'm taking her with me to see the guys about the whole court thing. I figure she needs her people right now, even if she won't admit it." I stop, pulling him in for a soft, deep kiss. I missed him well past what I tried to convince myself. His lips brush against mine like they don't want to leave again as we breathe each other's air. "How did Paris go?"

"Therapeutic, but I need this more." His hand snakes up my back, taking a handful of my hair as he holds me to him, kissing me harder as he backs me against the wall. Soft whimpers escape as he takes the control away from me, granting me a few moments of reprieve while he sucks on my neck and squeezes my ass. "Glad to see you remember your place like a good boy."

"You keep talking like that, and I might forget. Maybe you're a switch and need to open yourself up to the experience, Doc." The shower turns off in the other room and Theo and I break apart. We'll finish that later, I'm sure, but right now, there are more pressing matters. "We'll come by after and pick you up, check out a few of Xander's local spots."

"No need. I've got a few places I can check, a few numbers I can call. Keep me in the loop if you find anything, and I'll do the same." He brushes his knuckle down my cheek, and the weight on my shoulders from the last week lessens a bit. "You've done great, Skylar. No matter what you're thinking up here."

What I'd hoped to avoid, or at least hoped to handle in my own time, came smashing into my face a few weeks ago. Seeing people from my past was inevitable. They're all still friends with Dani and Xander, but seeing them all at once? It's been too long and I'm not sure what to expect. They might be so occupied with Elle's new charges to remember if they're mad at me for leaving or not. Or me being here might prove to be the outlet they need after getting that letter, taking out their frustrations with the legal system on me. Either way, I hoped to have backup. But Dani's mind is somewhere else, and she won't talk to me about it.

Jamie walks in first, filling the dimly lit bar with more sunlight than it's seen in a while as he's followed by Chase. I'm surprised to see Chase since he's supposed to be filming in

Canada, but with his arm still in a sling from the fallout with his stalker, he won't be filming anytime soon. To my knowledge, Elle never got to him. But he's the glue that holds the group together. Without him, Jamie would live as a recluse in a mountain somewhere, refusing to talk to anyone, and Steve would be…well, who knows where he'd be. Coop pushed Steve to ask me out in our senior year of high school. That seems like yesterday, but also a hundred years ago.

"Skylar?! You're here? Since when?!" Jamie doesn't bother reaching out a hand to shake. He pulls me in, much like Coop did, giving me a bear hug that's damn near cathartic. For both of us. "Fuck's sake, bro?" He asks Dani, before he turns to me. "Where the hell have you been? We need to hang out so I can catch up on what's going on. How long have you been back?"

"A few weeks now. I, uhm, I've been touring with Dani. She kind of picked me up in Fresno. I'm still working on getting around to seeing everyone again."

"Have you seen—"

"No. Not yet. You were next on my list. I wanted to save him for last. Guess that's pretty much out the window now," I sigh. "He knows I'm here, though."

"Wait, touring? You're back for good, though. Right?" His smile grows wide. "Please tell me you are."

I take Dani's hand away from her beer, which she barely notices, and lace my fingers between hers. "Yeah. I'm back for good."

"What?! Why am I always the last to find this shit out?" Jamie yells at Coop, who shrugs and offers no explanation as he brings over a round for everyone.

"Uh, because you've been AWOL in your studio for the last month, working on that commission for the mural downtown." Coop answers, putting a fresh round of beers in front of everyone. "I tried to call you to come hang with us, but you ghosted me!"

"It's not ghosting if I'm working. You could come over."

"You didn't text me back. That's at least *friendly* ghosting," Coop replies.

"That isn't even a thing," Jamie sighs.

"It is now!" He laughs, slapping Jamie on the shoulder before turning to Dani. "D, what the shit is up with you?"

"Nothing."

I shrug, mouthing Xander's name, and they both give knowing nods. The door opens again, sending my heart racing for my throat, ready to jump clear out of my mouth if I give it the chance. But it's a false alarm. An older couple, probably regulars, shuffle down to the end of the bar and take their seats.

"Don't freak on us, Sky. Steve's gonna be happy to see you. And if Ethan doesn't have practice and comes with him, you're gonna love him. That kid gives Steve so much of the shit he deserves." Coop smirks, shaking his head. "They're like an old married couple, I swear."

He means well, but the thought of the situation has me tensing up. I should be able to relate to Ethan, but so much of the relationship with Steve no longer exists in my head. I'm left with mysteries and questions, like how did we treated each other before the accident? Were we happy, did we bicker, were we sappy? Did I tease him, treat him poorly, make him laugh at jokes I don't remember? Hell, he had to remind me of what we used to do together in bed while desperately trying to ignite that flame again. Instead, one of us would end up on the couch, muffling sobs with the cushions. Only the chaos and unhappiness that came after remains.

The door opens again and a shorter guy, probably just under six feet, steps into the bar. He's got wild, shaggy hair he's trying to tame with a backward baseball cap. I side eye Jamie, who nods, telling me what I already know. Steve's husband—the guy who took my place after I bailed.

"Skylar, this is Ethan." Coop introduces us as Ethan walks up to greet the group.

We shake, like people do, but I'm sure he's doing the same thing I am—picturing each other with Steve. We both let out a chuckle. The pair of us are like night and day. I'm tall, tan, thin but muscular, with long brown hair. Ethan's short, built like a pale Irish brick, with sandy hair. I'm betting we have more in common personality wise, though. Steve has a type. Steve and Dani both have the same type—broken, but still fighting.

"I've heard Steve's back to his old self again," I break the ice and offer him a smile. "Dani says we have you to thank for that. That's enough for me."

"Thanks to you, apparently. The guys tell me you kind of helped shape a better Steve longer before I came along."

"Oh, come on, what could be better than this?!" Steve strides up, kissing Ethan hard before turning around and freezing. It takes a minute before his smile grows into laughter. He holds his arms out and I nod, knowing it's better to get this over with now. Steve's a hugger, and he claps me on the back at first, which makes the following hug a little too butch for either of us, before softening around me. "I missed you, Skylar. You didn't have to go so damn far away, you know."

"I did. You needed me to go, too. We both had to navigate the world without each other before we could try it in each other's way."

"Always the one with the words." Steve takes a step back. "God, you're still gorgeous, no offense, Sweets. I see you didn't quit working out, eh?"

"Ah, yeah. Did a lot of running, I guess. I've picked up the weights again once I got back here."

"What gym? Isn't mine, so isn't the best."

"Mine, fucker!" Coop yells out, handing a beer over to Steve. "Better than yours, because it's private!"

"Sneaky bastards," Steve flashes a suspicious glance toward Jamie.

"I didn't know. Don't look at me like that. Shit, I didn't even know he was back in town!" Jamie adds, throwing his arms up as he drops to a stool.

"Dude, you've been a hermit for two months. Like, you ghosted Coop and I, and I think the only person you see is Alexis," Steve points out, narrowing his eyes. "You better be seeing her, anyhow."

"I didn't ghost you! And yes, of course I see my wife. Every night, when she comes to check on me and distracts me, so I won't work through till morning." He winks and tips the bottle he's holding back. He nudges Dani with his elbow before he leans in and talks to her with voices so quiet, I can't make out what they're saying. I'm happy she's talking to anyone.

"So, the bitch came back. Again. Oh, and Elle, too." Steve jokes. "But also, does anyone else get the vibe she's luring us all in for some evil trap?"

"How can she have anything planned when she's in jail?" Ethan asks.

"Because she's not only the wicked bitch of the west, she's THE wicked bitch. She's got hidden assets and connections, crazy mad computer skills, and money with a capital M. Like Mommy. Cause that's who's holding onto her money while she's locked up." Steve laughs at himself, but Ethan and I both groan and shake our heads. "Oh, come on, Sweets! That one was good!"

"In no world, Pumpkin. In absolutely no world," Ethan teases. I am going to like him.

We spend the next hour playing the guessing game Elle wants us to play, trying to get ahead of her and knowing we're already three steps behind. We talk about not going, but we'll go. This could be the key to keeping her locked up, since right now they only have her on some lower level charges since that's all they could make stick. After a while, we're all tired of giving Elle Petrov any more of our time or energy. At least for today. As that conversation winds down, another one comes up.

"No, I don't want to talk about it! If I did, I'd talk to Theo, the shrink in this relationship!"

"Theo's the one breaking Xander's back, though." Steve points out in a way only Steve can. "You can't ask him. That would be messed up. Like hey, my boyfriend, also your boyfriend, is mad at me. Could you talk to him while you shove your dick in his mouth?"

"Eww, Steve! God, you suck."

"I do, but so does Xander." Steve cracks back, getting an eye roll from Ethan. "What? Just saying."

"It doesn't even matter since he's been in Paris, anyhow. At least he's trying to fix his relationship with his family." Dani scoffs. "What does he even tell her about the three of us?"

"He told her about us, and it sounds like it went well." I answer her. "I thought I'd wait for you and Xander before we get the full rundown."

Her shoulders slump and she mumbles, pushing away from the table. "I'll meet you outside. I don't want to drink anymore."

"Shit, I didn't mean to piss her off," Steve says, slouching his shoulders.

"She's in her own head," Chase answers, nudging Jamie. "Come on, Jimmy Jam, we got this."

HOLLYWOOD
Dani

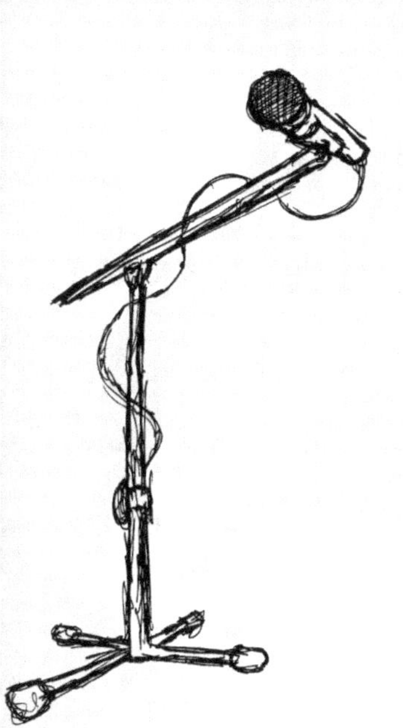

CHAPTER 43
DON'T TELL ME NO

MR BELLA

I CAN GIVE every excuse in the book, apologize a thousand times, beg on my hands and knees, but it won't matter. I said such awful things, things that I must have, at some level, believed. Why else would I say them to him? Why do I do these things to him, treat him like my emotional tackle dummy? We both already have the answer to that. We said so much the other day.

He comes back.

Ever since that first time he came back to me, I've pushed the boundaries further and further, until I broke through them the other night, completely disregarding the flashing lights and warning messages going off in my head that begged me to stop.

"Xander doesn't deserve that from anyone, but he especially doesn't deserve it from me," I explain to Jamie as I sit in his jeep, waiting for Skylar and the boys to come out of the bar so I can go home. "I knew what he'd been doing, so why now? I mean, I didn't know everything. I knew people paid to watch him online, and I knew he met up with guys for sex. Hell, we both did. Open relationship. But I also knew he paid for it with blood. How many times did he come home broken and bruised because

of them, because I wasn't enough? Why am I only mad about it now?"

"Because you're flying so close to the sun, the wings are melting off." Jamie replies. "Fly high, if that's what you want. I won't stop you. But you stole the wings off someone else, strapped them on, and expected them to work for you."

"What?"

"You work so hard on things for yourself, Dani. But anything that comes along that doesn't directly impact you, or, heaven forbid, causes you to stumble, struggle, or lose focus even for a split second? That shit throws you off your game instead of making you try harder."

"I *do* try."

"Yeah, you do. But you don't try *harder*. Not all obstacles are barricades." He checks over his shoulder to for the rest of the group. "I mean, listen to what you said. You're mad because you don't believe you're enough for Xander. But in an open relationship, that means you were sleeping with other people, too. Double standard."

"What if he means it, Jamie? What if, right when I'm finding the most epic poly fam ever, I screw it up by chasing away the one who means the most? The one who's my rock."

"You're already picking favorites, then?" He teases.

"No! I didn't mean…I mean…"

"I'm kidding, jeez. That's not how it works." He digs around in his jacket pocket and pulls out a bag of marijuana gummies. "Alexis left these in here the last time she borrowed my hoodie. Take one. It will help. I'll tell Skylar to drive you somewhere fun for the buzz."

"I don't need to be high, Jamie. I need to be less of a psychopath. You guys shouldn't be the only people I can keep in my life. And to be fair, you wouldn't even be IN my life if you hadn't fought to stay. I damn near sabotaged this, too! So many times!"

"Sleeping with Steve and then Devin to try to blow up a couple of friendships was a choice. I'll give you that."

"Ugh, don't remind me. I hate that I did that. I'm glad I haven't chased you guys away yet."

"Yeah, because you can't get rid of us, babe. We're like a rash!" Coop says, as he climbs into the other side of the jeep and gives me a hug from behind. "Sorry, had to pay before I came out here."

"Oh my god, who else heard all of that?"

"Nobody. They're making nicey-nice or whatever. I bailed so they could do it without me."

"You're in a mood," I snarl. Rolling my eyes and trying to pull out of his one-armed hug, and failing. "Anything new since you proposed to my sister?"

"Doc says she needs a few more tests, but she kicked me out of the room for a few hours so she could sleep. I might have gotten a little too high, but I don't care. Oh, did I mention I'm on about three hours of sleep over the last two days?" He grins, kissing my cheek. "So, how bad did it get?"

"Bad. Double bad. Super ultra bad. Like, I can't take this shit back kind of bad and now he won't talk to me. I wouldn't talk to me either, not after what I said. God, I'm awful."

"Want us to talk to him?" Jamie offers.

"You can't."

"Why not?"

"I shouldn't even be saying this to you guys, but I am, so don't make it extra weird next time you see him, okay?" They both nod. "He thinks you guys hate him. He calls you *my* friend, never his. Except for Steve, but those two have been playing a game of who gets to screw the new guy first for too long now.

Go figure, the one of you he considers a friend is the one I've slept with."

"You also slept with—"

"DON'T GO THERE, BRO!" Coop and I both cut Jamie off before he can remind me once again that I banged Coop's brother. Neither of us are over that mistake.

"Okay, okay!" Jamie throws his arms up like we're going to swing on him. "I get it. But it's true. So Xander thinks, what? That we don't like him, actively hate him, or somewhere in between?"

"Leaning more toward actively hate. It's his own fault for his entire phase of letting people believe he dealt drugs. He joked about it, how people judged him because of how he dressed. Of course, he actually supplied drugs to you guys once."

"Are you still pissed at me for that?" Coop asks. "It happened ONE time, and I had signed my first actual contract for that superhero thing. I had to at least *try* coke, didn't I? And I did it around people I trusted—Xander and Steve." He winks at Jamie and shrugs. "I knew you'd be pissed and kick my ass for it, so I never told you. Sorry, Dad."

"You're a dick." Jamie shakes his head. "Also, you're the one who told me he was a dealer!"

"He was. I mean, once, to me. And Steve. Plus, they were always the two who had the weed!"

"Why didn't he ever tell me he wasn't?" Jamie asks, that crease between his eyebrows getting deeper.

Xander enjoyed the game and would give nonsensical answers or walk away without denying a thing. The rumor started at one of Chase's parties, and seemed to grow from there, and it became a character Xander played to protect himself from the truth. To him, a drug dealer to Hollywood's elite had a better ring to it than the rich screw-up Dani pity dates. It gave him a reason to be there that wasn't me.

"He liked the attention. It got him a few clients for his other side hustle, too. The real one." I pull out my phone, still no response to the texts I've sent him. He's been gone a week, and I haven't told Theo about the fight yet, but I'm sure Skylar has. "What am I supposed to do? What if he doesn't want to come back? There's a giant hole in our wall connecting us to the place he considers safe, so he won't stay there."

"Add the door," Jamie suggests. I smack his arm for being a smartass. "I'm serious! Have Sky put the door in and lock the door. When Xander's back, make sure he gets both keys that come with the lock, so he's the only one who has access. That way, it's his choice when and how he literally opens up to you. The rest of you will use the front doors until you figure this out."

"Oh, my god." I stare at him, mouth agape. "That's actually brilliant. Well, it will be once I figure out where he is."

"Where who is?" Steve asks as he walks up to the jeep, arm around Ethan's shoulders and Skylar walking next to them. "Because if you're searching for me and all my awesomeness—"

"We're not. I need to build a door to find Xander." My mind won't slow down at the first real thing to give me hope in days. "I mean, Skylar, we need a magic door with keys to help get Xander back."

"Still no idea what you're asking me to do, Beetle."

We explain Jamie's plan to everyone and they all agree it's pretty solid. They also all agree that none of them hate Xander, they all assumed he didn't like them. That's something I need to fix after I deal with my colossal mess.

"I can tell you where he is," Ethan admits, rocking back and forth on his feet and shoving his hands in his pockets. This should be interesting. "He crashed at this guy's house, but that fell through after about a day, so he called me. I found him somewhere, so he and the cat are, well, they're at my teammates' place."

"Bro, seriously? That's awesome. But also, bro, love of my life, bright yellow sun in my daisy, beautiful husband of mine. Why didn't you say something?" Steve asks, arms folded. "Also, also—and more importantly—which teammate?"

"The new guy. Anders."

"Oh boy," Steve shakes his head as he stands as stiff as a board, putting on a drill sergeant persona. "Alright, we're splitting the party. We're in Ethan's truck, so we'll take that and Skylar and get the door. You two take little miss-bitchy pants, get her some ice cream, donuts, whatever she needs to cheer up, and get her game face on." I flip him off, but he's still going. "Do your whole buddy bit with each other, or whatever you do. Sky, you call the Therapy bro and have him pick up X and get him back to the house in a few hours. You have your assignments. Don't fuck this up!"

"Inspiring, Pumpkin. Get in the truck." Ethan turns to Skylar. "Are you okay with this? Be honest."

Skylar leans over, kissing my forehead. "I'll meet you back home, okay? We'll get him back. We will." They move to go with Steve, but only make it a few steps before turning back around, grabbing my face and kissing me long and hard. Steve teases them with little noises until Ethan elbows him in the gut. "I love you, Beetle." Skylar says, with a sad hope in their eyes as they step away and follow Ethan and Steve.

"What about my car?" I whine, sticking my lower lip out as I stare at the little yellow Fiat.

"She'll be fine. We'll come back and get it when we're done." Jamie ruffles my hair. His big smile tells me he's happy without a single word out of his mouth. Of all the boys, he's the one whose opinion matters most about stuff like this. Mushy stuff. He's an artist, and he's been lucky enough to find his muse, but he understands the struggles, too. It's now everyone's mission to get Xander back home where he belongs, and for me to get him to forgive me and never do this again. "Now scoot over so I can drive."

"He needs to do it on his terms, Dani. We all want him back now, but he said he needs a few days, and we can respect that." Theo says over my shoulder, but I'm ignoring him, shuffling the cards and laying them out. Picking them back up in a huff to shuffle and deal again. I understand that's not how tarot works. I just don't care at the moment.

Large hands close over mine before I can pick new cards, and I groan. Rolling my eyes until they meet his.

"Can we talk?" Theo asks.

"Are you going to bill me?"

"Is that joke ever going to get old?"

"Nope."

"Good. No, I won't bill you." His smile brings down my already crumbling walls. "You're on the road, Dani. You've got so many paths in front of you, and you can't figure out which one to take, so you're trying to take them all. Trying to spread yourself so thin that you accomplish everything and nothing all at once. That's the rub with life as a Jill of all trades."

"I know a little about a lot of things, but I'm not a master of any one thing."

"Including yourself." He sits beside me, giving me a moment to scoop up my cards and tuck them away. Along with the crystals, pendulum, unburnt incense, and the worry dolls. As if I opened a window into my mind and gave him a quick peek, he goes right to the heart of the problem. Me. "What happened first? The thing that happened when you were younger that scared you so much to fail, you gave up and picked something else?"

"I didn't fail!"

"No, you didn't. You don't fail. But that's a problem, isn't it? In order not to fail this time, you'll face giving up something precious to you, something you love so damn much. It's eating you alive to let them go." He leans his elbows on his knees and stares at the floor. "Dani, I'm going to tell you something, and I don't believe anyone said this to you before. If they did, you didn't listen to them, so I hope you listen to me. It's okay to fail."

"Of course it is."

"Don't play this off. You say that, but you don't believe it in your heart. I bet, when it came down to you, your sister, and your mother, you two grew close. She protected you and your mother, like many big sisters learn to do. But when she couldn't protect herself anymore from her husband, you became her guardian. Your roles are reversed."

I want to say something snarky and cruel to make him leave me alone, but that's what got me into this mess. When did I go from snarky and fun to hurtful? What happened to me? Theo's right. Skylar, too. Hell, everyone is right except me. I don't like it. I've let this all go on for too long, all the pain, the worry, the near constant internal struggles that I refuse to let anyone see. I used to be the baby, the one who could get away with murder. Then my sister left, marrying an absolute tool who didn't deserve her. He didn't deserve any of us and we shouldn't have fallen for his bullshit, but we did. Theo's right, I became the protector.

I had nothing that bastard Luis could take, so I used wit and sarcasm. Hurting me would have ended the relationship. He knew better. The protector angle fits me until it doesn't. Until I fail, which sends me down a dark, horror filled pathway of doubt and fear. And boy, did I fail.

"I'm going to guess you met Xander around the same time that your sister married or moved out? The strange new boy at school with no friends. He probably dressed different from everyone else and put on that cocky attitude of his. But you could see through that. You saw the naïve little lost boy that needed help?"

"He would have gotten his ass beat by the end of the week if I wasn't there."

He nods. "He doesn't make the best decisions sometimes, but they come from a good place. You're not mad at him for the porn site or getting paid for sex. You're angry at the times he came home beaten, in tears, scared. You blame yourself every time that happens, and it's been festering. Add the trip to Tokyo, and it gets worse. You're Wendy, collecting her lost boys."

"He came home a shell, Theo. He wouldn't let us touch him for days without jumping. He cried, and the nightmares. I couldn't help him; I couldn't see him like that. Where was I, Theo? Why wasn't I there? Because of some stupid concerts? Playing music that won't ever get me anywhere in life because I'll fail at that too if you give me enough time and rope to hang myself?" I can't stop as it all pours out. "I'm pathetic! I couldn't keep Ren safe, or Skylar, or Xander. I failed every one of them and—" I slam my hands over my mouth, unable to move or breathe. I said those things out loud.

"And it's okay, Dani. It's okay to fail. It's how we learn, how we grow. Humans start failing on the day they're born. They fail to walk and talk, so they learn how. They fail to read and comprehend, so they keep working at it until they can. Your music is going to take you places, Dani. You'll have bad days, but you'll move on and start again. As for the people? You didn't fail Xander or Skylar. You didn't fail your sister. You simply did the best you could. You're one incredible, resilient person with more strength and love than most people could ever comprehend. To think you could maintain that level of perfection? That's where you failed. It's the only place you failed."

"But I… I can do it."

"Just because you can do something doesn't mean you should. Just because you can scrape by and barely survive doing things alone doesn't mean you should live like that when there's an entire support system here ready to hold you up to the world and show everyone how much we love you and need you. How much we're there for you to help you when you fall, to hold you when you cry, and to remind you that you're not perfect, but you are right for us."

I throw my arms around him, bawling like a baby, because he's right. No one had ever told me failure was an option. I have so much to learn, starting with trusting my family with what's going on inside my head.

HOLLYWOOD
Theo

CHAPTER 44
SAVE ME

NOAH KAHAN

THE AIR in the apartment smells like melted butter and sugar because I've been baking non-stop today. Skylar brought Baggy home the other day, and she's been at my feet, pawing for scraps. Xander comes home today, and, to keep from pacing, I've been baking since six this morning. I'm so deep in my own head, I don't hear him come in until he drops his bags on the floor by the couch.

"Hey Xan!" I yell out, giving the batter one last stir. "Welcome home, baby. What do you think, chocolate or—" The words stick to my throat like molasses when I turn to see him. His face is a mess of blood, bruises, swelling, and tears. The bowl clatters to the ground, and I make it to him just as he collapses into my arms.

"Baby?" I wipe his matted hair from his face, slick with blood. "Who did this? What happened?"

I'm torn between calling Dani or dragging him to the hospital, unsure of which to do first. I get him back up and over to the couch to lean on while I turn the oven off. He's in bad enough shape. He doesn't need me burning the building down

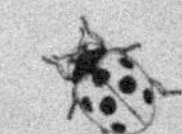

around us while I take care of him. When I turn around, he's stumbling into the bedroom and slamming the door.

Whether he wants it or not, I'm getting in there and helping him. I grab a few towels and a handful of bandages, making a mental note to buy a better first aid kit for the apartments since I'm pretty sure theirs has nothing but tiny bottles of booze. I don't barge in, even though that's exactly what I want to do. I force away the image of me charging to his rescue like we're in some kind of movie. Scooping him up and professing our love for each other as I tend his wounds.

I'm glad he didn't lock the door, but the relief that offers doesn't last long. The blood drips from his face, hitting the white porcelain of the sink and splattering to its edges as he stands there, watching it.

"Can you talk to me, or do you need me to patch you up and go away?"

Silence has never been so heavy, broken only by the faint outside noises and another drop of blood. There's a chance he's in shock, that he hasn't heard a word I've said. He's shaking, but hell, who wouldn't be?

"He followed me. He works there, or, pretended to," Xander whispers in a hoarse voice.

"Who? Work where?" I move closer, taking his hand first and inspecting the cuts and bruises there. The kid put up a fight, that's obvious. "Baby, tell me what happened?"

"I got hired by that security company. Computer stuff. I wanted to show Dani I could do it. I just wanted her to be proud of me, Theo. I wanted all of them to see I can handle myself." He stops, a painful sob racking his entire body, causing him to double over, grabbing his ribs.

"Take it easy, baby," I whisper, helping him stand up straight again. "I started a few days ago. It's why I didn't want to come home yet. I wanted to give Dani my first paycheck and show her I can be there for her. Prove I can help, and she doesn't need to do this all alone. He found me, though. He had these guys. I don't know where they came from. I never saw them until they were on top of me."

"Take your time," I keep the panic out of my voice, rubbing his back in slow circles. I need to see his face to get a better understanding of how much damage they did. "Xander, let me see—"

The sharp inhale I can't hold back makes his shoulders slump. Through his eyebrow and too close to his eye, I find the deepest cut. His eye has swollen shut in response, and the other eye doesn't appear much better. Three more cuts seep blood, so I staunch those first. Whoever did this broke his nose based on the caked blood under his nostrils. They also split his lip in two places, and that's what I can make out through the carnage.

"We should take you to the hospital, Xander. You need to file a police report," there's a crack in the last word, threatening to give away the icy panic racing through my bloodstream. But he shakes his head.

"I can't. I can't call them. What am I gonna tell them? Some posh prick followed me from Japan and hired a gang to come after me? Dani told me not to work there. I stayed behind a computer all day. How could that be dangerous?"

"You have to tell someone."

"What? Tell them the scrawny faggot didn't belong there and got what was coming to him? That's what they said, Theo. They knock me down and screamed it in my face as they hit me. He stood over me, laughing. Telling them how much I... how much I liked..."

"Who, baby? Who was it?"

"Oliver. He…he asked if I…if I missed how he… I'm gonna be sick."

He makes it to the toilet in time, and I wet the bloody rag in my hand, holding it against him gently. When he's done, I help him move over to lean against the wall while I run water in the tub. Kneeling in front of him, I dab at the drying blood. The realization of what he can't say hits me, knocking the wind out of me and sending my stomach to the floor.

Oliver. He kidnapped, blackmailed, and raped Xander in Japan. He's here.

"Xander, I need you to look at me, and don't lie. I won't be mad, neither will Dani or Skylar, but you need to tell me the truth. It's not your fault, baby. Okay?" His bottom lip quivers, he knows what I'm about to ask him. "Xander, did they—"

"Don't. Please don't ask," he sobs, reaching out for me. I pull him to me, holding him and rocking him in my arms as he continues to shake. "Why am I like this, Theo? Why am I like this?"

"It isn't your fault, Baby. It wasn't your fault before, and it isn't now."

"It is! I'm so stupid! Why can't I stop fucking up? Why can't I just be normal for once?"

I lean back and cup his face, staring into his one open eye. "There's nothing wrong with you, Xander. There's something wrong with them. The people who did this to you. There's something very wrong with Oliver, and we should call the police."

"If I wasn't a queer piece of shit, it wouldn't have happened." He slumps against me, his body shaking as he sobs. "The cops don't care. They'll think I'm a worthless whore."

"No, baby. You're so much more than that. You're brilliant and beautiful, Xander. You're carving out your own life out of this hate-fueled world, taking the harder path, and you are so brave for that. So damn brave. You're loved and you're so much better than those pieces of shit could ever hope to be. And the people that matter love you for who you are. We love all of you. Do you understand? Dani, Skylar…me. We love you exactly how you are."

It's not how I'd planned to tell him I loved him, but sometimes life likes to throw wrenches at your boyfriend's face and you end up pouring your heart out to him on a bloody bathroom floor. I do love him.

"You shouldn't. None of you should."

"We do, and we're not going anywhere, Xander." I take a deep breath. We need to rip this bandaid off now. "Xander, I need you to tell me if they…I can't let you take a shower if they—"

"It doesn't matter. I won't call the cops." He lifts his head and tries to keep his eye open long enough to meet mine before sliding closed again. I need to keep him awake, at least for now.

"I gotta know, Xander. I promise I'll take care of you no matter what."

"They…they tried. They pulled down my…they were going to. But some guy and his dog came by. He scared them off, so I ran. Like a coward."

"You ran for your life, Xander, that's not cowardice. That's brains." I kiss his forehead, tasting the iron immediately. "Okay. Let's get you off the floor and into the tub. Can you stand?"

It takes three tries to get him off the floor and I have him sit on the toilet as I undress him. Each article I remove boils my blood a little hotter. More bruises, more cuts, more blood. My guess is at least two broken ribs to go with his nose. It's likely he'll need stitches in some places, but for now, I bandage them as best as I can.

"Jesus," I say under my breath as I peel his shirt off. "Baby, you need to see a doctor. You could have internal bleeding."

"No, we can't afford it."

"I'll pay. You have to go, Xander!" My rage gets the better of me for a moment. "Fine. I'm calling in a favor, and if she says you need to go to the hospital, you're going to the damn hospital. Do you understand? I don't care how much it costs. You're going. I'll bill your damn parents. Now let's get you in the tub." I toss his clothes into the sink as he stands and stumbles, but I catch him, holding him to me again. "I'm not mad at you. I promise, okay? I'm scared, that's all."

"Did…did you mean what you said earlier?"

"I did. I absolutely did. I love you, Xander. I didn't think I could love like that again, but you've shown me how wrong I was. You've been nothing short of a beacon guiding me through my self-imposed darkness, and I don't want to lose you, Xander." He grunts as he brings his hands up and tries to hug me back. I press my lips to his forehead.

"Cool," he tries to laugh. He's deflecting, but right now it's a safety measure he needs to use like a crutch. "I worried I was too much of a weirdo for you."

"Never, baby. I love you, you strange little nerdy fuck. I love you so damn much."

"I—I love you, too, Theo."

I clean the last of the batter from the floor, shooing Baggy away from the kitchen. My bones are sore, that's how tired I am. But one thought keeps me pushing through, keeps me from curling onto the couch and passing out for the next forty-eight hours or so. Dani will blame herself for this.

As if I summoned her from the hallway, the door to their apartment opens and I rush through to catch her before she comes in.

"Keep it down, come on. Back outside. Quick." With the pain meds he's on, he'll probably be out for a few more hours, but I don't need him waking up to freak out again. I hold my finger up to my lips and lead her back out to the hallway, where Skylar stands with their bags from the show.

"What, is there like a surprise party for me or some shit? Bro, did you get hit by a bus? Please tell me you're not mad because I didn't come in and immediately get all cheerful and happy and yelling salutations or some shit. We had a breakthrough, sure, but I'm still me." She crosses her arms and stares at me. "We've had a day, man. Like a day where the van breaks down, the show gets moved around at the last minute, and we barely survive elimination kind of—Theo? Is that blood? Did you kill someone?"

"No, Dani. I…it's—"

"Xander?" Skylar asks, dropping the bags when I nod toward the door. They push past us and into the apartment, and I don't stop them.

"Theo?" Dani chokes on my name.

The dryness in my mouth makes it hard to swallow. "He's, uhm—" I stop and close my burning eyes. I've been holding the tears in since he walked in the door, but now that Dani's here, I can't hold them in anymore. She moves for the door, and I stop her. "Someone attacked Xander. Oliver, same guy from Japan. Xander's scared you'll be mad at him, or you'll blame yourself because you warned him not to work for that security company."

"That stupid son of a—" she can't keep the angry facade up for more than a second before she's breaking down alongside me. "He's okay, right? Tell me he's okay, Theo. I can't... I can't hear it if he's—"

"I called a friend of mine, a doctor. She left about an hour ago. We need to keep an eye on him, but she gave him something for the pain and stitched him up."

"STITCHED?! Oh my god."

"I had to tell you out here, Dani. I can't let you go in there until you work through this. It's... it's bad." I brush the tears with the pad of my thumb, running through the injuries with her slowly, not wanting to overload her. Taking care of one of them will be enough work. I don't need to send Dani into a spiral on top of that. When I'm done, she stares at me like I've just told her aliens are real and they live in the apartment downstairs.

"Can I see him?"

We walk back in to find Skylar on their knees outside the bedroom. Their shoulders shake, and Dani runs to them. When she reaches over to turn on the light, I catch her hand and shake my head. I want the lights off for two reasons, so she can't see how bad he is, and because Marie said Xander's headache would be like fifty hangovers all at once. I've even got a trash can by the bed in case he gets sick when he comes down from the shock. Dani helps Skylar up, and the pair creep over, cringing when they see how little isn't covered by bandages and ice packs.

I expect tears, frustration, and for the self-blaming to start— but this is Dani, after all.

"Frankenstein's monster on ice," she mutters, her shoulders dropping.

Skylar glances over at me again. "Get some rest. I'll watch him." Then climbs into the bed, curling as close to Xander as possible without touching him, other than to hold his bandaged hand.

"Well. If you'll excuse me," Dani says, voice low but not a whisper. "I'm going to call my brothers, buy the most badass metal bat I can't find at this time of night, and find the piece of shit who dared lay a finger on my boyfriend."

"Dani!"

"What? Oh, come on!" The harsh whisper full of poison comes out as she snarls. "He didn't call the cops, did he? Theo, he may be a stupid rich white boy, but he's my stupid rich white boy! No one hurts my Xander. I let that bastard do it once and get away with it, but he's in my town now. On my turf. I will end him."

"Our."

"What?" she snaps out of her rage.

"He's *our* stupid rich white boy. All of ours." Her face softens, and she blinks a few times. "You're our mouthy loud strong Latina. Sky is our confused, sensitive, taller white person. And if you'll have me, I'm your pretentious smug grumpy asshat."

"You forgot to say old," Xander croaks out a mumble from the bed. "You're fucking old."

"Don't give me that shit," I choke up as the words come out while I walk over and brush the hair out of his eyes. I don't care what he calls me, I'm glad he's awake and talking. "Morning, sunshine. How are you feeling?"

"Shit, is it morning?"

"No, assclown," Dani chirps in, holding his hand and running her thumb over the bandages.

"I'm sorry I didn't listen to you."

"Xan, if every man in history listened to what his much

smarter, much better-looking woman told him, we'd live in a utopia by now." Skylar replies, kissing the side of his head.

"Isn't that the car ride at the theme park?" Xander asks.

"That's Autopia. I'll take you there when you feel better if you want." Dani's smile weak smile stays hidden behind her hand, but Xander's eyes aren't open to see it.

"Alright, he needs his sleep," I interrupt.

"Don't go!" His hand latches onto Dani's, breaking both our hearts. "Stay. Please. All of you."

We exchange a glance in the darkness, and, as if climbing into a bed full of unbroken eggs, we all find a space. Dani slips between Xander and Skylar, careful of his bandages and broken ribs, and rests her head on Xander's shoulder. I move alongside him, nudging the side of his head. Skylar sets timers to make sure we wake up to check on him and give him meds.

"I love you. All of you. And I'm sorry I always fuck up."

"Oh, honeybee, you don't," Dani coos, one foot in dreamland already, exhaustion hitting her hard. "You're a novelty in a world that wants to classify you as whatever they deem to be normal. But it's okay, we've got you now. And we love you, too."

I couldn't have said it better, so I don't try to one up her. Why should I. Instead, I lean over and kiss the top of her head, and the side of his. "Get some sleep, sweetheart. Marie will be back tomorrow, and if she finds out we kept you up all night being sappy, she'll kick my ass."

"Who was she, anyhow?" His whisper crackles as he coughs.

"My sister-in-law."

"Cool. I didn't know…you had…siblings." The last word is hard to make out as his head lolls to the side and the meds take hold of him again.

HOLLYWOOD
Dani

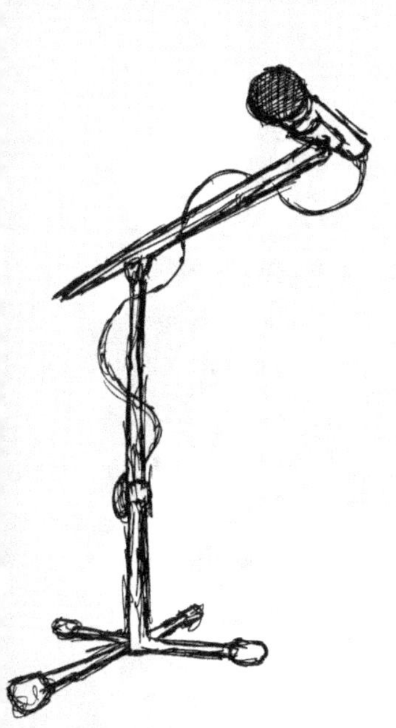

CHAPTER 45
LOOKING BACK

LORD HURON

I FINISH WRAPPING Xander's hand like Marie showed me the other day and tuck the supplies back into the kit Theo bought us. Pretty sure Xander's still asleep; I pick up the empty water glass and go to move, but his arm shoots out and finds me. He's getting a little too good at that.

"Stay?"

"I'll come right back. I promise. I need to get you some water."

"Please?"

I sigh and set the glass back down before I take my spot on the edge of the bed again. "How do you feel?"

"That's not why I asked you to stay. I want to say I'm sorry. For walking out. I shouldn't have done that to you." He coughs, the strain of talking still too much for his broken ribs. He's supposed to be resting, staying hydrated, and keeping quiet, but he's a terrible patient.

I've avoided this talk so far, so worried about everything I want to say, everything I need to say to him. Even more worried about the things he should say to me because I deserve each one of them.

"Xander, there isn't enough time to apologize as much as I need to. Even if I had a century, it wouldn't be enough time." I dig through my bag that sits next to the bed and pull out the pair of keys, running my thumb over the ridges. My heart races. I don't want to give him the keys because I don't want him to lock me out.

Failure is an option. Failure is okay. Everyone fails.

"We've put a door between our place and Theo's—"

"They built that before I left. You yelled about it, remember?"

"They built a nice hole in the wall. Now it's a full door." He turns his head and cracks open his working eye, struggling to keep it focused on me. "Do you want your glasses?"

"They're broken. What do you mean, a door?"

I pry open his hand, putting the keys in his palm and closing his fingers over them. I try to remember the way Jamie explained it the other day, but for whatever reason, it sounds like the dumbest idea ever now. I don't want to tell him what the keys are for, why there's a door, why I'm doing any of this, but I'm doing it because it's for him. He has the right to choose and I...I have the right to fail. Theo said this wasn't a failure if Xander locks the door. He called it an inconvenience I could overcome. A rough patch of water we'd learn to navigate. I don't want to navigate without Xander.

"The keys are for," my voice cracks. "For the door. These are the only keys for it, so we can't come in unless you want us to. I want to respect your privacy and your space, and what I said the other day will take time to recover from, but I—"

"Dani—"

"Let me finish, please? I've rehearsed this a thousand times. Just let me get it out?" He nods. "Basically, I may not deserve it, but I want you back, Xander. I'm willing to beg, plead, cry, whatever I need to do. But I can't do that unless I become a safe space for you. I can't be that toxic dump of fear, taking everything out on you until you had nothing left." I swallow hard, hoping this sounds better in his head than it does mine. "I don't want to do that anymore. I'm working on it, I am. But I understand if you don't want to be around me for a while. These are your keys, and you can lock the door whenever you need your space or whatever. I'll never argue with you about it."

He waits; his eyes closed. I'm about to see if he's fallen asleep again when he finally asks if I'm done.

"Yeah, that's...yeah. I'm done." I ask in a hushed tone, in case he is asleep. "Do you want me to go now?"

"No, but I think I need the trash can next to the bed now."

"Oh, no. Here!" I thrust it toward him and close my eyes, thinking he's going to be sick. Instead, there's a hollow thunk as he drops the keys into it. "Xander, that wasn't funny. I thought you were going to hurl because they said some of the medication could—wait. You did that on purpose?"

"Beetle, we fight. We make up. We're never physical, we're rarely hurtful. But no matter what you call me, your words are never, ever going to be enough to frighten me away. I thought we both needed space. Because we did."

"Really?"

"Yes, really. I needed space. I used the time away to finish the prototype website code so I can sell it."

"Sell it? I thought you were going to run the site?"

"It made you mad. I couldn't keep working on something you hated enough to go Chernobyl on me."

I bite my lip and frown. My Xander, the one destined to grow up to run multi-billion dollar companies and wear shoes that cost more than my car, almost gave up on a dream because he thought I didn't like it. I thought I'd neglected him by not protecting him from those men, by not being enough for him, but that's not it at all. It's because I don't talk to him. Keeping everything locked away, how I thought relationships worked. But doing that nearly cost me Xander and him his dream.

"You've got it all wrong." He shrugs, which causes him to wince, and reminds me how much pain he's hiding. "There wasn't a single thing I didn't like about your idea. The world needs your idea, your improvements to the original site. More money to the creators while saving them time, plus a safer and more inclusive environment for creators and users? Brilliant honeybee! I even think it's kind of hot that other people are watching my boyfriend—the guy I get to have sex with, sleep next to, kiss—to get themselves off."

"Skylar said you had an exhibitionist streak. So, why?"

"All the reasons you said the other night. And more. I took on too much, and I kept taking on more and more. I blamed myself for the apartment, for the way your parents treat you, for my sister leaving. All of it. But instead of telling you, instead of sharing the burdens with you like you've begged me to do, I couldn't stop. I wanted to protect people, and I couldn't allow myself to, well, fail. I didn't want you to see me as a failure, Xander."

"Beetle, you're my queen. You don't just call me honeybee because I got stung that one time. You call me that because you understand how much I need you. We both do. You've never failed me."

"I put too much energy and time into the concert stuff, but you were giving us money you earned with blood. If I lost, it would have all been for nothing. You bled for me, and I'd come home empty handed. Again. That sounds so dumb when I say it out loud."

"I'll bleed for you till I'm drained dry, baby girl. You're my life, my soul, my Beetle. I flew too far from the hive and this happened. I'm the one who failed."

"No. No, you're my brave bee. I love you, Xander. You're not a failure; you're not a fuck up. You're my everything."

"I'm gonna throw up." I whip my head around and see Steve leaning against the door, holding a couple of white paper bags. "You two done being sappy? I brought Zankou for those of us who didn't get our asses handed to us. And for the guy whose face ran into a brick wall, a protein bowl and a PB&H from Qwench."

"Yes!" Xander moans.

"Really? I thought you'd hate me for that?"

"Nah, man. I love those things, and I don't think I could eat anything real right now."

Steve climbs into the bed to hold the cup for Xander. I'm shocked by the tenderness as Steve tilts the straw down so Xander can take a cautious sip. A moment later, I tear into the bag and pull out the chicken wrap, smelling their famous garlic sauce and drooling. Steve waits until I take a huge bite and have my mouth well beyond full before he comes in hot with his next statement.

"So, you think the guys hate you, huh?" Steve takes a drink from Xander's cup and offers him more. "Because we heard from a little bird, or beetle, that you didn't call any of us when you needed a place to crash because we all hate you. Or, well, they all hate you. I'm cool, which is always the case and why I'm here." Steve boasts. "But anyway, bro, they don't hate you. You're part of the family, and you better call us next time. We know your girl, and we know she's a lot. Sooooo much. Fucking queen of a whole lotta mess."

I ball up a piece of the foil wrapper and chuck it at Steve's head before I flip him off.

"Don't make me laugh, it hurts!" Xander gasps as he tries hard to fight against the laugh growing in his chest.

"So, how's the show?" Steve asks after we clean up lunch and Xander falls asleep again.

"Skylar and I have a show in Chicago in two days. After that, we're in New York and Boston. And we're not to where we can book a bunch of flights, so we're driving."

"In Connor's piece of shit?"

"No, the van wouldn't make it on a trip like that. Chase got us a rental with a little more room, but still easy enough for all of us to take turns driving. Chase even had a stupid idea about a tour bus."

"Stupid or brilliant? Are you still worried about not winning?"

I punch him in the arm, but not hard. "You're probably right. I'll talk to Skylar tonight and see if they think it's dumb of me to turn him down. I should start letting the band make decisions with me, not making them all for them."

"She can learn! I'm proud of you, kid."

"Oh, shut up. Will you come to the show in a few weeks when we're here in Los Angeles?"

"Got the tickets the minute they announced it. So did everyone else." He flips to the ticket confirmation on his phone and holds it up for me to see. "Ethan's coming, too, since it's an off night for his games. See how much I love you? My husband has the night off and I'm taking him to see you instead of letting him break my back."

"Steven, you are a mess."

"Yeah, and you love it," he giggles.

"I always figured you'd be a top."

"Switch."

"Ahh. Yeah, I can see that. When Skylar wakes up, do you wanna walk down and get some pie with me? Jamie told me there's a pie place not far from here. He used to take Lexi there."

"Uh, yeah? Duh," He pauses, looking up from the game he's playing on his phone. "Wait, you said Sky, not Xander. Is Sky still sleeping? It's past noon."

"Yeah, they had a rough night. Between Xander, the re-opened case, and the stress of the tour, it's bringing back memories they weren't prepared for or something. The nightmares had dropped down to like once a week, but they're having them nightly again after Xander's attack." I peek in the door, checking on Xander. "There's also someone screwing with Sky on the tour, trying to spread rumors they're using again to get under their skin. The company keeps threatening to drug test them, not listening to us when we say they're not on anything."

"Shit. They've changed so much. They used to be early risers by Los Angeles standards. Up before eight most mornings."

"Now when they're up at eight, it's because they've been up all damn night. Like this morning." I glance over to the door to our bedroom, but still no light coming from inside the room. "I'm gonna go check on him. Will you keep an ear open for Xan, in case he needs something?"

"Absolutely, babe. I've got you."

Easing into the room while trying not to let too much light in, I'm able to make out the lump in the bed. I crawl in next to it, only to realize there's nothing but blankets and pillows. They haven't left the apartment, so they must be around here somewhere. I peek in the bathroom and find them asleep in the empty bathtub.

"Skylar?" They respond with something between a grunt and a whimper. "Hey, what are you doing in here, baby?"

They roll onto their side, facing away from me, but their breathing changes, signaling to me that they're awake now.

"I'm sorry I woke you, but seriously, why are you in the bathtub?" I reach in, pushing their hair back. They try to brush me off, but the heat coming off their body is so intense, I don't need to touch them to feel it. "Sky, you're burning up."

"S'why I'm in here," they finally answer, a slight tremor running through their body. "I'll be okay. Need some time."

"Time to what? Spontaneously combust? Come on, get out of there and tell me what I can do. Are you sick? Is it a recovery thing? Steve's taking care of Xander, so let me take care of you."

"It's the exhaustion and the stress." They say when I convince them to leave the tub, they hold me to them even though they're a space heater and their heart pumps to the rhythm of Wipe Out. They flinch and groan with every step. "Sometimes, it's like going through it all over again—the accident. Everything hurts and nothing I do stops it."

"How can I help?"

"If I get through the craving without doing anything stupid, it's a win. It doesn't last as long anymore, only a few hours usually. After that fades, I'm left dealing with the pain."

I wonder what will happen when all four of us board the struggle bus together. I say a silent thank you to the goddesses for not giving us that hill to climb yet, and tell them they can keep holding onto that for a while. Sky held on long enough for me, and now I've snapped mostly out of my funk in time for them to fall into one. As we walk into the bedroom and Skylar grabs the pack of cigarettes and lighter, I spot the letter sitting on the nightstand.

"You don't need to do this to yourself. I mean, she's in jail, there are pending federal charges that might still happen, and she's not your responsibility. Not if it's going to do this to you."

"It is my responsibility. I'll be worse if she ever gets out. I won't be able to handle that, even with all three of you and the guys by my side."

"Okay, let's figure this out. Pick one thing, the number one worst thing you can't get out of your mind about the trial."

"Seeing her," they say a little too fast. I cock my head to the side and give them a glare that tells them to try harder. This time, their answer comes slower and there's pain in every word. "Living through it again. They're going to ask me what I remember and force me to relive the entire ordeal. I avoided that last time, because they didn't go after her for my case. Not enough evidence."

I help them pull on some pants, kissing their legs and hips as I do, bringing a sweet hum that's almost a purr. We nod to Steve as we head out to Skylar's perch on the fire escape. I help them out the window, their balance wobbly and pain noticeable. After they light up, I lean against them, listening to his heart slow again.

"Would it help if you tell me about it? About her?" I reach under their shirt, letting my fingers play in their sparse chest hair. They like to shave it for the shows, but haven't been in the mood lately. I find it cute, especially when Sky and Theo both walk around shirtless. Those two are yin and yang.

They take a long pull and blow a few smoke rings. "I don't know, Dani. I mean, I'm not sure I can. Or that I want to."

"Have you ever told anyone? Because it helped with the nightmares, remember? When you finally started to tell me about them, about what you were going through."

Their finger hooks under my chin, tipping my head up. Their lips hover over mine and their eyes close as they breathe me in.

"I'll try. For you, I'll try. For you, I'll bare my soul and my secrets to the world."

"Good. We'll start as soon as I get back with some pie. Jamie says it always works for times like these and frankly, I'm not here to doubt the power of buttery crust and sweetness, but Theo's at work." I lick the tip of their nose and watch their mouth curl into a smile. "When I get back, we'll get through this. We'll have you so ready for this trial people will think I went to law school."

"You watch far too much true crime, Beetle."

"Or do you watch too little?"

HOLLYWOOD
Skylar

CHAPTER 46
NOTHING'S GONNA HURT YOU BABY

CIGARETTES AFTER SEX

THE BACK DOOR of the club opens, and we all look up to see the tour's head of security, Marco, and he doesn't look like he's bringing happy news. I light another cigarette, my fifth in the last hour, and Dani takes a drink of the beer she's nursing. She's nervous and angry. My intestines have been pulled into my chests and tied in knots around my hearts. Graphic, but accurate.

Our big night has finally arrived. Our time to shine the brightest with our home crowd here cheering us on. Instead, security has spent the last hour going through our things after someone tipped them off that there were drugs. This time, they decided to investigate the claims. There's a clause in the contract stated no drugs, which I can appreciate more than most. Eurovision does the same thing. It's hard enough running a series like this and dealing with all the drinking, the general idiocy, and the bands dropping like flies for less serious reasons, having them hauled away on drug charges or overdosing on the road wouldn't work well for publicity. They don't want another Woodstock '99 on their hands, since they're already starting to promote a second season of the competition.

We're in LA, so they're not worried about weed, but the

rumors going around the bands say the tip involved heroin and fentanyl. So far, it's delayed the show for an hour. At this rate, it might be two. They should have canceled, or made us get here early, but they picked tonight to start searching. At least it's not the entire lineup of bands. That would take all damn night.

Marco hops up on the stack of pallets with me and bums a smoke. He doesn't smoke, so I give him a bit of a side eye but still give him one and my lighter.

"That bad?" I ask. I'm not using, so I shouldn't have anything to worry about. But I'm also a recovering addict, and I've been open about that to people on this tour outside of the band. But that means they're looking extra close at me and my things. One well-aimed dropped pill, an empty baggie, or a needle slipped into my bag, and someone could end this whole thing for us. For Dani.

"They're still trying to figure it out, but it's looking like a false alarm. Or that people aren't hiding their stash in obvious places." He coughs when he takes his first drag. I scratch at my two-day stubble, trying to not get myself too worked up. "The crowd won't wait much longer, so I can't imagine they'll drag their feet on announcing something soon. Even if it's only to say they're pushing the show to tomorrow or—"

"No! Not tomorrow! Steve and Ethan are here because it's Ethan's night off and now they're already stuck waiting in line! On his night off!" Dani yells before waving us off and continuing her pacing and mumbling. She's back to herself, which we're all happy to see, but it's still going to take some adjustment before she trusts her pain, vulnerabilities, and problems with others.

"As for the other question, the one you asked before I went back in?" Marco continues. "They said it won't be enough to find something, they'll have to find it, and that person fails a drug test. That's the only way they'd bump the band from the tour based on the contract. They already anticipated the idea of someone hiding a stash to get a band knocked out, so at least there's that."

"So, have us all piss in a damn cup and move on!" Noah yells to no one in particular. She's worried they're inside messing up our gear since they don't have a clue how to handle it. I get it, but there's not much we can do about it. At least none of us have an acoustic guitar they might try to crack open.

"Drug testing all of us would be expensive, and a legal nightmare." I reply. "But they'll start asking for random tests after this. Bring it."

There's a shuffle from behind me and Dani turns toward the noise, ready to bite anyone's head if they try to tell us to go back inside again. Sometimes she's the scarab, sometimes she's the mantis. "Honeybee!!"

Xander and Theo sneak around the corner, holding their fingers to their lips as Dani wraps around Xander's neck, careful of his sling. Theo comes around next to me and pulls me into a hug.

"We had to bribe the guard to get back here," Theo laughs before he cups my face and kisses me. "How are you all holding up? Some kind of raid by the LAPD?"

"Fuckers! Profiling isn't legal!" Dani readies herself for a fight with no one, bouncing on her toes.

"Are you still going to do it?" Theo whispers, and I shake my head. He pushes my shoulder. "Why not?"

"Are you?"

"Yes!" He moves to his side, so he's not in Dani's or Xander's eye-line and pulls a ring out of his pocket. "Not tonight, but soon."

"She'll hate it. I returned the stupid ring last week anyhow."

"Sky, you worked your ass off in your friend's garage to save up for that ring."

"A passionate heat of the moment idea when we were all terrified about Xander's condition. I shouldn't be doing shit like that, messing around with Dani's head. My head." I offer Theo a faint smile. "Don't let it stop you, though. You two make sense, but our Beetle doesn't want to be tied down, and I'm not sure I'm ready for that even if she wanted it."

"She just wants to be tied up? Skylar, you said it yourself, it's not technically—" he's cut off when Dani and Xander come close enough to hear us. Theo clears his throat and changes the subject. "So, have they said how long before they let you all go on?"

I shake my head while Noah takes up the pacing where Dani left off. The only one of us that doesn't look like they're about to explode is Connor, but that's because he's busy making out with a groupie. I love that for him, because he loves the attention of strangers far more than I ever did and he takes a lot of the heat off me.

"Do you think they'll actually catch anyone?" Xander asks me, and I shrug before he leans in and kisses my cheek.

"Hopefully, no."

The doors pop open again. This time, two big cops come out and one of them has the bag for my bass. My stomach lurches.

"Mr. Beck? We're told this belongs to you?"

"Mx. Beck. Non-binary," Dani corrects him, no fear in her voice while I sit next to her, mouth dry and unable to form words.

I nod and the cop that hasn't spoken yet holds the bag up. I stare at it, nodding again, but still unable to speak. What if they did find something? What if there are drugs still in my system?

"Apologies. One of our dogs got a little rough going through everyone's things. He broke a pocket. You can file a complaint with the department if you'd like. They'll want pictures and other information, but for this, you're probably better off pretending it never happened. They'll likely string it out for a few months and —Shit, we just scared the piss out of you, didn't we?"

I nod again, letting out the breath I'd been holding so long I almost suffocated.

"Well, anyway, you're good to go."

I wait until they're back inside the door before I let myself fall back onto the stack of pallets. The flashing memories of the paranoia and the meltdowns I had over getting caught while living in Canada come flooding back. I never got caught, and that might be part of my problem. If I had, maybe it would have helped me sooner, or I'd still be sitting in jail. Who knows? But right now, my stress meter has maxed out, and my entire body trembles uncontrollably.

"Fuckers, seriously?" Dani yells, but they're long gone by now and I'm covering my face with my hands, trying to get my breathing to steady, along with my heart rate. "I mean, they could have led with a heads up that everything's fine."

Marco's phone buzzes. "Ah, our legal team arrived. Guessing that's why they even bothered to come out and tell you at all. Looks like they're shutting the raid down, and doors will open in fifteen. They've got LA Proper going second to last, and everyone will play shortened sets."

"Okay, Scooby Gang," Marco says loud enough to get Connor's attention. "See you inside. Sorry about the shit show, Sky."

"Connor! Get your disgusting tongue out of the groupie's throat and let her breath through something other than her eyelids! We gotta go!" Noah barks, but I don't register much of what's going on around me.

"We'll see you inside. Kill it up there, Beetle." Xander kisses her cheek and squeezes my arm. His eyes tell me he wishes he could climb up onto the pallet and reach me. After we watch them head back down the alley to the front, I watch Dani's lips moving, but I can't make out what she's saying. She whispers to Marco, and he nods. Before I stand up to follow everyone inside, Dani stops me.

"I got us a little time to help you relax. You okay?"

"Not gonna lie. I think that just ran my last spoon through a garbage disposal. I'll be okay, though. I can still play."

She holds out her arms and I take them as she pretends to pull me off the pallet stack and to my feet, wrapping my arms around her. She holds me there for a while, her head resting over my heart as it struggles to slow down. When I glance down at her, there's a familiar, wicked grin on her face.

"Oh, if you're thinking what I'm guessing you're thinking. Yes. Please."

She winks and grabs my pants, pulling at the button and unzipping them quickly. Her hand snakes in, wrapping around me as she bites at my chest through my shirt. Her big doe eyes look up at me, eyelids fluttering. "Can I be your good girl, Skylar? Will you let me suck your big cock for you? Put me on my knees and make me choke on you."

"Oh, you're going to do more than that, pet. But for now, get on your knees, open your mouth, and play with your tits." She lowers herself, pulling her shirt up so I can see she's not wearing a bra, allowing the silver jewelry glistens in the dark. Her knees spread wide, and her mouth opens in anticipation. She's so needy, starving for me. And I'm going to give her exactly what she needs.

Her tongue darts out like a lizard when I pull my cock out, running the tip over her lips. She's moaning at the taste of me, so I grab a thick handful of hair and pull hard. "I never told you to do that, did I?"

"No, my love. I'm sorry."

"You're going to be." I grin, pulling her up to her feet and dragging her further back in the lot to a short stack of road cases at the edge of the light's reach. I shove her down onto the case with her shirt still pulled up, and when her perky little tits press against the cool steel, she squeaks and gasps. "You're going to fulfill a fantasy of mine tonight, Dani. One I've been dreaming about since I watched you the first night."

"Do anything you need to me, Skylar. Everything you want."

There's a snap as I rip her panties off, leaning over her, I tap her cheek, "Open up, we don't need you making too much noise, do we?" I push her panties into her mouth, then flip her skirt up, exposing her glistening pussy. "Hands behind your back and don't move them unless I say."

Even in the dark I can see how wet she is, but I still slide one finger through her, from her clit all the way to her puckered asshole. If I had any lube, that's exactly where I'd be going tonight, but I don't, so we'll go with Plan B. I crouch behind her, making the same swipe, but this time with my tongue, listening to the whimper and wine as I slip the tip of my tongue into her tight hole. I won't fuck her ass right now, but I can sure as hell play with it. She pushes her hips back, wanting more. Spreading her cheeks wide, I spit on her puckered skin and push my finger in, relishing her gasps. I pump in and out of her, making her squirm and ball her hands into fists. My other hand teases her clit until it pulses for me. She's so slick, three fingers slip into her with ease. I don't even bother to take my rings off, letting her savor the warmth of my skin and the cold metal together until she's writhing, hips bucking.

"Oh please! Oh please, don't stop. Skylar, I can't! I can't!" she blubbers, pushing herself down on my fingers and begging to come. Crying out when I pull out of her and stand again.

"Quiet, pet. You have a choice to make," I hum, pressing the head of my cock against her asshole. "Are you going to be a good girl and take everything I give you? Let me paint your cunt with my cum so it can drip down your shaking thighs on stage. Or are you going to be a brat, and I'll bring you so close to the edge, you'll forget every one of our songs?"

I pull the panties from her mouth as she shakes her head. "No! Oh, come on Sky! No, no, please?"

"It's up to you. Think you can hold your legs together on stage so my cum stays inside you?" I flick her clit, and slide the tip of my cock through her wetness. "Or should I send you out there with ruined makeup and tear stains? No, can't do that. You won't be able to sing if I use your mouth."

"I'll be good, Skylar! Your perfect little toy. Please, just give me your cock!"

She thinks she knows what she wants, but I haven't told her everything yet. I lean in, pressing into her entrance. "You should learn to listen better, pet. No matter what you chose, naughty or nice, you're not coming before the show. Do you understand?"

"Skylar!" I push the panties back into her mouth and notch my cock against her dripping opening.

My teeth scrape against the skin of her neck as I let the four metals balls tease her. I bite down on her shoulder, squeezing my cock with my hand. It's almost painful how badly I want to be inside her, fully inside her. She tightens, desperate for me to go deeper, to lose myself to her. My free hand slides up her face, giving her a false sense of a soft moment between us until I grab her jaw and hiss into her ear.

"If you don't obey me, if you dare come on my cock, I will make sure no one lets you come for a week. Do you hear me, pet?" She nods, and I release her jaw, putting that hand to better use between her legs. "If you need to stop, tap me three times."

She squeezes her eyes closed and nods.

"I wish you could see yourself the way I do. How depraved and helpless you look with this monstrosity inside you, how needy your cunt is, how badly your entire body begs for me. Tell me what you want, pet." Her panties muffle her pleas, and I rip them out so she can answer me.

"I don't want anything unless it pleases you."

"Not super convincing. Maybe I should ask louder. Get the security detail over here to show them what a good little slut you can be for me. Do you want an audience? For me to fill your tight ass on stage while everyone watches?"

"Yes!"

"Don't tempt me, Daniella." I growl, watching my cock sliding in and out of her. "Shit, you're so fucking sexy when I'm inside you. I'll make you sing my name, my beautiful siren."

I slam against her so hard, the boxes we're leaning against shift, but she can only beg for more, balling her fists into my shirt, threatening to rip it. I bite down on her shoulder again, leaving marks for everyone to see. The guttural snarl that slips out of me as I fill her sounds damn near demonic. I don't stop, forcing my cum deeper inside her, causing harmonious wet sounds as I take her up the mountain and to the edge. When I can't spill anymore, I step back and drop to my knees. "Bend over, touch your toes for me." She shakes, having to lean her hip against the boxes to keep herself from falling over. My tongue slides through her, collecting our combined tastes before I spin her around and kiss her hard.

She sucks on my tongue, eyes open and watching mine struggle to stay open. Her hands play in my hair as I kneel before her beauty, praying to Loki that she's real and nothing takes her away from me. My light, my star, my siren.

"Good girl." my dark whisper sends shivers through her.

"I love you, Skylar," she whispers against my mouth as she clings to me. "We'll get you through this. All of us."

"We will, Beetle." I stand, stroking her cheek. "Now, let's go give the people what they want. Your siren song that sends them crashing against the rocks of the stage, begging for a piece of what they can't have. A piece of what's mine." I kiss the top of her head.

"Skylar," she stops me as I pull away, her voice softer than I've ever heard before. The sound scares me, and I worry I've taken this too far as I cup her face, holding it to mine. Her fingers wrap around my wrists as our foreheads press together. "You're ours, we're yours. Never forget that. No one will ever hurt you again unless they go through us, no one. Hang on, my dark deity, my perfect fallen angel. Please?"

It's like she can read my soul.

I close my eyes and nod. She recognizes how close I've been, and how hard it's been to hide it these last few days, even if I haven't told her. My finger has hovered over the call button to my dealer and my sponsor equal amounts, and each time it was my new family who pulled me away, saved me from falling.

"What's left of my soul and my fractured heart are yours, love. But you've clawed me away from the devil, and someday, he'll need his payment."

"I dare him to try me. He can't have you, any of you, because you belong to me."

"That's my girl." I kiss her forehead, relishing the sweet scent of her shampoo in her sweat damp hair. "Oh, and Dani?" She looks up at me, blinking her dark, mesmerizing eyes. "You have my permission to come. On stage."

HOLLYWOOD
Theo

IN ALL THE years I've had this cat, not once has she bolted out the door. Until tonight. It's like she knew from some weird cat senses that I needed to step outside at that exact moment to see Dani, my rockstar goddess, standing in the hall, keys sticking out of her door. Well, they were, until they fell to the floor making enough noise to scare Baguette and have her bolting down the stairs.

"I'm sorry! I'll go get her!" Dani yells out, dropping her things.

"It's fine!" I move toward her, picking up the bags of groceries she's dropped. "No Skylar to help you tonight?"

"No, they're at a meeting. Xander's there for support." She looks at the stairs like she's going to cry. "Poor Baggy, I didn't mean to scare her."

"Eh, she won't go far. She knows where the food is." Sure enough, as soon as I start picking up the remaining bags, the cat pokes her little nose around the corner with a soft meow. She follows us in and I help put everything away, before I find myself standing there awkwardly.

"Hungry?"

"For take-out, no. But I could cook us something." She sticks her tongue out at me and laughs. "I, uhm, actually I'm here for you. I got these tickets to a pop-up event tonight from my receptionist. She's using me to keep her from going out and doing stupid things. Impulse control problems."

"Sounds like my old co-worker, Kennedy."

"Kennedy? Well, I highly doubt the odds are high for two of them with the same issues. You worked with Alexis?"

"Still do. That's my day job. We took everything remote a few years ago, even my job as the receptionist. I never told you that?"

"No, I assumed when you came to work and hung around the coffee shop downstairs you were writing music and playing on the internet or something. Which sounds...terrible. I'm sorry."

"Nah, I mean, you're not totally wrong." She twirls her hair around her finger, biting her lower lip as she avoids looking at me. "I don't have a difficult job. And most of it involves playing around online and looking up new trends in music, fashion, and media. Research."

"So, you tag along to work with me because...?"

"The coffee doesn't suck?" I love the adorable way her face scrunches up, and I can't take my eyes off her. I can't keep my hands off her either, as they take on a mind of their own and slide under her shirt, rubbing against her hips.

"Do, uhm, we have time for a glass of wine before we go?" Her voice is so sultry and smooth, I could drown in it. When I nod, she giggles and reaches backward over her head, pulling down two coffee mugs.

I wish I could stop the laughter, but I can't. "My place. Let's go. I can't even take you seriously here because you're about to pull out a box of wine and it will, in fact, be the death of me, woman."

"Hey, there's nothing—"

"Nope. Don't finish that sentence. Let's go." I pick her up over my shoulder, smacking her ass as I walk through our passageway.

"Baggy, save me! I'll give you salmon!" The cat darts around us both to paw at the door of the refrigerator. "Traitor! Your betrayal will be remembered come exile day!"

I put Dani down on the counter, but before I can pull away from her, her hands are around my neck. She tastes like sweet lemon candy as we kiss over and over. Other than the days she works downstairs, we don't get much time alone together. It never works out with our schedules. Even then, it's not exactly easy to make a personal connection stuck in Los Angeles traffic. Her hands slip up my shirt and she works on the buttons, taking her time. I reach behind her and pull down a bottle of wine with one hand and two glasses with the other.

"Couch?"

"Couch." Her legs wrap around me and I manage to carry her into the living room without dropping anything. When she slides down my body, a tingle of sparks along my spine.

"Oh, holy shit! Theo!" she yells, running over to my wall of books and sliding her fingers over the spines. The shelves are overcrowded and probably a little dusty—it's been a while since my last deep cleaning. I've been…busy. She stops right where I knew she would, and the blush creeps up my cheeks as I pour the wine and walk up behind her. "I've never even noticed all these books before."

"Yeah, you're usually distracted by us or food when you're over here."

"You cleared this whole thing? Even with overflowing shelves?"

"They're overflowing because I cleared this case."

She pulls out the old but loved copy of The Hobbit, thumbing through it before she puts it back and takes out the next book in the series. "You haven't read these, any of them, have you?" I shake my head and she smiles. "You cleared an entire shelf for him. All these other books are clinical or baking or non-fiction. They're organized meticulously, except for what you've crammed into any available spot. All that to give him his own bookshelf?"

"He said he hasn't had one since he was young. His parents didn't think reading fantasy would help him get anywhere in life, so he snuck them from the library and read under the covers."

"He still does. He reads to me every night we spend together."

"And he reads to me the other nights. These are the oldest, rarest versions I could find. I haven't told him about the books yet. They came in yesterday and I've had to hide them. I've found others, too, but they're newer. Something about sea gods or living by the sea."

"Oh, I've heard some of those! He loves the, uhm, colorful word choices. They say things like '*by Poseidon's watery cold taint*' and stuff. Makes me giggle when he reads those. Especially in his voices."

"Careful, when I laughed, he turned the tables on me. Now I'm reading to him by the romantic glow of my tablet while he howls with laughter. What did we find the other night? Oh yeah, some Greek deity's *rock-hard anvil*. Ridiculous, but entertaining."

She hooks her hands into my half-unbuttoned shirt and pulls

me to her, so I press her against the bookshelves. She has to notice how hard I am as we stand there, staring at one another.

"It's hot. The way you and Xander are together." She runs her hands down my chest, licking her lips. "The way you two *love* each other so damn much. It turns me on watching you."

"I do. I love him."

"No shit, Doc. You can't hide those longing glances and not-so-secret touches when I'm around, big guy. He loves you, too. You couldn't have come along at a better time."

As a therapist, I'm supposed to be able to connect with people. But in my personal life, it's something I'm no longer equipped for because I've avoided it for so long. I tried, for a long time, but there's an ever-lingering pain that never fails to morph into my shield, reminding me that by opening up and getting comfortable around someone, I'm inviting the world up to yank them out of my life again. The inevitable reminder of why I live alone, why my relationships are rare, and why the walls around my heart shouldn't come down again, always makes an appearance. Any time I connect with another person, the chill along my back reminds me of what I had, what I lost, and how disappointed they might be if I moved on without them. How it would dishonor her memory and cheapen the love we shared.

Except, that hasn't happened yet. Not with Dani, Skylar, or Xander. Dani's personality, her strength, and confidence keeps my insecurities at bay, and for the second time in too many years, I'm not counting down the minutes or seconds until this interaction is over. I don't want it to end, the same way I didn't want Xander to leave that morning—any morning. And Skylar? The way they use that mouth leaves me speechless. No matter if it's full of poetry and prose, or my cock.

I had myself so convinced I enjoyed being alone, but I understand now how miserable I was before this. Before them.

"Uhm, that's good, because, I uhm, I need to ask you something important about our boy." I reach up, pulling the ring box from the top shelf. Hiding it there worked until Skylar spotted it the other day while we were making out in the kitchen and started asking questions. That fucker is too tall for their own good and reads me like a book. He chickened out on proposing to Dani—his reasoning made sense, though.

Dani gasps, letting go of my shirt to hold her fingers to her lips.

"It's, I want to, uhm, give it to Xander. But only if that's okay. I mean, if you don't want me to, or think I—"

"DO IT! AHH! Oh my god, this is so perfect!"

"You…don't think it's too fast?"

"Babe, who cares? You've lived through what can happen if you wait for the perfect moment or for other people's approval! Life is short, and crazy, and stupid. You just gotta do it." She flashes a toothy smile before biting at her lip ring, a nervous tick she has. "Is it, like, a gift or are you going to pop the big question?"

I sigh, putting the box back and running my hand through my beard. "I'm not sure, Dani. But I do want you to understand that I'm not trying to take him away from you."

"Again, with the obvious statements. I can't wait for him to see it. I hope you record it!"

"I could do it when you're there. Take some nervousness out of it."

"NO!" she squeals. "You can't! You need to do it all romantic or spontaneous or however you want, but it should just be you two. God, he'd love that. He tried to propose to me once, and I told him I'm not that kind of girl, but he is. He's absolutely that kind of boy. Oh, I'm so excited for you. Our little happy family!"

My crooked smile must confuse her by the look she gives me. "I'm not used to the acceptance. I'm used to the rejection. The rejection that you can love more than one person, you can love the idea of someone you love being in love, that this isn't cheating, it's… it's…"

"Beautiful? Magical? Anyone who thinks that it's not the most perfect thing in the world to watch someone you love fall in love with someone else while not falling out of love with you is missing out." She puts her glass down on a nearby table before putting mine next to it and taking my shirt in her fists. We're so close, I'm breathing in the wine on her lips. "Treat my Xander right, Dr. Clay. Always remember what he means to you, and don't fuck up like I do. I don't want to have to shank you."

"I'd like you to not shank me. In fact, I'd prefer if you kiss me instead," I whisper, dipping my head down as our mouths slot together. In a sudden movement I wasn't anticipating, she spins us around, shoving me hard against the bookcase.

"What time are these tickets for?"

"We've got hours."

"Good, because the idea of you putting that ring on my boyfriend has me tingling in all the right places. I want you to do to me what you do to Xander." She kisses my bottom lip, sucking gently for only a moment. "Show me how you make him lose control."

"No."

"No?" She pulls her head back and looks at me, pierced eyebrows pinched together.

"No," I growl, a firmness entering my voice.

I lift her up and claim every inch of her mouth with my tongue. Her legs wrap around me, heels digging into my back as

I grind against her, the sporadic chirps of delight driving me on. I take her to the couch and throw her down before climbing on top of her, only breaking the kiss for the shortest moment. My hand dives under her skirt and I push against the wet fabric between her legs, bringing a moan from her mouth to mine. I pull away and look at her, and she doesn't hesitate to nod.

Grabbing the hem of the tight skirt, I flip it up over her hips, and dive right into her with my face, licking and teasing her through the silky panties. Her thighs squeeze together as I nip and suck at her clit, fingers playing in my hair until I stop and glare at her.

"Oh, come on, please?"

"I have something for you."

"Yeah, I've felt that fat cock of yours."

I reach under the couch and pull out a box not much smaller than a shoe box, and her eyes go wide as I hand it to her. I nod when she hesitates and opens the lid, moving the tissue paper to the side. She giggles, pulling out the most ridiculous looking dildo I've ever seen in my life, and I'm the one who ordered it.

"Have you been snooping on my laptop?" She gives me a coy smile as she looks closer at the toy. To my surprise, she opens her mouth and sticks out her tongue, flicking it over the end of the purple and green monstrosity.

"It's, uhm, Xander..." I'm too flustered by the sight for words. "He said you have a thing for monster smut books. That's, uh, some demon—" I lose my train of thought as she parts her lips and slides it between them, her eyes rolling back as she does. My cock has never been so jealous of a piece of silicon than when she pulls it out and licks her lips.

"So, what's your plan with this, Doctor? Are you going to use it on me? Am I going to use it on you? Or can we do both?"

"All the above. I thought we could, uhm—"

"Stand up, Theo." The instant I do, her hand is against my bulge again, pressing and kneading my cock through my pants. "Now, take this pretty beast out and stand at the end of the couch. When you get the urge, join in however you want. Understand?"

I nod, moving like a robot she's controlling. The speed at which she disarmed me empties my head of all but one thought, pleasing her. I watch her shift so her head hangs off the end of my couch and her legs spread wide. The skirt is still bunched up around her waist and I love it. She takes the monster cock into her mouth again, pumping it in and out while I watch it bobbing in her throat. She moans and hums around it while I stand there, fantasizing that it's my cock. When she slides it out, it's dripping in her saliva and she looks up at me, breathless.

"Take off your pants, Doctor." The hypnotic colors of the toy pull my eyes between her tits and down her body while my pants fall in a puddle at my feet. She licks her lips again as she looks at me upside down, holding eye contact as she pushes the tip of the silicon dick inside her. "Fuck! It's so big, Doctor Clay. What should I do? This demon wants to screw my soul out of me and I can't say no!"

She starts panting, and I take two steps forward, grabbing the sides of her head and burying my cock in her throat while she chokes. My head spins, between the feel of her mouth, and watching that toy still sliding deeper inside her, it's fucking incredible. My hips rock, matching the speed of her own thrusts. Even with her mouth and her pussy full, she's still controlling me. Still in command of everything. She didn't even fight for it like Skylar does, she took it from me like she owns me.

She hums, rubbing her clit while I thrust into her mouth, and it sends a ripple up my spine. I pull out of her and grab her wrist, taking the dildo from her and rubbing the thick head over her lips. She stops me with a smirk, turning the toy to me. "This doesn't come out of your mouth until you've filled me with your cum. Do you understand, Doctor Clay?"

I nod, moving between her legs and opening my mouth as she slides the toy into me. The sharp taste of her cunt hits my tongue, and she starts pushing it inside my mouth. I match her motions, and push into her until I bottom out. We must be a sight, her spread out on my couch, impaled on my cock while she fills my throat with her new toy.

"Suck it, Theo," she commands in breathless pants. "Suck it like you do to Xander when you have him here, in your bed. Show me how good you treat my honeybee."

I'm thrusting wildly into her, her back arching as she shoves the toy further down my throat. I can't stop my mind from putting Xander there in its place. Wondering what it would be like to have them both at the same time. Would Dani and I fight for control, or would I give it all to her like I am right now? She's pulled her shirt open and playing with her perfect little tits, pulsing around me as she watches me take the toy deeper down my throat, thrusting into her so hard the couch shifts.

"Yes! Just like that. Oh fuck, I'm gonna cum all over you, Doctor Clay." She pulls the toy out of my mouth, and I chase it like a baby chasing a bottle, but she grabs my face and pulls me down to her chest. I find her nipple and bite down through her bra. She holds my head there as her body shakes beneath me.

"Oh god! Oh, God!" she shrieks, digging her nails into my arm when I pull her hair. "Just like that!"

"Tell me what depraved shit you want from me. I'll do it. I'll do anything for you, Dani."

"Oh fuck, yes! Harder, Theo! Don't stop!" Her hips rock in time with mine and her nails rake down my back, threatening to rip through the shirt as I pump my seed deep inside her. Her body shivers, holding me inside her as a second her orgasm rips through her, but I hold her down with the weight of my body as I collapse on top of her, kissing her hard until we're gasping for air.

"I like...the gift...Theo. Xander...will like it...too. Use it while you're watching Star Wars with him. Seriously," she sighs as I drop my head into the crook of her neck, staying inside of her as we fall asleep together.

HOLLYWOOD
Xander

I HAVEN'T SLEPT in two days, far too hyped up and nervous about the meeting with my first big investor. There are two cups of coffee, an energy drink, and the bottle of water Theo added to the mix sitting next to me as I work, plugging away at the last pieces of coding I need to finish before the presentation. I've run so many tests, trying to break anything I can so I can fix it before it breaks in front of the people that matter. So far, it's running smoother than I expected.

I'm about to start another pass through of the backend coding when the plate touches down on the table. I glance up from my spot on the floor, listening to the growl that emanates from my stomach.

"Baby, you need a break and some food. You've been at the coffee table for days without sleep, but I'm not going to let you starve, too."

"I'm almost done. I'll stop in a bit."

"You said that last night, around eight hours ago. You have a meeting tomorrow. You can't go into that running on caffeine alone. Come on, sit up here and have lunch with me."

"Lunch? Shit, what time is it?" I haven't checked a clock since

sometime around six. This morning, but now the sun sits high in the sky.

"Time for you to stop. Put it away. If it's not fixed by now, you're not going to get it fixed. You should practice what you're going to say tomorrow, but more importantly, you need to take care of yourself." He leans forward, closing the lid of the laptop as he glares at me. "Or, better yet, let me take care of you."

I huff out a slow breath and climb up from the floor, my back cracking in places I don't think should crack. At least the ribs have mostly healed. He pulls me down into his arms and we lay there for a while, enjoying each other's company—no words or worries. Dani and I don't do this much. She doesn't do well with silence.

"You know you're going to do great, right?" Theo says before sleep takes me.

"I dunno. I mean, maybe. There are bugs in the system and I'm not sure—"

"There are no bugs, Xander. It's a prototype, it's not meant to be perfect. Isn't the point of setting up this meeting to plan on ways to attract backers?" I nod. He sighs. "You and Dani are so good and yet so toxic for each other for this exact reason. Neither of you let go of your pride long enough to see that you need help."

I pick my head up and smile at him. "I won't, I promise. I'm beyond ready to let this thing go and go back to video games and jerking off all day for a few months." His laugh rumbles in his chest. It brings out the lines around his mouth and eyes and makes him look stunning. I shimmy up his body and the kissing starts. No rush, no need to hurry into the bedroom or rip each other's clothes off. We can do that later, for now, it's just tastes and teases.

"I got you something."

"Does it have tentacles and a demonic backstory like Dani's?"

"She told you about that?"

"Doc, she's used it on me." He laughs again, shaking his head until I leave a dozen more kisses on his lips. He tastes like coffee and caramel, his drink of choice. "So, what is it?"

His hand dips under the couch cushion that's holding his head up, pulling out a small red box. It's worn and tattered, traces of velvet clinging on in a last-ditch effort to remind people what the box had once looked like. He opens the box, but it's facing him so I can't see what's inside, only the glimmer of tears forming in the corners of his eyes.

The second he turns the box around, I'm pretty sure my heart stops. I've seen the ring before on the man who wore it last. I can't take my eyes off it as my mind goes blank and eyes well with tears.

"Xander, we haven't been together long—six months—but it doesn't need to be long when you know the person is right. You've brought back a spark I didn't think could ever catch again and turned it into a raging fire that could swallow the sun." He licks his lips, and I swipe away the tear from his cheek. "I don't care how the presentation goes tomorrow. I don't care if you come back with promises of millions, or a rejection and months more work ahead of you. I just want you to come back. Always."

"I… We…"

He takes the ring out of the box and slips it over my finger. It fits like it was made for me. Maybe he's right, maybe his lost love's ghost *is* inside of me. Reincarnation, but well after I was born.

"I don't care if it's official or only between us, just say yes. Please?"

"Yeah. I mean, yes. I mean, fuck yes!"

He pulls my face to his and we clash so hard we lose our balance and fall off the couch, still kissing. Still laughing. Still so deeply in love.

"I can't wait to show Dani." My face drops and panic comes rushing back. "Shit, what if this pisses her off again?"

"I already told her about it. Sky knew first. I hid the ring up high and that shit saw it. Both of them were over the moon happy. I wouldn't be surprised if they're waiting in the other room for you, or listening in on us right now."

I hurry to my knees and peek over the top of the couch, and sure enough, they're at the doorway, waving and giving me a thumbs up.

"Well, come over here, jerks. I'm pretty sure I just got engaged!"

Why the hell did nature decide an appropriate response to stress needed to involve sweating? That only makes it worse, and yet that's the response evolution decided to keep around instead of adapting to produce the scent of lavender or something relaxing? Sometimes, I agree with Skylar's concept when they wax on and on about Loki being the true god of the universe we live in. It explains so damn much about anatomy and bodily functions. I wipe my hand on my pants for the tenth time when my phone buzzes in my pocket. I glance up at the door. Maybe I should walk out, maybe this was a terrible idea. Pulling it out and trying to check without looking like I'm playing on my phone is difficult, but I pull it off. It's worth the risk as I stare down at a picture of the people I love holding a sign that says, 'You've got this, baby!'

It couldn't come at a better time.

"You must be Xander Maxwell." A tall guy with a goatee and glasses says as he heads toward me. I stand up, taking his hand when offered. "I'm Miguel. Come on up, we've got the team ready for you."

"The team? Great, that's…good."

"Hey, I wanted to ask, are you related to the Maxwells?"

"Uhm, will it help or hinder this presentation?"

"Neither."

"Okay, yeah. I'm their son. Sort of."

He stops, turning to give me a look I've seen too many times in my life. "Are they not interested? I assume you'd give them first denial?"

"I didn't. I didn't give them anything, honestly. They're in the dark about the project, and I don't want them involved in any way. Long story, but we're kind of estranged."

He smirks, swipes his badge, and presses the button. I'm expecting him to tell me to leave, to say I'm an idiot and toss me out. "Ballsy. I like that. Sorry to hear about the family troubles, but it happens to the best of us."

"Yeah? I'm thinking of a name change, to keep it separated."

"Oh, yeah? Probably a solid move. What are you thinking?"

"Not sure." My finger brushes against the phone in my pocket. "I've been playing around with Clay and Silva."

He thinks it over as the elevator climbs to the top of the high-rise, and as we walk toward the conference room, he turns. "What about Silva Clay Enterprises? There's a ring to it, and it flows better as a name with Silva reference first." He winks and holds the door open for me.

"Yeah, it does."

"Relax, kid. By the way, nice suit."

I don't text them until I'm almost back at our building, telling them nothing other than I'll be up shortly. I pop the trunk on Theo's car and pull the bag out, careful to shove something between the bottles so they don't clank around as I stick them into my backpack. As I expected them to be, Dani, Theo, and Skylar are all standing outside of our doors.

"Oh, honeybee," Dani comes to me first, throwing her arms around me as I keep my head down. I'm surprised she doesn't catch on that I'm faking it and hiding my smile.

"It's cool," I choke out. "I, uhm, grabbed lunch on the way back. Not in the mood to go out."

Skylar reaches around me and lifts the backpack, trying to take it off my shoulders. "Dude, what the hell do you have in here? A pound of bricks? I thought you said you stopped for lunch?"

"It's nothing." I shrug. "A couple of bottles of champagne to celebrate that they're on board to fund the project." They all step away from me and I pick my head up. "I'm going to talk to Laurie's guy tomorrow about contract negotiations. But they loved the concept. They're all in."

"Ahhh!" Dani screams as they all hug me. Their contagious excitement has me laughing and hugging them back. I'm not a fuckup. For the first time in a long time, I'm overwhelmed by the notion I've done something right, and now I'm being rewarded for it. Not for my name, or what my parents have done with their lives, but for me, for my ideas.

And I have a family to share it with, a family that's proud of me and believed in me from the beginning. A family that doesn't give a shit about the content I'll be working with or judge me for the things I like. In fact, they love me and all my weird little kinks.

"Hey Xan," Skylar says, biting their lip nervously. "I was, uhm—I asked Dani first, but what if…uhm…"

"They want to do a video with you!" Dani blurts out, causing Theo to choke and Skylar to blush.

"What? Seriously? Like, for the site?" I'm in shock. "You know what that means, right? I mean, the only way to hide your identity involves, like, a full body suit or something."

"No hiding. One stipulation." I narrow my eyes, curiosity eating away at me. "I want it to be live. I want to know people are watching us."

"Well look at that," Theo teases. "You've finally found a way to take care of that exhibitionist streak without the cops coming after you for indecent exposure. You were getting pretty close on stage, my friend."

"I'm not your friend, Theo," Skylar laughs. "I'm your lover, lover."

"Yes, to that request, Sky. In fact, we're going to be the first live stream for the site! Now come on, I'm starving."

Dani kisses my cheek. "I'm going to watch the hell out of that live stream while Theo eats me out. But yeah, let's get inside. Your man has been stress-baking since you left, and we have so much food right now!"

HOLLYWOOD
Dani

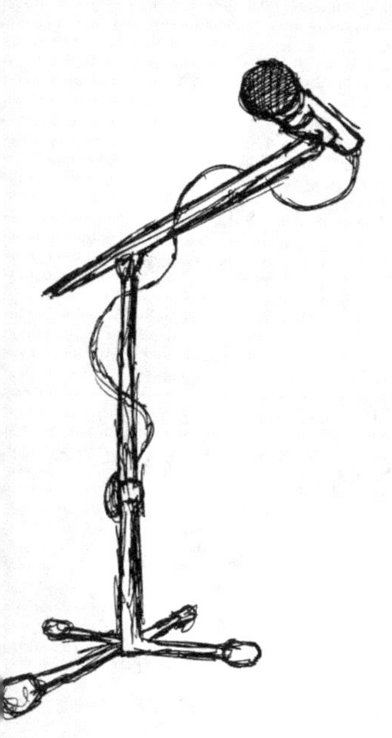

CHAPTER 49
TOO MUCH

DOVE CAMERON

"A CABIN? Like, in the woods and shit? Where wolves live?" I ask, lying across his bare chest as the sun rises. The sheets are loosely wrapped around us and his fingers play in my hair at the back of my neck.

"No wolves, Dani. And not exactly a cabin, but a house off the grid. It's not that eccentric of an idea. The peace and quiet of the trees, the trickle of water from the stream that runs through the back of the property. It's an oasis, a perfect retreat from city life."

"There are still bears, though, right?" His chest shakes as he laughs, deep and soothing. If I'm not careful, I'll fall asleep here in his warm, strong arms. He's like a bear in some ways, but not as furry once you get past the beard. The soft sprinkle of hair on his chest matches his head, and it tickles him when I run my ringers through the patch or try to follow it down to the other patch further south. The trail that leads to a sleeping monster.

"Yes, there are. Stuffed ones with little red shirts." He stretches his arms high over his head. In a panic, I nuzzle against his chest. I don't want him to leave the bed, not yet. "You're okay, sugar. I'm not kicking you out of bed yet."

"Are you a shrink or a mind reader?"

"Bit of both most days. We'll get out of bed when you're ready for breakfast, and not a moment before." His gentle kiss on top of my head sends a shiver down my spine and the smile it pulls from me has me blushing even if no one can see.

This isn't how mornings go with Xander. This is more like Sky, but even then, it's not the same. Xander rarely sleeps past sunrise and spends mornings on his computer either working on new programs, teaching himself code, or playing video games while he drinks his coffee. The only thing that can pull him away from the computer in the morning is sex, and he doesn't care where. Shower, bed, floor, couch, kitchen counter, anywhere. And that was just yesterday.

Skylar changes like the phases of the moon. In the hotels, they don't want to get out of bed or wake up early. Every time one of us finds ourselves awake before noon on the road, they crawl between my legs and I end up with some part of them inside me. Sleepily teasing and playing with me until we both finished and fell back asleep. They work at their own pace and no one else's, and that pace is slow and steady. They thrive on the experience, wishing they could view the world in slow motion. They take their time, mapping out freckles on my body, every noise I make, every piece of me that reacts to their touch. At home, though? They wake before the sun to watch it rise from his nest of solitude on the fire escape.

Maybe it's greedy to want to give in to these dark desires, but only because society has forgotten how we're programmed as people. Too many conservative minds run the show now, and that puts people like us under a microscope. Our lifestyle isn't new, unheard, or unnatural like they believe it to be. Of course, these are the same bastards that think the earth is flat and vaccines cause autism. The patriarchy has forced humanity into this monogamy idea, and no one wants to take a closer look at why marriages fail and people cheat—it would upset some religious organization's pockets. The ancients, even the Indigenous way of life, accepted that our brains aren't wired like that. It's a tribe, a group effort to keep everyone alive and happy, and these tie wearing assholes think there wasn't sharing going on back then? Take all the seats, madam.

I'm not greedy, I'm just a woman who knows what she wants. And one third of what I want happens to be lying in bed next to me right now.

"I wonder how Skylar and Xander are doing," I sigh, stretching as I check the time. We still have hours before I need to be back down at the studio for rehearsal, but I can't exactly lie around here all day.

Theo gets up and opens the bedroom door enough to let Baggy in. She doesn't waste time taking her place on the bed and staring at me until I pet her. "From the noises coming through the wall early this morning, they're fine," he laughs.

"Aww, wake me up next time and we'll go join them!" I snicker. Sometimes it's fun having separate bedrooms, but now and then all of us squeeze into one bed. Xander and Theo have talked about getting a larger bed for our apartment since that seems to be the communal bedroom, and I'm all for it. "I should shower," I announce, unable to tear my eyes away from his firm ass and muscular back. He hides his body behind a professional suit of armor, but it's obvious he works hard to keep in shape.

"I'll get breakfast going. Come out whenever you're ready." He pulls his sleep pants on and leans back into the bed, kissing just below my jaw in a way that curls my toes. "Over ice, three sugars, and two scoops of matcha? Or are we going with café de olla today?"

I'm not thinking about coffee or how to make it, I'm thinking of the three people I want in bed with me. The three people who could take me apart, put me back together, and work on each other while I remember how to breathe.

"Cream and sugar, lots of both."

"How do you do that? Different coffee every day?" He kisses me again, his hand squeezing my hip.

"You've seen how I date, and you still expect me to pick only one way of drinking my coffee?"

"Fair point."

The steam in the bathroom fogs up the mirror, so I swipe my hand across it, looking at the marks all over my body. I can match each mark with the person who left it. A chuckle escapes me at the thought of them. Most men are so consumed by their masculinity, if their partner came home with marks from someone else, they would lose their shit. Even someone they just met, if they took them home and found bite marks and sexy bruises, most of them would throw me out.

Skylar knew I had Xander. Theo knew Xander had me. None of that stopped either of them from welcoming me into their beds. It wasn't a competition for them, a way to prove they can satisfy me in a way other people haven't. Jealousy won't come for us, or at least I hope it won't. This is all I've ever wanted, enough people to share our love.

I open the door to the shower and step under the rainfall, letting the water tap gently on my head while it flows over my body. There's a moment of cool air before the arms wrap around me again, one dipping between my legs, gingerly testing his touch, making sure it's what I want and I'm ready for more.

I am. I always am.

"Breakfast will get cold," I moan, the tips of his finger drawing circles around my clit.

"Breakfast is in the oven for at least two orgasms." He nips at my ear as his body pushes me toward the shower wall. I hiss at the cold when my breasts push against the tiles and the sensation of his hard rod pokes me in the back.

"Is that an actual timer setting?" I tease.

"We never discussed your boundaries last night," he whispers, his free hand sliding up my body, wrapping his thick fingers around my neck. "Or picked a safe word, but Skylar said you like it like this."

"Pickles. And we haven't even come close to my boundaries yet."

"Oh?" His grip tightens at the same time as two fingers push inside me. "Xander had boundaries. He also had a thing for yelling out your name, Dani."

His deep voice makes my entire body spark with electricity. He squeezes again, but pauses to give me time to say the word and make it stop. I don't.

"Put your foot up on the edge," his voice drops to something lower, deeper, and I'm dripping for him. I'm saddened when he pulls his fingers out of me, drawing a whine from deep inside me where I miss his touch already. Once I've got my balance, he shifts behind me, his fingers trace through my slit, but they don't stop there, pushing against my ass and asking to be let in.

When I nod, it's not his fingers he pushes inside me. My back arches as I try to climb the wall. For the moment it takes the pain to become pleasure, he holds me against the wall, cutting off my airway as he pushes deeper into me. The transition to bliss happens in a blink, his cock still inching into me, his mouth closed around my ear, his hand around my neck, and his fingers pinching my clit.

"Atta girl. Take a deep breath when I let go. Ready?"

He releases my throat, and I suck in the heavy air. The distraction is enough for one last push, bottoming out as I scream and claw my nails through his hair. There's a sound from out in the apartment and he pauses, both of us aware of what that means.

"Do you want me to stop, Dani?"

"No! Don't you fucking dare! Shit! Please, don't stop!" A moment later, and another burst of cold air, more hands are on me, familiar ones. A mouth closes around me and that magnificent tongue swirls. I have one hand over my shoulder, holding Theo's head to me. The other plays in Xander's hair. I'm ready to explode when Theo moves me back and I have the perfect view of Xander as he stands up in front of me, mouth pressing hard against mine as he pushes into me, threatening to tear me in two.

"Jesus, Beetle! It's so fucking tight."

"Oh my god, it's too much. It's too much!"

"Shh," Theo tightens his grip around my throat. "He'll fit. Relax and let him in, pretty girl. Our Beetle."

My eyes flutter open as Xander pushes slowly inside, letting me adjust as Theo kisses him over my shoulder. My legs can't take much more, but Theo notices, grabbing me under my thighs and lifting me up. The move forces Xander against the wall as Theo bounces me on both their cocks and I've never felt so good or so damn full before.

They take turns thrusting inside me, all the control I had last night slipping away as they hold me in the air. Theo pulls out of me, and I throw my arms around Xander, who carries me out of the tub and into the bedroom. We're soaking wet, but he lays me down and rolls us over so I can ride him. A few moments later, the shower turns off, and a strong hand comes down on my back, pushing my chest against Xander.

"Let's really stretch her out, Baby."

My scream surprises even me when Theo push against

Xander's cock, sliding their shafts together inside me. Xander's head rocks back off the edge of the bed, mumbling around my screams. My nails claw at his arms, but I'm not saying the word. Not yet. Theo flicks his hips at the same time a third set of hands takes my head, filling my mouth with flesh and metal.

"I wanted to watch, but I couldn't resist." Skylar says, pulling their cock out of my mouth and sliding it into Xander's. They grab my hair and force me to look up, directing me to open my mouth. Their spit drops onto my tongue, but they don't let me swallow it, not until my mouth is full of him again. I don't even question it anymore, giving myself over to their pleasure, letting the three of them use me. I thought I'd hate it, but it's freeing to both my body and my mind. Skylar switches back and forth between Xander and me while Theo controls the thrusting.

Xander chokes on Skylar, his arm reaching out for Theo and warmth filling me. "Listen to them, Skylar. We've fucked them stupid."

"Give it to me, Theo!" Xander cries. "Don't stop! Oh shit, she's so close!" Xander's thrust snaps the band of pressure, and I can't hold back the orgasm any longer. The wave of release is so intense, my eyes roll back.

"Beautiful," Theo says from a million miles away. "She's soaked us both and the bed."

"I'm gonna come again!" Xander cries out as Skylar pushes between my lips again, fucking my throat until the salty sweet taste of him hits the back of my throat. Even Theo roars from behind me as he and Xander finish together. Skylar pulls out, letting the last few strings of cum decorate my face.

"Clean her up, Xander," they demand, standing over us and watching Xander's tongue slid over my cheek. I'm too tired to move, too tired to think. I'm ready to fall into a deep sleep covered in the blanket of warmth their love gives me. The three of them clean me with their tongues first, followed by a warm cloth. They're gentle, leaving the softest kisses on my skin and on each other as they tuck me into the bed. The shower starts up again—no wonder LA is always out of water—and I fall asleep to the panting moans of Xander echoing off the tile walls as they take him apart next. I smile, realizing that soon he'll be next to me, just as exhausted, just as satiated.

HOLLYWOOD
Skylar

CHAPTER 50
MY KINK IS KARMA
CHAPPELL ROAN

"SHE WON'T DISPUTE the charges if you do this."

The second the lawyer says those words, all eyes are on me. I go into the prison, let her say whatever she wants to say to me, and she agrees to plead guilty and write a full confession about my accident and what part she played in the accident that killed Jamie's father. Her father. One face-to-face visit and she'll take the guilty plea and rot in jail for the rest of her miserable life. How hard can that be?

"Sky, you don't have to do this," Coop breaks the silence that sits heavily over the group. Jamie has spent the last fifteen minutes quietly brooding in a corner, I almost laughed earlier at how much he and Dani look alike when they do that. Steve's across the room, staring out the window like the answers to life are in the clouds lingering over Los Angeles. "They've got enough on her to take her to court and—"

"That's not a guarantee." I shake my head, staring a hole into the carpet. "How many times have we seen that happen, slam dunk case and the bastard walks away? Those people had even more evidence against them."

"Yeah, but we're not in Florida," Steve replies over his shoulder, before once again staring at the clouds.

I shake my head, they don't understand. I don't expect them to. "It isn't even about that, Steve. It's closure. It's me finally understanding what happened that day instead of relying on my broken, messed up brain to try to tell the story."

"But you said you remember her. That you had a flash of a memory the other day," Steve says, finally turning away from the window.

"A dream, Steve. It's not enough. If we let this go to court, her lawyer could be a total douche and use my drug history. It's all the doubt people would need to believe I don't remember what the fact are. I mean, do I? This is it. This is the only way I find out the truth."

"And if it's a trap?" Jamie says. "What if she's lying?"

"I'll go with them," Xander says from across the room. He's been quiet, still adjusting to how they all treat him now. It's an emotional overload sometimes, but he's handling it well, and fitting into his new role in their family. "It's the least I can do—keeping you guys from going in there. Think of it as a thank you for your help with…Oliver."

His body reacts to the name with a shiver and a pained expression. When Coop and Jamie heard about what happened, they dropped everything and called an investigator they'd both worked with. Not only did he track down Oliver and get him arrested, but he also dug up ties to a human trafficking ring. Ties that included a buyer he had lined up in Tokyo for Xander. Oliver's parents were connected to the Maxwell corporation, too, but not how we thought. Xander's aunt found their employment records. She also found the prison each of them was serving time in for embezzlement, fraud, and identity theft. Oliver's grand plan involved skimming from the company, which he'd done quietly for years. But when Maxwell told him about the plan to introduce Xander as the next in line to head the new Tokyo office, Oliver made a new plan.

Xander understands my need for closure now more than he did before.

"You?" Steve questions him.

"I've been in prisons before. Not like locked up, but still. I can go. There's no way she'd plan on me coming along and I'd make sure Sky doesn't do anything stupid while they're with her." He shrugs before nodding at me. "Besides, I gotta go give a statement next week, and they already volunteered to go with me, so we're even."

"Are you sure you want to go with them instead of one of us?" Coop asks, looking between us.

"I can't go. I'm sorry, man. I mean, it should be me, it really should." Jamie says, and I appreciate his honesty. "But I'd lose my shit. We'd both end up locked up next to her."

"Same," Steve nods.

"Alright, it's settled." I announce and look back across the room at the lawyer. "I'll go."

"Okay, what now?" Jamie asks, ringing his hands and bouncing his leg. He's one of the most mellow, down-to-earth guys I've ever met. This entire situation has done a toll on him. It's his sister, and he doesn't want to hurt her, but the things she did? She threatened his friends, played a part in his father's death, and went after his future wife? He couldn't let any of that slide, but it's still his sister.

"James, breathe," Alexis tries to calm him, rubbing his back.

"We locked her up for extortion, conspiracy, identity theft, and a litany of other offenses, but if I'm being honest with you, which I'm trying to be, none of those has enough weight to keep her behind bars," The lawyer explains while she repositions her glasses and glances over some paperwork. "If she does sign this confession for the murder of Mr. Barton's father, there's no way she'll ever get out."

"What about what she did to Skylar?! We're gonna hand them over like a steak dinner?" Steve grumbles, Ethan at his side. That kid is one of the lucky ones who came around after Elle had gone to jail, avoiding her wrath. But from what Dani has told me, he's had his own share of traumatic experiences.

"I'm not dead, Steve."

"It's terrible to say, but they're right. It isn't murder and they're the only one she's asked for. Most of the evidence against her in Skylar's case was circumstantial." The lawyer says. "No one could place her there because she's too damn smart. The judge, I hope, has recognized that, too. As Skylar said, their part in this has to do with closure. After this, I'll want all of you to speak at her sentencing. To remind everyone of what she's capable of."

"Oh my god, seriously, you should have seen her face!" Xander cracks up, recounting the story one more time, a beer in one hand, Theo's hand in the other. "She turned whiter than white, like, so damn pale and just stared at Skylar!"

"I still can't believe your opening volley was to say *thank you. That accident ended up being the best thing that ever happened to me,*" Steve chuckles. "We finally got out ahead of her, or you did, Skylar. Gods, what a line!"

"I only told her the truth. No offense, Stevie. But to be fair, the whole thing worked out pretty well for you in the end, too."

"Oh, yeah. I mean, we were fun together, and if that hadn't

happened, we would have been good together for a long ass time. But if it had to happen, I'm glad we still got our happily ever after or whatever."

"Swing and a miss, pumpkin," Ethan snorts a laugh. "How did you let happy endings go? That was a softball for you."

"Oh, I'm getting my happy ending tonight. Don't you worry, pal."

"From who?" Xander jokes and Jamie gives his hair a tousle for that one.

Our group feels whole again. The damage that one spiteful woman did has been cleaned up as best as we can, and we all raise a glass for Jamie's dad, who finally gets justice. We were never supposed to make it here, but we fought for this. Our own demons, the demons of the world, and even the demons we'll never stop fighting.

"So, the big show happens in a week. How freaked out are you all?" Alexis asks Dani.

"We had our last rehearsal of the new stuff yesterday. It's epic." Dani boasts. "Noah and Sky played some of the new songs that she's co-wrote last week and I'm still not over how incredible it sounded. Seriously, shivers down my spine good. We're totally going to win this shit."

"And, if we don't," I say, reminding her of our promise.

"The hell with it, we go on tour anyhow, enjoy the benefits, and find a new label the second that contract expires! We might as well see the world on someone else's dime. It's better than crying in bed!"

"Atta girl," I wink.

"Speaking of bed," Theo breaks up the laughter and cheers. "It's time I get the kids home and in bed."

"So, it *is* just one bed?" Steve asks, wiggling his eyebrows like he's uncovered some hidden gem of a secret.

"Why don't you send Ethan over to find out?" Xander claps back as he jumps out of his chair and drops several hundred dollars on the table. "I've got this one. The numbers came back on the site's opening month, and we're fucking crushing it. The full version isn't even out yet. Dani and Skylar don't get to have all the fun throwing money around when they're famous."

There's another round of cheers and clapping Xander on the back before we pile into Theo's car and head home, exhausted and full of life and love. I've never been so sure about my decision to come back to Los Angeles as I am now. I love this crazy city.

HOLLYWOOD
Xander

THEO and I are the last in the group to get to the venue, but we're still an hour early. The line stretches for several blocks, and the people have started getting anxious. The tickets are either VIP, meaning you get a booth, or general admission, so some of these people have been camped out here for hours to guarantee they'll be close to the stage. I try to count the number of LA Proper shirts I spot, but I lose count. I'm floored at the outpouring.

Win or lose tonight, my girl has done it. She's famous, and no one can take that away from her. No one.

They beefed up the security detail and aren't letting people in early unless they've got a pass, which we do. As we flash them to the giant of a door guy, and he grunts his approval. The people waiting hiss with envy. I straighten my tie, and spin a few of my rings as we walk through the dark hallway that opens up to familiar faces.

"There you are!" If it wasn't enough that Dani could pull an A-lister like her best friend Chase Cooper, he's brought half the cast of the next film with him. That explains the tight security—

they probably work for these rich pricks. Chase winks and waves at us and so does his wife, Dani's sister. "It's about damn time. Come on, we've already started drinking! You gotta catch up!"

I shake hands with a few of the stars until Jamie pulls me in for a tight hug. "You look good, man." He beams at me when we part, his eyes bloodshot and half open. "Like, really good. All of you. I'm so proud of you and Dani."

"Come on, Jamie," his wife says with a smile and a hand on his arm. "You're now going to high cry on his fancy ass suit at a concert."

"Yeah, bro, what's with that? A suit to a rock show?" Steve asks, draped over his husband's shoulders. "Dude, look over there! Ethan brought the whole damn team!"

I glance across the way and sure enough, there sits the Pasadena Fighting Parrots hockey team, all sporting jerseys with LA Proper's logo emblazoned on their chest.

"They're gonna sign the jerseys and raffle them off to raise money for charity." Ethan explains before shrugging Steve off. He steps over to me and holds out a hand, but when I go to shake it, he also pulls me into a hug. "Talk to me later, when Steve's wasted. We'll pitch your website to him and we'll absolutely invest in that shit."

I pull away and can't mistake that sheepish grin. "You've watched me, haven't you?" The grin becomes a smirk as he nods. "You sick fucks. I love you guys. Glad you ended up with that meathead instead of me that night."

"Same!" Steve yells over the drumbeat of the band warming up.

There's a weight against my back before the arms encircle me. "Hey, Baby. Looks like she's brought one hell of a crowd."

"Yeah, she's probably losing her mind back there. Glad Sky's with her."

He presses closer and I notice how excited he is. Or maybe it's me in this suit that has him all worked up. I turn to face him and before I can lay a single word of snarky wisdom on him, he's got his hands on my face and his mouth slotted over mine.

"Mmm," I hum as our noses brush against each other. "Daddy's hungry, isn't he?"

"I told you not to call me that," he growls loud enough to be heard over the music. "Guess I'll have to keep that mouth busy since Dani's band isn't on for a while."

I glance down toward the stage and wonder what she's doing down there. Probably Skylar. Which gives me an idea. I tell the group we'll be back, take Theo's hand, and we head down the side stairs toward the stage. There's something electric about being let backstage when Hollywood elite and pro athletes have to sit up in the stands and aren't allowed back here. Theo and I meander the halls until we find someone to direct us to the right door. I poke my head in and find Connor and Noah playing video games, pointing to a door in the back when they spot us but not stopping their game.

"I knew it!" I whisper to Theo as we head for the door, debating on knocking or barging right in. "Fuck it!"

I barely have the door open when two hands reach out, the small one grabbing me, and the larger one reaching for Theo and pulling us into the small bathroom.

"Oh, fuck me. Please!" Skylar's shit-eating grin grows as they eye Theo and me. "You put one ring on it and all of a sudden, they stroll in here like the high dollar porn remake of Men In Black."

"Oooo, I like it!" Dani laughs, her makeup already a mess

and panties on the floor. "Does that mean we get to play with tentacles later?"

"What? Three cocks aren't enough? You greedy little slut!" Skylar spins Dani around to face me, squeezing her tits in their large hands. "What are we gonna do about that, guys?"

Dani squeals. "There's no shower in here and I am not going out there covered in, well, the three of you."

I step in front of her, brushing my knuckles down her perfect face. "Don't worry, Beetle. I promised you we'd take care of you, and we will. You'll stand on that stage with Skylar dripping down your legs, and I'll have Theo all over me." Without missing a beat, Theo's arms come around me again, but this time, they're undoing my belt. Dani's mouth crashes into mine as my pants are yanked down and her skirt flips up. We're pushed even closer together when Theo grabs Skylar by the hair and pulls them in for a rough, feral kiss, neither one slowing their thrusts. God, I can't wait to watch the two of them together after the show, while Dani and I cuddle together, ruined beyond recognition.

Our family might not be up to society's standards, but it's ours, and it's perfect.

There's a knock on the door and Theo pulls it open while Dani adjusts my tie, and I fix her hair to look like we didn't both just get a solid dicking down. Our people will spot it a mile away, but maybe the crowd won't. If they do, maybe that's to her benefit, too. Gotta love punk rock.

"You, uh, about done in here, Dani? You're on in five," the stage manager asks, fully aware of what he almost interrupted.

"Awww. Were you worried we'd miss the curtain? We're professionals, baby." Dani says as she walks past him, patting him on the chest. Skylar gives him a head bob as they follow her out.

It takes some pushing and shoving, but Theo and I make it back to our seats as their set starts. The tour started almost a year ago, and looking back, I don't recognize the lives we all lived before. Megan, the mice, and us trying to scrape by, no Skylar or Theo in sight.

"Damn, where the hell did you guys go? I want a pass to the sex room!" Steve teases as Chase hands us a beer.

Theo catches me spinning the ring he gave me on my finger as I sing along, taking my hand and threading his fingers into mine. They knock it out of the park, not missing a beat. The crowd loses their collective minds when Dani climbs on Skylar's shoulders for a song, and again for all the crazy shit Skylar and Connor do for the views and attention.

When the set ends, I lean over to Jamie. "How were the other bands?"

"The crowd wasn't as into their sets as they were LA Proper's." He points to the hockey team across the way. "Not one of them cheered for the first band. Honestly, I almost felt bad, but people need to learn what happens when they take on storm Dani, right?"

"Hell yeah."

The last band of the night goes on next, and we've already gotten word from Dani that we should stay up here and watch since they aren't letting people backstage anymore. It makes sense to not overcrowd the area before the big announcement.

All of us nervously watch as the competition comes on strong and doesn't let up no matter how hard we all begged for a string to snap or an amp to blow. Dani would have hated that, though.

She wants to win, but she's all about winning fair. If their tour bus broke down, she'd be finding room on their own to cram everyone in to make sure they all got to the show, that's how she is. She knew this was the band to beat, and she wants to beat them the LA Proper way.

This will be close.

To make matters worse, they're letting the crowd vote. Not by cheers or interaction, but with actual votes in these cheesy booths. It's a great tactic, they get to shut down the stage and set up for a big, streaming announcement while keeping the crowd entertained. Meanwhile, we're kept entertained by Ethan's continual shutdown of Steve's ideas for voting more than once.

An hour passes, the last of the crowd votes have been called for, and now, we're all too nervous to talk or joke around.

> BEETLE
>
> They're saying they want us all on stage in two minutes.
>
> They're totally going to try to drag this out even more.

> Yeah, I got that vibe from out here. How are you four doing?

> BEETLE
>
> Noah's got no nails left to bite. Connor and Sky are plotting what to do when the winner gets announced, and it will probably get them both arrested.
>
> I'm…weirdly zen.

> No matter what happens, we love you. Both of you. I may come shank people if you don't win.

> BEETLE
>
> Vacation after this?

The only thing close to a vacation we've ever taken was for Ethan and Steve's wedding, when they flew us out to Italy for a week.

I think we've earned it, babe

I'm proud of you, Dani.

BEETLE

I'm proud of you, too, Xander. We finally fucking did it!

And we're still together!

BEETLE

Always!

Oh shit, gotta go. See you soon-ish.

When the curtain pulls back, NotOkay Records has a huge stage production setup. Dani and Sky look up toward the booth and wave at us, even though I'm sure they can't see us. They're holding hands so tight, I swear I can make out the white knuckles from here.

"Okay, we're going to get right into this, folks!" The guy who introduces himself as the CEO of NotOkay Records yells into the mic. "We've got a ton of shit to go through, but as a thank you for getting your votes in, following the concerts, and being generally awesome, we're going to bring it down to two bands."

A mixture of cheers and boos comes from the crowd, although I'm not sure why they're booing.

"I know, I know! But we have a definitive gap between votes for third and second place. So, without any more stalling…"

When they announce the two bands leaving, a collective sigh of relief carries from our section and through much of the crowd. We're still in this. Dani should find that encouraging if she notices it. LA Proper has the advantage of this being their home turf. But will the hometown crowd carry them through?

Another hour of tour date announcements, upcoming bands and releases, videos of random people from the crowd filmed after they voted, and the anticipated but still cheered reveal that next year's contest will be filmed and streaming on some big service goes by. We thought the pre-show sex would help with the nervous energy, but that didn't last. The bands have come on and off the stage at least five times. Each time, I notice the combined worry and excitement on Dani and Sky's faces.

"Relax, baby. There's nothing we can do now, and especially not from up here," Theo reminds me, his hand on my knee. I'm not sure how he's keeping it all inside as he sits back and looks cooler than any of us. Meanwhile, everyone else in our box sits on the literal edge of our seats. If they make us wait much longer, these seats won't ever fold up properly again. The head guy comes out again, blabbering on and bragging about their company and how great it is.

"If they don't win, I'm starting my own damn label."

"You could. As much as you hate to admit it, you've got a great mind for business hiding up in that brain of yours." Theo holds his hands up to stop me from arguing. "Not like your parents, Xander. Nothing like that. You're young, smart, and capable. Someday, if you allow yourself, you'll be so big you could buy their company just to turn around and sell it back to them."

I lean over, kissing him softly. "Thanks, Doc. That means a lot coming from you. It does."

"Okay, so," Theo and I watch the stage. The bands are both back out there again and I swear if this isn't the announcement, I'm going down there and smashing people's faces in. "Time for what you've all been waiting for!"

We're all on our feet, crowding the edge of the box. Theo's hand finds mine as we hold on tight to see where this wild ride will take us next.

"The winner of the first, and best, Battle of the Bands Nation is…"

HOLLYWOOD
Dani

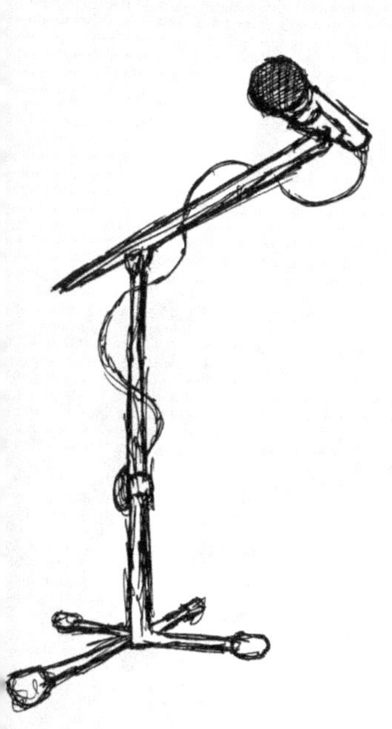

CHAPTER 52
WONDERLAND
CARAVAN PALACE

EPILOGUE

"Hey, Dani? Did you pack the tickets?" Xander asks and I flash him a look. He's asked me that question at least four times this hour. "Yes, asshat. I even showed them to you last time!"

"I wanted to make sure you didn't, I dunno take them out, put them on the desk, start to pack something else, and forget."

"Why the hell would I take them—" I groan when I notice the tickets sitting on the desk, right where Xander said they were. "Okay, why don't *YOU* pack them?"

"I have; every other time you've unpacked them." He gives me a peck on the cheek as he walks out the door with a small bag of things. "Hurry up, though. We're gonna be late for the flight, and Paris waits for no one!"

"Paris will still be there tomorrow," I mumble, stuffing one more thing into my bag and fighting with the zipper. I drag the last of my bags out to the living room and the three of them stand around, drinking coffee, and talking. "Where the hell is your luggage?"

Skylar nods to the small stack of three tote bags sitting by the door. "Beetle, we're going for two weeks, not two months."

I huff, looking at the three large roller bags, two duffle bags, purse, and carry on I planned to bring. I've done this every time Skylar and I leave for another leg of the tour, so they're not surprised. I do another mental inventory, shrug, and head toward the door, leaving the three large bags behind. The trio head for the bags the second I walk away from them, not a complaint between them about how much I packed.

"Leave them."

They all stop and turn, eyes wide. Xander does a double take, before he laughs, "No, you need this one. Or at least you need to get your passport out of it."

"What? I put my passport—" He opens the front flap of the large bag and pulls out my passport, wallet, and spare keys. "Fuck!"

"It's fine, I'll keep them in my bag," Skylar offers. "You're sure you want to leave all this stuff behind?"

"Yep. I'm working on that whole new leaf thing. Letting things go and seeing the other side of the coin. Whatever the stupid saying is." I open the front door and wave them all through it. Once we pile into the ride share, I turn to Skylar. "I'm kind of glad we didn't win. That band plays Arkansas for the next week and got roped into doing some radio talk show. Boring! We get two weeks off and a trip to get pastries!"

"We have pastries at home," Skylar laughs before kissing the side of my head.

"Better view, though," Theo laughs, watching the route on his phone until Xander swats at his hand. "And I have a surprise for all of you."

"Like what? Wait, let me guess," I shout out the first thing that pops into my head, "SYLVIE IS PREGNANT!"

"HA!" Xander doubles over in a fit of laughter. "I get to call you *Grandpa* instead of *Daddy*!" Theo rolls his eyes.

"No, it's not…wait, do you know something I don't?"

"Dani's a witch, Theo. Remember?" Skylar teases, braiding their fingers into Theo's, who looks like he's about to be sick. "An enchantress who's hexed us all, sucking our souls dry so she can see into the future!"

"Don't say it, Xander!" I snap.

He fights back a snort, "I don't think it's souls she's sucking out."

I'm already in awe when we board the plane, but when Theo turns the seats into a bed? My jaw hits the floor and I finally understand why Theo thinks Xander won't get airsick on this flight. He'll be too busy.

"Oh, I'm joining the mile high club today, baby," I giggle.

"You're already in the mile high club. Remember your plan to keep me calm on the way to Italy?" Xander says, exasperated that I could forget that.

"Yeah, it didn't work."

"No, but *it* did!" he whispers, pointing to his pants as the flight crew comes to check in on us. Theo sighs and reminds Xander to take his meds before we take off.

An hour into the flight, Xander and Theo are asleep, curled around each other and snoring softly. "They're cute together." I say, nuzzling closer to Skylar, who's enthralled by some documentary on Paris and only half listening. "I mean, we're cute, too. But look at them. God, I wanna squish them both."

"So do it."

"Are you trying to get rid of me?"

"No. But I have been trying to get you under the blankets for the last twenty minutes and you keep rejecting the offer."

"If I do that, I'll fall asleep! I don't want to miss my first time in first class by sleeping through it! Besides, there food to eat and so much—"

They cut me off with a kiss before smiling against my lips. "You're not going to fall asleep, Dani. I promise." They kiss me again while they reach up and close the curtain, and I catch on to what they're saying. I move quickly, digging for the opening of the covers and crawling under them.

"Whatcha doing there, Beetle?" Xander's unexpected voice makes me jump, almost elbowing Sky in the face as I do. It's a good thing they have fast reflexes. "Look, a partition so I don't have to watch you two going at it." He presses a button, and a screen starts to rise between us.

"Except, you like to watch," Skylar counters and the screen stops, slipping back down.

"Not as much as you do. Come on, if you're not banging, let's watch a movie together or something. I enjoyed the nap, but Dani's right. I don't want to waste this. I'm sure as hell not dropping this kind of money again on it, either. Bonkers." He flops down on his side of the divider and turns on the TV to scroll through the stations.

"Wait, you're seriously not ready to hurl your guts out?"

"Nope! I'm amazing!"

"Scoot over and give me the remote," Theo's gruff voice mumbles as he climbs in behind Xander. He flips it to a paid movie service and picks one out that none of us have seen, but he'll sleep through anyhow. We order too much food, and I only make it halfway through the movie before I'm sound asleep.

I wake up sometime later, the TVs are all off and the curtains are closed. Skylar's hand has dipped down into my shorts so they're holding my ass while they sleep. They love doing that. I poke my head up and see the lump of curled up Xander on top of Theo, they're both asleep again. They look so peaceful. I'm antsy, and I need to move. I crawl up Sky's chest and stare at them by the dimmed lights of the cabin.

"Why are you such a cat?" They mumble, squeezing my butt.

"Because I like seeing how long I can stare at you before you wake up."

"There are better ways to wake me up, love."

"Oh yeah? Like what?"

"Your mouth."

"I mean, screaming is always an option, but I thought it would be inappropriate on an airplane."

"Wise ass. You know what I mean."

I lick the tip of their nose before I leave a handful of small kisses over their face. I almost let out a squeal when they grab my hips and move me so I'm sitting on their stomach. At first, I'm excited we're about to have a little fun, but the look on their face tells me that's not what they have in mind. "What's wrong?"

"Nothing's wrong. Not really. I just…" They look over to where our partners sleep, a crooked smile forming at the corner of their mouth. "Dani, do you think we could ever…you know?"

"Sleep curled up like that? I mean, we were, but you had to—"

"Not what I mean, Beetle." They sit up, their hands traveling over my back until they lay back down, pulling me with them. They hold me like that for a while, letting the comfortable silence lay between us. "I'm scared of asking you. I want to, but I'm scared to go through with it."

"You are?"

"Yeah. I mean, shit, you've loudly proclaimed you're not the type for it. And look at the last time I asked someone. I couldn't survive that again, lose someone like that. Especially not all of you."

"Skylar, are you saying you…want to…"

"Yes." They whisper, struggling to say the word. It catches me off guard and I hold my breath. "I thought it would be cool not to. But the more I watch them together—the tender moments and sparkle in their eyes—the more I want to show you I'll never leave. Promise you I'm yours, and theirs, forever, you know?"

I cup their face and move up to kiss their forehead. "You think too much sometimes, my gorgeous deity. My perfect dark moth. Go on, do it."

"I don't have a—"

"I don't care. Do it."

They stare up, letting me get lost in the swirling amber of their eyes. "Daniella, my devious siren. Your wicked song has fatally wrapped itself around my heart and taken my soul hostage for all eternity. A part of me dies every time you kiss me, the part full of darkness, hatred, and loathing. You've taken my pieces, broken and scattered, and collected them one by one like shells from distant sandy beaches. You glued them to you, filling in your own broken pieces, building your armor and making me yours. Let me be yours forever?"

"Damn showoff," Theo mumbles, and Xander can't help but giggle.

"How am I supposed to say no to that?"

"I'm hoping you don't."

We seal the deal with a kiss as Xander and Theo both softly clap and cheer, not wanting to wake other passengers or draw too much attention. Skylar flips them both off and pulls the covers up over our head, and listen to the mechanical whir of the partition coming up. A moment later, my shorts are gone, panties pushed to the side, and Skylar slides inside me, their mouth over mine to keep me quiet as their piercings push all my buttons. I rock my hips, pushing him deeper, but he grabs me, slowing me down.

"I want to be inside you, Beetle. Just like this. Nice and slow."

"I don't do nice. Or slow," I whisper back. I'm about to add more when they cut me off, teasing my ass with his fingers.

"You will for me."

I wonder if Theo has his cock inside Xander right now. I'm picturing it, imagining what the scene must look like from above. Writhing sheets and silent screams, breathy moans and breathless moments. Theo's low grunt tells me he's finished first, a moment later comes Xander's shuttering gasp. Skylar's determined I'll be next, hooking two fingers inside me to the knuckle while their hips move slow and steady. They use their free hand to cover my mouth.

"Show me how good a girl you can be when I'm filling your greedy pussy." Even flying to foreign countries, they can't help their dirty mouth.

I shatter for them, quietly falling apart as my body shakes. I don't hear them, but I sense them follow me into the abyss. When they're done, muscular arms wrap around me, protecting me in this vulnerable state of bliss. They fall asleep first, their body more relaxed than normal, and their breathing just a bit softer. Everything about this moment is surreal.

We're engaged. I smile as I drift off, surrounded by their warmth.

Theo's so freaked out and excited he could explode. He's trying to hold it all in, but we all see it. His hands shake, his voice shakes, his entire body could be mistaken for a vibrator at this point. Marie picks us up in her adorably tiny car, and I'm glad I didn't pack all my things. We pile in, Skylar in the front since he's so tall, the rest of us nice and cozy in the back. Theo points out the restaurant where he first worked and smiles as he recalls the different places he went with Élodie and Gio. The sadness when he talks about them has lessened, replaced more every day by laughter and happy tears. But he and Marie both refuse to tell us where we're going.

I'm instantly in love with the city, and sad when it's nothing more than a distant skyline in the rear window. But the countryside is pure artwork. The colors are a palette of greens and browns spotted with brightly colored flowers in some areas. We pass by farmlands with rows and rows of grapes followed by a field of cows and flowers. Somehow, the scenery never changes but never looks the same. Xander pulls me close as I gawk out the window.

"Are you seeing how beautiful all of this is?" I ask in a whisper.

"I am." I turn to look at him and see he's staring at me, not out the window. My cheeks burn because no matter what, I'll always blush for Skylar, Xander, and Theo.

"Okay, everyone," Theo announces, waking Skylar from his nap. "Close your eyes. No peeking or you'll spoil it."

"I had my eyes closed just fine before you piped up."

"Don't be a brat, Skylar."

"Yeah, that's my job," Xander says, blowing Skylar a kiss.

Theo shakes his head, but laughs, and we all close our eyes. The car slows and turns, gravel crunching under the weight of the wheels. A rooster crows somewhere in the distance, which strikes me as odd since I thought they only did that in the morning. My mind races at what the surprise could be, and it doesn't help when Theo reminds us to keep our eyes closed as he gets out and shuts his door. I'm so tempted to open my eyes, but I don't want to spoil this for Theo, or myself.

One by one, he helps us all out and stands us by the car. The scent of country air fills my head, sending my mind on a wild ride of ideas from petting zoos to the thought that we're being lined up for a firing squad.

"Okay, open them."

None of us speak as we look around at a view that should be in a museum somewhere. The two-story house has a charming look that would never work in the wilds of Los Angeles, but here in the French countryside, it's perfect. Butterflies flit around the garden in the back near a swing hanging from a tree branch, and row after row of grapevines grow as far as I can see.

The sound of a door opening has the three of us turning to find a radiant woman who looks to be a few years younger than me. She's got her dark hair swept up in the most carefree updo I've ever seen, the epitome of a French woman in my mind. Her familiar eyes dart between us as one hand mindlessly rubs circles over her belly and the other holds onto the man next to her. He's tall and thin with a mustache and an outfit that reminds me of old Italian movies my mother would watch late at night when she couldn't sleep.

Theo's mouth drops open as he looks between the woman and me.

"Sylvie. Luca. This is Xander, Dani, and Skylar," Marie introduces us since Theo's forgotten how to speak. "This is Theo's house, where he lived with his family once, and can now do it again."

"I told you," I say with a smirk to Theo, before I let out a scream and run over to them, throwing my arms around Sylvie's neck while being careful not to squish her belly. Everyone else behind us exchanging hellos with Luca, and when they're done, I scream again and switch to hugging him.

"Hey, hey. He's spoken for," Xander teases.

"Yeah, and I have the three of you, don't I?"

They lead us into the house and everything smells amazing. A mixture of sweet baking that reminds me of Theo, and rich, savory flavors that have me salivating and craving the biggest dish of pasta ever.

"In the traditions of both the French and the Italian people," Luca says once everyone gathers inside, pouring glasses of wine at a long table. "The best way to get to know one another is over delicious food and a good drink."

"Oh fuck, I like those traditions."

"You like food," Skylar quips, pinching my ass.

"Yeah, and apparently, food is a tradition!" When I turn to say something to Xander, I find Theo trying to fight back sobs of joy as Xander holds him close, kissing his cheek and whispering. The sting in my eyes hits just as Skylar sniffles and pulls me closer before taking Theo's hand.

"You built this home without judgement, left it abandoned in sadness, and allowed the echoes of love to dim in your absence. It welcomed your family before, Theo, a refuge from those that don't understand, and it longs to be that for you once more. To share your happiness and love in these walls." Marie says with tears in her eyes as she holds up a glass and looks around the room. "Welcome to the family, and welcome home. All of you."

The Hollywoodland Series
will continue with
Devin Cooper & Bex Strauss in

BOOK FIVE:

LIKE WHAT YOU READ?

Let others know how much you enjoyed this book by sharing your favorite scenes or moments! It's a quick way to support the author, and only takes a few seconds.

So be sure to leave your review and help spread the word about Never To Suffer, and all the other books by Jordyn Barnes on Amazon and Goodreads today.

Thank you.

MENTAL HEALTH RESOURCES

IT'S OKAY TO NOT BE OKAY.

This book deals with several instances of mental health issues and struggles seen frequently in the LGBTQIA+ community. If you or someone you know is struggling, the following are free and confidential resources to help.

National Domestic Violence Hotline
www.thehotline.org
1-800-799-7233 | Text **LOVEIS** to 22522

Suicide and Crisis Hotline
www.988lifeline.org | Call or text 988

Prevention & Treatment of Child Abuse
www.childhelp.org/hotline/
1-800-4AChild (1-800-422-4453) | Text 1-800-422-4453

From hrc.org:
Transgender Community
translifeline.org | 877-565-8860

LGBTQ+ Youth

www.lgbthotline.org/youth-talkline | 1-800-246-7743

www.thetrevorproject.org/get-help-now
1-866-488-7386 | Text START to 678-678

All Ages
www.lgbthotline.org/national-hotline
1-888-843-4564

For more information on Mental Health:
National Institute of Mental Health (educational)
www.nimh.nih.gov | Chat: infocenter.nimh.nih.gov
1-866-615-6464

For International Mental Health resources:
dbtselfhelp.com/resources/international-resources

Find more resources on my website:
www.jordynbarnes.com/resources

ACKNOWLEDGMENTS

Mom, you're the best. Thank you for supporting me, encouraging me, and for reading my silly stories. You've listened to me ramble out my ideas, and encouraged me to keep them coming. I'll never get tired of handing you a first draft only to get it back two days later and hear *"Okay, where's the next one?"* I love you.

My **alpha readers**: Kate, Tara, Andrea, your feedback was incredible and helped me see how wonderful this book would be.

My beta readers: Tara, Stacey, Sami, Andrea, Tiffani, Melissa, Ash, Nalia, Taylor, and Erin. You shaped this book and gave me so many encouraging words when I needed them the most. I love you all!

My street team, thank you for opening my emails, sharing my posts, making super rad posts, and being the best support squad an author could ask for. Without you, I don't think I could have finished this book. I love you!

Very special thanks to **Stacey Kelley**, you've been one of my biggest cheerleaders, brought me new readers, and helped me in ways you'll never even imagine. Thank you for volunteering your time to make my books shine! Best PA ever!

Thank you also to **SafeHaven Author Services** for stepping in and taking over so I could finish this book and not have to juggle ARC reader signups and more. If you're an author looking for help, I highly recommend SafeHaven. Deb, thank you for believing in my books!

To **White Rose Books & More** (Kissimmee, FL), **The New Romantics** (Orlando, FL), **The Moirae Sister Booktique** (online/physical store coming soon), **Spellbound Books** (Sanford, FL), **Barnes & Noble** (Orlando, FL), **Words On Pages** (Paw Paw, MI), **The Spice Cabinet (**Mobile Bookstore in CT), **Scribbles Bookstore** (online), **Lady Lair Booktique** (online), and everywhere else that has my books on your shelves. Thank you for believing in my books and letting me bring them to your customers. You are all incredible and amazing.

As always, extra bonus thanks to to my **editor** (Danielle), and my **muse** (seriously, you should all know who he is by now). Also to Måneskin and Damiano David, thank you for giving me the vibes for Skylar.

And, as always and with the deepest love, thank you to everyone and everything that is **Los Angles, California**.

These business don't sponsor me, or even know I exist, however, they do appear in this story:

Irelands 32- Sherman Oaks, CA (my therapy office)

Portos- Burbank, CA (the cases of delicious things!)

Santee Alley- Fashion District, Los Angeles, CA

Zankou Chicken- All over LA (the garlic spread!)

ABOUT JORDYN

*Giving Broken Characters
Their Happily Ever Afters.*

Jordyn Barnes is an author, graphic designer, nerd, & elder goth. She loves Halloween, creepy things, morally grey characters, and writing about the flawed and beautifully broken people she creates in her mind palace. When she's not writing or reading, she's rearranging the growing collection dedicated to her favorite Disney Princess: Bucky Barnes/Winter Soldier. She also enjoys Marvel movies/shows, true crime everything, and, occasionally, sports. She's a long time Disney adult who relates most strongly with Madam Mim's dislike of sunshine while envying her forest hag lifestyle.

For updates on upcoming releases, join Jordyn's mailing list at jordynbarnes.com. Don't forget to follow her on social media:

instagram.com/jordyn.writes.and.reads

tiktok.com/@Jordyn.writes.words

facebook.com/jordynbarnesauthor

goodreads.com/jordynbarnes

amazon.com/author/jordynbarnes

bsky.app/profile/jordynwrites.bsky.social

bookbub.com/authors/jordyn-barnes

THE HOLLYWOODLAND BOOK SERIES

Let Me Love You Anyway

Faith in Fools

Love the Stars Fondly

Never to Suffer

In the Hatred of a Minute

Dream Only by Night

www.ingramcontent.com/pod-product-compliance
Lightning Source LLC
Chambersburg PA
CBHW070259310726
48976CB00005B/1485